Battle
Beyond
the
Rim

Also by Jess Levins

Starship Named Demon Book 2
Battle Beyond the Rim

Standalone
HOSPITAL ANGEL
To The Stars
My Pet Werewolf

Watch for more at https://www.JessLevins.com.

For my daughter

Jill A. Levins

And my son

Brian A. Levins

BATTLE BEYOND THE RIM
Starship Named Demon Book 2
By
Jess W. Levins

Publisher
OMEGA WRITINGS LLC
Ω
FLORIDA

COPYRIGHT & DISCLAIMER

Library of Congress Cataloging-in-Publication Data
ISBN 979-8-9867-7324-7 Paperback
ISBN 979-8-9867-7325-4 eBook

CHAPTER 1 NEW STRATEGY

The name of the ship was Demon. It was slightly larger than a military destroyer in size and power. For protection, the vessel had military-grade shields, six rapid-fire particle beam cannons mounted on turrets with full rotation, four missile launchers, two torpedo tubes, and two rail guns. The railguns pointed toward the stern of the ship to protect against an enemy trying to approach from the rear.

The name and symbols of demons were prominently displayed in bold red lettering on both sides of the ship. However, the depiction of the demons was more angelic, showing a human body with wings, a shield, and a sword. The same display appeared on the crew's uniforms.

Captain Thomas Wilson was on the bridge of the Demon halfway through Middle Watch. They had accomplished a lot, but he felt disappointed with the results. He always thought better on the bridge. Pirates and marauders constantly attacked the Outer Planets and the Rim Worlds. The pirates would attack ships and steal their cargo, but marauders would take the entire ship and murder everyone onboard. Also, marauders attacked planets with superior arms and killed those who resisted.

Thomas was operating under a clandestine agreement with the navy to provide arms to certain factions within the Outer Planets and the Rim. The profit from selling arms was excellent due to of the additional dangers associated with transporting such cargo.

Thomas had made progress reducing piracy in the Outer Planets, but to have a significant impact on piracy would require a new strategy.

Thomas had just received an encrypted message from Agent Sicarius. Agent Sicarius, the navy's top intelligence agent, had assisted the Demon in the past. The coded message from the agent said Rigel was more crowded than normal, which meant pirates or marauders would be waiting for them when they exited hyperspace.

Thomas had just completed an outline of a viable strategy when Amanda, his three-year-old daughter, walked onto the bridge and climbed onto his lap. He reclined the seat. She curled up and was soon asleep. The junior bridge officers kept their voices low so they would not awaken their favorite crew member.

A short time later, Suzanna showed up and spoke softly, "Our bed is lonely without you." She had moved into the captain's cabin shortly after Amanda's birth. The temporary arrangement was still in place after three years.

"Sorry, I couldn't sleep."

Suzanna picked up Amanda to take her to her bed. "Make sure she is secured," Thomas whispered.

Suzanna knew Thomas would not make such a statement unless he expected trouble. After Suzanna left, Thomas stood up.

"Deck Officer Olsen, take over. I suggest you and the bridge officers practice using combat simulation Epsilon Tau Omega." Thomas stood in the background and watched.

Thomas had surprised the deck officer. She moved from the first officer's seat to the captain's seat. Epsilon Tau Omega was a challenging simulation, even for the senior officers on Day Watch. However, it would be a distraction and add excitement to Middle Watch.

They scored poorly in the first battle. The Demon was destroyed after taking out eight enemy ships. The deck officer told everyone the score was unacceptable as she started the countdown to repeat the simulation. The computer would use the same difficulty level, but the battle would be totally different. This time, the Demon took out fourteen enemy ships before being destroyed. Deck Officer Olsen congratulated the other officers. Olsen turned to the captain, expecting him to commend them, but Captain Wilson was frowning.

"Sir, you seem disappointed."

"You lost the Demon, and everyone onboard died. Such a loss is not a cause for celebration."

She had not expected the response. "What would you have done differently?"

Thomas motioned for her to return to the first officer's chair as he took the captain's chair. He increased the difficulty level and started the countdown for the third time. In the simulation, the Demon faced thirty-four enemy ships. Thomas took only a second to examine the enemy's positions before giving directions to the helmsman. The Demon used flank speed to run from the enemy vessels toward the nearest Star Gate. The enemy ships chased the Demon. Before entering the Star Gate, the Demon cut power, rotated 180 degrees, and fired both torpedoes and all its missiles. Then, it turned back toward the Star Gate. The torpedoes and missiles took out four ships. The Demon reduced speed to one-half impulse, and the enemy ships rapidly approached the Demon. Right before entering the Star Gate, the Demon fired both railguns. The enemy ships were too close to take evasive actions, and nine more enemy vessels were destroyed. While in hyperspace, the railguns had time to recharge. The Demon exited the Star Gate, turned around, and waited for the ships. Only one ship could come through the Star Gate at a time, and the Demon destroyed all the remaining vessels, one at a time, as they exited the gate. When the simulation ended, everyone on the bridge was clapping and cheering. Thomas stood up and motioned for Deck Officer Olsen to return to the captain's chair. She took the offered seat, but now she felt utterly inadequate.

"The purpose of the simulations and all forms of practice is to learn and improve your abilities," Thomas said. "The goal is always to protect the ship and its crew. Winning is surviving to fight another day."

A little over an hour remained before they would exit hyperspace. However, Middle Watch would end in three hours. The senior officers started arriving since they always took over when it was time for the Demon to exit hyperspace. However, Thomas directed the senior officers to sit at the back of the bridge so they could observe. Exactly one hour before the exit from hyperspace, the Communications Officer sent an audio message throughout the ship, "General Quarters, General Quarters, report to your station."

The countdown reached thirty minutes. "Battle Stations, Battle Stations," Officer Olsen announced over the ship's common channel. "Attention, we will exit hyperspace in thirty minutes. All hands, we will exit hyperspace in thirty minutes." Every crew member would ensure all items were stowed for extreme maneuvers before securing themselves to avoid injury.

The navigator brought the Demon out of hyperspace a few seconds early, placing them two days away from their intended destination. A good navigator would have plotted the coordinates for the ship to come out of hyperspace a few hours from their destination. However, by coming out of hyperspace several days travel from the planet, they could cautiously approach with sufficient time to plan a battle strategy. Also, it gave the Helmsman more experience maneuvering the ship using the impulse engines. It had become their standard policy to always come out of jump early.

All four impulse engines were online and operating in the green as the helmsman steered the Demon toward Rigel at one-fourth impulse power.

"Sir, there are two ships to our stern on an intercept course," the Tactical Officer said. He immediately brought all weapons to bear on the approaching ships. He knew the Demon never fired first, but he became concerned as the two ships continued on an intercept course.

"Hold course and speed, don't fire unless fired upon, but be ready to return fire," acting Captain Olsen said. "The two ships continued their approach, and she did not want them to have a clear shot at their engines.

"Sir, they're family ships," the Communications Officer said. "Pirate ships are chasing them, and they're asking for help. I have confirmed their identification."

"Our sensors are picking up two additional ships at extreme range," the navigator said.

"Helm, cut power to our engines and rotate the ship to face the enemy." The helmsman complied with the order given by Olsen. Inertia caused the ship to continue toward Rigel even though it was now traveling backward. The helmsman made minor corrections with the lateral thrusters to keep the Demon pointed at the approaching ships.

The senior officers were worried and anxious. They kept waiting for their captain to signal them to take over. Thomas appeared calm on the outside, but it took all of his willpower not to take command.

Olsen continued to watch the approaching family ships. As the ships passed by on either side of the Demon, each ship fired two missiles at point-blank range. The Demon could deploy none of its defenses because of the proximity of the missiles. Also, the ships were moving at flank speed, and the Demon had no time to return fire before the attackers moved to a safe distance. The port side shields dropped to thirty percent, and the starboard side dropped to twenty percent. Additional missile strikes would cause the shields to collapse.

They received a communication over their general channel. "Captain Wilson, this is First Officer Torrance. You should have killed me when you had the chance. You are too weak to be captain of such a fine vessel. I knew you wouldn't fire upon a family ship. They were also weak and begged for their lives as we spaced them. It'll give me immense pleasure to see your ship destroyed." Torrance was a former member of their crew and part of a mutiny group. The mutiny failed. Thomas had paid him for time served and left him at a space station instead of executing him. Thomas did not respond but knew his past weakness in failing to kill the mutineers had resulted in the murder of hundreds of innocent lives.

They watched the ship's rear display and saw the attacking ships turn around for another pass. Officer Olsen started to order the helmsman to turn the ship, but stopped.

"Tactical, fire missiles at the family ships as soon as you have a firing solution. Helm, keep our stern pointed toward the nearest ship. Tactical, launch the missiles." Each enemy ship approaching from the bow launched a missile. Olsen waited until the enemy ships from the stern were too close to take evasive action.

"Helm, line up our stern at the nearest ship," Olsen said. "It only took a moment using the thrusters to align the ship.

"Fire railgun number one," she said. "Helm, line up the other ship."

The helmsman used the lateral thrusters to achieve alignment. "Fire railgun number two." Only a few minutes separated the firing of the two railguns. The railguns' magnetic fields launched the projectiles at twenty-four hundred meters per second. The projectiles hit each enemy ship. Shields were designed to absorb energy from exploding ordinance, not thousands of hardened projectiles. The two attacking ships never had a chance. However, they had launched two missiles before being destroyed.

Tactical used their particle beam cannons and laser battery to destroy the incoming missiles at a safe distance.

Officer Olsen switched the monitor to the two known pirate ships. The enemy ships changed directions away from the Demon and engaged their jump engines.

"Secure from battle stations," acting Captain Olsen said. There were shouts and cheers throughout the Demon.

Thomas returned to the captain's chair and congratulated the crew. He issued new orders. "In the future, approaching ships are to receive two warnings. If they fail to heed the warnings, we'll fire first."

The Demon approached the former family ships, and it was apparent there would be no survivors. Also, because of the damage, the vessels did not warrant salvage. As Thomas approached the bridge the following day, he received a signal on his wrist communicator to meet with his senior officers in his Ready Room. All his senior officers, including the department heads, greeted him as he entered the room. He had just sat down when Suzanna entered and took a seat.

"Is this another mutiny?" Thomas said with humor. No one laughed or even smiled.

First Officer Miller said, "Captain Wilson, I'm speaking on behalf of all your senior officers regarding a matter in which we're unanimously in agreement." His uncle addressed him using his formal title, so Thomas knew he was serious.

"Middle Watch performed admirably last night in the battle against the pirates. We understand the need to give our junior officers experience taking the ship into and out of hyperspace. However, when the ship faces a potentially dangerous situation, you need to be in the captain's chair, and your senior officers should be at their stations. Each officer here is prepared to give you a statement about why this is necessary."

Thomas raised both hands with his palms facing outward. "That won't be necessary. I agree with your assessment. I'll immediately take charge anytime the ship is threatened, but we have a problem. Demon alone cannot eliminate the pirate threat or handle the trade needed by the Outer Planets and the Rim. I recently purchased all the ships at the Navy graveyard. Those ships are being converted into merchant ships. We'll need captains, bridge officers, department heads, shuttle pilots, and crews for every position on those ships. We need to run bridge simulations regularly, with each junior officer acting as captain to see if they can command a ship. These new ships will serve three functions. Reduce, or eliminate piracy, provide needed trade to the Rim Worlds, and support the navy in the event of an invasion by the Hostis."

Everyone seemed relieved as they left since they had convinced their captain to do his job, but they also understood the urgency of advanced training for the crew.

Thomas joined Suzanna and Amanda for lunch. "I was born in space," Suzanna said, "but the Familia Primum traded only within the Outer Planets. Tell me about the history of the Core Planets and the Rim, since my entire knowledge is based upon rumors and childhood stories."

"As you know, the human part of the Galactic is divided into three discrete areas of space: the Core Planets, the Outer Planets, and the Rim Worlds. There are over a thousand Core Planets, and there's little crime. People go unarmed, and there's no poverty. Food, healthcare, and minimum housing are available for those not working. However, individuals with jobs have a higher standard of living. There are also extremely wealthy individuals. An elected planetary governor is the top politician on each planet. Each planet has a Senator with a seat in the Imperium to handle interplanetary issues. The Senators select the Premier. I've only visited a dozen Core

Planets when traveling with my family on joint business and vacation trips. Each planet has its unique differences."

Thomas was thoughtful as he considered the Rim. "Like you, my early knowledge of the Rim is based upon rumors and superstitions. The average Core citizen thinks the Outer Planets are inhabited by poor, uneducated savages who are to be pitied. By contrast, they believe the people in the Rim are murdering monsters to be feared. I'm fortunate to have received copious amounts of factual information on the creation and colonization of the Outer Planets and the Rim Worlds. The average person is unaware the minimum terraforming standard of all Core Planets was 95 percent before they considered it fit for colonization. Those standards are based on the conditions of the planet on which humans evolved. The standard time, day, and year are all based on the measures of that planet. The standards allow us to compare humans from any planet against each other regarding age or the time it takes to travel a certain distance. The standards for a planet are based on temperature, air quality, gravity, radiation from the sun, soil composition, water quality, and many other measurable parameters. The terraforming standards for the Outer Planets started at the same level as the Core Planets but were later dropped to 85 percent. For the Rim, it was set at 70 percent from the beginning. The worlds inhabited in the Rim are not referred to as planets, since the terraforming did not fall within the Imperium's range for classification as earthlike. It's also why the living conditions on many of the Rim Worlds are extremely harsh. The humans, plants, and animals changed over time because of the genetic code within all species to survive."

"Why did they reduce the terraforming standards?" Suzanna asked.

"I don't know," Thomas replied. After lunch, Thomas went to the bridge while Suzanna and Amanda returned to the cargo bay.

———— ✦✦✦✦✦ ————

TWO STANDARD DAYS LATER, the Demon arrived at Rigel, their fifth stop, a planet centrally located within the Outer Planets. Rigel was above average when compared to other Outer Planets.

Rigel welcomed the Demon. Suzanna was in charge of trade and quickly sold all their weapons and trade goods. She purchased a variety of rare earth metals, which were highly valued within the Core. Thomas convinced the political leaders of Rigel to petition for membership in the Imperium. Membership would allow the Imperium to establish a military base on the planet and install a space-based planetary defense network. Suzanna negotiated a trade agreement with the planet and took advanced orders for future deliveries.

They secured the ship for the long jump back to the Core. Thomas let Night Watch make the jump into hyperspace. The senior officers attended as observers.

The Demon's cargo bay had rack spaces for fifteen hundred thirty-six containers, making it the largest freight hauler with jump engines. This gave them a tremendous advantage in negotiating trade at locations without a Star Gate. Large barges could hold ten times more freight, but barges were too large for jump engines. Thus, a barge could not import or export to planets or stations without a Star Gate.

Demon picked up a full load of weapons from the two primary arms manufacturers who had exclusive contracts with the navy. The navy had granted a purchase waiver to the Demon. The sale of arms proved extremely profitable to the Demon since they sold the weapons at five to ten times their costs. The arms were military grade and superior to the weapons sold illegally through the underground economy. The Demon was the only option if someone wished to purchase quality munitions. The navy wanted to arm certain planets in anticipation of an invasion by the Hostis aliens. Humans fought a war with the Hostis over a hundred years earlier, but it ended in a draw with no peace treaty.

Admiral Nelson had previously given Thomas the decommissioned navy ships stockpiled at the navy graveyard for old ships. In return, Wilson Enterprises agreed to build the navy a new cruiser paid for by the Demon. Wilson Enterprises was already refurbishing the retired navy ships to serve as merchant traders. Also, Thomas hoped the navy would like their new cruiser enough to order additional ships from his family.

After purchasing a shipload of arms, the Demon jumped to Melius, a corporate manufacturing planet. The planet was inhospitable to human colonization but contained raw materials critical to manufacturing a nearly infinite variety of products. The employees lived in highly automated domed facilities and received high salaries for working on the planet. In addition, they received commissions and bonuses based on the profits generated.

Unknown to the navy, upon arrival at Melius, approximately half the weapons were unloaded and stored in warehouses assigned to the Demon. Melius manufactured vast quantities of trade goods explicitly for the Demon. Also, Melius stored products it purchased from other Core Planets for Demon. These were products that could not be mass-produced profitably by Melius.

Demon used all its shuttles to load the products from Melius. The cargo consisted of power units, healing chambers, medical supplies, food processors, universal computer chips, and nutrients used by the food processors. They filled every cargo rack and overloaded the ship with an extra eight hundred containers stacked to the ceiling between the racks.

The Demon's helmsman could feel the extra load as he powered the ship using the impulse engines. He would be happy once they entered hyperspace. He hoped they would not encounter enemy ships until they sold off the excess cargo. No civilian ship had the firepower or the speed of the Demon. However, if they faced multiple enemy ships, the added inertia of the excess cargo would hamper their ability to take evasive action in the event of a battle.

Over the past four years, pirate ships that made the mistake of attacking the Demon were destroyed. As a result, the Demon had earned the reputation of being ruthless when attacked.

Several years earlier, the Demon had fallen into a trap where the ship was surrounded by fifteen pirate ships as it came out of a Star Gate. The crew never tired of telling the story of how their captain had hired four of the best pirate ships. Then, Thomas convinced all except two pirate ships to flee in fear. Demon easily destroyed the two remaining ships. The four former pirate ships now had lucrative trade routes provided by the Demon, and they paid the Demon a five percent commission on the trade conducted under the contracts.

The crew knew an attack could occur at any time since no ship carried a more valuable cargo than the Demon. Captain Thomas Wilson notified the crew they would make numerous stops within the Outer Planets. None of the planets to be visited had accessible Star Gates, and only limited information existed for these planets. Thomas issued standing orders that no one could take shore leave except in groups of four or more. The Demon planned to sell portions of their cargo at each stop and take volume orders for future deliveries while making purchase commitments for each planet's exports. At each stop, they would try to set up long-term trade agreements. Many Outer Planets struggled to survive and were ready to support an interplanetary trade arrangement. Thomas was confident he could build a trade network throughout the Outer Planets. Then he would attempt to do the same within the Rim Worlds.

The navigator performed the calculations for the first jump and wondered why the captain had given him the coordinates for the next eight jumps. He already had the coordinates for the second destination entered into the ship's AI in case they needed to make an emergency jump after arriving at Domum. In an emergency, they would still need to accelerate to a minimum velocity using the impulse engines before entering hyperspace using the ship's jump engines. But, they would not lose time waiting for the navigator to plot the jump coordinates.

THOMAS WAS ON A FIRST-name basis with all his officers, but most still called him Captain Wilson unless they were alone. Thomas called a staff meeting after they entered hyperspace.

The senior officers and department heads joined Thomas in the Ready Room.

Thomas smiled at Suzanna as she took a seat next to him. All the senior officers believed Thomas and Suzanna were Yuanfen, a relationship by fate or destiny. They had fallen in love with each other before they became separated on the same day Suzanna became pregnant with Amanda. They were reunited seven months later when the Demon returned to the same planet. Suzanna was from the family ship Familia Primum and had become an invaluable crew member. She handled all the purchases and dispositions of their cargo. Suzanna had been trained for the position by her parents, who held similar positions on the Familia Primum.

Thomas looked around at his officers. The crew was loyal to the ship and to their captain. "As you all know, we will exit jump at Domum, the first of nine planets we'll visit on this trade route. The nine planets are Domum, Oceanum, Cunabula, Geminor, Bigna, Hermosa, Desetum, Laumar, and Smeraldo. We'll only need to make eight jumps since Geminor and Bigna are in the same system."

"Sir, you normally keep future destinations secret from the crew," the navigator said. "For security reasons, we announce our next stop after we enter hyperspace. This is the first time you have disclosed our future destinations to the entire crew."

"I believe we can trust the crew," Thomas replied. "Before the recent attack, no ship has attacked the Demon in over two years. The extra precautions are no longer necessary. However, I still expect to be at Battle Stations each time we jump into or come out of hyperspace. Also, I want to spend the minimum time at each destination. Does anyone have additional questions or concerns?"

The room was full of concerned expressions, but they respected their captain and would not question their orders.

"The meeting is over," Thomas said. "I'd like Suzanna, Ralph, and Grayson to remain."

Ralph Miller, the Demon's first officer, was Thomas' uncle. Grayson was the commander of the marines and head of security. They wondered why Thomas asked them to remain.

"I've received a message from Agent Sicarius," Thomas said with a solemn expression. "The pirates have put together a fleet to attack the Demon. They want our cargo, but primarily they want to eliminate the Demon since none of the pirates acting alone can survive an engagement with our ship. This fleet comprises well-armed ships, and I expect them to attack us at one of our future destinations. The elimination of these ships would end most of the piracy threat in the Outer Planets. Also, it would support our goal of providing the planets with needed supplies on a consistent basis. These pirate ships are from the Rim, and eliminating these ships would reduce the threat when we decide to establish trade routes there."

"How many ships are in this pirate fleet?" Grayson asked.

"Sicarius has identified six ships but says there are ten."

"I believe we can handle six, but ten is a lot. Was it wise to let the entire crew know about our future destinations? If the enemy finds out about our route, they could use the information to wait for us at one of our stops."

Thomas had anticipated the question. "I would prefer to face our enemy now, rather than give them time to add more ships to their fleet. Also, if the Demon is damaged or we need to escape, I would rather be within the Outer Planets instead of the Rim. We have friends in this sector of space."

"Ralph, I want to have battle simulations daily until we eliminate this threat. Also, determine our best strategy against the six identified ships. Let me know when you have a battle plan."

After Ralph left, Thomas motioned for Grayson to step into the corridor.

"Suzanna, please remain here. I need to speak with Grayson privately, but I'll only be a minute."

Thomas kept his voice low. "I expect the pirates may have contacts on various planets we'll be visiting. I sent unencrypted messages to various family ships detailing our destinations and the cargo we would be selling. During shore leave, it'd be helpful if your most trusted marines were overheard discussing our future destinations. I expect the marines to complain about the problems we have with our shields and engines. Tell them to be creative."

Grayson smiled as he finally understood. "You want the pirate fleet to attack us."

"A bug in the Ready Room recorded the first part of the meeting," Thomas said.

"No way," Grayson replied. "We scan the entire ship on a regular basis."

Thomas smiled, and Grayson realized Thomas had recorded the meeting. A crew member would sell the recording at one of the destinations.

Thomas returned to the Ready Room, and Suzanna saw the concerned look on his face. Suzanna embraced Thomas and gave him a passionate kiss. Suzanna smiled mischievously.

"You seem a little stressed, and I know the perfect remedy to relieve the stress if you have the time."

Their cabin was close to the Ready Room, and Thomas planned to enjoy relieving his stress with the woman he loved.

Suzanna used meditation techniques to control the hypothalamus, amygdala, and septal areas in her brain. It allowed her to concentrate better during work or study. It was a common practice among spacers. The reverse happened when she relaxed to prepare for sex. Her body would become sexually aroused, the desire for her mate would increase, and reaching a climax was instinctive.

Suzanna was fully aroused when they entered their cabin. She was burning with a barely restrained need as they removed the last of their clothing. She loved Thomas and only him. He had the strength of a grounder but the balance of a spacer with an overpowering animal magnetism. Their lips touched, then their mouths parted as they passionately kissed. Thomas could not believe he had such a beautiful, sexy partner. They made their way onto their bed. The sex they experienced at night was good but could not compare to the complete abandonment they experienced when they took time to meet during the Day Shift.

Afterward, it took a few minutes before their heart rates and breathing slowed down. Thomas was lying on his back. She put her hand on his well-muscled chest and moved her leg over his.

"We need to do this more often," she said. "At night, we're both tired from pulling a double shift. During Day Shift, we're both full of energy, and the exercise is good for us."

"Let me know anytime you're in the mood for a little exercise, and I'll be there," Thomas said as he grinned.

Suzanna smirked. "What if I'm in the mood and you're not?"

Thomas laughed. "That'll never happen!"

They both enjoyed their intimate moment of relaxation. Suzann knew Thomas was concerned about the lack of progress with the pirates. She gave him a knowing look.

"The rest of your staff are concerned about an attack by the pirate fleet. They think you're getting careless, but I know you have a plan."

"Suzanna, we've made only a small dent in the pirate problem. We can barely honor our trade agreements and can't afford to continue losing family ships. We need more ships, not less. I checked with your former ship, and Captain Javier says they may have lost another ship to marauders. Their ships now travel in groups of two or more for added protection. While it increases their safety, it limits the number of destinations they can service and lengthens the time between visits to the planets waiting for needed cargo."

Suzanna shook her head. "You have done so much for the planets, stations, and the family ships, but the Demon is just one ship. What else can you do?"

"A new strategy is needed to deal with the pirates. We need to hurt the pirates in a big way. I plan to send a strong message to all pirates to make them think twice about attacking a trade ship. I want to convince them it is safer and more profitable to join us in honest trade. We need a critical event to make all the pirates realize their survival depends on not attacking innocent ships, stations, or planets."

"What type of event are you planning?"

"A major confrontation," Thomas said with a predatory smile.

Suzanna knew Thomas did not make idle comments. She worried about her former ship and other family ships being preyed upon by pirates. The family ships did not have the defensive or offensive capability of the Demon.

"I saw you received an encrypted communication," Suzanna said. "I assumed Admiral Nelson contacted you to complain about something."

Thomas sighed. "The Admiral complained we're not recruiting enough Outer Planets to join the Imperium. It's strange, but he sounded desperate. He is anxious to establish military bases on the planets, install planetary defense grids, and arm the citizens. The Admiral wants us to deliver more arms as quickly as possible. He further complained we're wasting too much time providing the planets with trade goods instead of weapons."

Suzanna shook her head. "If he's so concerned, he should recruit other ships to assist Demon. How can he expect so much from a single ship? Also, would it hurt to have the navy deliver weapons he insists the planets need in case of a Hostis attack?"

"It's politics," Thomas said. "The navy can't be seen delivering arms to civilians. He is restricted until a planet becomes a member of the Imperium. Also, there are barely enough votes in the Senate to allow an Outer Planet to join the Imperium. We need Rim Worlds in the Imperium, but the Senate would never allow a Rim World to join the Imperium. They don't seem to understand these worlds will be the first to be attacked in a Hostis invasion. There have even been insane motions on the Senate floor to offer the Rim Worlds to the Hostis as a peace offering. There was a recent motion to disband the navy by a group who believe the Hostis threat is pure propaganda to get more military spending. Fortunately, the group had little support."

"Why do you think the Admiral is complaining more than normal?" Suzanna asked.

"The Admiral is certain a major attack by the Hostis will occur before we're ready. If an invasion took place now, the Rim would offer little resistance. The Outer Planets would hold for a short while. Once the Outer Planets fall, the Core would be defenseless.

Lethal weapons are illegal on most of the Core Planets. Also, only a few Core Planets have space-based defense grids, and even fewer have military bases. The human race could become extinct since the Hostis do not take prisoners."

"What are the Admiral's plans?" Suzanna asked.

"The Admiral does not have a plan. He will fight to the last ship when the Hostis invade and hope for a miracle. He hopes we can improve his odds."

"I believe in miracles, and I believe in you," Suzanna said before they separated and returned to work.

Thomas went to their cabin during the latter part of Middle Watch. Suzann was already asleep. Thomas sat at his desk. He had studied the history of battles, where a smaller group with superior strategy overcame a larger force. He needed such a strategy to prevail in the current situation.

CHAPTER 2 OCEANUM OBSERVERS

The Demon came out of hyperspace several seconds early as they arrived at Oceanum. The early exit resulted in a delay of three days to reach the planet. They put the extra time to good use, communicating with those in charge to determine trade opportunities.

Oceanum had just one small continent, but it had a thriving economy. It was named Oceanum because water covered ninety percent of the planet, and the settlers were not resourceful enough to create a better name. The ocean provided the primary food source consisting of both plants and fish. Farms provided the balance of their diet. The entire population was pescatarians, since fish was the only meat in their diet.

Citizens of the planet seemed happy and healthy. They referred to themselves as Oceanums. They bought sufficient arms to protect themselves against future attacks by pirates. Unfortunately, they were not concerned about a Hostis invasion and had no desire to join the Imperium. The Oceanums believed a navy occupation would be just as harmful as the pirates. The planet's primary buyers purchased power units, solar chargers, universal chips, and other products. It surprised Suzanna when the buyers did not seem interested in buying any medical supplies or healing chambers.

Even though Thomas failed to persuade them to join the Imperium, they agreed to a long-term trade agreement. The overall happiness existing throughout the planet bewildered Thomas and the rest of the crew. There were no prisons or organized law

21

enforcement. The planet had no crime except for the occasional pirate raids. As the exchange of goods neared completion, the President of Oceanum asked Thomas to join him to discuss an urgent but delicate situation.

Thomas and Suzanna arrived mid-morning with a contingent of bodyguards. The President, his wife, their two adult children, and various governmental officials socialized with them through lunch.

After lunch, the President invited Thomas and Suzanna to join him as they walked toward the back of the residence. They were on the second floor and walked out onto a balcony. They were about fifty meters from the deep green ocean. The ocean was spotted by sea life breaking the surface of the water.

Thomas wished the President would disclose why he requested the meeting and felt relief when he said, "It is time for me to explain why I asked you here. The delay gave us time to decide if we could trust you. In all of humanity's space exploration, the only advanced species we have encountered are the warlike Hostis. As a result, most humans have a negative view of aliens. Humans found evidence of an advanced civilization that is now extinct. We refer to them as the Ancients and credit them with building the Star Gates. Archeologists have evidence the Ancients were destroyed in a great war. Humanity is fearful that whoever destroyed the Ancients may still be out there. What do you think would occur if humans discovered an alien race on one of the Outer Planets who were intellectually superior to humans?"

"I suppose the first concern would be to determine if they were a threat to humanity," Thomas said. "Scientists would want to study them, and hopefully, we'd welcome them into the Imperium."

"What would be the worst-case scenario?" the President asked.

"Out of fear, I suppose the Imperium might decide to destroy such aliens." It was not difficult for Thomas to imagine such a scenario.

"When we arrived on Oceanum from Panteen, the planet had been successfully terraformed. The terraformers seeded the ocean with all forms of plant and animal life for the eventual colonization by humans. They moved the planet closer to the sun, the rotation was modified, and a slight tilt was added to allow for moderate changes in the seasons."

"I reviewed the history of the planet," Thomas replied. "I am aware of the planet's terraforming and colonization history."

The President frowned. "What isn't in any report is that an intelligent species already inhabited the planet. The species survived the changes to the planet because they are adaptive and can even modify their genetic structure. They studied the new inhabitants, and over the years, they changed their body structure to be more acceptable to humans. They provide us with fish and sea plants. In return, we agree not to pollute the ocean. Because of our concerns, we've kept their existence a secret." He did not tell how the vocal cords of the species had been genetically altered to allow for human sounds.

"We informed the Nereides of your visit, and they'd like to meet with you. I assure you there is no danger from the Nereides."

"Nereides?" Thomas asked with raised eyebrows.

"Nereides is the name we gave them since they are protectors of the sea. They are smart, creative, and intuitive. At their request, our ancestors assisted them in changing their DNA and the DNA of certain species of sea life to improve the food supply for both the Nereides and humanity." He avoided mentioning the telepathic abilities of the Nereides.

The disclosure intrigued Thomas. "I'd be happy to meet with the Nereides."

Thomas was concerned about the DNA changes since the Imperium prohibited changing the DNA of all animal life, including humans. They strictly regulated changes in the DNA of plants, and it took years to get approval for a plant DNA change.

Thomas followed the President as they took the stairs to the ground floor and walked to the ocean. The ocean was calm, with small waves rolling across the white sand. The slight breeze brought a subtle smell of salt, seaweed, and marine life.

They stopped at the ocean's edge, and five Nereides emerged from the water. They had four webbed appendages for swimming with a tail for guidance. The front appendages had five finger-like claws with full rotation. Their hind appendages were shorter, with four finger-like claws. The eyes were human-like, with both eyes in the front so they could look forward, unlike fish with eyes on either side. Their elongated snouts were blunted. It surprised Thomas they were not more alien in appearance.

The Nereides came forward and stopped in front of Thomas. "Thank you for meeting with us," the largest Nereide said, using the Galactic language without a translator. "We live here in peace in a symbiotic relationship with humans. We provide them with food and live in harmony with them. They provide us with equipment. The equipment allows us to cultivate and excavate the ocean floor to our advantage. The humans told us there are other worlds in the heavens similar to this one. We wish to improve the survivability of our species by spreading our seed to other worlds."

A different Nereide leaned forward. "We ask you to drop us in the oceans of the worlds you visit. We can hibernate in a frozen state without damage in specially prepared containers. Each container would contain our weaned offspring, thousands of Nereide zygotes, seeds of ocean plants, and the fertilized eggs of a wide selection of sea life. We hope you'll deposit ten or more containers of Nereides on planets you visit that have an acceptable ocean. We'd like you to deliver one hundred containers. In return, we'll help with the survival of the humans on each planet by providing food and medicine from the sea. We understand the payment concept and will pay for passage on your ship. We've spent years collecting gold, platinum, and other precious metals from the ocean floor. Again, we'll commit to improving the lives of the humans on the worlds you select."

"How do we know your presence will not harm humans on another planet or humans in general?" Suzanna asked.

"We are empaths. We feel the emotions of others of our kind and the emotions of humans. We'd never intentionally harm humans since we would feel their pain."

Thomas kept a straight face as he placed his hands behind his back and slowly bent his finger without outwardly showing discomfort.

"Please stop," the Nereide said. Thomas stopped twisting his finger. It had been painful, but he wanted to test the truthfulness of the Nereide's statement concerning his empathic ability.

Thomas knew several worlds with oceans where life for the human population could not get much worse. He would use those planets as a test and hoped he would not regret his decision. He looked at Suzanna to see if she felt the same way, and she nodded.

"If we agree to the one hundred containers of Nereides, what do you propose as an adequate payment amount?" Suzanna asked since she was the Demon's primary trade representative.

The Nereides had only used a slight mental push to convince the captain since Thomas was already inclined to help them.

The Nereides had the entire ocean to locate and collect elements. They had been planning this event since the humans first uplifted them. The Nereides offered twenty containers of gold, ten containers of platinum, and seventy containers of rare earth metals as payment.

The agreement included bringing along two hundred Oceanums who would accompany the containers and have final authority on which planets would be selected for colonization by the Nereides.

Also, they made accommodations for two hundred adult Nereides who would be in hibernation. Twenty adult Nereides would be awakened when an ocean was selected. They would remain on the planet to guide the Nereide children.

First Officer Miller reassigned the ship's cabins so the Oceanums would be housed in the same section. Certain crew members became aware of the Nereides since the containers had to be monitored to maintain the health of their sleeping guests.

The Demon cargo crew had experience handling sub-zero containers for liquid hydrogen, liquid oxygen, frozen foods, and special commodities. The containers to house the frozen Nereides required maintaining the temperature at the level specified by the Nereides and providing a brine solution with the correct salt content.

Thomas hoped he was making the right decision in allowing the Nereides to settle on other planets. He wondered if the Nereides could help the humans struggling for survival on certain Outer Planets and Rim Worlds. He was impressed with the intelligence of the Nereides. Such intelligence could help provide new inventions to deal with the Hostis or any other invaders since their survival would be tied to the survival of the human race.

After much consideration, Thomas decided the Nereides could significantly benefit humanity. However, he was concerned. If he were wrong, the Nereides could pose a threat to humanity similar to the Hostis. Regardless, humans must learn to coexist with other species, or war would be the only option. With the vastness of space, humanity would meet other species. It was critical to have as many friends as possible. He hoped the Nereides would someday be a partner in advancing both their species.

The top politicians and scientists were concerned about the disappearance of the Ancients. How could a race so powerful vanish? Their greatest fear, to the point of paranoia, was the possibility of a planet or group of individuals discovering a new weapon of the Ancients. Such a weapon could be used against the Imperium. This resulted in laws prohibiting civilians from possessing any technology of the Ancients. Their second primary fear was any species not classified as human. Their third fear was any humans outside the Core Planets, with the greatest phobia directed against the Rim. It would be easy for such fears to include the Nereides.

THE DEMON COMPLETED their trade with Oceanum and left the planet behind. They accelerated to the minimum speed needed to engage their jump engines and enter hyperspace. Thomas took the time to get better acquainted with their guests from Oceanum. Doctor Adler spent several days examining the Nereides, then requested a private meeting with Thomas.

"Thomas, the Oceanums and the Nereides have lied to us," Doctor Adler stated with concern. "I conducted a remote scan of the Nereides and took DNA samples. The Nereides are not aliens. The Nereides are modified bottlenose dolphins and one percent human. The DNA of the Oceanums has also been changed. Like the Nereides, the Oceanums are also empaths. I watched as they all cringed when a cargo handler dropped a box on his foot. Modifying the DNA of the Nereides and Oceanums has improved their intelligence and communication ability. Extrapolating, I suspect the modifications are responsible for their empathic abilities, but I suspect they may have other abilities not readily observable."

"Recommendations?" Thomas asked.

"I don't know what to recommend," Doctor Adler replied. "I like the Oceanums and the Nereides, but I fear what we have brought aboard the Demon. There was a time in human history when anyone exhibiting paranormal abilities was hunted down, imprisoned, executed, and blamed for all manners of evil intentions. They may have lied to us out of fear or for a nefarious motive. Regardless, the Imperium's penalty for DNA modification is death."

Thomas was thoughtful and frowned. "Don't mention this to anyone else."

Thomas did not want to involve anyone else since he didn't know if the abilities of the Nereides included mind reading, mind control, or physical manifestations such as telekinesis. He traveled within the ship as far from the Nereides as possible and had a private conversation with Omnia.

Thomas had Omnia use her AI controlled nanites to create a specific cage made of multiple layers of various materials. The cage prevented penetration by radiation, sound frequencies, vibrations, and all forms of communication. Omnia made a tiny hole for a microwire to allow for voice communication outside the cage. She built another larger enclosure around the first cage. Thomas was inside the first cage. A micro-opening was made in the second cage opposite the hole in the first cage. Omnia used the nanites to connect a microwire to an electronic converter outside the first box. It converted Thomas' voice to digital. A wireless transmitter in the outer cage converted the digital signal to analog. Outside the second enclosure, a wireless computer transmitter converted the analog signal back to digital.

The Demon had four cargo bays. The crew vacated Cargo Bay One and Four. Thomas left a message for the Oceanums to meet in Cargo Bay One. Once they were in the cargo bay, Omnia locked access to the bay with the override blocked. No one could open any of the cargo doors except for Omnia. The containers holding the Nereides were in Cargo Bay Four, and it was similarly secured.

Thomas had left a high-volume wireless speaker on a table in the center of Cargo Bay One. Thomas formally addressed his audience.

"This is Captain Thomas Wilson. You've lied to me. The Nereides are not aliens. You have modified the DNA of both the

Nereides and yourselves. You're locked in Cargo Bay One, and the Nereides are locked in Cargo Bay Four. There are explosives on the containers of the Nereides and poisonous gases ready to be pumped into your bay. Finally, the cargo bay doors will open. You, and the containers, will be dumped overboard into hyperspace. I don't know what will happen to you when we exit hyperspace, but I would not expect you to survive. The Imperium penalty for DNA manipulation is death. You'll get only one chance to explain why I should not carry out the death sentence. Any attempt to use mind control won't affect the outcome since the person operating the controls can't be controlled by you."

Thomas did not have visual access outside his cage and could not see what was happening in the cargo bay. Omnia informed him the Oceanums were in deep concentration until they shook their heads informing their pseudo leader they could not locate Thomas.

Demato assumed the role of speaker for the Oceanums. "We felt our survival, and the survival of the Nereides required us to obnubilate our true nature. As you stated, the actions of our ancestors merit the death penalty. Our ancestors lived on Panteen when a research facility studied those individuals with higher brain wave activities. However, extreme human modifications were made on Ithea, which resulted in a war where millions died. Their acts resulted in the establishment of the death sentence for any human DNA manipulation. Anyone with unusual brain activity was executed without a trial, even if their DNA had not been changed. Our ancestors decided their survival required them to leave Panteen. They settled on Oceanum to escape the persecution prevalent throughout the Core for those who were mentally different. Our top scientists wanted to find out why we were different. They experimented on the dolphins since the dolphin, and human genomes are the same. Also, dolphins have similar personality traits. The dolphins have slightly larger brains than humans but were close enough to generate results comparable to human tests. What happened was beyond expectations. The dolphins advanced past humans intellectually. We could communicate, but it was difficult. Using their superior brains, the dolphins devised a method to combine human DNA with their DNA to allow their descendants to speak the human language. They then taught us how to modify our DNA to improve our psychic abilities. Our intelligence and psychic abilities improved, especially in the empathic area. We are strong empaths. Also, we can sense others and their whereabouts. We don't wish to harm anyone and apologize for deceiving you, but our very existence is at risk. None of us have performed any DNA modifications. Our ancestors conducted the DNA changes. Should we, as their descendants, be executed because of their crimes? Our ancestors broke the law, but we haven't. Will you let us live?"

There were several minutes of silence. "You must never use your powers to influence the decisions of anyone on this ship," Thomas said. "You're not to use your psychic abilities except among each other unless specifically requested. Such a request is not to be influenced by anyone in your group. There's an entity onboard the Demon that can't be affected by any psychic abilities. If you violate this rule, the death penalty will be carried out. I'll be unable to prevent such punishment. Do you agree to those terms and understand the consequences of a violation by any member of your group?"

"Yes, we do, and thank you," Demato said.

"Meet me in Cargo Bay Four." The locks to Cargo Bay One and Four were retracted. Thomas was standing in front of the containers holding the Nereides when the Oceanums arrived. An explosive device was attached to the top of each container. Thomas had already told Omnia to get rid of the explosive devices. The Oceanums witnessed the bombs disappearing as the nanites were put to better use. The Oceanums were in awe, thinking Thomas was manipulating matter.

Omnia noticed a special coating on the outside of the containers and knew the only reason for the layer would be to protect the sleeping Nereides from being bombarded by emotions while hibernating. Omnia decided to protect Thomas. He immediately replicated the material and directed Thomas to touch one of the containers. Omnia had the nanites travel subcutaneously through Thomas and form a microscopically thin layer around his skull.

The fear generated by the Oceanums overwhelmed Thomas. "Stop. You agreed you would not try to influence me."

"We aren't," Demato responded quickly. "You are just receiving our fears. It's not being directed toward you."

The fear disappeared. "That's better," Thomas said as his headache dissipated and his mind cleared. The Oceanums looked at each other. They could not detect Thomas. It was like he was not even present.

"We apologize again. We'd never have perpetrated the deception if we'd known you were one of us."

Thomas started to say he was not one of them but stopped when he remembered Sun Tzu, *All warfare is based on deception.* Thomas remained silent since their false belief in his ability could prevent them from taking inappropriate action in the future.

"I have work to do," Thomas said. "The containers will be placed back in the racks and secured." Thomas turned and left the bay. The Oceanums discussed the situation among themselves. Their leader said what they were all thinking.

"He has a perfect mental shield," Demato said. "His psychokinesis and telekinesis abilities allow him to manipulate matter at the subatomic level. He is what our ancestors had hoped to achieve. We need to find out more about Captain Thomas Wilson. Whatever you do, never challenge the captain. Also, we need to be extremely careful around our captain. We don't know what other abilities he might possess. Whatever happens, we don't want him as an enemy. Search his background, talk to the crew but be discrete."

They separated in wonder at what they had just seen. After two cycles, they met in small groups to discuss what they had discovered about Captain Wilson. The crew had shown them the results of the confrontation between the Demon and the large fleet of pirate ships. They believed Thomas used his mental abilities to cause the enemy ships to flee from the Demon. They watch a vid of the championship hockey arena game played in zero gravity. They interpreted what they saw as Thomas using his mental powers to win the game. They watched the crowd of fans shouting his name as he simultaneously controlled the emotions of over fifty thousand spectators. They detected the total loyalty of the entire crew aboard the Demon and believed Thomas used his mental abilities to create such loyalty.

The Oceanums' primary purpose in coming aboard the Demon was to help find good planetary homes for the Nereides. The second clandestine reason was to find an additional home for the Oceanums. They were hoping to find a home in the Rim. It was the furthest point from the Core Planets and the death penalty of the Imperium. Now, they thought gaining some of the powers shown by Thomas would enhance their safety.

The Oceanums decided to have their most potent females copulate with Thomas in the hope of having his child. Children of such unions could be psychically powerful. The gene manipulation by their ancestors resulted in attractive, superior bodies that were resistant to disease. The Oceanums onboard the Demon comprised one hundred females and one hundred males. There was no shortage of females volunteering to have Thomas' child since witnessing his abilities had acted as an aphrodisiac.

WHILE REVIEWING REPORTS on pirate activities, Thomas received a request to meet one of the Oceanums in her cabin. He figured it was a benign request. Thomas reached her cabin and placed his hand in front of the sensor. The door opened, and he took two steps inside. As the door slid shut, he sensed a presence behind him and went into full combat mode. Thomas completed a forward roll and turned around in a fighter's stance to face his adversary. He faced a smiling, scantily dressed, beautiful female. He could feel her desires as she approached him. She put one of her hands behind his head and the other around his waist as she passionately kissed him while pressing her body firmly against him. Thomas was returning her passion when he realized what he was doing. He took each of her hands and disengaged himself from her.

"You're beautiful, and I'm attracted to you, but I'm committed to another,"

It shocked her when he walked out of the cabin. The door closed automatically, and she collapsed on the bed. She had felt his rapid heartbeat and was overwhelmed by his emotional desire. Her heart was still beating fast, and she wanted him even more. She had used her mental ability to ovulate and knew sex with Thomas would have resulted in her becoming pregnant. She reported her failure to Demato.

SUZANNA WAS REVIEWING potential sales and purchases associated with their next destinations when a female Oceanum sat down next to her.

"How may I help you?" Suzanna asked.

"I'm Marta, and I tried to seduce Thomas since I want to have his child. When he came to my cabin, I felt his desire for me, but Thomas rejected me. He told me he was committed to another. A crew member said you were the committed person, but I still don't understand why he rejected me. I wasn't asking him to break any commitments to you."

Suzanna grinned. "Thomas was originally a grounder. He is from a planet where monogamy is the norm between committed couples. Having sex with someone other than your mate is against their religious code. They may still break the code, but it could result in the couple severing their bond. I don't fully understand it since I was born a spacer. As a spacer, we expect to have a child from a sleepover with a stranger during shore leave to increase the gene pool. It's expected and would not affect the bond a couple might have on their ship. Thomas is faithful to me even though I don't require it. I am faithful to Thomas because I know about his beliefs. Plus, I'm happy to have his and only his children. I noticed you Oceanums all look alike, and I understand your need to increase your gene pool. Thomas is an outstanding individual in every measurable way, and I can understand your desire to have a child with him."

"I still don't understand how he could leave my cabin without having sex with me. Will you help me?"

"I'd be happy to tell Thomas it's okay for him to have sex with you, but I don't think it will make any difference."

"I agree," said Marta. "He has incredible self-control in addition to his other powers. Would you mind wearing this inside you the next time you have sex with Thomas? Please!"

Suzanna knew what Marta was trying to accomplish and knew the joy of having a child. She nodded her head and took the small flexible sperm collector. It would not collect all the sperm but would provide several hundred million more than Marta needed.

Omnia observed the conversation and felt any reproduction associated with Thomas should have his best chromosomes.

The next day all the female Oceanums volunteered to have Thomas' child. Still, they limited the pregnancies to six females with the most potent mental abilities since having one hundred females become pregnant simultaneously would raise too many questions.

The Oceanums became part of the crew by taking jobs no one else wanted. They used the training center to develop expertise in ship skills. The Oceanums excelled at engineering and filled openings on Middle Shift and Night Shift. Maintenance openings were available on all shifts, so Oceanums became qualified to fill those vacancies. Further, they took courses to become qualified as bridge officers even though they did not expect to be offered such a position.

CHAPTER 3 SETTING A TRAP

As their standard practice, the Demon exited jump early at Domum. The planet was friendly and conducted trade with family ships.

The communications officer turned to Thomas. "Sir, I'm receiving distress messages from two family ships, the Sojourn and the Viking Star."

"Helm, take us to the nearest ship," Thomas said. Thomas leaned forward and increased the magnification on the forward monitor.

"Call Suzanna to the Bridge." The Communications Officer contacted Suzanna, as requested by Thomas, and told her about the distress signals they were receiving.

"Have you raised anyone?" Suzanna asked as she arrived on the bridge and took a seat.

The Communications Officer shook her head. Then her face lost all its color. "Sir, I'm getting a voice recording from the captain of the Viking Star. A fleet of pirates attacked them. Pirates boarded the Sojourn first and killed everyone. The crew begged for their lives and the lives of their children. The pirates laughed as they raped, tortured, and killed the crew. The captain of the Viking Star refused the boarding demand, dumped their cargo, and performed an emergency override sealing all doors throughout the ship. The message is repeating."

The Demon slowly approached the Viking Star, and the crew silently observed the damage. The pirates had fired missiles into the bridge, the engines, and the middle of the Viking Star. Commander Grayson took half the Demon's shuttles to the Viking Star.

It was another two hours before they reached the Sojourn. The Sojourn had merited only a single missile to the engines. With a contingent of marines, Sergeant Jackson took the balance of the shuttles to the Sojourn.

Suzanna asked for a status report on survivors. There were only six children on the Sojourn who survived. They had been shoved into ducts before the last of the crew were killed.

There were seventy-two survivors from the Viking Star. Only seventy-eight had survived out of over a thousand who had lived on the two ships. All survivors suffered from malnutrition and dehydration. Many had injuries from the missile blasts. Doctor Adler and her staff provided medical care to the survivors.

Suzanna met with the survivors and received more information on the attack. The pirates had been utterly ruthless with no signs of compassion. The survivors were severely traumatized from the horrors they had witnessed and from being adrift for over thirty days. They thought they would die and had given up any hope of rescue. They sent distress calls to the planet with no response. Suzanna knew some of the survivors, and they all recognized her. She assisted with getting them assigned to cabins so they could rest and recuperate.

Suzanna contacted her father onboard the Familia Primum and gave him the details on the vicious attack against the family ships. They got Captain Javier and the senior officers of the Familia Primum on a group communication and discussed the situation. They knew no one would be safe against such a large pirate fleet.

"The Demon will keep a watch for the pirate fleet," Thomas said.

Thomas told Javier the names of the planets he would be visiting. Captain Javier reminded Thomas they should not discuss their travel plans over an open channel. Thomas said he was distraught over the murders and had temporarily forgotten to keep such matters secret. They knew the pirates had devices capable of listening to their long-range transmissions. Suzanna let Captain Javier know the survivors would be safe aboard the Demon and would be welcomed to become part of their crew. Also, the survivors had the option to move to a family ship willing to take them.

Thomas did not mention he planned to offer the survivors a new ship since he did not want to get their hopes up prematurely.

THE TACTICAL OFFICER used long-range scans to search for pirate ships and continued the scans as they approached the planet. No ships were detected.

The helmsman established an orbit around Domum. The Communications Officer sent the standard greetings on various frequencies to establish contact with the inhabitants, but they did not respond. There were three continents on the planet. Thomas had Grayson send two military shuttles to each continent to determine the status of the inhabitants.

Grayson contacted the shuttles before the end of Day Watch, and the reports were quite gruesome. Thomas reviewed the information. There had been a volcanic eruption twenty years earlier, resulting in the beginning of an ice age, and it was continuing to get colder. The planet's top climatologists estimated the ice age would last a hundred and fifty years. The growing season would shorten annually. In another fifty years, they won't be able to produce enough food in the northern and southern continents to feed the people. The scientists determined the central continent at the equator would be the best location for survival. The northern and southern continent people decided to move to the central continent, but all the land was already owned.

The northern continent sent its army across the isthmus, connecting them to the central continent. Millions died in the resulting war. The central continent prevailed, and they destroyed the isthmus during the war. Both armies bombed the towns and villages of each other's continents. After the surviving soldiers of the northern army surrendered, they were executed out of revenge and to eliminate having to feed them.

While the war in the north was taking place, an army from the southern continent invaded the central continent using thousands of ships but did not engage in battle until the war in the north was over. Then, the southern army attacked the depleted army of the central continent. The central and southern armies were evenly matched in the number of soldiers. However, the fatigued central army had depleted their weapons in their war with the north. The central army destroyed the ships containing supplies for the invaders. However, the southern army prevailed in a devastating battle and summarily executed all the survivors of the central army. The invading army continued to kill central citizens as they took over the farms.

Overall, a little over half the populations of the north and central continents were dead. The manufacturing facilities, fuel depots, and utilities on all three continents had been bombed. Nearly all the watercraft and aircraft on the planet were destroyed. The smaller southern continent fared a little better, but still lost a third of their population.

The north and south continents were now isolated, with populations consisting primarily of older men, children, and females. These groups kindly received the representatives from the Demon and asked for their help.

The situation in the middle continent comprised the survivors of the southern army made up mostly of men who knew little about farming, and they attempted to enslave the population. Two shuttles landing in the middle continent were attacked when they refused to turn over the shuttles to a local commander but lifted off with only a minor injury to one marine. Thomas directed all shuttles to return to the Demon. He scheduled a staff meeting for the following morning.

The senior officers assembled in the Ready Room. Grayson and the six shuttle pilots gave a detailed report with vids. When they finished, Thomas asked for recommendations. Several officers suggested they leave since the planet's inhabitants could have solved their problems if they had worked together instead of going to war. Also, an analysis projected there would never be profitable trade with the planet. However, other staff members wanted to help.

Discussions lasted through most of Day Watch, and Thomas approved their recommendations. The Demon would provide power units, food processors, and medical supplies to the northern and southern continents. The power units would help them repair the less damaged facilities. The inhabitants would need to grow as much food as possible, store the food in silos, and build thousands of greenhouses. There were not enough minerals and nutrients for the food processors to feed the entire population, but it could supplement the diminishing crop yields if rationed. However, their survival would still be tentative.

They agreed the Demon or one of their representative ships would return with hybrid seeds adapted for cold climates. Crops from such seeds would further supplement their food supply. Even without the ice age, the populations of the northern and southern continents would drop to less than half within a generation. This would occur because of the natural deaths of the older inhabitants with fewer births. Their future population would be from the surviving children. This dire situation would reduce the food requirements. However, every simulation showed a low probability of survival for both the northern and southern continents.

The middle continent would fare only a little better even though the climate would be less severe. The invaders were failing in their attempt to force local citizens to grow food. Theoretical projections showed the military dictator would be unable to rule the middle continent since the local population would continue to attack the soldiers of the occupying army.

Every time a shuttle from the Demon tried to land in the central continent, they were attacked by local militias or the invaders. Therefore, they left the central continent alone but would check periodically in the future to see if the situation changed.

The staff meetings discussed transporting the seventy million surviving inhabitants to another planet, but it could not be accomplished since resettlement ships no longer existed. Such one-way settlement ships separated into modules and landed on designated areas once the passengers were transferred to the planet. If the citizens of the planet had worked together, it would have been possible to survive the mini-ice age without the heavy casualties resulting from the two wars.

Thomas discussed the situation with the Oceanums, and they decided Domum would be an adequate planet for the Nereides. The Oceanums said the weather would not be a problem for the Nereides since only the water close to shore would freeze, and their population would be established before the worst of the ice age ravaged the planet. They felt the inhabitants of Domum would welcome the food they could supply from the ocean.

They awakened twenty adult Nereides and delivered them to the ocean. The adults surveyed the depths before deciding where to start the two habitats. As directed by the Nereides, ten containers were dropped near the coast of the northern hemisphere and another ten containers off the coast of the southern continent.

The adult Nereides opened the containers and awakened the children. The children helped the adults spread the plant and animal seeds in their new home. They secured the incubators for birthing the Nereide zygotes. After reaching adulthood, the Nereides would proceed with their natural mating and no longer need the incubators. As the initial two colonies grew, they would divide to form new colonies.

The Nereides assured Thomas they would help the humans on the planet survive. Thomas provided communication devices to allow the Nereides to contact them during future visits by the Demon. The sealed devices were waterproof and would only require periodic exposure to the sun to recharge. The devices would last for hundreds of years, barring physical damage.

The Demon had only planned to spend several days at each destination, but it was three weeks before they departed Domum. They made friends in both the northern and southern continents. They were realistic and knew the aid they provided now and, in the future, would not guarantee the survival of the inhabitants. However, with the Nereides' help, Domum's future looked considerably better.

After all the shuttles had returned and were secured, Thomas directed Middle Watch to accelerate to jump speed. Demon reached jump velocity and entered hyperspace. Everyone was hopeful their next destination would be less depressing and provide for a trade agreement.

While in hyperspace, Demato approached Thomas. "The survivors of the family ships are suffering from the traumatic experience. We're experiencing their pain. We ask your permission to lessen their pain using meditation, exercise, and our parasympathetic ability to release certain hormones within their body to assist in their mental healing." Thomas initially hesitated since he did not completely trust the Oceanums, but he finally agreed to their request.

THE DEMON'S NEXT STOP was Cunabula. The Demon exited hyperspace and approached the planet. They were immediately greeted when they contacted the planet. Suzanna sent Cunabula a cargo manifest and asked about the planet's available exports. Thomas scheduled a meeting with the planet's top politicians.

Thomas and Suzanna met with the current rulers of Cunabula. Thomas explained the navy's concern regarding the likelihood of an invasion by the Hostis. He discussed the advantages of joining the Imperium for their protection and access to the resources of the Core. The meeting went better than expected, and they expressed an interest in joining the Imperium. The planet's representatives purchased a sizable number of arms. The planet's traders purchased Demon's regular cargo, including power units, medical supplies, and universal computer chips. They could have sold a large order of food processors at a good profit, but they had given all the processors to the people on Domum for free. The Demon stayed in orbit for five days selling and purchasing cargo. Thomas granted limited shore leave to the crew with the same restrictions requiring they travel in groups of four or more while on the planet. Even while granting shore leave, the ship maintained sufficient crew onboard to remain at battle readiness.

Grayson and Jackson took three marines each as they made the rounds of the planet's bars and restaurants. Grayson and the three marines accompanying him entered their fourth bar. Grayson saw two unsavory men following them. They sat down at a table in the center of the bar.

A server came over. "What would you gentlemen like to drink?"

"We have been in too many fights to be called gentlemen," Grayson answered with a smile. "Bring each of us a beer."

Every planet had produced a liquid they called beer. While the taste might be exotic, there was sufficient alcohol to get drunk if you overindulged.

After the server delivered the beers, the youngest marine spoke loudly. "Commander, if we make it back to the Core, I'm jumping ship. We are carrying over two thousand containers. Captain Wilson has been making millions in credit but refuses to maintain the ship. The shields keep failing, and the engines are barely holding together. The last two battles severely damaged the ship, and it needs to go to a shipyard for repairs."

"I know the ship needs to be repaired, but it's the captain's decision," Grayson replied in a loud disgruntled voice. "Your job is to follow orders and not raise questions about other issues regarding our ship. I'll talk to the chief engineer to find out if the captain has scheduled the ship for repairs at a shipyard." They changed subjects and started discussing their future destinations.

Jackson and his three marines had similar discussions in other bars near the spaceport. Tonight, Jackson's group comprised Lawrence and two other former players from the legendary World Champion Demon Arena Team. They had been spending heavily and had bought drinks for different spacers who were down on their luck with little to no credits. Jackson decided it was time to return to the ship and paid the final bar tab.

They left the bar and proceeded down an empty street when a group of five men came out in front of them. Jackson looked behind him and saw four more men positioned to prevent any attempt to escape. The men were carrying clubs with several displaying knives. Jackson started laughing.

"You guys seem to have excess universal credits," the largest man said. "You will download all your credits onto this wafer." He held up a computer wafer for all to see.

"This is going to be fun," Jackson said as he laughed. "Lawrence and Jasper, take the four behind us. Tyler and I will take the five in front."

Jackson spoke to the guy holding the wafer. "As long as you don't pull a blaster or other firearm, we'll let you live. Anyone of you who pulls a gun will die."

The guys should have turned around and left, but they made the mistake of accosting four marines. The marines did not wait for an invitation. They simply attacked. Jackson rotated and kicked the nearest person in the stomach while ducking under a club. He hit the next person in the jaw so hard he was unconscious when he landed on his back. Tyler made quick work of one adversary, who fell to the ground with a broken arm, but one of the other assailants sliced him in the side with a knife. Tyler turned and disarmed the man by breaking his wrist. The biggest guy dropped the wafer and landed a blow to Jackson's head. He expected him to go down, but Jackson just grinned. Then Jackson took a step forward and buried his fist in the guy's stomach. The guy looked sick. The next blow hit the center of the guy's face, and blood flew everywhere from the broken nose. The guy landed on his back in a daze. He had never lost a fight and had never been hit so hard. The marines were trained to hit using their entire body when delivering a punch, whereas most fighters only use their arms. The guy previously holding the wafer started to reach for his blaster when he remembered what the spacer had said about killing anyone who pulled a gun. The fight was over, and all the assailants were on the ground. They were either unconscious or moaning in pain. Tyler was the only one with an injury, and his hand was pressed against his side. Jackson placed a first-aid patch on the wound.

They returned to the ship and reported to the hospital. The attending nurse could not understand why the men seemed so happy while she attended to Tyler's injury. Grayson and his team dropped by the hospital. Jackson's team excitedly told them about the fight. They showed vids from their body monitors. The marines who accompanied Grayson were disappointed they missed out on the fun.

Grayson reported back to Thomas. Several individuals at two of the pubs had seemed interested in the ship's future destinations. They had asked about the mechanical problems with their shields and engines. One man had even joined them at their table and bought several rounds of drinks.

While the marines were completing their mission on Cunabula, the Oceanums sent probes into the oceans. They awakened the adult Nereides, who explored the seas and were delighted with the waters. At their request, the Demon dropped thirty containers of Nereides, ten in each of the three oceans. This left Demon with fifty containers of Nereides.

As the Demon was leaving the system, the Tactical Officer reported their extended sensors detected four ships, but they were too far away for identification. As Demon reached jump velocity, the Tactical Officer reported the four ships were also accelerating to jump speed but were too far behind to be a present danger.

THEIR NEXT DESTINATION was to a system with two inhabited planets. Geminor had a larger land mass but a smaller population than Bigna. Both had well developed democracies with thriving economies. Both planets had defense satellites and a space-based trade center for off-world imports and exports.

Thomas decided they would approach Geminor first. Suzanna provided a cargo manifest and set up a meeting with the local authorities. Thomas and Suzanna, along with their bodyguards, attended the meeting. Thomas immediately provided the details he had presented to prior planets concerning the need to join the Imperium for the benefits and the protection they would receive in the event of a Hostis invasion.

The youngest delegate asked, "If we join the Imperium and allow the navy to maintain a base on Geminor, will the navy join us in defending our planet against a potential incursion by Bigna?"

"If you're a member of the Imperium and Bigna is not, then the answer is yes, the navy would join in your defense," Thomas responded. "However, if both you and Bigna are members of the Imperium, then the navy would remain neutral unless they are directly attacked."

The group asked Thomas and Suzanna to give them time to discuss the issues in private. A follow-up meeting was scheduled for the following morning.

They arrived the following day, and while drinking the local equivalent of coffee, the representatives provided purchase orders. The orders included a large quantity of their heavy-duty arms. Then, they said their planet would like to join the Imperium. Suzanna presented the group with a list of the planet's exports they would like to purchase. It took eleven cycles for the trade goods to be delivered and the planet's exports to be brought to the ship.

Grayson and Jackson again made their rounds of the local bars. The marines accompanying them enjoyed the free drinks being funded by the Demon since it was a work mission. They made the mistake of complaining the following morning about their hangovers.

Grayson and Jackson shook their heads. "You children are a poor excuse for marines," Jackson said. "A real marine could drink twice as much and still report to duty ready for battle. A little exercise should take care of the hangover."

The workout was extra gruesome, and none of the marines complained again, at least not in the presence of Grayson or Jackson.

The Nereides did not consider Geminor a suitable planet. The salinity of the ocean was too low and only covered twenty percent of the planet.

After completing the final freight deliveries to Geminor, the ship used their impulse engines to travel to Bigna. The trade was conducted efficiently. Bigna indicated they did not wish to join the

Imperium until Thomas told them Geminor had already agreed to join. Thomas described how the navy would support Geminor in a conflict between the two planets. The following day, Bigna decided they would also seek membership in the Imperium.

The ocean covered eighty percent of the surface of Bigna, and they dropped twenty containers of Nereides. Because of the size of the ocean, they discussed the possibility of dropping more than twenty containers. Terraforming of the planet had only been partially successful, resulting in a somewhat barren sea. Edible sea life did not exist in sufficient quantities to generate any interest in fishing by the human inhabitants. High winds and gigantic waves made the ocean dangerous for humans, but the Nereides loved it. The one continent only had minimum boating close to shore for occasional visits between coastal communities.

The Nereides knew they could help grow the sea life to provide for their survival. If they stayed away from the single continent, they would go unnoticed for generations. After considerable discussions, they decided to deliver ten additional containers of Nereides to Bigna since the ocean covered so much of the planet. Only twenty containers of Nereides remained aboard Demon.

After fourteen days, Demon was ready to leave the system. Demon accelerated to jump velocity. The Tactical Officer again informed Thomas that their long-range scanners detected four ships. However, the ships were in front of them at maximum range. The ships entered jump ahead of them.

HERMOSA WAS THE DEMON'S next stop. The Demon exited hyperspace two days from the planet. As the name indicated, it was a gorgeous planet. Hermosa had two continents on opposite sides of the planet. Seventy percent of Hermosa was covered by water. Thomas directed the helmsman to slow to one-half impulse power.

He directed the Tactical Officer to go to General Quarters and to maintain the condition for all three watches. General Quarters was one step down from Battle Stations. The crew believed in Thomas and his ability to win regardless of the opponent. They knew if Thomas called General Quarters, there would likely be a battle. Their sensors were extended to their maximum range in all directions. At their reduced velocity, it would take four days to reach Hermosa instead of two. Thomas felt apprehensive about the enormous asteroid belt in the system, and he directed the helmsman to keep a distance of at least one standard astronautical unit from the belt.

Thomas woke from a deep sleep when he received a call from the Tactical Officer on Night Watch. He eased out of bed to avoid waking up Suzanna. Thomas took a quick shower, dressed, and when to the bridge. He asked the Technical Officer to bring up the screens. Thomas adjusted the screen to maximum magnification. Their advanced sensors barely detected the heat signatures from nine ships hiding within the asteroid belt.

Thomas looked around at the Night Watch officers. "Good job, no use sounding battle stations this far out. Send a message throughout the ship. We'll go to battle stations in six hours."

There were smiles throughout the Bridge. Even though it was dangerous, his crew was young and looked forward to going into battle. Thomas knew there was no guarantee of winning in any engagement, but this battle was necessary if he wished to eliminate or reduce the pirate threat. The rest of his crew did not realize the nine ships could destroy the Demon if properly commanded. However, Thomas did not plan to lose.

Five hours later, Day Watch relieved Night Watch. One hour later, the ship sounded battle stations when the nine pirate ships exited the asteroid belt. Thomas watched the approaching pirate fleet on the main screen. The enemy ships were too far out for optimal firing. The Tactical Officer laughed when the pirate ships prematurely launched missiles that were easily avoided.

"Helm, I want you to reduce our speed to one-fourth impulse," Thomas said. "Use thrusters to move the ship slightly to starboard until we have two enemy ships in a line. Once the ships are aligned, I want you to maintain the line."

The helmsman established the line and did an excellent job maintaining the line as he compensated for each movement of the enemy ships.

"Rotate the ship one hundred and eighty degrees," Thomas said with a raised voice.

Everyone had secured themselves when the ship announced battle stations, but the quick turn of the ship pressed everyone against their harnesses. The enemy ships mistook the maneuver as a sign that they had turned to run, and several enemy ships accelerated toward the Demon.

"Prepare to fire both rail guns," Thomas said as he intently watched the monitor. "Helm, keep those two ships lined up."

Thomas concentrated on the monitors. "Wait, wait, get ready, fire rail guns!"

Both rail guns fired simultaneously. The rail guns used an advanced electromagnetic force to launch high-velocity projectiles. The projectiles contained cluster munitions that would detonate before impact to cover a wide area of destruction. The only defense was to use evasive action to avoid being hit. Only heavily shielded ships with thick hulls survived an impact from a rail gun. However, rail guns took a long time to recharge and typically could only be fired once during a battle unless there was an extended engagement. The rail guns on the Demon were reversed to guard the ship's stern. The pirate ships did not realize what was happening until the projectiles passed the halfway point, and the pirate ships no longer had time for evasive action. Thousands of projectiles hit the enemy ships and overloaded their shields. The two enemy ships directly behind them were filled with thousands of holes from bow to stern, destroying systems throughout the ships. The ships did not explode but lost their engines and maneuverability as they drifted in space.

"Helm, turn the ship around and accelerate at flank speed toward the enemy," Thomas ordered. "Tactical, take out those two lead ships, fire when you get a lock with the torpedoes, and follow each torpedo with a missile."

The Demon completely surprised the enemy fleet as the engagement changed from chasing the Demon to seeing it coming straight at them. The two lead pirate ships fired two missiles before they exploded. The enemy missiles missed the Demon.

The Demon opened up on the five remaining pirate ships with their entire arsenal of six particle beam cannons, four missile launchers, and their laser battery. The two torpedo tubes were reloaded and launched. The five remaining pirate ships fired two missiles each and opened up with their cannons. The Demon's lasers and cannons took out seven of the inbound missiles. Three missiles impacted the Demon without damage, but the shields dropped to sixty percent. The Demon and the pirate ships passed each other, going in opposite directions.

"Tactical drop shields," Thomas shouted. "Helm, reduce velocity to one-fourth impulse power."

Thomas called engineering, and the chief engineer responded. "I need an emergency shutdown on three of our four engines," Thomas shouted.

Only three pirate ships survived, and the pirate commander had decided to flee the area until his first officer said, "Sir, we got him. The Demon's shields are down, and they lost three engines."

The leader of the pirates signaled all three ships to pursue the Demon.

Thomas smiled as he watched the pirate ships turn to chase the Demon. "Captain, the three pirates are following us," First Officer Miller said, "but four ships in front of us are approaching on an intercept course."

"Don't fire on the four ships. They are friendly. Reduce velocity. Turn around and match speed with the four ships."

Thomas asked his Communications Officer to contact the four ships using a unique frequency. The bridges of the four vessels were displayed simultaneously on the large forward screen, and Thomas addressed the captains.

"Greetings, Captain Cube of the Interco, Captain Sultana of the Libras, Captain Turro of the Bitrates, and Captain Albertus of the Frampton. Go to battle stations. Three pirate ships will be joining us. Six additional pirate ships are no longer operational. As per our prior agreement, you'll receive the salvage along with any cargo or other valuables on the nine ships."

"Tactical, raise shields," Thomas said. "Helm, point us toward the enemy."

Thomas contacted engineering. "Chief, restart the engines."

The three pirate ships raced toward the Demon at maximum velocity. Then they realized the Demon had full shields and were accompanied by four additional vessels.

Thomas looked around his bridge. "Do you want to let our friends handle the remaining ships, or do you want the honors?"

All the bridge officers responded together. They wanted to continue the battle.

Thomas nodded. "Fire when ready."

The Demon fired a torpedo and a missile at each of the two closest ships and four missiles at the third vessel. The pirate ships tried to turn and flee, but it was too late. One ship managed to fire two missiles at the Demon. The Demon used their lasers and particle beam cannons to destroy the incoming missiles.

Thomas advised the four captains to join him on Hermosa when the salvage was under control and agreed to buy the drinks.

The Bridge Officers all looked at Thomas. They figured out their captain had made the Demon look vulnerable to get the pirate ships to chase them.

The Demon proved to be more than a match for the pirate fleet. The four friendly ships did not surprise Suzanna. She suspected Thomas had a backup plan to protect the ship. The crew throughout the ship had been following the battle.

Everyone on the Demon was celebrating their victory. A yeoman entered the bridge with non-breakable glasses and two bottles of champagne. There was a strict rule of no alcohol on the Bridge. The yeoman looked at Thomas with a sheepish grin.

"Is this the good stuff?" Thomas asked.

"Yes sir," the yeoman grinned even wider.

Thomas took a sip. "Remind me to put the entire bridge on report, including myself. Otherwise, I might forget."

The yeoman was still smiling as she shared the champagne with the officers. Thomas pulled up the yeoman's personnel file and noted she had recently completed officer training. She showed initiative even though it involved breaking a rule. He executed a promotion to offer the yeoman a junior officer's position on Night Watch.

"Sir, one of the pirate ships failed to show up," First Officer Miller said.

"Make a note in the log. We'll find and destroy the missing ship or consider it for future inclusion in our trade network." Thomas sent an encrypted message to Agent Sicarius with a note concerning the missing pirate ship. Thomas got a refill on his champagne as Suzanna walked over to join him.

TWO DAYS LATER, CAPTAIN Cube, Captain Sultana, Captain Turro, and Captain Albertus joined Thomas, Suzanna, and Amanda for dinner on the planet. They informed Thomas the salvage of the nine pirate ships would take several months, and they were delighted with the value of the salvage. They toasted Captain Wilson and told him the best decision they ever made was not firing on the Demon when they surrounded him with fifteen ships. They were looking forward to telling others about the Demon's one-sided battle against nine ships since some spacers still called them cowards for not attacking the Demon during their previous encounter. Suzanna introduced the captains to the local trade representatives, and they worked out schedules for future trade.

Hermosa had two separate oceans. They transported ten containers of Nereides to each of the oceans on Hermosa. All the Nereides had been delivered as agreed. Four adult Nereides received permission from Thomas to remain on board the Demon. They wanted to stay with the Demon in the hope of finding additional oceans to colonize. They were happy and wished to inhabit every world with a suitable ocean. The two hundred Oceanums onboard the Demon had accepted positions on the ship and were now serving as crew.

Later, Thomas sent a coded message to Admiral Nelson and Agent Sicarius. He informed them the Demon had met nine ships at Hermosa for a social gathering, but the nine ships departed permanently because of a minor disagreement. He provided the identification for all nine ships. Thomas also provided the Admiral with the contacts for the Outer Planets wishing to join the Imperium.

Suzanna sent a similar message to Captain Javier of the Familia Primum. She told him the Sojourn, and the Viking Star had been avenged. The crews who died on the Sojourn and the Viking Star would not be forgotten. The survivors could take some comfort in knowing the pirate fleet would not attack another family ship. Captain Javier notified the rest of the family ships. The family ships acknowledged their debt to Captain Thomas Wilson, the crew of the Demon, and Suzanna.

THE DEMON MADE THEIR next jump to Desetum. They entered an orbit around the planet but received no answer to their communications. The ship sent out all ten military shuttles to visit the planet. They found old dwellings that had been vacant for decades. The planet was mostly desert with limited plant and animal life. The scientists took several days before reporting their findings to Thomas. They determined the people died from multiple sources. They analyzed the bone remains and found a complete lack of Iodine and Selenium. The water supply was contaminated with high levels of mercury and arsenic. Such contamination was not present when the planet was settled. Also, the water could have been purified, but the lack of certain trace elements would have dulled the senses of the people. This caused them to lose the ability to solve basic survival problems. Thomas sent the information on Desetum to Melius, including the analysis they had conducted. It was perfect for a corporate world since it was ideally located for providing goods to the Outer Planets. Also, Melius could use its resources to clean up the environment, eliminating the need for domed facilities. Advanced production techniques were pollution-free.

The Core Planets had eliminated hunger. The people received free housing and free healthcare. The free housing was modest, but everyone had a place to sleep. Public schools provided free education, but private schools were available for a fee. The life expectancy was approaching two hundred years. In addition, a more robust lifestyle could be had by those enterprising enough to seek employment.

Unfortunately, the word, free, didn't exist in the vocabulary used by the Outer Planets or the Rim. Shortages were the norm on most planets, and healthcare was minimal or unavailable. The Demon continued reestablishing trade routes but had to keep returning to the Core for critical trade goods. Thomas saw a future where the Outer Planets and the Rim could have a living standard equivalent to the Core Planets. However, the Imperium would see such a future as a threat. Thomas knew the Imperium needed all humans united against the impending alien invasion, but what action would the Imperium take once they concluded the war with the Hostis?

CHAPTER 4 SPECIAL TORPEDOES

The Demon entered hyperspace and exited jumped near Laumar. They immediately spotted an old mining vessel situated between them and Laumar. The craft maintained a stationary position and did not appear to be a threat, but Thomas had learned not to take any chances. No asteroids were in the area to attract a mining vessel, and the ship did not appear damaged. The Tactical Officer identified the mining vessel and its captain. Thomas directed the Communications Officer to open a channel to the miner.

"This is Captain Wilson of the Demon; do you need any help?"

After several minutes they received a response. "This is Captain Erling, and I'd like to meet with you concerning an arms purchase."

"We normally don't sell arms to individuals," Thomas replied. "If you'd like to join us at the station, I'll consider your request."

"No, you don't understand. I wish to sell you some weapons."

"I doubt you have any weapons I'd be interested in acquiring."

"Captain Thomas, you'll absolutely want the weapons I have," Captain Erling said with confidence. "Nothing you or the military have can compare to what I offer. I can't legally offer these weapons to anyone else. You have a reputation for honesty and are probably the only ship willing to pay a fair price for what I offer."

Thomas became intrigued. He glanced at his Operations Officer. "Sir, he's no threat. I completed a full scan, he has a pulse cannon for breaking up asteroids for mining, but it would not be effective against our shields. Also, he's the only person onboard his ship."

Thomas nodded to the Communications Officer, and she reestablished communications with Captain Erling. "You've piqued my interest. How do you propose we proceed?"

"Well, I suppose the best route would be for you to come aboard my vessel to inspect the weapons."

"I'll come aboard using one of our shuttles and with four bodyguards."

The old miner laughed. "You may bring all the bodyguards you like. I mean you no harm."

Thomas suited up in his armor along with the four marines. They entered the shuttle bay and saw Pilot Seymour standing by the designated shuttle. Thomas had reviewed the vids of Pilot Seymour's emergency landing when she brought the shuttle in hot for a perfect landing. She impressed him with her flying ability. Her flying ability saved his life and the life of Suzanna.

Thomas paused in front of the pilot. "Pilot Seymour, can I assume you'll not break any flight regulations today?"

She grinned. "Only if there are no emergencies, sir."

Everyone boarded the shuttle, and the shuttle exited the ship at minimum power. The shuttle slowly approached the mining vessel and entered the ship through an open cargo door. As soon as the shuttle landed, the ramp door opened, and they exited the shuttle. They did not have long to wait until Captain Erling approached.

Thomas stepped forward. "I'm Captain Wilson."

"Please follow me," Captain Erling said.

They did not have far to go. Captain Erling pointed to a stack of missiles secured in a rack against the wall. Thomas noticed the missiles seemed strange. Then he leaned in close to observe the writing and felt a chill go through his body.

He motioned for his bodyguards to stay by the missiles and asked Captain Erling to follow him. They moved to a distance where they could talk without being overheard.

"Those are weapons of the Ancients," Thomas stated. "Where did you get these missiles?"

"I got them off an Ancients' ship. I found the ship half-buried on the dark side of a moon. I also found two other ships at the site. I checked out those ships first and found the skeleton remains of the crews. They'd been dead for hundreds or perhaps thousands of years. Then I visited the ship of the Ancients. It was huge. Hundreds of missiles were in racks, and twenty-eight missiles were lying on the floor. I started loading the loose missiles on my ship. After loading twenty missiles, I took a break and explored the alien ship. I took vids throughout the ship. Writings covered all the walls. At times, I thought someone or something was following me. However, when I looked around, there would be nothing there. Then I would hear a soft sound. You'll think I'm crazy, but the ship was haunted. I returned to my ship to eat a meal and noticed the ship's power reading was lower than I remembered. Then while I watched the display, the power dropped further. I panicked. I rushed to secure the missiles I'd already loaded and took off. As I left the moon, the power drain stopped. If I had stayed, I'd have ended up like those other two ships. There's no way I'll ever return to the site."

Captain Erling shivered before continuing. "My partner died years ago, and a miner's life is hard, especially when you get old. I want to retire. I have savings, but only enough to live in a low-income area where safety would be a concern. If the government finds out I have artifacts of the Ancients, they'll take them and either execute me or lock me up for the rest of my life. If I try to sell these missiles to ships that do not care about the law, they'll take the missiles without paying me, and I'd be lucky if they didn't kill me."

"You're probably correct."

"I'm a miner, and like many miners, I'm superstitious. The symbol on your ship is the same symbol I saw in the ship of the Ancients and on these missiles. You're my best option. I want to sell these missiles to you. I'll even throw in the location of the Ancients' ship."

Thomas was thoughtful. The location of a ship of the Ancients would be worth a fortune or a life sentence on a prison world. After a million years, the missiles may not even work, and he would have to figure out how to use such missiles. However, he did not want the missiles to fall into the wrong hands.

"Captain Erling, there's no way of knowing if these missiles still work. What is your asking price?"

"I want 100,000 credits per missile?"

Thomas stared at Captain Erling. "Now tell me how much you need."

"I need 50,000 credits per missile. Adding the credits to what I can get for my ship will cover me for the rest of my life."

"Okay," Thomas replied, "but I'll need a copy of the vids, the location of the ship of the Ancients, and I'll need to have a tech specialist wipe the jump coordinates from your navigation unit."

It took two trips to transfer the twenty missiles. The Demon's top tech wiped the jump coordinates, and Captain Erling gave Thomas the only recording of the vids.

Thomas was puzzled. "The funds have been transferred to your account. I need to ask you how you managed to meet us at this location?"

Captain Erling smiled. "There are other old miners like me, and it's a pretty lonely job. We communicate with each other to keep our sanity. I sent messages to other miners asking if they'd seen your ship. You were seen at several locations connected in a fairly straight line. So, I got here first and waited. I've been waiting for three months but figured you'd get here, eventually."

Thomas nodded his head. "I shouldn't have to tell you the importance of never speaking about this transaction."

"I understand completely. Thank you, Captain Wilson."

Thomas had an idea. "Captain Erling, would you consider postponing your retirement for a profitable venture?"

Captain Erling smiled again. "I suppose I could delay my retirement for the right opportunity."

"A planet in the Hermosa system collapsed and formed a huge asteroid belt. We scanned the asteroid belt searching for hidden pirate ships. The scans showed rich deposits of valuable ore. It'd be perfect for a mining operation. I can provide a list of the ore I'd like to buy. I'll purchase everything you and your fellow miners can process."

Captain Erling's smile had turned into a grin. "If you provide me with a contract, I think you have better be prepared to purchase a lot of refined ore." They executed an ore contract, and Thomas paid one million credits for the missiles.

Thomas suggested Captain Erling's first stop should be at Wilson Enterprises to have his ship serviced. Captain Erling agreed. Because of a lack of funds, his ship hadn't received an overhaul in over forty years. He entered the coordinates and jumped to the shipyard of Wilson Enterprises.

THOMAS RETURNED TO the Demon and immediately asked Chief Engineer Anderson to meet him in the cargo bay. He asked the engineer to figure out a way to test the missiles. He advised the engineer to take his time and to be extremely careful.

Officer Anderson spent several weeks examining one of the missiles from the Ancients with no success in understanding how it worked. He felt sure the ancients' missiles would explode if anything impacted the nose of the missile. The missiles were smaller than their ship's torpedoes and too big for their missile launchers. He considered firing it from a rail gun but decided the force generated during the launch could detonate the missile. Therefore, he cradled a missile inside a torpedo housing so it could be fired it from a torpedo tube. The torpedo would explode upon impact and hopefully detonate the missile. The chief engineer received approval from Thomas for a trial experiment.

Thomas did not want another ship to see the explosion, so they traveled to a remote system with an asteroid belt. They located a large asteroid and positioned sensors at various distances from the asteroid. Then the Demon moved to the maximum range that would still allow the torpedo to lock onto the asteroid. The bridge was crowded since everyone wanted to watch the explosion. Thomas gave the order to fire. The missile blew the asteroid apart. Their sensors registered the missile had twice the capacity of their existing torpedoes, but Thomas had expected a bigger explosion from a weapon created by the Ancients. Thomas considered the possibility the Ancients' technology was less advanced than everyone believed. The chief engineer asked to see Thomas in private.

"I have something interesting to show you. These are the sensor readouts from the test. Each sensor has a separate power supply. Watch what happens to the power readings on the sensors shortly after the explosion."

Thomas watched the explosion in slow motion. The power was drained from all the sensors. The closest sensors ceased working first, followed by the sensors farther away. Each time a sensor was depleted, there was a slight increase in the explosive power of the missile. Also, the explosion continued longer than it should have.

The chief engineer excitedly exclaimed, "What if the technology of the Ancients is in their ability to pull energy from other sources to generate power? For example, if this missile hit a ship, the explosion might be catastrophic if it used a ship's energy to enhance its explosive power. If my theory is correct, one of these missiles could destroy any size ship regardless of shielding."

Thomas was intrigued by such a possibility. "How can we test this theory of yours?"

"We could weld some of our power supply units together and couple them to a small energy shield. Then we fire another torpedo and see if there's any change in the output of the explosion."

Thomas authorized another test. Two days later, the chief engineer informed Thomas he was ready to proceed with the second test. They took the same precautions as before. Thomas gave the order to fire, and everyone waited to see if there would be an increase in the power output of the weapon. This time they were not disappointed. The explosion was five times greater. Putting the missile inside a torpedo had worked well. Thomas wondered how big the explosion would be if a missile impacted the shield of a destroyer or a cruiser. Thomas had the chief engineer prepare torpedo housings for the remaining eighteen missiles of the Ancients. He wondered about the ship of the Ancients resting on the dark moon.

Thomas reviewed the writings of the Ancients he received from Captain Erling. He used Omnia to help with the translation. Omnia found examples of the symbols from multiple dead languages and a few complete words. Still, the same word would appear in another language with a slightly different meaning. The AI collected research papers showing limited translations of a few words and phrases. Thomas added the translations to his research but made little progress. He developed more complicated search patterns for Omnia to run in the background. Thomas used an innovative approach suggested by Omnia to allow the AI to generate its own search parameters. It would attempt a translation by using a multiple variance analysis program. Omnia would use a best-guess scenario, refine the results, and then extrapolate to the most reasonable solution using all active and dead languages. This approach would take a long time, so Omnia would only contact Thomas when there was a reasonable probability a word or phrase translation proved statistically relevant by requiring two separate languages to show the same or similar translation.

THE DEMON'S NEXT DESTINATION was Laumar. It was a short jump. As they approached the planet, they saw a ship leaving the system. "Can you get an identification of the ship that's leaving?" Thomas asked.

The Tactical Officer Terrance answered. "It's the Lamia. It's one of the fifteen ships we encountered at Schlimm. It seems Captain Connic has repaired their shields."

They contacted the planet and received a warm greeting. Suzanna sent them a manifest of their cargo.

A while later, the planet's Secretary of Trade contacted the Demon and asked to speak with Thomas. "We're aware of the exploits of the Demon. Thank you for scaring off the pirate ship. They attacked three of our smaller towns. We're caring for our dead and wounded. Besides medical supplies, we'd like to purchase enough weapons to defend ourselves against future attacks. I've sent you a copy of the trade good we wish to purchase."

"We have medical personnel on board to help with your wounded. The severely wounded can be brought aboard our ship and placed in our healing chambers."

"We appreciate the help. I'm transmitting the coordinates for the locations hardest hit by the pirates."

Shuttles brought the worst medical cases to the Demon. Doctor Adler and her assistants stayed busy for the entire time of their visit. After hearing about the healing chambers, several doctors from the planets visited the Demon. They added fifty healing chambers to their order for future delivery. Thomas advised them of the opportunity to join the Imperium, which included a space-based defense grid. He discretely suggested they ask for a thousand healing chambers as a condition for joining.

Thomas granted rotating shore leave to the crew. The planet was primarily rural with a moderate climate. The crew enjoyed the food and hospitality. Laumar executed a long-term trade agreement and looked forward to the Demon's next visit. Thomas sent a message to the Admiral letting him know Laumar might consider joining the Imperium and mentioned they were interested in acquiring healing chambers.

CHAPTER 5 THE ENVIRONMENT WINS

The Demon jumped to their next destination, the planet Smeraldo. The name Smeraldo means green, and the name fits the planet. The planet, including the oceans, was entirely green. The terraforming had been phenomenally successful in establishing a vibrant plant population over the entire planet. Tributin, one of the Demon's scientists who was also a botanist, begged to go to the planet to establish contact on behalf of their ship. Thomas finally relented. They could not find any vacant land, so they landed the shuttle in the branches of a Sequoia Tree they estimated to be over a hundred meters tall.

Tributin exited the shuttle with a backpack, walked approximately ten meters from the shuttle, and sat down. He wore a waterproof jacket since a drizzle of rain appeared to be the constant weather for the planet. Standard protocol required him to stay close to the shuttle in case the inhabitants were hostile.

Tributin sat for over two hours before a young man walked across the large branches and sat down facing him. The pilot and a platoon of marines monitored the situation from within the shuttle. The sensors showed locals hiding a short distance from the shuttle. Tributin had reviewed the history of the planet. When the planet's terraforming results reached the Core Planets, a group of religious environmentalists got funding to claim the planet and turn it into an environmental utopia. The terraform team seeded the Smeraldo with a wide variety of trees, vegetables, and grains to establish a healthy ecosystem. The environmentalists brought in a vast collection of endangered animals they received or acquired from animal sanctuaries, zoos, ark storage facilities, and private owners. They established prey for the predators comprising everything from rodents to boars. The planet proved to be environmentally friendly to the extreme. The sun provided perfect sunlight, constant rainfall provided perfect moisture, and the planet's surface provided the ideal soil. The original colonists struggled to keep the plants from overgrowing the towns and villages. The humans on Smeraldo were extreme environmentalists and refused to use chemicals to kill the vegetation. Thus, they worked continuously to dig up the plants, or the plants would ultimately grow over the homes, covering the windows and doors before taking over the inside of the houses. After several generations, the inhabitants started living in the trees of the forest.

The human inhabitants lived a vegetarian existence and appeared to be very healthy. However, lions, tigers, leopards, jaguars, and other predator animals flourished. While the predators ate rodents, boars, and other prey, they preferred the taste of humans. The inhabitants used spears, bows, and arrows for defense since they opposed any weapons not provided by nature.

"There are others here who are hiding," Tributin said.

"They are here for your protection against the local animal population. Why are you here?"

"We're here to see if you want to establish a trade agreement."

After getting over their initial distrust, the inhabitants allowed more of the Demon's scientists to visit the planet, and adventurous inhabitants visited the Demon. Several dignitaries visited the ship. The dignitaries were members of a council who set the rules governing the planet's inhabitants. They said the food grew wild throughout Smeraldo and only had to be gathered. Each family had the freedom to grow vegetables within the forks of the trees and in boxes made of wood. A wide variety of fruit and vegetables were plentiful and required little cultivation. Everyone on the planet became a member of the Environmental Faith when born. Their religion dedicated their existence to the furtherance of the environment and the endangered animal species.

The inhabitants said it had been over thirty years since a trade ship had visited the planet. They were peaceful people with a homogenous population. A quasi-central government comprised a leader from each village who reported to a religious council to handle the rare disagreements. They had no desire to join the Imperium and stated the original settlers had left the Core because they wanted their freedom.

They had no desire to enter a trade agreement. They would be happy to trade with the Demon during future visits but without a contract. They purchased communicators, hand tools, and medical supplies in small quantities. In the end, Suzanna and her team told Thomas the inhabitants did not need trade since they were self-sufficient and had nothing to export.

However, Smeraldo had a wide variety of predators on the Core's endangered list. Many of the species existed only on Smeraldo. The inhabitants expressed interest in any opportunity to export animals to planets with a good ecosystem or planets with an animal sanctuary since they wanted to assure the survival of the endangered species flourishing on Smeraldo. Within the predatory cat family, Smeraldo had millions of each of the thirty-seven species the colonists had brought to the planet. Having the animals on multiple planets would increase the species' survival if anything happened to Smeraldo. On several occasions, they warned the Demon of the dangers from the wild animals and suggested they not venture outside a village when visiting the planet.

Tributin believed the warnings were exaggerations. He and two assistants ventured to ground level, where they excitedly collected plant samples. A marine corporal and private accompanied them.

After spending the day on the planet, the corporal told Tributin they needed to return to the shuttle. The shuttle rested on heavy branches over seventy meters above them. They had used motorized hoists to lower themselves after the marines cut through the top canopy. The trees and vegetation filtered much of the light from the sun, leaving the lower levels in semidarkness.

Tributin stood up with a bright smile. Just as he spoke, a large animal landed on his back. He fell to the ground and made only a partial scream before an Amur Tiger bit through the back of his neck, killing him instantly. Another tiger simultaneously attacked one of the female assistants with the same results. The second assistant screamed at the top of his lungs while the marines opened fire on the two cats. Then it was total confusion as a pack of hyenas attacked. Multiple hyenas ripped apart the second assistant before the marines could react. Hyenas knocked the Private to the ground. Luckily, he had activated his helmet, and his armor protected him. The corporal stayed busy sporadically firing his gun as the smell of blood drew additional animals. The private regained his feet just as several animals knocked the corporal to the ground. The private killed the animals on top of the corporal and helped him get up just as another group of animals attacked. They stood back-to-back and kept up a continuous fire. When the attack ceased momentarily, they saw that little remained of Tributin and his two assistants. They prepared quick vids, and a different species of tigers attacked as they made their way to the hoists. Their body cams would provide additional vids. They hooked themselves to the hoists and started their ascent. Leopards attacked them as they powered their way to the shuttle. Every predator in the area smelled the blood on their armor as they hurried to the shuttle.

They called ahead, but the pilot did not answer. They reached the top branches and saw blood splatter and other streaks of blood as they neared the shuttle. The marine corporal opened the shuttle ramp while the private dropped to one knee facing the jungle. The pilot was not inside the shuttle. The corporal ordered the private to enter the shuttle and secure it for takeoff. He checked the pilot's locator. The monitor pinned the signal at over two hundred meters from the ship. He knew the locator was in the belly of a predator.

On the flight back to the Demon, the corporal gave Grayson a report on what happened and apologized for failing in his duty. Grayson informed Thomas and immediately notified all ship personnel of the death of the three scientists and the pilot.

The dignitaries had been given several communication devices to discuss potential trade opportunities. Thomas notified the council of his crew members' deaths.

A representative for the council responded. "You have our condolences, but we warned you about the dangers. Predators kill our citizens every day."

Thomas ordered everyone to return to the ship. Additional orders required anyone visiting the planet to be in full armor with a marine contingent.

Suzanna completed her research and determined nearly every planet within the Core had one or more natural habitats for endangered animals. The habitats within the Core Planets worked together. The habitats were well-funded and had special ships designed to transport animals. They were excited when Suzanna said they could have as many animals as they wanted for free. They wanted several thousand animals of each of the endangered species and would send multiple ships to visit Smeraldo. Since their ships lacked armament, they would use their political influence to get a navy escort.

A delegation member from Smeraldo arrived by shuttle and approached Suzanna.

"I'm Viberius. I understand Captain Wilson is in charge of this ship, and I need his help."

"Thomas Wilson is the captain, but maybe I can help you."

"Only the captain can help me, and I'll be killed if anyone finds out I asked for help."

Suzanna called Thomas to let him know a visitor from Smeraldo wished to see him on a matter of some urgency. Thomas agreed to meet with the visitor.

Suzanna escorted Viberius to the captain's ready room. Suzanna kept it formal since their guest was a government representative. "Captain Wilson, this is Viberius, a member of their ruling council."

"How may I help you?" Thomas asked.

"This is a confidential matter and must be kept secret. My life would be forfeited should certain parties become aware of our conversation."

"Suzanna is a trusted member of my senior staff, and we'll not disclose the nature of our conversation to any of the inhabitants of your planet."

"I've learned you carry many weapons as part of your cargo. Are these weapons available for sale?"

Thomas put his palms together with the tips of his fingers touching his chin as he contemplated his response.

"Yes, we sell arms to governments and other parties when it benefits a planet's inhabitants, but we don't sell to terrorists or those who wish to use the weapons for criminal acts. Why do you wish to purchase weapons?"

Viberius took a direct approach. "You know we have a wide variety of predator animals on our planet, but you have not been told the whole truth. Over the years, the number of predators has grown to number in the billions. The predators eat boars, rats, and each other, but all animals prefer humans as their most sought-after prey. Our population, in the beginning, grew each year. In the distant past, our population exceeded twenty million. Today, I'd estimate our population at less than three hundred thousand. We have two continents connected by a small strip of land. The northern continent used to be more populous than the southern continent, but no human survivors remain in the north."

Viberius continued in desperation. "If there's no change, the human population will become extinct on our planet. I had four children, and only one is still alive. Predators killed my other children. Spears and arrows are not enough. We need actual weapons if we're to survive. You're our only hope."

"How many people on Smeraldo feel the same way?" Thomas asked.

"It's difficult to determine the exact number due to the power of the church, but I'd say twenty to thirty percent." Thomas needed more information.

"Suzanna will show you our weapons and the prices." Suzanna saw Thomas tap his ear and understood.

"Follow me," Suzanna said. She took him to their shooting range and allowed him to fire a variety of their small arms, including handguns and rifles. Suzanna loaned him a portable projector and a vid showing the small arms being fired against stationary and moving targets. She did not show him the listening device incorporated into the projector.

TWO DAYS LATER, SUZANNA played selected passages from communications between Viberius and a group of co-conspirators. At first, the individuals in the discussions were excited about protecting their families and friends. However, the meetings became darker as they realized the council would order their arrest and execution. They planned to kill all the council members except for Viberius. The law allowed the council to appoint temporary members to serve until the next elections. With Viberius being the only survivor, he could appoint like-minded individuals to the council. The new council would declare martial law until they killed off enough predators for their survival. They would grant amnesty to everyone assisting in the reduction of the predators.

Thomas called a staff meeting and summarized the discussion he had with Viberius. He then played selected recordings of the conversations Viberius had with his supporters. Thomas asked for recommendations.

"Arming roughly twenty to thirty percent of the population will result in a civil war," Grayson said. "The larger population with primitive weapons will be at a disadvantage against the smaller group with military arms. The fighting would result in guerrilla warfare since the combatants can hide behind tree trunks and in the vegetation. They will fight three-dimensionally by simply climbing higher or lower. The death toll would be high on both sides, and the predators would kill the survivors. We'd hasten the elimination of human life on Smeraldo."

"What about using marines to reduce the number of predators," Thomas asked.

"We considered that," Grayson said. "Let's assume the number of marines available was not an issue, and we could send ten thousand marines in full body armor to the planet. Each marine would need to kill 100,000 predators. The forests are too thick to get a clear shot, and the predators are fast. Also, predators are intelligent. There's no way the military would provide marines for animal hunting. A military solution is not feasible.

"If twenty to thirty percent of the population are non-believers, then we're talking about roughly a hundred thousand people," Ralph said. "Would it be possible to get the family ships to help move the disgruntled population?"

Suzanna spoke up. "The family ships would help with a relocation, but they refuse to leave their planet. We considered deforesting a section of the planet, but it would not help since chemicals strong enough to destroy the trees would contaminate the soil and prevent crops from growing. The people would have to go into the forest for food and be killed by the predators."

"Maybe it's best to let nature take its course and simply leave them alone," the helmsman said. Several of the staff sadly nodded their heads.

"We just lost four crew members," the Tactical Officer responded with anger. "I hate to think of everyone on Smeraldo being eaten by these animals. I favor arming those who want a gun, but I don't want them to use the guns for a coup or a civil war."

Chief Engineer Anderson spoke up. "They have little in the way of technology. Our sales of smart guns include a programmer. We could program the guns to prevent the weapons from firing at humans. We can provide handguns and rifles with embedded restrictions. Without a coder, it'd be impossible for anyone on Smeraldo to modify the guns."

"I like your proposal," Thomas said. "But it doesn't prevent the majority from taking the guns away from the people trying to defend their families."

Thomas broke the staff into four groups and asked each group to work separately to find a solution. The following morning, they reconvened and quickly arrived at a solution. They would provide arms to anyone who wanted to relocate to the northern continent. They would show the faithful the killing power of the weapons. They would not disclose how the guns were non-lethal against humans. They would provide marine escorts and shuttles to assist in relocating those furthest away, while the bulk of the relocation would be done on foot.

Thomas met with the council and presented his proposal with a slight modification. "You have a group of individuals who are unhappy with the status quo and believe human life is more precious than animal life."

"Non-believers," shouted the council.

"They've approached our ship and asked to purchase guns to protect themselves from the predators on this planet."

"You can't seriously consider such a request. It'd result in civil war. Thousands would die."

Thomas waited for the council members to calm down. "We propose all non-believers be allowed to travel to the northern continent. We'll sell them guns for their protection. The projectile guns come with a thousand rounds of ammunition, and the blasters are recharged using solar panels or power units. Even with guns, killing the predators will be difficult. Using our weapons won't result in a significant reduction in the overall population of the predators. Also, the guns will only be given to non-believers who cross into the northern continent. Thus, the animals in the southern continent will be unaffected."

"And if we refuse?"

Thomas took out his sidearm and fired it at a midsize tree. "Then we'll give the guns to the purchasers and leave."

The council called a meeting of the village leaders. The eldest council member announced to those in attendance. "This is against our religious laws. The Demon will give the non-believers unnatural weapons to kill the sacred animals. However, at the council's insistence, the guns will only be given to the non-believers who move to the northern continent. The northern continent will serve as a prison for non-believers, but any non-believer may return if they regain their faith. Captain Wilson has offered to arrange transportation for anyone who wishes to move off-planet. Anyone interested in leaving Smeraldo must decide quickly since the Demon will leave once the relocation is completed."

The ship spent twenty days at Smeraldo using all their shuttles to assist in the relocation. They would have completed the relocation task sooner, but the population moving to the northern continent exceeded sixty percent. Many of the devout believers wanted to save their children. They sold the guns on credit to the non-believers knowing they would never be paid.

The scientists asked Thomas to join them, and they presented specific findings regarding Smeraldo. Extrapolating the history of the planet and using a modified anthropology approach, they determined Smeraldo would ultimately be devoid of human life. The planet was environmentally structured to support plants and wild animals but was detrimental to humans and domesticated animals. The probability of the hypothesis that human life would cease on the planet within sixty years exceeded ninety-five percent. The small population of humans did not stand a chance against several billion predators. The guns we provided will allow those in the north to last about thirty years longer than those without weapons. Therefore, guns will have a negligible impact on the statistics. They discussed their finding with the inhabitants but were not believed.

Only two thousand and twenty inhabitants asked for asylum to leave the planet. The rest adamantly opposed leaving Smeraldo. Suzanna contacted the non-profit group responsible for the animal habitats, and they gladly offered employment to the asylum seekers. Thomas made a note to check back with the inhabitants at a future date to see if more would reconsider their opposition to moving to another planet. Thomas and the rest of the crew gladly left Smeraldo and hoped their calculations were wrong.

THE DEMON HAD TRAVELED a long way from the Core. They had sold all their cargo and entered into good trade agreements. Also, they had made some good friends on most of the planets. Thomas gave the order to make the long jump back to the Core.

Thomas felt satisfied with the progress they had made in the Outer Planets. They had established additional trade contracts and eliminated the pirates in the Outer Planets. They were now ready to proceed with establishing trade within the Rim.

Thomas and Suzanna continued to be in love with each other. Even though they were not married, they continued to share the oversized captain's cabin with Amanda, their daughter. They had made a door into the adjoining cabin so Amanda could have a separate bedroom.

Amanda was precocious, and with the help of the onboard training module, she exceeded the grounders of her age in education. She enjoyed helping her mother with the second most important job on the ship, which involved buying and selling products. The most important job was the defense of the ship. As part of Amanda's training, Suzanna gave her the responsibility for buying and selling certain small accounts where errors would not appreciably affect the ship's profitability. Suzanna had learned using the same approach. However, unknown to Suzanna, Amanda had help from the ship's advanced AI to assist her, and it provided additional training.

Amanda searched for the trade items she needed to purchase when they returned to the Core Planets. She saw items listed at half the standard pricing. She saw the seller was a salvage company.

"Omnia, why are the prices so low at this company?"

"Why do you think the prices are low?" Omnia asked.

"Mom always says if the price is too low, then the quality is most likely low, or the product may be stolen, or the seller is desperate for some reason."

"Could there be another reason? How do you make a profit?"

"By selling higher than your total costs," Amanda replied after thoughtful consideration.

Amanda pulled the full description of the items for sale and read the disclaimer. The disclaimer for the product said the product contained contaminants, but it did not list them.

"Omnia, see if you can determine the contaminates and find out how much they paid for the product." Omnia had expected the question and immediately displayed the results. "Omnia, if we purchase the product, can you remove the contaminates?"

Omnia affirmed his ability to remove the contaminants and repair the damaged containers. He displayed how the salvage company had purchased the product from an insurance company for twenty percent of wholesale pricing. The product had been part of a large warehouse complex recently damaged by an earthquake. The warehouse caught fire. The sprinkler system was damaged and failed to put out the fire. A response team used robotic equipment to spray the building with fire-retardant chemicals. The containers of product became buried underneath the building's rubble. The fire-retardant chemicals penetrated the walls of some containers, and there were cracks in other containers. The salvage company bought four hundred of the eleven hundred containers at twenty percent of wholesale pricing. Amanda contacted her mother.

"This is your product line," Suzanna said. "Call the insurance company and make an offer on the seven hundred remaining containers."

Amanda grinned and had Omnia put through the call. The insurance company's AI answered the call. Amanda offered to purchase all the remaining containers at five percent of the wholesale price. The AI responded at twenty percent. Amanda responded at ten percent as the best and final bid. The AI rerouted the call to a human agent who noted the offer originated from the Demon. Everyone was aware of the exploits of the Demon.

The agent quickly confirmed a fifteen percent price as their best and final offer. Amanda looked at her mother and responded. "The best containers have already been sold at twenty percent. The remaining containers have more damage and contain slower-moving products. Plus, we'll take all seven hundred containers at ten percent."

There was a pause. "Twelve and one-half percent."

Amanda looked at her mother, who smiled and nodded her head. "Agreed."

Suzanna processed a twenty-five percent down payment with the balance due upon transfer of the containers.

Suzann suggested Amanda contact the salvage company. The salvage company would have selected the least damaged containers that were likely free of contaminants.

Amanda again had Omnia put through the communication and submitted an offer to purchase all four hundred containers for twenty percent. The AI for the salvage company replied with a price of fifty percent. Amanda submitted a final bid of twenty-five percent.

A human agent made the subsequent response. "If you take all four hundred containers, we'll accept thirty-five percent of the current wholesale price."

Amanda looked at the current wholesale price being displayed. It was slightly higher than the price when the salvage company purchased the product from the insurance company.

"You only paid twenty percent when the wholesale price was lower," Amanda responded. "My offer will allow you a nice profit, and you won't have the cost of spending years trying to sell all those containers."

The image of the negotiator for the salvage company showed a rough-looking middle-aged lady with short brown hair and piercing hazel eyes. She asked for a visual to see the person making the offer. Amanda reluctantly switched to visual.

"Is this a prank? Do your parents know you're interfering in trade matters? I want to speak to one of your parents, and don't hang up since I'll call back using the same frequency."

"I'm Amanda Wilson, and my father is Thomas Wilson, captain of the Demon. He's quite busy. He or my mother will approve whatever agreement we may reach. Do you really want to talk to my father? He gets upset when bothered by minor issues while on the bridge."

The lady swallowed and said, "No, that won't be necessary. If the Demon takes all four hundred containers, we will sell at thirty percent if you take an additional fifty containers of the same products at the same price." Amanda looked at her mother again.

"Agreed," Amanda said. They executed the standard purchase agreement. Suzanna signed below Amanda and transferred the deposit.

After disconnecting, the lady laughed. She owned the salvage company and had enjoyed negotiating with the child. A child who had all the facts and was a tough negotiator. She chuckled and took a coffee break before returning to work.

"What are we going to do with all this excess product," Suzanna asked Amanda. "The product you just purchased is more than our ship would use in a hundred years. Rather than sell to the planets, you might check with your grandparents on the Familia Primum."

Amanda contacted the Familia Primum and asked to speak with her grandparents. Her grandmother appeared on the screen. Then, her grandfather appeared next to her grandmother.

After the pleasantries, Amanda said, "I've just purchased eleven hundred and fifty containers. I'm sending you a list of the products and quantities. We'll consider selling nine hundred and fifty containers at the right price."

Omnia transmitted the product information for the containers. Amanda and her mother had already selected two hundred containers they were keeping for the Demon. Amanda gave her grandparents time to review the products. Her grandparents looked at her, and she knew it was time to negotiate.

"We'll sell at a discount to a buyer who will take all the containers," Amanda said. "The containers are listed with certain contaminates, but the products will be pure when delivered. Plus, we need to make a slight profit. If you take all the containers, you can have them for eighty percent of wholesale pricing."

Her grandfather grabbed his heart. "My granddaughter would rob her dying grandfather."

Amanda started laughing. "You're not dying. Okay, I will lower the price to seventy percent since you are family."

"It'll take us a lifetime to resale all the products," her grandmother replied. "Even at thirty percent, we'll lose money. Surely, you can lower the price some more for your grandmother."

Amanda knew she would lower the price, but negotiating with her grandparents was fun. "For grandmother, I'll lower the price to sixty percent."

Then her uncle appeared on the screen. "How's my favorite niece?"

Amanda laughed. "I'm your only niece."

"Yes, but you're still my favorite. Will you lower the price to fifty for your favorite uncle?"

"Okay, but that's the final price." Amanda completed the transaction with a note letting them know the product would be available for pickup on Arabath.

"We're family. What's your cost basis?" her grandfather asked.

"A seller should never let the buyer know their cost basis, but because we're family, our cost is around nineteen percent." Her grandfather, along with everyone else, was impressed.

"For family, you could let us have it at cost."

Amanda giggled. "Don't be silly. I'm a spacer."

Her grandfather, grandmother, and uncle all grinned. Amanda was definitely a spacer. Their family would gain additional ship honors with the profits of this purchase, guaranteeing the survival of their ship for years to come. They contacted the family ships and sold the just purchased cargo at seventy-five percent of standard pricing. They kept sufficient containers for their use and sold the balance before the end of Day Watch.

Captain Javier of the Familia Primum called for celebrations for the next three cycles. Everyone knew Suzanna's child followed in her mother's and grandparents' footsteps. Suzanna's parents and brother continued to be treated like celebrities on the ship while the crew practically worshiped Suzanna. Everyone on a family ship lived the same basic shared lifestyle. It took profit for a ship to survive. Over a hundred family ships existed in the distant past. Now, only sixty-five remained. Ships disappeared because of accidents, pirates, marauders, and insufficient profit. Family ships looked out for their ship first and secondarily for other family ships. They considered the Demon, an honorary part of their family. The support provided by Thomas benefited the family.

SUZANNA HUGGED AMANDA and sent her to tell Thomas about the trade transaction. She called Thomas and gave him all the details. After Amanda left, there was something Suzanna remembered during the negotiations. She brought up the video and played it twice before realizing that Amanda had lowered her voice to a whisper when talking to the AI. Suzanna played it back again and increased the gain. She barely heard Amanda referring to the AI as Omnia. However, everyone else referred to the AI as Jewel. Thomas had selected the name.

"Omnia," Susanna said. There was no response.

"Jewel, who is Omnia?"

Jewel responded. "There is no person on the ship named Omnia."

Everyone on Demon was having fun discussing Amanda's trades. Later in the day, after Amanda had completed her session in the education module, they met in the cafeteria for dinner. Thomas sent a message saying he would join them.

"Amanda, who is Omnia?" Suzanna asked.

Amanda looked surprised and said, "It's a secret."

"You can tell me, and then it'll be our secret too."

"One day, while sleeping in our cabin, I woke up and heard dad talking to Omnia. Dad and Omnia were discussing secret things. When I asked dad about Omnia, he said it's a secret. Omnia is my friend, and she's very smart. Dad said we must not tell anyone."

Suzanna saw the concerned look on her daughter's face. "Don't worry. I'll keep our secret." Amanda relaxed and smiled.

That Night, after Amanda was asleep in her room. Suzanna closed the door to Amanda's room and crawled into bed with Thomas.

"Who is Omnia?" Suzanna felt Thomas' body go rigid.

"What have you heard?" Thomas avoided the question.

"I heard Amanda whispering to Omnia, and it answered her. She told me it's a secret. She says only you and her talk to Omnia."

Thomas did not know how to respond to Suzanna. "It's our backup AI."

"Why is it a secret?"

"Omnia will take over in the event our primary AI becomes inoperative. It has data and certain information not accessible by anyone else. Information I don't want anyone else to know about."

Suzanna understood. "You mean information about the Ancients."

"Yes." Thomas remained quiet.

Suzanna understood. Anyone with information regarding the Ancients was required to turn it over to the authorities. Having such information was treasonous.

"Your secret is safe. I'll delete the vid containing Amanda's discussions with Omnia. Amanda seems convinced we can clean the contaminants from the containers she purchased today."

"She's correct. We have a built-in extractor on the ship. It can purify the containers."

"Great, it'll save us the costs of paying for the service. I thought I knew everything about the ship. It would have been nice to know about such capabilities." Suzanna was upset with Thomas for not telling her about such an extraordinary aspect of the ship.

Thomas did not want anyone to know Omnia's true nature and abilities. "I'm sorry, there are so many operations on the ship I take for granted and forget others may not know about all the things the ship can do. Are you mad?"

"Yes, but I'll get over it." Suzanna found it difficult to stay mad at Thomas, but how could he fail to understand how this ability gave them a tremendous trading advantage? For someone so smart, how could he be so stupid?

Thomas was still concerned as he listened to Suzanna's breathing and knew she was asleep. However, he knew Suzanna would keep their secret. He'd fallen in love with Suzanna and couldn't contemplate life without her or Amanda. Amanda was growing up so fast, and she had a fun day. She was so excited when she told him about buying and selling the cargo.

THE DEMON ARRIVED AMONG the Core Planets and made their first stop at the planet with the eleven hundred fifty containers. As soon as they docked at the space station, the 700 containers from the insurance company and the four hundred fifty containers from the salvage company were delivered. Suzanna had the handlers place them in the corner of the cargo bay designated by Thomas. Omnia immediately used the nanites to remove the impurities and repair any damage to the containers. It only took a single cycle to purify the contents.

They made two stops to pick up munitions before arriving at Melius. Melius had manufactured the quantities to fill their purchase orders. It took five cycles to transport all the purchases onto the ship. The ship was double loaded with containers stacked from floor to ceiling in every aisle. They needed to lighten the loan.

Thomas took his seat in the captain's chair. "Enter the coordinates for Arabath," Thomas said to the helmsman.

"All hands make your final checks to verify everything is properly stowed." Thomas waited the time allotted for the crew to conduct their final inspection. No one asked for extra time since the time for leaving Melius had been previously posted.

"Helm, take us out of orbit and proceed to jump speed, but Demon is overloaded, so take it easy." They slowly left the orbit of Melius. They could all feel the extra vibration of the ship as the engines responded to the heavy load. Because of the added inertia, it took longer to reach jump velocity.

"All readings are green, and we are at jump velocity," the first officer said.

"Engage," Thomas announced. The ship entered hyperspace without issue.

"First Officer Miller, you have the bridge." Thomas stood and left the bridge.

CHAPTER 6 ASSASSIN

Thomas and Suzanna discussed the cargo they would sell and buy at Arabath. It was the richest of the Outer Planets. They met each other on Arabath. It held both good and bad memories. They did not expect any problems since there was little to no crime on Arabath compared to other Outer Planets. Suzanna was looking forward to seeing Terrell. When Suzanna had missed her family ship's departure, Terrell got her a job. She also lived with Terrell for seven months before hiring on as crew with the Demon.

Demon received preferential treatment for dock assignment since they carried products not available from any other ship. Also, they conducted a higher volume of trade than any other ship.

Suzanna spent the first day organizing the major exports and imports before turning over the work to her crew. She had already offloaded the containers purchased by Amanda. The containers would be warehoused on the planet until picked up by the family ships. She then surprised her staff and told them she was taking a holiday. The following morning, Suzanna and Amanda left the ship with their assigned bodyguards. She noticed nothing had changed at the station as she went to the restaurant where she used to work. Suzanna and Amanda sat down at a table and waited. It was not long before she saw Terrell delivering an order to a nearby table. Terrell was wearing the same type of dress she had worn five years earlier, and the years simply disappeared.

"How about a little service over here?" Suzanna shouted.

Terrell turned with a frown on her face. She stared and then screamed, "Suzanna!"

Everyone in the restaurant was startled but settled down when they realized the station was not coming under attack. The disturbance was just two crazy females showing their excitement at meeting each other after a long absence. Suzanna stood up as they embraced each other. When they separated, they both had tears in their eyes. Terrell joined them at their table, and Suzanna introduced Amanda.

It had been over five years, but the years had not diminished their friendship or the bond they had formed when they worked and lived together. They finally dried their eyes. Terrell wanted the details of Suzanna's life aboard the Demon. Suzanna knew Terrell was not interested in the mundane ship duties associated with the ship's trade. Suzanna told Terrell how she and Amanda shared the captain's cabin. She told her how much she loved Thomas and how happy she was on the Demon. Terrell needed to know the sacrifices they shared had made a difference.

They had been talking for a while when the cook came out. "Terrell, the orders are backing up," he said in a raised voice.

"Shut up and come over here," Terrell said. "Suzanna, you remember Ruddee, the cook. The two of us bought the restaurant and then got married. Ruddee, you remember Suzanna. This is her daughter, the one she was carrying when she worked here."

Ruddee looked shabby with a dirty apron and a big belly from sampling his cooking every day. However, he had a twinkle in his eyes, which gave him a jovial appearance.

"Wow, you have turned into a queen since leaving here," Ruddee said. "This must be a princess sitting next to you." Ruddee left to go back to the kitchen after taking their orders for two specials.

"I need to get back to work," Terrell said. "I've wondered almost every day what became of you. I always hoped you were happy out there sailing through the galactic."

"When you get off, I want to pick you up so we can go shopping for expensive clothes at a high price," Suzanna responded. It was an inside joke. When they worked together, they bought cheap clothes at a cheap price.

Terrell laughed. "Sounds great. We have a small home on Arabath."

Terrell transferred the location to Suzanna's wristband, and they set a meeting time.

"Once I get off, it'll just take a moment for me to go home and change clothes. Suzanna, it's so great to see you, and we'll have a wonderful time spending the afternoon together."

After finishing their meal, Suzanna and Terrell hugged again before they left. Suzanna took Amanda to see and ride the space elevator. Then she took Amanda to the tourist sites while waiting for Terrell's shift to end.

Suzanna and Amanda picked up Terrell at her home at the end of Day Watch, and they had the rest of the evening to socialize. Terrell explained how Clarence, the restaurant owner, wanted to retire but could not find anyone interested in buying the restaurant. Terrell and Ruddee told Clarence they wanted to purchase the restaurant but did not have any money. Clarence provided the financing, and they had been making the payments even though it was difficult at times. They had regular loyal customers who worked at the station and recommended their restaurant to visiting ships. Also, Arabath continued to be a busy port, and the only other restaurant served a different expensive cuisine and was not a direct competitor.

Suzanna said she wanted to visit the prior owner and thank him again for giving her a job when she needed it. They visited Clarence without calling ahead. He recognized Suzanna and appeared happy to have visitors. He told them to come in and sit awhile. After talking for a while, Suzanna whispered into Amanda's ear.

Suzanna turned to Terrell. "You've been here before. Would you mind showing Amanda to the bathroom?"

When they left the room, Suzanna asked, "How much do Terrell and Ruddee owe on their note?"

"Well, I suppose it is okay to tell you since you're such a close friend."

She saw the amount and asked him to provide his access code so she could make a payment. Ruddee thought Terrell might have trouble making the next payment and figured Suzanna was helping her friend. Then he looked at the account and saw the remaining mortgage balance had been paid. He was shocked and graciously thanked her.

"The amount I just transferred could never cover the debt I owe Terrell. I owe my existence to her. She was a friend when I desperately needed one."

When Terrell returned, they told her the loan had been paid in full. Before Terrell could say anything, Suzanna said, "You were there when I needed help, and I don't know how I'd have survived without your help. You never asked for anything and spent your last credit getting me a dress when I went onboard the Demon. Because of you, my daughter and I are spacers. Now, no more talk about me helping the best friend I ever had."

"Thank you," Terrell murmured while hugging her friend.

"Let's go shopping," Suzanna said.

They enjoyed shopping and purchased several outfits for themselves. Then they had fun buying items for Amanda, Thomas, and Ruddee. Suzanna provided the dock location for her and Amanda's purchases since the upscale establishments offered free delivery to visiting ships. Then, they had dinner together at an upscale restaurant. The time passed too quickly as Suzanna dropped Terrell back at her home with all her packages. They hugged again and cried again as they said their goodbyes.

WHILE SUZANNA WAS VISITING her friend, Thomas saw
Suzanna's department had already taken care of offloading the
freight. He approved the shore leave schedule. Everyone was
efficiently handling their assigned duties, and no one seemed to need
his help.

Thomas exited the ship and figured he would visit the planet.
Although he felt safe on Arabath, he was armed when he left the
ship. Before the last jump, he received a communication from Agent
Sicarius. Duke Winsor had put out another contract to have him
killed.

This time the Duke had hired a female contract killer. The killer
had many aliases, and she usually traveled with four or more
accomplices. She took the most difficult cases but guaranteed results.
Supposedly, she had never failed to fulfill a contract. As a result, she
charged a very high fee. This gave her the funds to get information
not readily available to most assassins. The file contained copious
details on a dozen accomplices she had used in the past.

There was considerably less information on the assassin, but
Agent Sicarius had somehow located her birth name as Opaline
Couyon. Not only was she a high-priced assassin, but she liked to
seduce her victims before killing them. While she was an expert with
all weapons, she could kill with a scratch of her fingernail or a bite.
Out of curiosity, Thomas searched to see the origins of her last name
and could not help but smile. The Cajun French meaning of Couyon
was 'foolish,' which was not too bad, but it translated to 'dumbshit'
in the Mauritian language. Thomas chuckled and could not blame
her for changing her name. He saw the lengthy list of kills associated
with her were all in the Rim. There were considerable rewards offered
for her and her accomplices. Thomas figured he would not have to
worry until he returned to the Rim.

Thomas took the space elevator to the planet. It was simply a gorgeous day. The temperature at twenty degrees Celsius was perfect, with low humidity and a cloudless sky. He could not remember a more beautiful day. Toward the evening, he went to the restaurant he had taken Suzanna on their first date. The place was not very crowded, so he took a table for four close to the wall. An attractive server dressed in black pants, a black matching vest, with a white shirt asked if he would mind moving to a smaller table, but she ceased when he gave her a large tip to stay at the table. He asked the server to give him a minute to review the menu.

Thomas was reviewing the menu when an outrageously gorgeous lady entered the restaurant wearing a red dress. It hugged her large breasts and slim waist. The dress had a slit along one side, exposing her long, beautiful legs. Everyone watched her as she walked over and sat at a nearby table. Thomas glanced around and felt a cold chill run up his spine as he noticed the four men who had come in shortly after the lady. The four men split up, with two men taking a table between him and the entrance to the restaurant. The other two men walked past Thomas and sat at a table blocking the back exit. Thomas was effectively boxed in. He immediately sent an emergency code through his armlet. It would go straight to the Demon and light up all the screens. He then muted the device but left it on audio out.

Thomas looked around and noticed a large, heavyset male with bulging muscles wearing a black shirt with the restaurant's logo, who had to be the bouncer. The bouncer had a physique typical of someone from a world with a higher than standard gravity.

The server came back over to take his order. "I'm going to transfer ten thousand credits to your account," Thomas said.

She gave him an angry stare. "I'm sorry I gave you the wrong impression, but we only serve food and drinks here. Establishments within walking distance can take care of your physical needs."

"The fee is to help me get out of here alive. Don't turn your head. The four men who just came in and who are sitting at separate tables are wanted criminals. There is a one hundred thousand credit bounty on each of their heads, dead or alive. The beautiful lady in the red dress who just sat down has a million-dollar bounty on her head. If you and the bouncer help me, you can have all the reward money. Be careful of the female. Her fingernails and teeth can kill. Talk to your bouncer sitting close to the two men at the door and see if he can take out those two. I'll handle the rest. Hold out your risk band and open your account to receive. I'll transfer you the pictures and the rewards. Please bring me a glass filled with one-hundred-ninety-proof grain alcohol. When you return, say yes if the bouncer will help. If he isn't interested, say no."

She looked at him strangely. "If you drink a full glass of pure alcohol, you'll not walk out of here."

"I don't plan to drink it. Please remove the two chairs on the side of the table. When she comes over, I want her sitting as far away from me as possible."

The server moved the chairs to other tables. She left to get drink order and talk to the bouncer.

As soon as the server left, the assassin got up slowly and walked toward him. Every eye in the restaurant turned to watch her. She was beautiful and sexy to the extreme. She moved her hips just enough to be enticing.

"I hate eating alone. Would you mind if I joined you?"

"A gentleman would never turn down an offer from such a beautiful lady," Thomas answered as he tried to think of a way to provide time for reinforcements to arrive.

Grayson received the emergency code at the same time as everyone else and used a continuous stream of derogatory words to refer to the captain. He quickly had a dozen marines grab their guns and rush out of the ship toward the space elevator. Because of a previous assassination attempt, his weapons and the guns of the primary bodyguards carried armor-piercing rounds. They did not take time to suit up in their armor. Using his wristband, he directed a platoon of marines to suit up in their armor and follow in a shuttle. They moved as fast as they could but were slowed by the crowd. The space elevator was on its down up when they reached the entry point. Various people complained when the marines broke in front of the line but stopped when two of the marines turned toward them, gripping their guns. It took a long time for the elevator to return to the station. As soon as the elevator doors opened and the passengers departed, the marines rushed into the elevator and told the conductor to descend. The conductor took note of the weapons and started their descent. Grayson continued to listen to the conversation between Thomas and the assassin. He informed the marines they had two friendlies assisting them, a heavy-worlder bouncer and a server. The restaurant was not close to the space elevator.

THOMAS STOOD UP AND greeted the beautiful assassin but did not come around the table to help her with her chair.

After she sat down, she prepared to introduce herself. "I'm."

Thomas immediately interrupted her. "No, don't tell me your name. I want to play a game with you. We'll talk, and then I get to ask five questions. You must answer each question honestly with a yes or a no. After each answer, I'll try to guess either your first or last name. If, at the end of our meal, I guess either of your names correctly, then you have to grant me a wish."

She smiled seductively. "And what type of wish would I have to grant you?"

"Nothing criminal," Thomas replied with a fake grin. "It's not like I'd ask you to kill someone. I'm a man, and you're a very sexy woman. I'd just ask you to do something of a physical nature."

She readily smiled at the comment. "What do I get if you fail."

"If I fail, I'll give you a choice of receiving one hundred thousand credits, or you can ask me to do your bidding as long as it is nothing criminal."

The server returned with his drink. "Yes," she said.

Thomas turned his head toward the server. "I'd like to order the special, and please put whatever the lady is having on my tab."

"I'll also have the special," the assassin said.

"Would you like wine with your dinner?" Thomas asked the assassin. "Again, it's my treat. Get whatever you like."

The assassin selected the most expensive bottle of Cabernet Sauvignon on the menu. She read it off to the server to see how Thomas would respond.

He impressed her when he nodded his head. "An excellent selection."

He was very handsome. Opaline planned to enjoy having sex with him before she killed him.

"I'll play your game. It'll be entertaining."

"You have a slight accent," Thomas said. "Your hair, body type, and skin color are unique. My first question is if any of your ancestors are Cajun French or Creoles French?"

"Yes," she said with a puzzled expression.

Thomas looked at his armlet and completed a search. He then put his elbows on the table and rested his chin on his hands in thought. He needed to prolong the time.

"The most common last name is Beeharry. Is Beeharry one of your names?"

Opaline relaxed as she laughed and said, "Not even close."

The wine arrived along with a sommelier since it was an expensive reserved estate wine. The sommelier showed his expertise as he opened the wine and described its history and why it ranked as one of the best wines in their wine cellar. He first took a small amount of the wine and swirled it around in his glass to let it breathe. Then, he took a taste and smiled. He poured each of them a small sample for them to taste. Thomas was not a wine connoisseur, but he had watched his parents order and drink wine when the family would eat at gourmet restaurants. Thomas took his time and smelled the wine. Then, he drank the sample.

"The wine's reputation is well deserved." The sommelier smiled and filled each of their wine glasses.

"The second question. Were you or either of your parents born on the planet Mauritius?"

This time she failed to hide her shocked expression. How could he successfully guess her homeworld? She had studied his background to prepare for completing the contract. Thomas and his ship were held in extremely high regard. She had listened to a copy of the conversation when he had faced sixteen ships. His knowledge was uncanny, and his survival against prior attempts on his life had resulted in her demanding double her usual fee. She looked at him with a deadpan expression. "Yes," she replied.

"Well, the most common first name on Mauritius is Aurelie. Is Aurelie one of your names?"

Opaline had been holding her breath. "No," she said softly with concern.

Then she berated herself for actually believing he could guess her name.

Their dinner arrived. "Let's enjoy our meal while I think of the next question." Thomas took his time eating.

Halfway through their meal, Thomas asked, "Do either of your names have a religious meaning?"

"No," she replied with a predatory expression.

Opaline felt certain she would win the bet. Then, she would invite him to her hotel room for sex and death. She would naturally be on top and would enjoy watching his face when he knew he was going to die. Opaline had a different chemical under each fingernail. She would enjoy stretching out his death. Opaline would paralyze him at the appropriate time, but he would still feel the pain she would inflict. She would spend most of the night pleasuring in his agony until she became bored and killed him.

As they were finishing their meal, Thomas saw Grayson and half a dozen marines slowly enter the restaurant.

Thomas took another sip of his wine, draining the glass. "I have my next question. Does your last name have a derogatory meaning?" She looked at him and did not answer.

Thomas had already pulled his gun. He held the gun under the table in his right hand and had his left hand on the untouched glass of grain alcohol.

Thomas gave her a knowing smile. "I can tell by your facial expressions the answer is yes. Therefore, your name must be Opaline Couyon."

She screamed as she jumped up from her chair and tried to scratch his face, but Thomas had already jumped up and backed away while throwing the alcohol in her face. He then upended the table as he turned to face her two closest associates. Both had pulled their guns. Thomas shot one, but the other fired before being gunned down by Grayson and the marines. Thomas turned back as a man at a nearby table tried to assist Opaline, but her eyes were still stinging from the alcohol. She scratched him across the face. He fell backward and was dead before he hit the floor. She pulled a gun from a holster strapped to the inside of her thigh and started firing at Thomas. Opaline was shot multiple times and fell facedown onto the floor as a female marine walked up and kicked the gun away from her hand. She checked Opaline's pulse and nodded to confirm her death. Thomas looked toward the far door and saw the other two accomplices were lifeless on the floor and correctly assumed they were dead. Then he noticed the blood on his shirt and thought, not again. Grayson rushed over while the marines took up defensive positions. The server and the bouncer came over. Thomas told Grayson the server and bouncer were entitled to the rewards.

"I know," Grayson said. "I heard your agreement."

The bouncer showed him the reward posters or his wrist display for the assassin and her four associates. A marine told Grayson one of the assailants was an android. Without the armor-piercing bullets, they would have been in trouble. Also, the dress Opaline wore was made from a lightweight armor material that even their armor-piercing rounds failed to penetrate. The armor allowed her to shoot Thomas multiple times before a headshot killed her.

"They're assassins hired by Duke Winsor," Thomas said.

Grayson wanted to shoot Thomas himself. "And you didn't think to tell me."

"She was supposed to be in the Rim."

Thomas turned to the server and the bouncer. "Thank you for your help. I recommend you put bags over her hands before moving her."

Thomas turned back to Grayson. "I'm not feeling well."

Grayson motioned to two marines who came forward and helped support Thomas as they left the restaurant. Grayson received a communication. One of their shuttles had landed a short distance away. As they approached the shuttle, a platoon of fully armored marines took up defensive positions. As they boarded the shuttle, the marines helping Thomas told Grayson that Thomas was unconscious. Grayson spewed out an excessive amount of profanity as he called the Demon. They connected him with Doctor Adler, and he asked her to meet them in the shuttle bay.

"What's the nature of the emergency, and who's injured?" Doctor Adler asked.

"Who do you think?" Grayson replied.

"Not the captain, not again," the Doctor said with a groan while shaking her head.

AFTER AN ENJOYABLE day, Suzanna and Amanda returned to the station via the space elevator. As they got off the elevator, Suzanna saw Demon marines rushing past her, and she stopped one of them.

"What's going on?" Suzanna asked.

"You haven't heard? The captain has been shot. All the marines have been recalled to the ship."

"Where is Thomas now?"

"A shuttle is bringing him back and should be landing shortly."

Suzanna took Amanda's hand and started running toward the ship, followed by their bodyguards. After they reached the Demon, Suzanna asked one of the bodyguards to pick up Amanda, and they raced to the shuttle bay. She saw the shuttle had already landed. Doctor Adler was rolling a stretcher away from the shuttle. As Suzanna reached the stretcher, she saw Thomas was covered in blood and unconscious with an IV in his arm. The blood loss caused him to look pale and lifeless.

Suzanna turned to Grayson and shouted, "How did you let this happen?"

Grayson rolled his eyes and asked himself the same question.

Suzanna and Amanda watched as Doctor Adler cauterized one of the wounds, and her assistant put a second IV into Thomas' other arm.

"Is he going to be alright?" Suzanna asked.

"He's lost a lot of blood," Doctor Adler said without looking up.

Then Doctor Adler saw Amanda with a worried look in her big round eyes. "Your father will be fine." The Doctor hoped she had not lied.

Doctor Adler looked back at Suzanna and shrugged her shoulders. She needed to get to the hospital and pushed the stretcher at a fast pace. Suzanna and Amanda followed at a slower pace until one of the marines picked up Amanda, and they took off running behind the stretcher. A marine ran ahead of the stretcher to clear the path. When they arrived at the hospital, Suzanna and Amanda waited in the recovery room while they wheeled Thomas into surgery.

Doctor Adler and her assistants placed Thomas on the operating table. They quickly removed his clothing. Doctor Adler scanned his body and located three bullets. She found an entry and exit wound for a fourth bullet. Doctor Adler, with her assistants, performed surgery to remove the three bullets.

Two medical assistants had already prepped a healing chamber. They gently eased Thomas into the healing chamber and hooked up all the monitors. Doctor Adler injected tubes of nanites directly into the three wounds in his chest. She removed the two IVs and wrapped chamber injectors around Thomas' wrists and ankles. Next, she put a breathing tube down his throat. Doctor Adler sealed and activated the chamber. Once the chamber filled with fluid, she checked to verify all the monitors were active. Unfortunately, the monitors showed the patient's condition as life-threatening. Now, they could only wait and hope.

Doctor Adler set up a schedule for a medical assistant to be with Thomas around the clock. She asked Suzanna to step out into the corridor so they could talk without being overheard by Amanda.

"Thomas hasn't fully recovered from his previous injuries," Doctor Adler said. "We'll have to see if the nanites can work their magic once again."

Doctor Adler broke protocol and sent a communication to Admiral Nelson. She provided full details of the attack by the five assassins hired by Duke Winsor. Doctor Adler was still secretly on the navy's payroll in addition to being paid as the Demon's doctor. She told the Admiral this was the second time Duke Winsor had hired someone to kill Captain Wilson.

When Admiral Nelson received the communication, he forwarded it to Agent Sicarius with a message asking the Agent to discuss the matter with Duke Winsor without delay. *Discuss the matter* meant the Duke was to be eliminated. *Without delay* indicated it was to be done immediately.

GRAYSON HAD A SPECIAL meeting with everyone assigned to security. Next, he called a crew meeting in the cargo bay. He used the ship's open channel to reach everyone not in attendance.

"Everyone on this ship is personally responsible for the captain's safety," Grayson said. "Under no condition is the captain to leave this ship without his bodyguards. You're to physically restrain the captain if he refuses to wait for his bodyguards. Every senior officer supports this position" The crew would rather face discipline from the captain than Grayson's wrath.

Grayson knew they must do something about the Duke. He visited the Technology Intelligence Department. He told them what had happened and how they needed to locate the Duke.

Grayson shook his head. The captain had a blind spot for his own safety. How could Thomas go to the extreme to protect the crew and then take no precautions for his personal safety? Nothing was more important to Grayson than the captain's safety, and he must do a better job. No one else could command the Demon and get the results obtained by Thomas. Plus, he and the former teammates of Thomas held a special bond with their captain.

THOMAS LOOKED AROUND and could not believe he was in the healing chamber again. He saw Doctor Adler's face and heard her as she said, "Don't say a word! You should be ashamed of yourself for scaring Suzanna and your daughter to death. Were you mindless when you left the ship without your bodyguards? Don't bother answering. Wiggle your toes, wiggle your fingers."

Doctor Adler checked his vitals and then put him back to sleep. She was furiously pissed at the captain. How many times did he think he could cheat death? She looked down at Amanda, asleep on a mat next to the healing chamber. She leaned down and tucked the blanket around Amanda. Suzanna was sleeping in the next room. She notified her assistant she was going to her cabin. She told them to call her if any of the alarms went off.

AGENT SICARIUS LOCATED Duke Winsor on a planet in the Demaron system. After landing on Demaron and spending a few credits, he found the Duke was living in a sizable home in a rural area outside the capital. The Duke had hired a group of fifteen mercenaries to provide for his protection. Also, the Duke had hired two females to keep him company.

Agent Sicarius rented a ground vehicle and drove to the home where the Duke was staying. He got out of the vehicle and approached a mercenary standing guard at the entrance to the driveway. The Agent told the mercenary to have the person in charge of the mercenaries meet him at the small local pub located a short distance up the road. He told the guard he would buy the beer and give the person in charge ten thousand credits for an hour of his time. He then said he would be at the pub for one hour, and then he left.

Agent Sicarius arrived at the bar and did not have long to wait. Five of the mercenaries entered the bar. The Agent motioned for them to join him. Agent Sicarius signaled the bartender. One of the servers brought a pitcher of beer and six glasses to the table.

Agent Sicarius took a sip of his beer. "You have a problem. Duke Winsor has upset the wrong people, and he will be terminated. If you stay with the Duke, you and your men will be eliminated. I'm offering you one option and only one option to stay alive. You all are former military. You know or suspect there's a special branch handling off the books, clandestine operations. I'm part of such a unit. I have a cloaked ship in orbit. We prefer to keep casualties to a minimum whenever possible. However, our mission will be completed regardless of collateral damage. I'll give you one million Galactic credits to pack your bags and leave within the hour, or you can die within the hour."

"When would we get paid?" The mercenary in command asked.

"I'll pay you upfront right now."

"Can you give us a moment?"

"Sure, I'll be at the bar."

As soon as the Agent walked away, they started talking among themselves. An older mercenary said he had met a person who had seen an elite group in action. The men in the group were efficient and completely ruthless, with unlimited credits backing them up. After further discussions, they all agreed they believed the Agent. The leader of the Mercenaries motioned for the Agent to rejoin them.

"We'll take the deal. Here's our account number." Agent Sicarius completed the transfer, and the leader saw the deposit in their account.

"You have one hour starting now."

The mercenaries left the bar and returned to the home. They spoke to all of their fellow mercenaries and packed their gear. As they were leaving, they saw a person in full military armor standing by a ground vehicle. They heard a roar as two shuttles came in for a landing on either side of the homes. They were glad they had accepted the deal as they left the area at maximum speed.

Armored individuals exited the shuttles and surrounded the home. Agent Sicarius used his throat mic to inform the team to wait outside and stay alert. He had been earnest with his offer to the mercenaries. They would have died if they had failed to take the buyout offer. He approached the home and entered through the unlocked door. He searched the house until he found Duke Winsor in a bedroom with the two females. Agent Sicarius retracted his helmet and grabbed the foot of first one lady and then the next, to get their attention. He put his finger to his lips to indicate they should remain silent, and then he motioned for them to leave. He told an agent outside to give a bonus to the two ladies and tell them to use his vehicle to return to the city.

Agent Sicarius went into the kitchen and located a bucket. He filled it with water and returned to the bedroom. Then, he threw the cold water on the Duke. The Duke sat up screaming. It was apparent the Duke had a hangover.

"I'm a Duke and will not stand for such treatment," he shouted. Then he saw the gun pointed at him and stopped talking as he became suddenly fearful.

"Your mercenaries are all gone," Agent Sicarius said calmly. "I'm here to kill you." The Agent pointed the gun at the Dude's head.

"Stop, I have funds," the Duke said quickly. "I'll pay you whatever you ask, just don't kill me."

"Show me your account." The Duke pulled up his account. "Transfer the entire amount to the following account," Agent Sicarius said as he displayed the destination account.

"No way," The Duke replied.

The Agent shot him in the kneecap. After the Duke stopped screaming, he started crying. Then he transferred the entire balance as directed. After the transfer, Agent Sicarius dragged the Duke through the house and out the backdoor.

Agent Sicarius pointed his gun at the Duke. "Your wife sends her regards, as well as the families of the freedom fighters and all the people you've killed over the years. You could have just left and maintained a low profile. No one would have cared, but you sent assassins to kill Thomas Wilson. He is working on behalf of the navy, and we protect our own."

Agent Sicarius shot the Duke through the head. Two of the men with him knew what to do. They sprayed the body with liquid acid and then set fire to the remains. When they were done, nothing remained except a burnt spot on the ground.

Everyone, including the Agent, entered the shuttles and left the planet. The Agent sent a message to the Admiral letting him know he had a successful discussion with the Duke, and the Duke voluntarily transferred his remaining funds to a needy charity.

ONBOARD THE DEMON, Thomas awoke and realized the medical assistants were removing him from the chamber. He tried unsuccessfully to help. He decided not to say anything to the Doctor until he found out if she was still mad at him. Once they had him dressed in a hospital gown and resting in bed, they let Suzanna and Amanda enter the room. Amanda wrapped her arms around his neck and held him as hard as she could. Thomas hugged her back and asked her what had been happening during his stay in the hospital. He learned he had been in the chamber for twenty-nine days. Thomas asked why he had been in the chamber for such a long time. Suzanna explained how previously they had let him out early with the understanding he would take it easy while his body recuperated. This time Doctor Adler left him in the chamber until he was completely healed. Thomas admitted he felt stronger this time compared to his two previous experiences in the chamber.

Thomas worked on his exercises each day until he exceeded the requirements for release. Finally, the Doctor told Thomas he could return to light duty. Then she gave him the lecture he had been expecting.

"I don't want to see you in my hospital again as a patient. Do you understand?" Thomas was afraid to speak and showed his intelligence by meekly saying yes and nodding his head.

He finally spoke to the Doctor as he was leaving. "Thank you."

The Doctor grimaced. "You're welcome. Now, get out of here."

It was Day Watch, so Thomas made his way to the bridge. Everyone welcomed him back. The next several months were uneventful as they handled exports and imports among planets. Then the Technology Intelligence Department said they needed to see him. When he arrived, they gave Thomas a report on their efforts to locate Duke Winsor. They had finally found the Duke, but then he had simply disappeared.

They informed Thomas the navy was assembling a large force in the Rim. They were concerned it was preparation for a major battle with the Hostis.

CHAPTER 7 RIM WORLD CONTRACTS

With less threat from pirates within the Outer Planets, Thomas figured it would be a suitable time to return to the Rim to conduct some serious trade. They made a jump to one of the arms manufacturing planets to purchase military munitions. They filled up over half of the cargo racks before jumping to the second arms planet and purchasing enough containers of additional munitions to fill every rack space and the aisles.

Then, they jumped to Melius. Similar to previous trips, they unloaded half their munitions into their warehouse on Melius. They loaded the Demon with high-value standard cargo, including power units, universal chips, food processors, solar generators, under armor, medical supplies, and other specialty items. The under armor had become a top seller on planets with uncomfortably cold or hot climates. In addition, to protecting the wearer against small caliber weapons, the under armor warmed or cooled the body depending upon the ambient temperature. Besides their standard cargo, they added eighty of the expensive healing chambers.

The Demon jumped to the nearest Sector Star Gate for transport to the edge of the Outer Planets. As soon as the navy gave their approval, the Demon entered the Gate. With the reduction in piracy, Thomas felt safe using the Star Gates for the long jump from the Core Planets to the Outer Planets. Thomas was surprised to see only four frigates guarding the Gate. The six Sector Star Gates connected the Core Planets to the Outer Planets. These Gates were usually guarded by a minimum of four destroyers and a cruiser. The same was true for the four Sector Star Gates connecting the Outer Planets to the Rim.

Thomas met with his staff to discuss the Rim Worlds they would visit on this trip. When the Demon exited the Star Gate, Thomas was again surprised to see only frigates greeting them. Usually, the Demon would jump to an Outer Planet to start their trade route, but this time the Demon headed to the nearest long jump Sector Star Gate for travel from the Outer Planets to the Rim. It only took two standard days to reach the gate.

Upon arrival, Thomas received immediate authorization to enter the Gate, but the captain granting the gate access seemed worried. The navy captain uncharacteristically wished him good luck and told him to be careful.

During the transit, Thomas selected the Rim destinations. When they exited the Sector Star Gate, there were no navy ships, and Thomas began to worry. He told First Officer Miller to keep the Demon at General Quarters until further notice. He wanted the Demon ready to go immediately to battle stations if needed. Thomas saw the concerned faces on his bridge officers.

THE DEMON MADE ITS scheduled jump to Suerte. There were defense satellites in orbit, courtesy of the navy. Suzanna sent Suerte a manifest of their cargo. Suerte immediately asked to meet with the Demon's representative to discuss trade and said they wanted to purchase all their arms. Thomas and Suzanna, in full body armor with twenty marines, landed on the planet next to a building as requested by the President of Suerte. Thomas was surprised to find Suerte operated under a quasi-democracy. Thomas and his trade team were uncomfortable since the planet's gravity was a hundred twenty percent above standard. Because of the gravity, the people of Suerte were shorter but very muscular compared to Thomas and his crew. There was no socializing, and everyone took a seat at the conference room table.

"We were informed over a year ago by the navy to expect a trade ship to arrive with much-needed items and weapons," the President said. "We've been stockpiling rare earth elements and excess minerals in anticipation of your arrival."

An advisor to the President provided a list of the elements and minerals, along with the quantities of each. Suzanna performed a quick calculation and provided the President with the credits they would have available for the purchase of the Demon's cargo. It only took a moment for the advisor to create two purchase orders for Suzanna. The first was a military order for three hundred and ten containers of arms, including six Aysal Attack Helicopters. The second was a civilian order for two hundred containers of food processors, a hundred containers of medical supplies, including twenty healing chambers, and fifty containers of power units. The advisor asked if Thomas would sell them some shuttles. Thomas reluctantly agreed to sell them two of the non-military shuttles. They worked around the clock. It only took three cycles to unload the ship's cargo, but it took four additional days to load the rare earth elements into containers and transport the containers to the Demon. The President provided over two thousand workers to help unload and reload the containers. While they transferred the cargo, Suzanna negotiated a long-term trade agreement.

The President took Thomas aside for a short private meeting. "One of your crew said your family is in the shipbuilding business. Would it be possible for our planet to buy a ship from your family?"

"As you say, we're in the business of building ships and would be happy to sell you a ship. The ships are quite expensive, but the ships would immediately be profitable since you can buy direct for your planet's needs. The cost of your imports would be half your current costs. You could recover your entire investment in less than ten years.

We have three standard merchant ships designed for trade between planets. For your planet, I'd suggest you start with our midsize design. I'll transfer you the design specs for all three models and the price for each ship. You can decide which ship you would like. We require progressive payments with twenty-five percent upfront."

"How long would it take to deliver such a ship?"

"The normal delivery is eighteen months from the receipt of the down payment and execution of the contract," Thomas said. "You need to have a trained crew ready when construction is completed. If you'd like, we could hire some of your citizens as crew on the Demon. They would go through training and should be ready to crew your new ship when it is ready."

"We'll have the down payment ready before you leave orbit. How many of our people are you willing to hire?"

"You need at least sixty, but one hundred eighty would be better if you want to cover all three shifts with a minimum crew size."

"We'll have a hundred eighty of our best people ready by this time tomorrow and thank you. Also, we'll pay a premium if you can deliver the ship in less time. The navy was recently here and believes an attack by the Hostis is imminent. We want to purchase fifty thousand surface-to-air missiles, a hundred thousand portable rocket launchers, and ten million 50-caliber machine guns. With such weapons, we may be the first planet to survive a Hostis invasion."

The visit to Suerte was a complete success. The crew was happy to be back aboard the Demon since the heavy gravity of Suerte had exhausted them. The new crew personnel from Suerte were excited to be aboard and were already using the training modules.

The Demon accelerated to jump velocity. The navigator had previously entered the coordinates for their next destination, and they made a smooth transition into hyperspace.

Their next Rim destination was Acheron, which translated to the name for hell. The name fit since the planet was hot and humid. The temperature seldom dropped below thirty degrees Celsius, with the humidity remaining above eighty percent. The crew seemed thankful the gravity was standard, but no one looked forward to visiting the planet. Small dictatorships ruled Acheron, and there did not seem to be anyone in overall authority who could make decisions for the entire planet.

They located a continent in the southern hemisphere with a single ruler. As soon as the shuttle landed, assailants attacked the ship using bolt-action single-shot rifles. The shuttle returned fire using the cannon mounted on top of the shuttle. They aimed the cannon so no one would be injured. After a brief wait, a lone person approached the shuttle with his hands held straight up. Grayson exited the shuttle in full armor with his helmet engaged as a precaution against snipers. The person asked Grayson to accompany him to meet with their leader.

"Your leader can come to our shuttle if he wishes to meet with us," Grayson said. "He lost our goodwill when you attacked our shuttle. We're here to conduct trade if you have anything of value to exchange. Tell your leader we have an assortment of lethal arms and a wide range of common trade goods for sale. He'll have to come here to discuss the possibility of trade."

Grayson handed the guy a hard copy of the cargo manifest. He watched the person as he retreated out of sight. Grayson reentered the shuttle. The armor maintained a comfortable temperature as long as a person kept the helmet closed. The shuttle also stayed at a comfortable temperature. After several hours, a large caravan arrived. Grayson again exited the shuttle and waited for the approach of the group.

A male stepped forward. "I am Betar, a servant of Premier Alexander. He's interested in purchasing a large quantity of your weapons. First, I need to know if you're a man or a machine."

"I'm a man," Grayson said as he retracted his helmet.

"It's as we hoped," Betar said with a smile. "The list of weapons indicates you sell them in large quantities. My Premier wishes to purchase two hundred of your containers of arms and is offering two hundred of our finest female slaves in exchange. They will provide you and your men with a lifetime of pleasure."

Betar motioned with his hand, and the two hundred females he mentioned came forward. Most of the females stared fearfully at Grayson, but some looked on with curiosity. Grayson was appalled and utterly disgusted. He stayed quiet as he decided what to do. He wanted to kill Betar along with the other men and free the females but knew good intentions could make matters worse. Grayson looked over the females. Most were young and attractive, but many had scars. Most of the females suffered from malnutrition. He noticed the men were armed and ready to attack if he gave the wrong answer. He was not concerned about his safety, but some of the enslaved women might be killed in an exchange of fire.

"The ladies are attractive," Grayson said. "But our weapons are exceptional. I'll need to present your offer to my captain since he makes the final decisions. Besides the ladies, do you have anything else to trade, such as rare earth elements, minerals or other commodities?"

"We don't have any of the items you mentioned, but we have male slaves who can serve as laborers. If you consider our offer insufficient, we'd be interested in hearing what you feel your weapons are worth. Please come and inspect the females."

Grayson walked over and listened as Betar described the ladies. The ladies were scantily dressed, but he noticed everyone wore little because of the heat. Again, it took all Grayson's self-control not to kill Betar. Grayson noticed the ladies kept their eyes looking down, except for one female who watched him continuously. Grayson was uncomfortable with her intense stare and tried to maintain a neutral expression.

Betar then surprised Grayson. "Please select your choice of a female as a gift to you or your captain so you can see the quality of the females we offer in trade."

Grayson was trying to decide how to respond when the lady staring at him stepped forward. "The warrior has already made his selection. I'll go with him to encourage him to accept your trade proposal."

She then walked over to Grayson and whispered in his ear. "If you refuse to take me, they'll kill me for speaking without permission."

"Thank you for your generosity. My captain will consider your offer."

Grayson closed his helmet and walked backward toward the shuttle. The lady walked with him. Two of his marines were on one knee to either side of the shuttle, ready to open fire if necessary. Grayson and the lady entered the shuttle, followed by the marines.

Grayson retracted his helmet and said to the lady, "Come with me."

She followed him to the cockpit, and he directed her to sit next to him since he was concerned she might become afraid during liftoff. This was likely the first aircraft she had ever seen. Grayson reached over and buckled her harness.

Grayson announced over the speaker. "Prepare for immediate lift."

Grayson checked all the gages. The shuttle lifted off and continued accelerating as it left the planet below.

Grayson engaged the autopilot and turned to the lady. "I'm Grayson, and we don't buy or sell slaves."

"My name is Mila. I wasn't always a slave. The slavers raided our village and killed my parents. You're a great warrior. Please do not return me. I'll do anything you ask. Just let me stay with you."

Grayson did not know what to say. "I promise you'll be protected, but you can't say with me."

"You already have a woman?"

"No, but on our ship, you'll be free. We have many people on our ship. No one is a slave. You decide if you wish to be with someone."

"If I'm free to choose, then I choose to be with you," Mila said.

Grayson saw they were getting close to the Demon and took the shuttle off autopilot. He landed in the shuttle bay. All the marines were smiling at him as he left the shuttle bay with Mila. He decided to postpone his meeting with the captain. He took Mila to the cafeteria and showed her how to use the food processor. While eating, Grayson had her explain life on the planet or the lack thereof. He noticed she was shivering from the cold. He became angry at himself when he realized she had little clothing and was accustomed to a hot environment.

Grayson took off his pullover shirt and slipped it on over her head. She ate tentatively but seemed to enjoy the food.

"Come with me," Grayson said after they finished the meal.

Grayson took her to ship stores and filled up a cart. He then took her to his cabin and showed her how to operate the shower. She was in the shower for a while before coming out smiling. While Mili was in the shower, Grayson had one of the female marines bring him a set of marine clothing.

Mili came out of the bathroom completely naked without any modesty. Grayson tried unsuccessfully not to look.

Grayson pointed to the clothes. "I had one of our female marines loan you some of her clothes until we can get you some clothes of your own."

Mili dressed, and Grayson thought she looked so cute in the oversized clothes and could not help smiling. He decided she should be checked out medically and asked her to follow him to the hospital.

When they got to the hospital, Grayson talked privately with Doctor Adler about Mili and the situation on the planet. He asked the Doctor to examine Mili to see if she was all right medically while he reported his findings to the captain. As he prepared to leave, Mili panicked and joined him. She grabbed hold of his arm.

"You need to stay with the Doctor," Grayson said.

"Please don't leave me. I promise I'll do whatever you ask. Just let me stay with you." Mili started to panic as she continued to grasp his arm.

"Grayson, it's best she stays with you until she has time to adjust to shipboard life. It'll only take a moment for a medical evaluation."

Grayson did not want to leave her, but he wanted her to realize she was free and did not owe him anything.

After Doctor Adler completed her tests, she administered an injection. "She is slightly malnourished, but all she needs is a few days of proper food. I gave her an injection to balance out her nutritional needs, but overall, she is healthy."

"Mili, you can come with me, but you need to understand you're free. I'll not take advantage of you sexually or otherwise. Do you understand?"

"Yes, I understand."

On the way to see the captain, Grayson called ship stores and told them to set up a second bed in his cabin. As a senior officer, he had a slightly larger cabin and a desk with full access to ship systems. Thomas was waiting for Grayson in his Ready Room when he entered with Mili.

"Captain, this is Mili. I sent you a summary of the situation on Acheron. Doctor Adler said Mili needs to stay with me for the time being until she understands ship protocol."

Grayson told Thomas about the situation on Acheron. Mili provided additional details when questioned. At the end, Thomas asked for a recommendation from Grayson.

"I believe we can eliminate slavery in the southern continent. One individual controls the entire area, and the population is less than a million, but the other continents are too fragmented. The small villages operate autonomously except when the slavers come by to collect goods, supplies, and additional slaves. Anyone who objects is summarily beaten or killed. Our aerial reconnaissance has located a fertile valley surrounded by mountains. It could serve as a base of operation and home for up to a hundred thousand inhabitants. Give me four military shuttles and two hundred marines, and I believe we can replace the tyrant who is presently controlling the population."

"Will the population support our efforts to free them?" Thomas asked Mili.

Mili, without hesitation, replied. "Yes, the people will fight to be free of the slavers. I'll go with you when you visit the villages so they'll not be afraid. Give them weapons, and they'll help you defeat the tyrant and his followers."

"The problem is, what will replace the tyrant?" Thomas said with a concerned look.

"Whatever replaces the tyrant will be better than what we have now," Milo answered.

"I agree," said Grayson.

"Okay, Grayson, you may prepare a strategic plan of action for review by the staff. You have two days."

Grayson and Mili left the room. Thomas had his elbows resting on the table with his fingers interlaced, supporting his chin. He wondered if he was making the right decision.

Grayson made his rounds with Mili in tow. During lunch and dinner, he had her explain more about the daily activities on Acheron.

The following day Grayson presented a plan to Thomas and the senior officers. The plan of action was approved with only a few minor changes. After the meeting, Grayson and Mili had lunch. After lunch, they approached the deck where the marines were practicing. Someone shouted, "Officer on Deck," and the marines snapped to attention. Grayson had told them they did not need to interrupt their training every time he came on deck.

"Gather round," Grayson said. "On Acheron, a tyrant is abusing and enslaving the population. I sent everyone a list of the marines I plan to take to the planet to remedy the situation. Jackson will accompany me. Marine Sergeant Lawrence will be acting commander during my absence."

"Sir, may I speak freely?" Lawrence said. "Sir, I've been with you since before you joined the ship. We played on the same world championship team. How would you feel about being left behind if you were me?"

Grayson raised his voice and said, "Belay the last order. Sergeant Alice York, you'll be acting commander during my absence."

"Sir, may I speak freely?" Sergeant York said. Grayson rolled his eyes and nodded. Sergeant York stood straight and remained at attention. "Sir, over sixty percent of the population are female, and according to your summary report, the enslaved women have been treated horribly by the males. You need me and all the female marines on this mission."

Grayson thought about it for a moment and realized she was right. "Very well, belay my last order as well. Sergeant York, you and the other female marines will join us on this operation."

Grayson looked around the room. "Sergeant Ross, you'll be acting commander during my absence, and don't you dare say a word, or I'll shoot you where you stand."

The marines laughed since they knew Sergeant Ross would decline the temporary promotion since he didn't want to be left behind. Grayson asked Jackson to determine the supplies needed for the mission.

While Grayson talked with Jackson, Mili when over to Sergeant York. "Will you teach me to be like you so Warrior Grayson won't be ashamed of me?"

Sergeant York had watched how Mili looked at Grayson. She felt everyone on the ship should know how to fight and be able to defend the ship. Also, she did not want to turn down anyone who wanted to be trained, and they could always use another marine.

"If Grayson has no objections, you are welcomed to join us at oh nine hundred tomorrow." York saw the confusion on Mili's face. "Come here tomorrow morning after breakfast."

The sergeant spent three cycles teaching Mili how to shoot using the marine rifle and handgun. She also fitted her with a suit of armor. York taught Mili all the general commands and hand signals. Hand-to-hand combat took years to master, and she did not have enough time to develop anything except a few basic moves. Mili was in good physical shape and did not seem to mind the hard work.

On the fourth day, Mili sat across from Sergeant York in the cafeteria, waiting for Grayson to join her for dinner.

"I'm sharing Grayson's cabin, but he doesn't touch me," Mili said. "He looks at me like he wants me but then looks away like I'm not there. I thought he'd want me if I were more like you. I'm afraid he'll put me in another cabin since he mentioned it last night. I begged him not to, and he said he'd wait until I'm ready, but I'll never be ready."

"Grayson, for all his toughness, is a gentleman," York said. "He doesn't want to take advantage of you. He's from the same planet as our captain, and they have some archaic beliefs. You may want to try the Suzanna approach."

"What is the Suzanna approach?"

York grinned. "When this ship first launched, our captain was unattached, handsome, and owned this ship. He was rich and a good man in every measurable attribute. All the ladies onboard waited for the captain to select one of them. Suzanna was not even part of our crew. She walked up to the Demon while we were docked at a space station. She asks for a tour of our ship. The next thing you know, she's sharing his cabin, and he's unavailable. She's now the second most powerful person on this ship. Sometimes, you must make the first move if you want a specific man. If you want advice on Grayson, I suggest you talk to Suzanna. It might help to let Grayson know how you feel about him." They saw Grayson as he entered the cafeteria.

York got up to leave as Grayson came over. "Mili is going to make a fine marine. She's an excellent shot with a handgun and rifle, so don't piss her off."

Grayson chuckled as he asked Mili, "Have you had dinner yet?"

"No, I've been waiting for you."

They ate and talked about what each had been doing during the day. They finished dinner, and Mili said she would meet him in their cabin later. Grayson watched her walk away. It had been a while since he felt such an emotional attraction to a woman.

MILI LOCATED SUZANNA, and they discussed Grayson's background. Suzanna had studied the customs and talked to other crew members about the home planet of Thomas and Grayson.

When Mili entered their cabin, Grayson was working at his desk. They smiled at each other. Mili went into the bathroom and took a shower. She would typically get dressed in her sleep attire immediately since she had not adapted yet to the ship's temperature. Tonight, she came out of the bathroom with no clothes and sat on the edge of her bed. Grayson looked at her and then turned back to the monitor on his desk.

Mili stood up and walked over next to him. "Am I so repulsive you cannot bear to look at me or touch me?"

"No, you are beautiful, but you've been through so much. It would not be proper for me to take advantage of you."

"I have loved you since the moment I saw you. You're a fearless warrior who showed compassion to the other slaves and me. I share your hatred toward the men who abused us. It is fate that we're together. I want you and only you. I'll never be happy with anyone else. I was only recently captured. You may not want me because of what I had to do as a slave. Suzanna told me that people who want to be together get married on your world. I was told the male normally proposes marriage, but the female could also propose. Warrior Grayson, will you marry me?"

Grayson stood up and embraced Mili. They kissed passionately, and as their lips parted, he said, "You had no control over the abuse you received as a slave. Yes, I'll marry you, but we'll wait until after we get rid of the slavers. Then, you can decide between living free on your planet or living aboard a starship with me." Milli joined Grayson in his bed.

Two days later, two hundred and twelve marines with over two hundred containers of supplies landed on Acheron in a valley they named Heaven.

The marines knew the Demon would travel to its next destination. It could be months before the Demon returned. Mili proved indispensable as she met with the villagers and talked them into moving to Heaven for combat training. She showed them how to use the weapons, and they agreed to fight alongside the strangers from the heavens.

THE DEMON JUMPED TO Pax, a low-gravity planet with minimum technology and limited manufacturing capabilities. The inhabitants were tall but very slim, with an average weight below fifty kilograms. They wanted the medical products, nutrients, and vitamins but had no interest in weapons. Their life expectancy was only fifty years. The inhabitants suffered from calcium deficiency even though there was no shortage of calcium. However, the low levels of vitamin D, the low level of ultraviolet light from the sun, and the elevated level of phytic acid in their diet prevented the absorption of calcium necessary for proper health. Unfortunately, the Demon did not have the supplies needed by the population, but Suzanna, with Thomas' support, agreed to provide the planet with the required products on their next visit. They needed to bring sufficient quantities of vitamin D and supplements to reduce the acid. Such a minor change would significantly improve the health of the settlers. Thomas was not concerned with the small losses they would experience on Pax since the survival of each world increased the overall survival of the human species.

The Demon had better luck with Gemma. The inhabitants had been successfully trading with the pirates. The people were hardy, and everyone was armed at all times. The pirates behaved themselves since the local population swiftly dealt with any problems. However, it took a considerable time to conduct trade since the towns and villages were spread out, and they had to trade separately with each location. While it took considerable time compared to other worlds, the trade was worth the effort. The inhabitants were aware of the Hostis threat and ordered heavy-duty ground-to-air weapons. The jump distance between Pax and Gemma was short enough to consider it one stop. Averaging the expected losses from Pax and the high profit from Gemma resulted in a good overall average. The more trade they conducted, the more disillusioned Thomas became with the Core Planets. The standard of living throughout the Outer Planets and the Rim could have been significantly improved with just a little help from the Core Planets.

The Demon returned to Acheron to check on the success of Greyson and the marines. It had been over nine months since they had departed from Acheron, and Thomas hoped the marines had made some progress in reducing the slave trade. As soon as the Demon entered orbit around Acheron, they sent out messages to Greyson on their dedicated encrypted frequency. Grayson answered almost immediately.

"Have you had any success in achieving any of the primary objectives?" Thomas asked.

"We were very successful," Grayson replied. "Shortly after you left, we made a nighttime raid. We killed the leader of the slavers and all of his staff. After that, the entire organization collapsed. Mili led the villagers in tracking down and eliminating the rest of the slavers. The enslaved people represented about ninety percent of the population and are now in charge. Females now hold most of the critical governmental positions. Mili became the hero who brought the marines, and she's now the President. Milli says she still loves me but has responsibilities to her people and can't leave. She plans to use their superior weapons to wipe out slavery everywhere. I'll not be getting married, and I support her decision. I'm proud of her. She's a fine marine."

"Fantastic, not the marriage part, but the success with the mission. I'm glad to get you guys back onboard the Demon."

"We have a slight problem," Grayson said after a moment's hesitation. "Mili told the ladies how she planned to marry me. Eighteen of our marines accepted marriage proposals from the ladies and are now married. Some plan to stay here, but the balance wants your permission to bring their new wives to the Demon."

"Permission granted," he said, even though he was shaking his head.

It only took a few days for the marines and their new wives to board the Demon. Thomas told the new wives he would return them to their planet if they got tired of life aboard the Demon or got tired of their new husbands. The new President executed a long-term trade agreement. She provided a list of all the items they wanted to purchase in the future and gave them a list of items they would have ready for export.

While waiting, Thomas received messages from several sources that numerous navy ships were en route to Carcerem. Carcerem was the furthest planet from the Core and was a prison planet without supervision.

Thomas reviewed the files on Carcerem. For hundreds of years, the most notorious prisoners were simply dropped on Carcerem and forgotten. History says many of these prisoners would have been sentenced to death for the most heinous crimes. These prisoners were considered too evil to be rehabilitated. Shuttles that brought the prisoners to Carcerem did not even land. They would come close to the surface and shove the prisoners out of the shuttle. No one cared if the prisoners were injured in the fall. The governments did not want to be considered entirely inhumane. The shuttle would dump a few hand tools, some seeds, and thirty ration bars with each prisoner. Each ration bar provided the daily requirements of nutrients. It was not unusual for prisoners to kill each other to make the provisions last longer. The prisoners were tough and resourceful. Somehow, they survived.

Approximately eighty percent of the original population was male. Still, after hundreds of years, the original prisoners would have died off, and it was assumed the descendant population would be equally mixed. No additional prisoners had been sent to the planet in over a hundred years. Armed satellites orbited the planet. The satellites issued warnings and described the nature of the inhabitants. Even pirates were afraid of landing on Carcerem. There was an abandoned space station circling the planet. Even though the descendants had never committed a crime, no government wanted to risk a landing to check on survivors.

Carcerem was only an intermediate jump from Acheron, so Thomas decided to check in with Admiral Nelson. Thomas informed all hands they would make a brief detour before returning to the Core as it appeared the navy was conducting exercises on the edge of the Rim. Following their standard procedures, they would come out of jump early so they would not interfere with the navy ships. As always, they would be at battle stations when they exited jump. The Demon achieved the required velocity and engaged their jump engines.

CHAPTER 8 INTERSPECIES WAR

As the Demon came out of hyperspace at Carcerem, they observed a major battle between the Imperium fleet and a Hostis armada. Over a thousand ships were involved in the battle. Debris from hundreds of destroyed ships showed the two sides had been engaged in the conflict for some time. It did not take Thomas long to determine the Imperium fleet was outmatched and losing the battle. The entire human fleet was here. If they lost, it would only take a short time for the Hostis to destroy all the civilian ships in the Rim before moving to the Outer Planets. While the ships in both the Rim and Outer Planets were armed and would fight back, the civilian ships were no match for the military ships of the Hostis. Then the Hostis would move against the Core Planets, which had several thousand civilian ships without armament. Humanity would be wiped out if the Hostis reached the Core Planets since the Hostis did not take prisoners.

Thomas knew they were lucky. Intentionally pulling out of jump a few seconds early left the Demon outside the battle. Thomas knew they should turn tail and run. However, if the Hostis destroyed the Imperium's fleet, the human race would be wiped out.

Thomas looked around his bridge. They were already at battle stations when he announced on the general channel. "Prepare for battle. This is not a drill."

The alarm sounded throughout the ship. The Bridge Officers turned toward Thomas, waiting for him to say something.

Thomas said what they were all thinking. "If the Imperium's fleet is destroyed, all our home planets will be in danger."

Thomas knew every member of his crew would give their best. He looked over at his Tactical Officer. "Terrance, have the crew load our tubes with the new torpedoes, and let me know when the loading is complete."

"Sir," Terrance announced, "the torpedoes are loaded, racked, and ready for launch. The torpedoes had been loaded before receiving his order. Thomas looked at his Tactical Officer with a knowing smile, and Terrance grinned back. He had anticipated his captain.

Thomas looked straight ahead while addressing his helmsman. "Francis, slowly move us toward the battle. I want to get as close as possible without attracting the enemy's attention."

They were approaching the left flank of the battle when he nodded to his Communications Officer. "Put me through to Admiral Nelson."

"I have their first officer on the com."

"This is Captain Wilson of the Demon. My ship is outside your left flank. There's a battle where three of your destroyers are engaged with five Hostis destroyers. We'd be happy to help if you'll cover any damage to my ship and grant us full salvage."

First Officer Wen, aboard the Battleship Independence, addressed Admiral Nelson. "Admiral, Captain Wilson of the Demon is offering to help our ships fighting on the left flank."

Wen superimposed the battle taking place at the edge of the left flank so the Admiral could see the engagement. "Sir, Captain Wilson wants us to cover any damage to his ship and grant him salvage rights."

The Admiral glanced at the minor battle with a grim expression as he saw another destroyer explode. Now, five enemy ships were firing against their two. He had over four hundred ships committed to this battle. If their flank was destroyed, enemy ships would circle around their formation and attack from the rear, resulting in a strategic disadvantage.

The Admiral gave his first officer an icy stare. "One ship won't make a difference but agree to their request. It's doubtful he'll be alive at the end."

Wen sent the confirmation. He immediately focused on another part of the battle and directed ships to fill a new hole in their formation. They had already lost a third of their ships, and he knew they were in trouble. They had fallen into a trap. They had assembled an armada with their largest battleship, eighty-four cruisers, two-hundred-thirty-two destroyers, and over a hundred frigates with an accompaniment of over a thousand fighters.

The navy's spy ship sent a transmission showing less than two hundred Hostis ships. But, after the battle started, over four hundred additional enemy ships lifted off the surface of the moon circling Carcerem. Over half the additional enemy ships were cruisers.

Officer Wen and his fellow officers practically worshipped Admiral Nelson since he had won every battle. Also, the Admiral looked after the people in his command. Officer Wen knew they would fight to the last ship. But, barring a miracle, none of them would survive. Wen transmitted the ID for the Demon to all ships. She sent a separate message to Ellen Gaffney and Gabe Lewis, the captains of the two destroyers, to let them know the Demon would be joining them.

"SIR, WE HAVE TORPEDO lock on the two closest ships," Terrance announced. "None of the ships have turned to engage us."

Thomas continued to wait as they moved closer to the enemy ships. Then one of the enemy ships started to turn toward them.

"Fire torpedoes," Thomas shouted. "All gunners open fire and continue firing as long as you have targets."

Everyone on the bridge watched as one of their torpedoes impacted the closest ship that had only completed a partial turn. The flash was blinding. Just as their eyes were adjusting, the second torpedo hit the other enemy ship. Even with the optics dampening the flash, it was still blinding. As the second flash faded, there was no sign of either of the ships they had targeted.

"Sir, two more torpedoes locked and loaded. We have a firing solution, launching. Sir, all three of the remaining enemy ships have us targeted."

Terrance watched his screens carefully. "Sir, six missiles are heading our way. Sir, it is still too far away for our lasers."

Thomas gave the order even though the bridge officers had already taken action. "Helm, take evasive action. Tactical take out those missiles."

They watched as the torpedoes and the missiles crossed, going in opposite directions. Their torpedoes would arrive first. One of their torpedoes destroyed another destroyer. The second torpedo was hit by enemy fire, but all the pieces continued on the same path with the Ancients' missile still intact. Again, upon impact, nothing remained of the enemy ship. The explosions took out the enemy fighters that were close to the exploding ships. However, sixteen enemy fighters survived and were coming straight at the Demon.

The Demon's missiles, torpedoes, and artillery cannons were effective against ships but were useless against the smaller, faster fighters. They depended on their six particle beam cannons and laser battery to defend the ship against the enemy fighters and incoming missiles.

Terrance directed their gunners to target the incoming missiles and inbound fighters. They opened fire with their particle beam cannons and their laser battery.

The captains of the two Imperium ships were firing on the remaining Hostis ship, and their captains had directed their fighters to assist the Demon. However, the enemy fighters would reach the Demon first. The two Imperium ships disabled the fifth destroyer by targeting its engines, and it was no longer heading toward them.

The Demon gunners were firing continuously at the incoming missiles and fighters. Thomas watched as three of the incoming enemy missiles and nine of the sixteen fighters were destroyed. The remaining enemy fighters fired their missiles and took out two of Demon's forward guns. The shields dropped to eighty percent. Thomas redirected all energy to the forward shields. The next missile shook the ship, and the shields dropped to sixty percent. Everyone on the bridge sighed with relief, but it was short-lived when another missile hit one of the weakened gun positions. The shields dropped to forty percent. The next missile struck before the shields could be rebalanced, and the shields dropped to less than ten percent. The remaining incoming missiles had been destroyed. The enemy fighters circled back to make another pass but could only use their guns since they were out of missiles. The Demon continued to fire with its remaining cannons and laser battery.

The friendly fighters arrived and started taking out the enemy fighters. Then, the two destroyers arrived and started firing on the enemy fighters. It did not take long for the remaining Hostis fighters to be destroyed.

Damage reports were coming in from engineering. Maintenance reported major damage to the outer hull, and three inner hull penetrations were losing air. Those areas were immediately sealed off from the rest of the ship. Engineering reported one of the four engines was damaged and being shut down for emergency repairs. First Officer Miller coordinated the maintenance repair crews while the Tactical Officer worked with engineering to get the shields up.

Thomas received a call from medical. Thomas expected a medical report when Dr. Adler asked if Amanda was on the bridge.

Suzanna had been on the bridge since the beginning of the attack, and Thomas turned toward her and shouted, "Suzanna, Amanda is not in the hospital."

The children were taught to go immediately to the hospital when Battle Stations sounded. The hospital was located in the center of the ship and was the safest place during a battle. A patient room in the hospital had been designated as a safe room for the children. The hospital staff had a list of the children assigned to the hospital during a battle. However, sometimes Amanda would take her special seat on the bridge since it represented the second safest place on the ship.

Both Thomas and Suzanna started scanning the ship. "She's in section 44E," Suzanna shouted.

Suzanna jumped out of her seat and took off running. Thomas switched his viewer to the same section and saw it was one of the sections that had been hulled, and it was sealed off. He followed Suzanna's path and directed the AI to open doors in front of her and close the doors behind her so she could run at full speed without slowing down. Suzanna reached their daughter. Thomas watched as Suzanna sealed Amanda's helmet, which had not been properly mated to the suit. He finally breathed. He had not realized he had been holding his breath.

Suzanna held Amanda. The corridor where they were located was sealed in both directions. There was a small hole in the hull, which was opened to the vacuum of space. Safety compartments were spread throughout the ship. Suzanna went over to a compartment and grabbed a repair kit. She looked through the small opening of the inner hull and saw a much larger opening in the outer hull. She felt a chill when she realized how close she came to losing her daughter. Suzanna opened a repair kit, selected a patch, and placed it over the hole. She sprayed the quick-drying sealant over the patch. A few minutes later, a door opened, and a maintenance worker entered the compartment. He examined the patch and nodded his head. He spoke into his wrist communicator, and air started hissing through the vents as the area was repressurized. They all retracted their helmets.

Once the helmets were retracted, Amanda looked up. "Hi Andrew, mom fixed the hole."

Andrew looked relieved. "I'm glad you are okay. You gave me a scare. You need to stay in the hospital or on the bridge."

"Okay," Amanda said as she smiled at Andrew.

Suzanna took Amanda's hand, and they headed for the bridge while Andrew headed in the opposite direction to return to engineering.

Thomas asked for a status report from his first officer. "Sir, the three inner hull breaches have been sealed. The engine taken offline only had minor damage and will be restarted shortly."

Tactical Officer Terrance responded without being asked. "Sir, our shields are back up to thirty percent."

The two Imperium destroyers pulled up on either side of the Demon. The Communications Officer informed Thomas that the Lennox wished to talk to their captain. Thomas nodded, and the call was placed on the main screen.

"Captain Wilson, I am Captain Ellen Gaffney of the Lennox on your port side, and Captain Gabe Lewis of the Ardent is on your starboard side. You have our thanks for joining us. I've never seen a weapon with such destructive power. How does it work?"

"It works using a reverse explosion principle," Thomas said. "It absorbs the energy from the enemy's ship, leaving the targeted vessel with no shielding, and it detonates using nuclear transmutation to complete the destruction. The bigger the ship, the greater the destruction."

Thomas had discussed the matter with his engineers, and none of them had a clue regarding the action of the missile, but he had given one of the theories they debated. He did not want to tell her it was Ancients' technology, and he had no idea how the weapon worked.

Captain Gaffney laughed. "I have no idea what you're talking about, but I like the results. Shall we rejoin the battle?"

"I'm sorry," Thomas replied. "Our ship is too damaged to continue. Our shields have only returned to thirty percent, and the Demon would not survive another torpedo or missile impact against our damaged hull."

"Captain Wilson, we need your help," Captain Gaffney said. "The Lennox and Ardent will extend their shields around the Demon, and our fighters will provide additional cover for your ship. All you have to do is fire your torpedoes. We'll protect the Demon."

Thomas looked around his bridge and saw his officers nod their support. Suzanna had retaken her seat, and Amanda sat in her customary chair next to her mother.

"Once either of your ships starts to lose shielding, we'll depart," Thomas replied.

"I understand."

The ships and fighters formed up and headed toward the nearest group of engaged ships. This was another small but slightly larger battle on the edge of the armada. Four cruisers and ten destroyers on the Imperium side were battling against six enemy cruisers and fourteen enemy destroyers. The Demon approached the enemy ships from the side and from slightly behind. The approach exposed the engines and the broadside of the enemy ships where there was less shielding. The broadside also provided a larger area to target. This represented a classic fleet commander's strategy where you have part of your fleet attack an enemy head-on while having the balance of your ships attack from the side. If the enemy turns to engage the ships attacking their fleet from the side, then they expose their flank to the enemy in front. Also, the enemy ships would have difficulty shifting power between shields since they would be absorbing damage from both the bow and the broadside of their ships.

The Demon approached the enemy ships, with the two destroyers providing the Demon with additional shielding. Captain Gaffney advised all the Imperium fighters to withdraw from the enemy ships and dampen their screen sensors as the Demon launched two torpedoes against two enemy cruisers. The first torpedo took out a cruiser and two enemy destroyers that had moved close to the cruiser for added protection. The second torpedo took out a second cruiser. The two torpedoes also took out over a hundred enemy fighters which were flying close to the cruisers and destroyers. Plus, all the enemy ships were temporarily blinded by the flash from the explosion. The Imperium ships took advantage of the enemy's disorientation and took out another six destroyers during their confusion. The Demon fired two more torpedoes, and two more enemy cruisers were vaporized. The Imperium ships surrounded and destroyed the remaining enemy ships. This second small battle with the enemy was successful without any missiles reaching the Demon.

Fleet Commander Myers of the cruiser Seawolf contacted the Demon. "Captain Wilson, thank you for the two victories. How do you think your weapons would fair against a battleship?"

Thomas thought for a minute. "Sir, I'm not sure."

"Well, let's find out. Captain Gaffney informed me about your shielding. We'll protect you with four cruisers, ten destroyers, and over two hundred fighters. Please follow the coordinates and flight plan being transferred to your helmsman."

Thomas realized it was not a request. Fleet Commander Meyers had given him an order.

"Helm, follow the flight plan." Thomas hoped the added protection would be sufficient.

They circled well behind the enemy's lines and avoided contact with the enemy. Thomas noticed his chief engineer was calling, and he took the call.

"Sir, the offline engine has been repaired, and we are restarting it, but it'll only run at eighty percent."

Thomas thanked him as his monitors showed the engine restart. Thomas noted their shields were back to sixty percent, but he was still concerned about the damage to the outer hull.

Their flight path took them around the planet, and they emerged directly behind the Hostis armada. The rear of the enemy's battleship was straight ahead. However, there were enemy ships they would have to target first.

The enemy ships surprised Thomas when they opened a corridor to the battleship. Then he realized the enemy was letting them get close to the superior firepower of the battleship while moving in behind them to cut off any escape.

"Sir, torpedoes locked and loaded," Tactical Officer Terrance announced.

Thomas decided not to take any chances and directed Terrance to fire both torpedoes at the battleship. The battleship did not even attempt to shoot down the torpedoes believing they would pose no threat against their superior shields. Fleet Commander Myers ordered all friendly ships and fighters to retreat while dampening their sensors.

Thomas did not wait for the torpedoes to impact. He asked the fleet commander to clear the area to the rear of his ship so he could fire the rail guns. As soon as the area was clear of friendly ships, the Tactical Officer fired both rail guns and cleared the path behind the Demon.

Thomas sent another communication to the fleet commander as he gave orders to turn the Demon around and accelerate at maximum velocity. Fleet Commander Meyers gave similar orders to the navy ships and matched speed with the Demon. Thomas displayed the rear monitor to his screens so he could watch the torpedoes' impact. At first, he thought the torpedoes were ineffective. Then, he was stunned as the explosion continued to grow and grow. The blast blew a hole in the entire enemy armada.

Fleet Commander Meyers had never witnessed an explosion of such magnitude. The blast took out the battleship, over forty cruisers, and at least a hundred destroyers that were close to the battleship. Over a thousand enemy fighters were vaporized in the explosion. The fleet commander heard the cheers throughout the ship since everyone had watched the blast from a monitor.

Fleet Commander Myers contacted Admiral Nelson and described the Demon's role in destroying the enemy's battleship.

With the enemy's battleship gone, Admiral Nelson used the superiority of his own battleship to slice up the enemy's formation. The human ships became hunters, and the Hostis became prey in what turned into a lopsided battle.

It did not take long for the deeds of the Demon to spread throughout the Imperium's ships. Religious fighter pilots started a rumor that quickly circulated that the bright flashes were of fire and brimstone when the Demon opened the gates of hell to consume the enemy.

Fleet Commander Myers continued to protect the Demon, and they used two more of the Demon's torpedoes when they found a cluster of Hostis ships. Multiple enemy ships were destroyed with each torpedo fired from the Demon since the enemy ships made the mistake of being too close together.

Some navy pilots and captains could not believe a civilian ship could destroy a battleship. However, they quickly changed their minds when they witnessed one of Demon's torpedoes impacting an enemy ship and destroying everything around it.

The cruisers, destroyers, and fighters of the Imperium were everywhere, hitting the enemy ships. When an Imperium ship started losing shield strength, it would withdraw until the shields recovered, and another vessel would take its place.

The Hostis ships did not have such luxury and were constantly bombarded by multiple ships. The enemy fighters were similarly destroyed since they were outnumbered and were taking fire from ships and fighters. The Imperium fighters avoided enemy fire from the Hostis ships by only engaging enemy fighters that were separated from their ships. The destructive power of the Demon spread through the Hostis fleet. Any time the Demon approached a concentration of enemy ships, the ships would flee, making it easier for the Imperium ships to destroy them. At the end, only about fifty enemy ships remained when they tried to escape. The Imperium forces continued to give chase, and only a dozen enemy ships reached jump velocity and escaped. None of the enemy fighters escaped. Fleet Commander Myers had kept his word and protected the Demon.

All the crews of the Imperium ships were cheering, and the Demon's Communications Officer was overloaded with calls thanking them for their help.

The Demon's maintenance and engineering crew were busy putting temporary patches on the outer hull while sealing off the destroyed weapons sections. Thomas directed the torpedo crew to remove and store the remaining ten torpedoes of the Ancients.

The Demon's crew was celebrating, but Suzanna looked at Thomas and saw his sad face.

Suzanna walked over to Thomas. "How many casualties?"

"Four dead, another fifteen with serious injuries, but they should recover."

Amanda came over to her father and held out her arms. Thomas picked her up and hugged her harder than normal.

The Imperium ships started collecting escape pods, attending to the wounded, and repairing the repairable ships. Thomas was surprised to learn the Hostis did not have escape pods.

Admiral Nelson kept his word, and Thomas contacted Wilson Enterprises to begin salvage operations. He knew the salvage operations would take several years. The salvage would be very profitable, and they might acquire new technology from the enemy vessels.

On the morning of the third day after the battle, Admiral Nelson invited Thomas and his senior officers to dinner aboard his Battleship, the Independence. Thomas instructed his officers to wear the dress uniforms they wore when attending dignitary events, and of course, they would go armed. Four of his bodyguards would accompany him and be in full body armor. His officers had already choreographed their exit from the shuttle. He and Suzanna were to exit the shuttle after the marine bodyguards.

The shuttle entered the Independence and turned around so the front of the shuttle pointed toward the exit. The pilot made a perfect landing. The ramp at the rear of the shuttle was lowered. Thomas' bodyguards exited the craft first and stood at attention. Thomas walked to the bottom of the ramp and took two forward steps. He turned toward the shuttle. All eyes were focused on Suzanna as she proceeded down the ramp. She wore a custom-made evening gown with a beautiful necklet and matching stud earrings. She walked up next to Thomas and took his arm. The officers then proceeded down the ramp, two across, until they had all exited the shuttle. The officers and crew of the Independence were standing at attention. At a given signal, they honored the Demon officers by saluting.

Admiral Nelson walked forward, and Thomas introduced each of the officers who had joined him and named the senior officers still aboard the Demon. The assembled naval group cheered and clapped their hands when Thomas finished the introductions.

Admiral Nelson introduced Thomas to Fleet Commander Myers and other senior officers. They followed the Admiral to the reception area for drinks, hors d'oeuvres, and socializing prior to dinner.

At the reception, Admiral Nelson commented to Suzanna. "It appears you're the only member from the Demon who is unarmed."

Suzanna gave the Admiral a demonic grin. "I'm fully armed and dangerous."

The Admiral laughed. "Somehow, I'm not surprised."

Suzanna reached up with both hands and straightened the Admiral's tie while planting a listening device.

Thomas removed two glasses of champagne from a nearby table and handed one of the drinks to Suzanna.

"My apologies," the Admiral said to Suzanna. "I need to talk to your captain in private. We'll only be gone for a few minutes."

Thomas followed the Admiral to a conference room. Two additional officers joined them. They took their seats around the table.

"This room is secure, and what we discuss is private," Admiral Nelson said. "I want you to tell me about the torpedoes you used in our recent battle."

Thomas did not know if the Admiral was entirely truthful or whether they were setting him up for possible arrest for possessing the technology of the Ancients. He thought carefully before answering.

"They are nothing special. I picked them up at a junkyard and figured they might come in handy under the right circumstances." The Admiral chuckled and shook his head.

"Am I under arrest?" Thomas asked.

"No, if I tried to arrest you, I'd have a mutiny on my hands. Without your help, we would all be dead. However, at some point, I hope you'll trust me and provide me with certain information. You'll have my full support when that time comes, and I'll do everything within my power to protect you. Also, any information or equipment you provide will be classified as top secret, and your name will be redacted or left out. You, your crew, and your ship will be protected. However, we can't allow certain technologies to fall into the hands of the Hostis. Therefore, while we'll not seize your ship, we'll shadow your ship with sufficient naval support to make sure another party doesn't capture your ship."

"I understand your position," Thomas said. "I welcome your discreet support. However, would such support not compromise your ability to deny involvement in our gun-running operation?"

"Yes, it could, but I'll take that risk over the risk of losing your ship and your ship's contents. To further that effort, I'll provide you with an untraceable transmitter. It'll allow you to contact me should the need arise."

The Admiral did not disclose they were secretly going to put a transponder on the Demon to allow them to track his ship.

Thomas looked at the Admiral with a grave expression. "Sir, as long as we're friends, you'll have my loyalty, and we'll be available should you need us."

Admiral Nelson stood up. "Let's rejoin the reception. It's about time to move into the dining room."

Thomas took a deep breath as they could have placed him in restraints and marched him to the brig. They exited the conference room, and one of Thomas' bodyguards was right outside the door. The bodyguard fell in behind. As they turned the corner, another of the bodyguards stepped to the side and joined the first guard. At the next entryway, a third guard joined the first two. Finally, the fourth bodyguard stood at the entry to the reception area and joined the other three bodyguards. The Admiral noted what had taken place. They rejoined Suzanna, and she asked Thomas to get her another drink.

As Thomas walked away, Suzanna turned to the Admiral. "You would have failed if you had tried to arrest our captain. Thomas looks up to you, and you have his complete loyalty, but he's sometimes naïve and too trusting. Your decision to shadow our ship is good. Because of your incompetence, some of the Hostis ships escaped, and as a result, the Hostis will find out about the Demon's capabilities. You should have followed their jump signatures and destroyed them."

"You listened to our private conversation?" The Admiral said with a frown.

"All of us listened to your conversation with our captain. We have not survived this long, by chance."

Thomas returned with the drinks. "So, what have you two been discussing?"

Suzanna smiled as she took her drink. "The Admiral complimented me on my dress, and I was boring him by discussing our trade arrangements."

The Admiral raised his eyebrows. "It looks like it's time for dinner."

As they proceeded to the banquet area, the Admiral looked at Suzanna and realized she was the most dangerous person in the room. She reminded him of a younger version of his wife. He fought the battles, but his wife significantly helped his career as she handled the politics that could have prevented his rapid advancement. He wondered if Captain Thomas knew how lucky he was to have Suzanna looking out for him. Admiral Nelson liked and respected this young captain and his entire crew. After talking to Suzanna, he was thankful he had not seriously considered arresting Captain Wilson. He remembered when they had initially talked Captain Wilson into handling the arms shipments. Everyone figured he would be lucky to last a few months. After getting a better measure of this captain and his crew, he understood how they had survived for over six years in an extremely dangerous business.

Once everyone took their seats, Admiral Nelson addressed the group and spoke about the glorious victory and how they had triumphed over their enemy. He stated the gathering was to honor Captain Wilson and the entire crew of the Demon for their role in defeating the Hostis armada. Loud cheers and clapping filled the room as the Admiral took his seat.

While eating, Thomas raised his voice and said, "Admiral, you have a lot of damaged ships. You should have your ships repaired by Wilson Enterprises. Unlike most repair yards, you'll pay about twenty percent more at my family's yard, but the ships are remanufactured. The engines are taken apart and rebuilt or replaced with more powerful engines. The hulls are seamlessly repaired. The ship's exterior is recoated with a proprietary blend of Iridium to increase its strength. All electronics throughout the ships are upgraded or replaced. When complete, you essentially have a new ship that is stronger, faster, and more powerful. Let Wilson Shipyards repair several of your ships. Once you see the results, I guarantee you'll not let any other repair facility touch your ships."

The Admiral was thoughtful as he turned to his Procurement Officer, who had been listening to the conversation.

The Procurement Officer stated the obvious. "Admiral, over half our ships were destroyed. We have the maintenance budget from those ships we could use to repair the other ships. Over half of our surviving ships are no longer battle-worthy, and we need to have those ships repaired as soon as possible."

Thomas took advantage of the opportunity. "Admiral, you should consider placing a large order for new cruisers to replace the ones you lost. A properly built cruiser can outperform two or three destroyers."

The Admiral choked on his water and took a moment to wipe his mouth.

Fleet Commander Myers asked, "If the navy entered into a contract for the repairs and the new ships, could we get some of those torpedoes the Demon used against the Hostis?" Everyone stopped talking at the Admiral's table and held their breath.

Thomas considered the fleet commander's request and decided to be magnanimous. "The Independence only uses missile launchers. We'd have to create a special missile enclosure to accommodate your launchers. If the navy entered into a decent size contract with Wilson Enterprises, we could provide you with four of our old missiles for free."

The Admiral laughed and then stared at Thomas. "Are you trying to blackmail the navy?"

"No sir," Thomas said with his famous innocent expression. "Wilson Enterprises is a family business. Anytime a customer places a large order and does business over time, they become like family. As part of our family, the missiles would be a gift from one family member to another."

This time the entire table laughed as they dreamed about using such missiles in future engagements with the enemy. The Admiral wanted all the missiles, but he would start with four and put their top scientists on a project to reverse engineer the missiles.

THE DEMON NEEDED A complete overhaul. Thomas had been captain of the Demon for seven years while running guns for six years. Thomas decided it was time to go home. However, it would take weeks to complete sufficient repairs to allow for a safe jump.

Thomas called a staff meeting to discuss the status of the repairs going on throughout the ship. They were not surprised when he announced they would take the ship to Wilson Enterprises for repairs due to structural damage. The crew members from Fidem looked forward to visiting their home world. They would enjoy an extended visit with family and friends since repairing the Demon would take considerable time. However, they needed to repair the Demon to jump status before making the long jump home.

Thomas put the crew to work collecting salvage data on the Imperium and enemy ships. The information would be forwarded to Wilson Enterprises. The Demon's hospital stayed busy assisting the navy in caring for the injured. Identifying the living was the only way to get an accurate account of the dead.

The Hostis refused to surrender and committed suicide to prevent capture. Doctor Adler completed an autopsy of a Hostis at Admiral Nelson's request but shared the results with Thomas.

CHAPTER 9 PRISON PLANET

Thomas decided to review the history of Carcerem and learn how it became a prison planet. He researched the information provided by Jewel, the ship's primary AI. He was puzzled by the lack of information on why the government established it as a prison planet. Thomas switched to Omnia, the ship's sentient backup AI. Omnia provided the missing information for Thomas. He became angry with what he discovered. The planet's core was unstable, resulting in earthquakes and volcanic activity. Natural pollutants covered the entire world. Also, the planet had excessive quantities of radioactive tritium and plutonium. The initial surveyors sent in a report saying the planet did not meet the requirements for terraforming. Terraforming would not rid the planet of dangerous radiation. The surveyors recommended quarantining the planet since it had unique animal and plant life. However, the planet contained vast quantities of scandium, lutetium, jadeite, painite, platinum, gold, and a wide variety of flawless gems. This made Carcerem the richest planet ever found. The environment resulted in a short life for all electronics, which required laborers for mining. A powerful family wanted to exploit the planet's riches, but they knew no one would be willing to work on the planet at any price if they knew their life expectancy would be significantly reduced.

The investors murdered the survey team, changed the planet's description to meet the minimum requirements for settlement, and deleted all mention of the planet's wealth. They then used their influence with politicians to establish the planet as an ideal place for housing the worst criminals with their company managing the prison. They seeded the oceans and provided a hybrid potato that would grow in the harsh environment. They increased the population of Carcerem by offering reduced sentences to select criminals with no family ties without telling them of the danger. Then, they secretly rounded up female youths from the slums and dumped them on the planet. They wanted the population to have sufficient females to give birth to future generations of miners. The investors figured if a child started mining at fifteen, they could work for twenty years on average before dying. They never planned to let anyone leave the planet. They built a space station to collect the ore from Carcerem and export it to the Core Planets.

During the Hostis war, the space station was abandoned, and the investor family lived on one of the planets where the Hostis killed the entire population. Thomas directed his science department to send probes to the planet. They found humans living in a settlement near the equator.

Thomas surprised his staff when he announced he planned to visit Carcerem while waiting for the ship to be repaired for the trip home. Everyone was opposed, but Thomas insisted the descendants on the planet should not be condemned because of their ancestors. He planned to take a military shuttle and several bodyguards. Suzanna, supported by his entire staff, objected and stated he could not take such a risk. Doctor Adler said she would declare him medically unfit for duty and confine him to his quarters if he insisted on going.

After accusing everyone of mutiny, he had little choice but to let Ralph and Grayson devise a plan to visit the planet.

The Demon orbited the planet for several days and sent dozens of additional probes. The results of the investigations were not encouraging. The two moons created thirty-meter tides. Active volcanoes resulted in acid rain and daily earthquakes. The planet's thin upper atmosphere resulted in hot, humid days followed by cold nights with snow and ice storms. Tornadoes, hailstorms, and hurricanes were common. They found only one town on the entire planet.

Animals had been provided to support the miners. However, the animals adapted to the environment and bared little resemblance to their progenitors. The mutated native animals were vicious. There were ample freshwater sources, an ocean with plenty of sea life, and an abundance of plant life. However, natural pollutants resulted in unhealthy concentrations of metals in the plants and animals. After considering a variety of options, Ralph and Grayson met with Thomas.

"Life on Carcerem is extremely harsh," Ralph said. "We estimate the average life expectancy is around thirty-five. This is because of the poisons in the soil and water. The background radiation also contributes to a shorter life expectancy. Secondarily, many inhabitants are killed by the planet's physical hazards and predators. As you pointed out, all inhabitants were born on the planet, but they're still the descendants of the Core's worst criminals and may have the same dispositions as their ancestors. While we can't clean the planet of the natural pollutants poisoning the population, we have the technology to increase their life expectancy by providing them with purification equipment to remove mercury, arsenic, and other harmful metals from their drinking water. We can remove the same impurities from the top layers of soil where they are farming, but we can't remove the harmful metals from the fish or animals they eat. However, we can provide chelation and other drugs to remove these metals from their bodies to reduce some of the damage. If they remain on the planet, they'll have to take these drugs daily for their entire life. Implementing these changes would more than double their life expectancy, but it would still be only a third of the life expectancy in the Core Planets. The question is whether we should attempt to help them when the only long-term solution is moving them to another planet. None of the inhabited planets will want them. There are partially terraformed Rim Worlds that are now devoid of life, but they're not much better than Carcerem. We need more information before we offer to help them. Also, they may not want our help."

"What do you propose?" Thomas asked.

"We propose to drop one of our marines on the planet as if he was a convicted criminal," Grayson said. "We'll provide him with a good cover story. He can spy on the people and provide us with information to decide what type of help we should provide. Being on the planet for several weeks will not affect his health."

After further discussions, Thomas agreed to their plan. He told Grayson and Jackson to select the best marine for the assignment. They reviewed the files of their marines and found the ideal candidate. However, because of the nature of the assignment, they wanted a volunteer. They wanted someone who grew up on a rural planet with experience in farming, hunting, and fishing. The person would need to have an amiable disposition. After reviewing the background of every marine, they selected Kyle Murdock as the perfect choice. He was smart, well-liked by his fellow marines, stayed out of trouble, was good in all forms of combat, and was nineteen years old. Plus, he was from an agricultural planet. They called together thirty-nine of their younger marines from eighteen to twenty-five. Grayson described the mission and asked for volunteers. Everyone except Kyle volunteered.

"Kyle, is there some reason you're not volunteering?" Grayson asked.

"When I enlisted, my father told me to obey orders, do my job, keep my head down, and never volunteer for anything." The rest of the group tried not to laugh but failed.

Jackson walked over and stood in front of Kyle. "I'm ordering you to volunteer," he shouted.

Grayson asked for volunteers again, and this time every hand went up. Grayson asked Kyle to step forward and thanked him for volunteering. Kyle had a sick look on his face as they told him to report to the hospital for special inoculations before being transported to the planet.

When Kyle finished at the hospital, they told him to report to the captain. Kyle went to the bridge and was informed the captain was waiting for him in the ready room. Thomas offered Kyle a cup of coffee as he made a cup for himself. Kyle declined and took a seat when directed by Thomas.

"I want to thank you for volunteering." Thomas had watched the vid and knew Kyle had been forced to volunteer. "First, my entire staff is opposed to this mission. They don't believe we should help the descendants of criminals. This is a dangerous mission. I wanted to go on this mission., but my staff refused to let me leave the ship. They even threatened to have me confined to my cabin or placed in the brig."

Kyle considered the captain's decisions to be absolute and could not imagine anyone having the courage to oppose him.

"Kyle, you'll be given a small but powerful communication device. I want you to contact me each night and update me on your progress. This communication is not to interfere with the mission or your reports to anyone else. Do you have any questions?"

"No sir."

After being dismissed, Kyle returned to his cabin. Today was the first time he had ever been to the bridge and the first time he had a conversation with the captain. He was now fully committed to the mission. It must be important if the captain wanted to go on the mission. Whatever happened, he did not want to disappoint the captain.

The following morning, Kyle met Grayson and Jackson in the shuttle bay. He had dressed as ordered in under armor which would pass as long underwear with his marine pants, shirt, and boots. They had studied old court sentencing for prior convictions, which allowed for a six-shot revolver, a marine knife with a sheath, and a backpack. The gun and bullets had to be specially manufactured in the ship's machine shop. Kyle would have preferred having his rifle with a thousand rounds of ammunition and a blaster as a sidearm. The backpack contained a change of clothes, and survival food bars. He had a smaller gun strapped to his ankle, and a second collapsible knife was hidden in the inner pocket of his pants.

A HIGH WALL SURROUNDED the town. The area outside the wall had been cleared of trees and scrubs for a hundred meters. The shuttle hovered five meters off the ground, and two marines carefully threw Kyle off the shuttle's rear ramp. Kyle was wearing leg and wrist shackles. His gun, knife, backpack, and a key were thrown from the shuttle. The shuttle headed straight up and disappeared. Kyle knew the shuttle would return and land three kilometers from the town at a preselected site. Kyle used the key to unlock his restraints, picked up the gun, and placed it in his holster. He put the large knife in the sheath on his left side. He hoisted the pack on his back. They had dropped him near the farthest edge of the clearing close to the forest. They had timed his arrival for midmorning. People working in the fields outside the walls had watched as the shuttle disappeared. Guards watched from the top of the walls with crossbows. The main gate stood open, with a guard standing on each side of the gate.

Kyle walked toward the compound. The people in the fields stopped working and intercepted him at the gate. Kyle stopped ten meters from the entrance and waited.

One of the men who had been working in the fields stepped forward. "It's been over a hundred years since a prisoner has been dropped from the sky. The last one was executed after only three days since he had an evil disposition and murdered a member of our society. What heinous crime did you commit to land on this god-forsaken planet, and do you have any skills?"

"I am Kyle Murdock. I'm a marine and had the misfortune to kill a man in a bar dispute. I beat him in a fair fistfight, but he pulled a gun. He missed, but I didn't. Unfortunately, his parents had political influence, and I was found guilty of murder. The military intervened and prevented my execution. They planned to appeal my case, but I was dragged out of my cell in the middle of the night. After several months, I was dumped here. I need transportation to the nearest city. If you help me, I'm sure the military will reimburse you when they come for me."

The people who had gathered around shook their heads. Several were chuckling.

Kyle acted confused. "Did I say something funny?"

More people had gathered around from inside the walls and from the farms. A male who appeared to be in his forties stepped forward and told him their town was the only city on the planet.

"I'm the town's mayor. What did you do before you became a marine?"

"I lived on a rural planet. My family are farmers, and I hated it. I joined the military when I turned sixteen. I'm only two months from the end of my enlistment and had considered going home before they arrested me."

"As the mayor, I'll allow you to become part of our community on a trial basis. You'll need to give me your gun."

Kyle was unsure how he should respond. As he looked around, everyone was armed with knives and bows. A criminal would not meekly hand over his weapon.

"I think I'll hang onto my gun," Kyle replied as he took a defensive position.

"You can keep your gun, but then you'll have to stay outside the town walls," the Mayor said as several bows were pointed at Kyle.

"This seems like a dangerous place. If I give you my gun, I'll be the only person without a weapon."

One of the men stepped forward, gave him his crossbow, and mentioned he had another at home. Kyle reluctantly unbuckled his gun belt and handed it to the mayor.

"I hate politicians," he said with a disgruntled voice.

The mayor laughed. "We all do. All the political jobs are part time without pay. We all have to work to survive. If you work well, you can stay. If not, we'll ask you to leave." Kyle was thankful they did not ask him to turn over his knife.

"Does anyone want to be responsible for our newest town member?" the mayor asked.

A man in the back stepped forward. "He seems strong. I'll take a chance on him."

The man stepped up to Kyle. "I'm William. This is my daughter, Kaylyn."

"We need to search your backpack to see if you have any other guns," the mayor said. "We'll not take any of your other possessions."

After going through his backpack, they gave it back to him. He followed William and Katlyn to their small cabin. William and Kaylyn sliced several potatoes into a pan and placed it on a coal-fired stove. The temperature had been cold when he first arrived, and now it was turning hot.

"You should take off your outer shirt," William said. "It'll get hotter during the day, but you'll need to put it back on at sunset. Keep your long sleeve undershirt on since you need to keep your body covered when outside."

Kyle removed his outer shirt and hung it next to two coats hanging on hooks next to the door. Kaylyn divided the potatoes onto three plates and placed the plates on the table. William saw Kyle staring at the worn four chairs. "There used to be four in our family. My wife died two years ago from the cough, and my son died in one of the mines last year."

During lunch, William provided Kyle with basic information about their town. "The town survives on farming potatoes, fishing, and coal mining. There used to be a group of hunters, but they either died from predator attacks or decided it was too dangerous and switched to one of the other occupations. We are potato farmers. Any potatoes harvested over our needs are sold in a general market, and the pay received is used to purchase other items. The primary items sold are coal, fish, and potatoes. Each item is sold in baskets, with each basket receiving one coin. Coal is sold in the larger baskets, the potatoes in midsize baskets, and the fish in the smallest baskets."

William said their family survived well when all four were working. They brought home four baskets per day and sold two. Over the years, they had saved the excess coins not used to purchase coal. They had used up all their savings, and their coal bin was running low.

William said with complete candor, "I didn't take you into our home out of charity. I'm hoping you can work hard enough for us to survive. We only have two bedrooms since it would take too much coal to heat a larger home. You can sleep by the fireplace. It'll be the warmest place in the house."

They finished the meal and rinsed the dishes. Kyle followed them as they returned to the fields to continue gathering potatoes. Even though Kyle worked only half a day, he filled a basket. William and Katlyn were happy since together they had only filled one basket. They sold both baskets and purchased two baskets of coal. William and Kyle each carried home a basket of coal. They used a basket of coal each day for cooking and heating the cabin at night. William told Kyle a full coal bin would last thirty days. He liked to keep it full in case he or Katlyn became sick, but it had not been full since his son died. While they were eating, the temperature continued to drop, and Kyle put his shirt on over his under armor. His soft under armor would keep him comfortable in any temperature, but he did not want anyone to know he had a self-regulating garment. After dinner, he walked outside and reported to Captain Wilson. Thomas thanked him for the update.

Katlyn saw Kyle outside and joined him. "You need to come in before you get sick from the cold. We need to buy you a proper coat." Kyle said he did not need a coat, but Katlyn thought he was just being chivalrous.

The following morning they had breakfast and went to the fields. Kyle was stronger and healthier than any of the town's people. He filled a basket during the morning while William and Kaylyn together filled one. They dropped off the two baskets at the market on the way home for lunch and picked up two baskets of coal. During the afternoon, Kyle filled two more baskets while William and Kaylyn filled another. Everyone started talking about Kyle when rumors circulated that he had filled three full baskets in a single day. They kept one basket of potatoes and sold the rest for one coin each. The rest of the town's people at the market told William how he had outsmarted everyone in town by taking in the stranger.

The young girls were giving Kyle enticing looks when Katlyn walked over and put her arm through his. "We need to head home," she said.

William placed the extra coins in a small box when they arrived home. Kyle asked about the small empty barn and the corral behind the house. William told how they once had a yak to pull the plow, but it died, and now the planting was more difficult. During dinner, Kyle expressed his confusion over their form of government.

William told the same story told to him by his parents. "During the early days, we had individuals who tried to become a de facto dictator. However, nearly all the original inhabitants were criminal bosses or leaders, and none were followers. Each dictator only lasted for a brief time. Their own followers killed them because they wanted control, or they were killed by the people they tried to subdue. Anyone attempting to take over was killed. There was even a female dictator for a short while. She assumed the position after gruesomely killing the former dictator who took her by force. After a while, everyone became too smart to take the position. Then a person stepped forward and announced there would be no government. It was a pretty easy sale since the life of a dictator was not significantly better than anyone else. There were no luxuries, and no one would give up their meager property without a fight. Our first law was each person would trade with others whatever they produced, and anyone who tried to steal from another would be executed. Over time our ancestors created a market for the essential items needed to survive. Because of the shortage of females, a second law decreed that a woman could divorce her husband at any time for any reason. Also, any male harming a female was executed. After several generations, the number of males to females became somewhat equal, and there was less violent competition among the men for a wife. Our government, if you can call it that, slowly evolved into what it is today. There were issues with each new criminal they dropped on the planet. They either accepted our laws and adapted or were left outside the wall to die. If they refused either option, they were killed. Survival is difficult for everyone, and we work hard each day to maintain a minimum existence.

"What about crime today," Kyle asked.

"The town is like one extended family. Crime is practically non-existent. There are no jails. If there is a disagreement, the elders listen to both sides and resolve the issue. This only happens once or twice a year. Everyone depends on each other for food and protection. You're the first prisoner to be dropped on our planet in a hundred years. The prior prisoner only lasted a few days since he refused to work and killed a family when they refused to feed him. That was our last murder."

"With the town's prior experience, I'm surprised you accepted me into your home."

"My daughter and I are desperate, and you seemed like a decent person. Also, my daughter and I, along with the rest of the town, have been watching you."

Kyle helped with the dishes and walked outside the home to make his reports. William and Katlyn joined Kyle. Together they practiced using their crossbows on a target. Katlyn and William were hitting the target dead center with each shot. Toward the end of the practice session, Kyle was hitting the target but not in the center. Kyle was disappointed since he was a marksman with guns. William gave him some encouragement and said he just needed a little practice.

The next day, Kyle finished two baskets by noon and dropped them off as they went home for lunch. Kyle found the farm work was not as bad as his childhood memory. They went back to work after lunch. Kyle thought the work was peaceful when he heard a horn blow twice. Kyle looked around, and everyone was grabbing their crossbows. He noticed everyone was looking up at what looked like a flock of birds. However, as the birds got closer, Kyle realized they were flying reptiles with clawed feet and long sharp teeth. The farmers gathered quickly into small groups for protection. Kyle found himself with William, Katlyn, and six other farmers. Williams took Kyle's crossbow and told him to help with the reloading. Two of the reptiles dove at their group. No one fired until the beasts were only twenty meters away. Each arrow was accurate, and the injured creatures prowled into the ground a few feet from the farmers. The farmers reloaded and fired several arrows into the heads of the beasts until they stopped moving. Kyle reloaded the two bows Willian had fired. One group had a fatality and two injuries. Five flying reptiles were killed and dragged inside the walls. Katlyn told Kyle that every part of the creatures would be used. Nothing was wasted on Carcerem. Kyle spent several hours practicing with his bow after dinner, and his accuracy was much better.

The next morning, ash fell for several hours. At midday, they took their baskets to the store. While William and Katlyn were socializing, Kyle went out to the water well. He took off his shirts and poured a bucket of water over his head. It felt good to wash off the ash. The marines had demanding daily workouts, and Kyle was well-muscled with a flat stomach.

Katlyn heard all the females oohing and aahing. She turned around and saw all the girls were watching Kyle. She ran to Kyle. "Put on your clothes," she shouted. "You're half naked." The other females told her to leave him alone so they could enjoy the view. "We're going home!" The females were making offers to Kyle as Katlyn dragged him down the road.

When William came into their home laughing, Katlyn was telling Kyle how he made a spectacle of himself by taking his clothes off in public.

After Katlyn calmed down, William explained that everyone covered their body outside their home to protect their skin against the climate. Ash, acid rain, hail, and falling hot pebbles from volcanoes could occur without warning. Thus, everyone remained fully dressed when outdoors, which resulted in a prudish culture.

They returned to the fields after lunch. Much to Katlyn's displeasure, Kyle received smiles and enticing comments from the ladies. Kyle apologized for his indecency, but they laughed. He received multiple offers to meet after hours at the bar.

After dinner, Kyle said he wanted to check out the town's bar. Katlyn was mad until Kyle asked her to join him. There were two bars in town. One bar was more sedate. Kyle watched the people sitting around tables telling stories, laughing, and drinking. The only alcohol was vodka. Many drank it straight, but there was a type of fruit you could use to water it down. Kyle was surprised the people were relaxed and having a good time. Kyle could not understand how anyone could enjoy themselves since there was so much hardship. Then he saw a writing in large letters along the top of the back wall. *The mind in its own place and in itself can make a heaven of hell or a hell of heaven.* It was credited to someone named John Milton, and Kyle figured he must have been born on Carcerem to have such a strange idea.

The second bar was filled with single people. It was loud, with music and dancing. Kyle drank slowly to avoid getting drunk. He danced one dance with Katlyn, but then every girl in the bar took turns asking him to dance with them. Kyle saw Katlyn frowning and decided to make it an early night. They held hands as they walked home.

The next morning was another work day. After lunch, Kyle asked William if he could take the afternoon off, and William readily agreed.

"Are you going to meet some female in town?" Katlyn asked.

Kyle laughed. "No, I just want to look around."

She did not find it funny and was still sulking when he left. Like everyone in town, Kyle carried a crossbow wherever he went. He stopped by the mayor's home and spoke to him as he was getting ready to return to work. Kyle said he wanted to explore the woods and needed to borrow his gun. The mayor told him the woods were dangerous but retrieved the gun from his home and gave it to Kyle. The mayor spent a few minutes describing the animals in the woods. The mayor said goodbye since he did not expect Kyle to survive. Kyle started jogging once he entered the woods. He saw large rodents eating bugs and digging up worms from the earth. Later he saw two howlers eating one of the rodents and a vulture devouring a howler pup. While jogging, he called the shuttle and told them what he had planned. All the areas close to town were void of anything worth hunting, but further from the town, there were wild boars and even herds of wild yaks. He saw several howlers following him as he neared the shuttle.

When he arrived, the marines had killed two wild boars and had already butchered the animals, which reduced the weight. Kyle provided a soil sample, a water sample, a potato, and hair samples he had collected for their analysis. They agreed to capture some yaks and boars. He would be back in two days to pick them up. He hoisted a boar over each shoulder and started back to town.

Kyle was walking at a brisk pace when he had the feeling he was being followed. He moved faster and managed to jog even with the added weight on his shoulders. Kyle heard the growls and saw several howlers following him. Soon the number of howlers increased. He started running as fast as he could without dropping the boars. He reached the clearing and hoped the howlers would not leave the forest, but they were in full pursuit, lured by the scent of the blood. Eight howlers ran after him as he raced across the clearing for the town. The guards saw him and started ringing a bell. Anyone outside the walls hurried to the gates. The guards knew Kyle did not stand a chance as they watched him running for his life.

Kyle was only halfway across the cleared area when he knew he had to make a stand or be brought down from behind. He spun around, dropping the boars as he pulled the crossbow from across his back. He fired the bow and missed the howler he was aiming at, but it buried into the chest of another howler that plowed into the dirt. Kyle dropped the bow and pulled his gun just in time to fire at the closest howler. He had to be accurate with each shot if he hoped to survive. He fired all six rounds killing four howlers. The three remaining howlers attacked him. He shoved his gun into the mouth of one of the howlers. He raised his left arm to keep another howler from his throat, and the howler bit into his arm. He remembered his backup gun. He landed on his back and brought his knee up to his chest. A howler bit into his leg just as he pulled out the gun from his boot. The third howler was going for his throat as he fired three shots into the howler. He then emptied his second gun into the howler biting his leg. Somehow, he dropped his gun and found his knife. He reversed his grip and stabbed the howler biting his arm. On his second attempt, the howler died when the knife went through its eye and entered its brain. Three howlers were lying on top of him when the townspeople arrived. They stood around him in awe as he shoved first one and then another of the howlers off of him. Kyle could feel the blood running down his face and realized one of the howlers had clawed his face.

Kyle staggered to his feet. The town's people picked up the howlers and boars. The guns and knife were handed to him. After entering the town, Kyle sat down on one of the benches, his adrenaline rush was gone, and he felt weak. The mayor walked over to Kyle.

"You need to see our doctor, then you can explain about the second gun." Kyle was worried, but when he looked up, the mayor was smiling.

Kyle thought everything would be all right until Katlyn ran up, screaming and crying simultaneously. Several of the wives told her it would not be proper to kill him until the doctors patched him up. William helped him to his feet and walked him to one of the homes. A young boy had run ahead to inform the doctors. When he arrived, they were expecting him and helped him lie down on a table. He understood the man and his wife were both considered by the town to be doctors. Kyle began to relax until the female doctor poured liquid on the cuts on his face. He screamed and would have fallen off the table if not for both doctors catching him. He sat up and continued to scream until he had used every foul word in his vocabulary.

Finally, when he stopped, the female doctor said, "I've had ladies delivering a baby who did not scream as loud. I just applied a little alcohol to keep the cuts from getting infected."

At his request, she told him it was the same alcohol from potatoes they served at the bars. Kyle grabbed the bottle of vodka out of her hand and took a big gulp. She shook her head and took back the bottle.

She picked up another bottle with a colored liquid. "I'm going to apply some liquid to deaden the spot so we can stitch up the opening."

Kyle watched her approach with a needle threaded with a thin twine. He grabbed her arm. "I'm fine. Just put a bandage on it, and I'll be good to go."

"You just fought a pack of howlers and are afraid of a little needle? I can put you to sleep if you wish, and you can sleep through the procedure." The needle was within inches of Kyle's face, and then he did not see anything.

Her husband felt Kyle's pulse and listened to his strong heart. He smiled at his wife and said her patient had fainted. She poured another liquid on a cloth. She placed it over his mouth and nose to keep him sedated. They removed his clothing to check for other injuries. His outer clothes were ripped in several places, but they were surprised to see his underclothes were in perfect condition. They gave his outer pants and shirt to one of the ladies for patching.

They removed the remainder of his clothes and noted the bad bruising all over his body. They saw several scars and knew this was not the first time their patient had been injured. They applied healing cream to his bruises and moved him to one of the beds. The sun had set, and it was already starting to get cold as they added coal to the fireplace.

They examined his clothing. The husband took the shirt over to the fireplace for added light. "This material is remarkable," he said.

He showed his wife how his hand inside the sleeve did not feel hot next to the fire. His wife tried with equal success. He took off his shirt and put on Kyle's shirt. It easily stretched to fit him, and he walked into the backyard. His wife put on her coat and joined him. He told her only his hands were cold. The rest of his upper body felt comfortable. She tried it next and was equally amazed. They placed the undergarments next to where Kyle was sleeping and decided to keep the clothing a secret.

The following morning Kyle was stiff but felt much better. William and Katlyn stopped by to see him on their way to work. After they left, he saw his clothes on a small table beside the bed. Kyle noticed his outer garments had been patched. The doctors asked if he wanted to join them at the kitchen table or if he wanted breakfast in bed.

"I'll join you at the table as soon as I get dressed." He was surprised when he saw meat next to the potatoes.

"Thanks to you, we have howler meat with our potatoes," the doctor said with a laugh. "Your undergarments are unusual."

"Yes, they are," replied Kyle. "Off planet, the garments are readily available. The two of you are doctors, and I hope you'll believe what I tell you. On most planets the life expectancy is considerably longer. The food and water contain impurities that are bad for your health."

Both the doctors were quiet as they considered what he had said. "Even if what you say is true, what can we do about it?"

"Filtration devices can remove all the harmful items from the water. Specialized machines can remove the poisons from your farm soil so the potatoes can grow without harmful impurities. You now have domestic animals. You could feed them grain from the field and eat the meat without adverse effects. Unfortunately, nothing can be done about the fish in the ocean. There are medicines that can remove harmful metals from your body. Doing these things would more than double the life expectancy of everyone here."

"How would we get the machines, equipment, and medicine you talk about?"

"If I can get a message to one of the military ships and if I'm rescued, would you be able to convince the people here to accept the help I mentioned?"

"You're a dreamer, but I like your dream. No one here would trust anyone who offered anything for free. Also, how would we pay for the equipment or medicine you describe?"

"I have another question. If the people here were offered an opportunity to move to another planet, would they?"

"You ask such ridiculous questions," the wife replied. "No one has ever gotten off this planet."

Kyle figured he had pushed enough. He thanked them for attending to his injuries and left. They watched him go. He was so full of energy and unlike anyone else in their town. How could anyone be so optimistic?

When he reached the home of William and Katlyn, they had already eaten lunch and returned to the fields. He laid down on his floor bedding and quickly fell asleep. He awoke when William and Katlyn came home. When dinner was ready, he joined them at the table and saw they had potatoes and howler.

Katlyn was so excited she could not sit still. "Tell him pa, tell him," she exclaimed.

William grinned from ear to ear. "The townspeople figured the howlers and boars were rightfully ours since you're part of our household. We sold the boars at two coins for each half and the howlers at one coin each. We kept one of the howlers and cured the meat. Everyone agreed to give us the skins to make a warm coat for you. We should have let you decide whether to keep a boar or a howler, but I couldn't refuse four coins for each boar. I hope you agree."

"Of course, I agree. I assume you filled the coal bin?"

"Yes, and the townspeople helped deliver the coal to our home. Our coin box is nearly full. All the town's people regret not asking you to join their home. You have saved us. I'm not a religious man. But I prayed, and you're the answer to my prayers."

"Thank you, but I don't think your prayers had anything to do with it."

"While you were with the doctors, I turned eighteen," Katlyn said. "I convinced pa to wait until you were well to announce my birthday. On a girl's birthday, all the guys can ask her to marry them, and a female can decide if she wants to accept. You can ask someone to marry you anytime, but birthdays are special. I think you should ask me to marry you."

Kyle choked on the water he was drinking. "We've just met. You can't possibly want me as your husband. Have you seriously looked at my face? I was never handsome, but I'm downright ugly with this scar on my face. Plus, you're too young to get married."

"You're so ugly that every girl in town wants to marry you. I'm not too young. Most girls are married by the time they're sixteen. At eighteen, I'm practically an old maid. Just think about it."

Kyle knew he had to be careful and did not want to hurt her feelings. "Right now, I'm too tired to think about anything. William, would you mind if I took the day off tomorrow to rest?"

"Of course, you take all the time you need."

The following morning, they had breakfast together with potatoes and howler. It was barely daybreak when William and Katlyn were ready to leave. William went out the door first. Katlyn, still inside the cabin, grabbed Kyle and kissed him hard. She grinned. "Think about me during the day. I'll certainly be thinking about you."

Kyle stared after her. She was undeniably a young lady any man would want. She was not beautiful, but her personality made her attractive and desirable. He needed to control the relationship since he did not want her hurt when he left in a few weeks.

Kyle filled his guns with bullets from a hidden compartment in his pack and checked his knives. He felt guilty as he took one of the coins from the box and headed to what passed as the general store. No one was present at the store, but the prices were on each item. He found the rope he wanted and a dozen burlap sacks. He left a coin behind the counter with a short piece of rope he had cut off with his knife. He put the sacks in his backpack and wrapped the long rope around his neck and shoulder. Then, he headed for the gate. The town's people took turns guarding the gate. He did not know the two men at the gate, but they recognized him and asked what he planned to do with the rope.

"I'm going to rope some howlers and bring them home. I'm going into the howler-raising business. At a coin each, I figure to be rich in no time." He was joking, but the two men thought he might be crazy enough to try it. They laughed and shook their heads as they watched him head to the woods.

Kyle traveled fast and reached the campsite at midmorning. There were four shuttles and a platoon of marines. They had eight yaks and a pen full of young boars. The yaks would use their horns to fight the predators but were unafraid of humans. The marines put the boars in the breathable burlap sacks. Each yak carried two sacks tied together with a short piece of rope. A sack was placed on each side for balance. The largest yak had no boars and was the yak Kyle planned to ride. Several marines had already ridden the lead yak, but Kyle found himself face down in the dirt a few seconds after climbing on the yak's back. Everyone laughed, and Kyle had a red face but did not say anything as he got back on the yak.

Kyle headed back to town with eight yaks and fourteen boars. The platoon followed to make sure he had no problem with predators. When they got close to the town, the marines left Kyle and headed back to the shuttles. As Kyle approached the town, he heard the bell ring but thought it strange since everyone would already be inside the wall. As he approached, the gates swung open, and the townspeople came rushing out to greet him. He dismounted and asked everyone not to scare the animals. He gave each person a smelly boar bag and led the yaks to the center of town before stopping.

The mayor came forward, shaking his head. "What are you up to now?"

"I figured the town needs a boar farm. You need to let the animals grow and produce more boars until you have enough for the entire town. The boars can have two litters per year, with about ten boars per litter. In a couple of years, this town will be overrun with boars. The yaks can be bred. In time, every farmer will have two yaks to help with the plowing. I believe some yaks are already bred." He did not tell them the females were already been bred and would have their foal in eleven months.

"How did you catch these animals," a neighbor asked.

"On my last trip, I found a rockslide had trapped them in a small clearing. The small area made it easy to catch the yaks, but the boars are mean, and they bite." The people laughed, which was rare due to their harsh living conditions.

"What you brought the town is priceless," the mayor said. "Name whatever you want, and it's yours."

"First, the yak I rode in on, one of the female yaks, and four boars should go to William and Katlyn. I give the rest of the animals to the town to raise until every home has at least two yaks and two boars. The yaks and boars are to be distributed by a fair lottery. Second, when a family receives their first boar, they will give William a coin. When they receive their first yak, they will give William three coins. Third, once every family has two boars and two yaks, then all future births of the animals will be equally divided among the families."

They all knew the price being asked was ridiculously low, and they recognized he had asked nothing for himself. Every head nodded in agreement, and the mayor said no vote was necessary.

Everyone in town wanted to thank Kyle, and he received considerable attention from the young girls his age. Katlyn stepped forward and told Kyle it was time to head home. William, Katlyn, and Kyle headed home with their two yaks and four boars. Kyle asked for the next day off, and William just laughed. He asked Kyle not to take any more chances in the forest.

Later after dinner, Kyle went out back and gave his report to Thomas and then to Grayson. Katlyn joined him outside. She had her coat on, but she shivered just a little until Kyle put his arm around her waist.

They both looked at the stars. "I know your home is up there, and you miss it. Are you going back to the stars?"

He stayed silent for a few minutes. "Yes," he replied with a little sadness.

"When you go, can I come with you?"

"I'd like that," Kyle replied. "I'll get out of the marines in a few months, and I plan to go home to the farm on my homeworld. I think you'd like it there. Farm life there is easier than here. There's no food shortage, and you'll live to be over a hundred while having good health. The land is plentiful, and there've been twelve hundred acres in my name since I was born. When a child of one of the founding families is born, the parents get to select twelve hundred acres in the child's name. It'll be a long time until all the land is taken, if ever. Our children will get the same size farm if they are smart enough to stay home or return home. However, you may not want to come with me when I tell you my secret."

"Nothing you say will change my mind."

"I've lied to you and everyone here."

"Is everything you told me about your home a lie?"

"No, that's the truth."

"You're not a marine?"

"Yes, that part is true. I am a marine."

"You didn't kill a man in a bar fight?"

"Yes, I killed a man in a bar fight. There was a hearing before a judge, but I was acquitted since it was self-defense. I'm a marine serving as a gunner on a ship called the Demon. We were in a battle involving hundreds of spaceships. Our ship was damaged and is currently being repaired. I was sent here as a spy to see if we should try to help the inhabitants. I'm a spy. You're the only person I've told. Do you still want to marry me?"

"Yes," she answered before kissing him. She pulled her head back to catch her breath. "But, you being a spy, should be our secret," she said with a grin before kissing him again. Katlyn made sure everyone knew Kyle was her man, and the single girls were told to keep their hands to themselves.

Kyle spent each day talking to the various families. He would meet with them at meals and enjoy light conversations. Everyone wanted to spend time with him, and he was a good listener. None of them could believe he had asked nothing for himself. Kyle would casually mention he was trying to contact a military ship. He showed them the small transmitter and told them he had hidden it on his person before being dumped on the planet. He told them if a ship came, there was a chance they would provide equipment to make life easier and medicine to cure the cough. No one ridiculed him since they were indebted to him. Most believed it was impossible, but others would mention how Kyle had already achieved several miracles. The younger people started believing as Kyle continued using the soft sell approach by simply letting them know it was possible. He visited the mines and used his wrist monitor to analyze the discarded ore piled up outside the mines. He told them the waste was extremely valuable on other planets. He transmitted his finding to Thomas.

THOMAS, SUZANNA, AND Amanda were having lunch. "I reviewed some of the vids from Kyle's body cam," Suzanna said. "They work so hard, and the children are so thin. I watched the family Kyle is staying with as they ate dinner. They were giving thanks for such a small amount of food. You were right about Carcerem. The descendants are good people, and we need to help them."

Finally, Thomas thought it was time. Thomas, Suzanna, and Amanda came down with six shuttles full of gifts for the inhabitants. When a shuttle was emptied, it took off and was replaced with a full shuttle. As the townspeople came forward, they were told to take whatever they wanted.

The mayor came forward and asked loudly, "Why are you providing all these items?" He wanted the townspeople to hear.

Thomas answered with a straight face. "You have one of our officers, Kyle Murdock. He contacted us and said he was being held as a prisoner. We were told of your ransom demands. We'll provide what is requested. We ask that he be brought to us unharmed after we have provided the items demanded for his release."

Kyle had explained to the mayor how he should respond. "Kyle Murdock won't be harmed as long as you meet the ransom demands."

The mayor motioned for everyone to haul the merchandise inside the walls. Doctor Adler, with her staff, asked to meet with their doctors. They provided four shuttles loaded with medical supplies. They delivered cultivating equipment they had manufactured in the ship's machine shop. They installed water purification subsystems throughout the city. They cultivated the land and removed all the poisons from the top two meters of the soil.

They planted seeds of a wide range of vegetables that would grow well in the planet's environment. They installed power units throughout the city to provide heating and cooling for every home.

The townspeople were skeptical at first but started helping with the installations. An education center was built with training modules. Food processors were provided with all the nutrients necessary to provide food for the town until the new crops were ready for harvesting.

Kyle and Katlyn asked William if he would bless their marriage, and he hugged them both. She told William she would be leaving with Kyle. William would miss them but was happy to see them leave the planet when Kyle told him about his own farm. They were married, and the entire town celebrated with no outsiders present.

Finally, on the thirty-second day, they brought Kyle to Thomas unharmed. Kyle introduced Katlyn to Thomas as his wife and said she would join him on the Demon. Kyle had offered to take William with them, but William did not want to leave the planet. Even though it was a horrible planet, it was still his home.

Before Thomas left the planet, he and Suzanna met with the town council. They provided a list of things the town might consider exporting. The town had been mining coal for hundreds of years and discarding enormous quantities of precious metals as byproducts with little value. Suzanna gave them the value for each item and agreed to purchase their entire supply. They loaded containers full of ore which was transported to the Demon. The town set aside ten tons of the most valuable ore as a wedding gift for Kyle and Katlyn.

First Officer Ralph Miller told the inhabitants of opportunities to travel to other worlds and explore employment opportunities.

"A while back, we saw bright flashes of lights and streaks of fire in our sky," a middle-aged female said. "Do you know what caused such a sight?"

"There was a great battle in the heavens," Ralph stated. "The enemy we fought was planning to destroy all of humanity. We successfully defeated the enemy this time. Our captain was a major factor in helping to defeat the enemy. The lights in your sky were the weapons being used in the battle. The streaks were debris from the battle burning up in your planet's atmosphere."

"You said the enemy is not human," she said. "What is the appearance of such a foe?"

"I'll show you," Ralph responded.

Ralph used his suit's electronics to display a holograph of a Hostis in full size. Everyone was initially startled by the display and fearful until Ralph explained the holograph could not harm them.

"Why has no other ship visited us?" another man asked.

Ralph had hoped to avoid the topic. "Do you know your planet's history and how your planet was settled?"

The same man said, "Yes, we know this is a prison planet, and we have many tales but no written history of our founding."

Ralph had studied earth history in one of his school courses and used an analogous situation as an example. "On a very distant planet, a mostly uninhabited large landmass existed. People who had broken the laws were rounded up and abandoned on this large landmass. At first, there was much violence, and no ships ventured there because they were fearful of the inhabitants. After many years, the descendants built a great civilization. It was rich in beauty and culture. Your planet was similarly settled. No one came here because they were afraid of you and did not know of the valuable metals found on your planet. There are also mobile weapons circling your planet capable of destroying any ship attempting to land. Our ship can avoid such weapons."

Ralph noted the listeners had considered what he said, but no one seemed angry at his explanation. They could not understand how people who commanded the heavens were afraid of them.

"It must be wonderful to travel among the heavens," one of the younger ladies said.

"Would you like to visit our ship and see the heavens?"

She was surprised and responded, "Yes, I'd like that very much."

"Our ship will be here for several days," Ralph said. "Each of our shuttles can hold several hundred people. We'd be happy to conduct tours for anyone who would like to visit our ship."

They discussed the possibilities among themselves. They reached a consensus with Ralph's input. Whoever wished to travel to the ship would show up at dawn the following morning.

THOMAS MET WITH THE Town Council and told them his family was in the shipbuilding business and would be happy to sell them a spaceship.

"It'll take over a year to build a new ship. However, you can purchase a used ship for about half the price, and it would be available in about four months. You'll need trained spacers to operate the ship. The training modules we set up for you will let your citizens learn the basic skills necessary to pilot such a ship. We can also provide trainers with the ship to assist you until you gain the experience to handle the ship without assistance. The Demon is preparing to return to our home planet for needed repairs. The ore you currently have is sufficient to pay for the supplies you need and purchase a used spaceship. Wilson Enterprises will conduct salvage operations in this system for several years. They'd like to engage in direct trade with you. The ore you provide during the salvage could be used to purchase a second ship. We have prepared a standard agreement used by other planets, but it is strictly voluntary. A planet being terraformed will be available for colonization in twenty years. No one else knows about the planet. It's yours if you want it. Moving your small population to the new planet using your own ships would take around a year. You have twenty years to think about such a move. In the meantime, you can significantly improve your living conditions on Carcerem. The rough repairs on our ship will be completed in six days. You have until then to decide how you would like to proceed."

There were questions after Thomas finished his explanation, but all the questions were positive. Thomas leased Carcerem four shuttles with an option to buy. The inhabitants of Carcerem took possession of the space station, and they immediately started delivering ore to the station. The shuttles were parked on the station when not in use to minimize corrosion from the planet.

Thomas entered into four agreements with the representatives from Carcerem. They executed a general trade agreement, a contract to purchase two used, refurbished spaceship from Wilson Enterprises, an agreement to supply materials for the salvage operation, and a multiyear lease for Wilson Enterprises to use part of the space station.

The doctors from Carcerem were shown the healing chambers during a tour of the Demon's hospital. Doctor Adler explained that the chambers would not last long on Carcerem due to the environment but would work perfectly on the station. They ordered twenty healing chambers and would use the shuttles to bring the people to the station. Adding the healing chambers to all the other changes on Carcerem would significantly add to their life expectancy.

Thomas informed Wilson Enterprises of the large market in the Outer Planets and the Rim for used ships. The poorer Rim Worlds would be happy to get a reliable used ship at an affordable price.

After the shuttles left, the mayor called a town meeting. He told them Kyle had been convicted of murder and sentenced to their planet. However, Kyle's parents were high-ranking royalty on his home planet and got the charges dropped. Kyle's parents were prepared to spend whatever it took to bring their son home. He told them it was Kyle's idea to require a ransom. Some of the townspeople said they should have refused the ransom and kept Kyle.

BOTH GRAYSON AND THOMAS congratulated Kyle on the results of his mission. At Doctor Adler's suggestion, Katlyn spent three cycles in one of the healing chambers.

After her time in the chamber, she looked at Doctor Adler. "I can't believe how great I feel. I have never felt so good. What did you do?"

"We removed the heavy metals and other impurities from your body. Plus, the nanites in the healing chamber repaired the damage to your organs. We have a purchase order to deliver healing chambers to the station so all the inhabitants of Carcerem can be similarly cured."

Kyle met privately with Grayson and said he would not be re-enlisting. He quoted his enlistment papers as providing a free trip home at the end of his service period and asked if his wife could be included in the free ride home. Grayson agreed but hated losing a good marine.

Thomas asked Kyle and Katlyn to join his family for a farewell dinner. Suzanna and Katlyn enjoyed each other's company. Toward the end of the meal, Thomas decided it was time to discuss Kyle's and Katlyn's future.

"If you ever get tired of farming, you could use a small portion of the credits from your wedding gift to purchase a spacecraft. You could use the ship to become merchant traders. There's a real need for trade ships, and such a ship would be beneficial to both your planets."

"Do you need an answer now?" Kyle asked.

"No, spend time on your homeworld with your family. Send me a message if you get bored with farming, and Wilson Enterprises will build you a ship."

Katlyn whispered into Kyle's ear. "I'll consider your offer," Kyle responded with a smile.

Grayson provided a shuttle. Kyle and Katlyn said their goodbyes. The military shuttle had jump capability, and they were soon on their way to Kyle's home. Kyle and Katlyn were both excited about buying a spaceship at a future date. First, Katlyn would meet Kyle's parents and his two older sisters.

The salvage crew representing Wilson Enterprises arrived and took inventory of all the battle debris. The lease at the space station was perfect for supporting their salvage operations and provided Carcerem with additional income.

The battle against the Hostis had been fought in the Rim. However, it did not take long for the results of the Demon's participation to spread throughout the galactic. The stories of the Demon's part in the battle were discussed over drinks in every bar whenever the navy granted shore leave. The reputation of the Demon continued to grow. Individuals no longer doubted the earlier stories told by pirates about the invincibility of the ship. The pirate ships fleeing previous confrontations with the Demon gained added respect from other ships.

It was time for the Demon to make the long jump to Fidem, the home planet of Thomas and his original crew. They would generally make several jumps and conduct trade along the way, but the ship was in no shape for the extra stress it would be subjected to for multiple jumps.

Shortly after entering hyperspace, Suzanna visited Doctor Adler. She mentioned how she had made hundreds of jumps over her lifetime and never felt more than a slight disorientation. Doctor Adler did a complete examination and told her what she had already suspected. She was pregnant. The Doctor further told her six Oceanums were also pregnant.

"Do you know why all seven pregnancies appear to be around the same day?" Doctor Adler asked. Suzanna explained how she had loaned one Oceanum some sperm from Thomas without his knowledge.

Suzanna was disgruntled. "I didn't expect them to have a sperm party." She then asked the Doctor to keep it a secret until she found the right moment to tell Thomas.

ADMIRAL NELSON HAD his maintenance and engineers work round the clock to repair the ships to flight status. He selected thirty-two ships needing major repairs and sent them to the Wilson Enterprises shipyard.

After additional communications, the navy gave a ten-year contract to Wilson Enterprises to repair damaged navy ships and serve as their maintenance provider for all navy vessels. A separate order was placed for twenty new cruisers under a five-year contract. However, it was understood the agreement would be extended before it expired. The twenty cruisers were part of the navy budget, which was approved before the battle with the Hostis. Admiral Nelson needed over a hundred cruisers and over two hundred destroyers to replace the ships he had lost in the battle. However, replacing the vessels would require the Senate to approve a separate appropriation. Hopefully, he would get the approval after the Senate learned of their glorious victory against the Hostis.

Admiral Nelson received a message to meet with the Premier and address the Senate on their victory over the Hostis. Admiral Nelson took the Battleship Independence to the meeting since it was his flagship. He hoped the Senate would be impressed enough with their success to approve funding for the additional cruisers and destroyers.

Shortly after his arrival, the Premier requested Admiral Nelson's presence for a private meeting. The Admiral took a shuttle to the planet, and a governmental ground vehicle picked him up when the shuttle touched down. It was not long before the Admiral took a seat in one of the Premier's secured conference rooms. Admiral Nelson noticed the Premier was wearing one of his famous neutral political expressions. The Admiral immediately knew the meeting was going to be difficult.

"Admiral Nelson, let me congratulate you on a glorious victory."

The Admiral addressed the Premier formally. "Thank you, your Eminence."

"Please watch the following vid," the Premier said.

The Admiral watched a vid showing the end of their battle with the Hostis. It clearly showed the part the Demon played in the victory. Anyone watching the vid could see the naval fleet would have lost without the Demon's help.

When the vid ended, the Premier said, "At our last meeting, you emphatically insisted the Demon did not possess superior weapons. Do the weapons used by the Demon in this battle look like standard military-grade weapons to you?"

The Admiral sighed. "Your Eminence, I swear, I didn't know the Demon possessed such weapons."

"We can't have such weapons in the hands of a civilian," the Premier said. "What action have you taken concerning this matter?"

"Your Eminence, as you saw, without the intervention by Captain Wilson, we'd have lost the battle, and the Hostis would be in the Core right now, wiping out the human race. Captain Wilson is very loyal to the government and you. It's important to maintain his loyalty. You saw the power of the Demon. I didn't want to go to war against his ship. However, I agree with you. We can't allow a civilian to have such power. I have entered into a military contract with Wilson Enterprises, owned by Thomas' family. In return, Thomas turned over four of the torpedoes to us. I'm hopeful our scientists can reverse-engineer the technology. Also, I plan to obtain the additional torpedoes diplomatically. I don't want to force the turnover since it could be a tactical mistake. Also, I don't want to be on the receiving end of one of those torpedoes. The Demon only has a few special torpedoes left, and I want to locate the origins of those weapons. I have a tracker on the Demon, and I'll follow him when he picks up additional weapons. Thomas has agreed to let a convoy of navy ships accompany the Demon. As you know, we lost a lot of ships in the battle with the Hostis. The navy needs replacement ships. Assuming the Senate approves a budget for a hundred new cruisers, I'll offer the contract to Wilson Enterprises for the remaining torpedoes and the location of the site where he obtained the weapons. Regardless, we need the additional ships. So, we're not giving up anything to get the weapons and the site information. With the additional ships and the new weapons, we can take the fight to the Hostis. We can attack their system and end the war."

The Premier was thoughtful. "I can get the Senate to approve fifty additional cruisers now and the rest later. With the twenty already approved, you will have seventy new ships. I'll get the Senate's support for the additional ships when we have the new missiles. Tell me, what will you do if Captain Wilson refuses to provide the weapons and the site information?"

The Admiral knew what was expected. "Then we take it by force and dispose of the captain along with his crew!"

The Premier nodded his head in agreement. "Very well, tomorrow you and certain of your officers will be present for an award ceremony in the Senate where we'll celebrate your victory. At the same time, we'll ask the Senate to approve an appropriation for your new ships in anticipation of future attacks by the Hostis. Also, if we can reverse engineer those weapons, we can go on the offensive without waiting. With such weapons, we can attack the planets of the Hostis and wipe out the entire species."

CHAPTER 10 PRODIGAL SON COMES HOME

Alina Wilson was about to tell everyone to sit down for dinner when the door chimes sounded. She looked over at her daughter. "Joan, will you please see who's at the door."

Alina directed everyone else to take a seat and enjoy their once-a-month family reunion dinner. Alina enjoyed spending this time with their daughter Joan and Joan's husband Finley, and her son Stephen and Stephen's wife Melanin. At each of these gatherings, she would think about her son Thomas, who she had not seen in seven years, and wondered if she would ever see him again.

Joan was wondering who would bother them on a Saturday night. She opened the door.

The young man standing in the doorway smiled and said, "Hi Joan."

Joan paused and suddenly realized her younger brother was standing in front of her. She screamed and jumped into his arms. She held him tight and did not want to let go.

Amanda looked around at the inside of the largest home she had ever seen. She decided to explore while the adults continued with their discussions. After Joan released her brother, Thomas introduced her to Susanna. Then, he looked around for Amanda and looked at Susanna.

Suzanna lifted her eyebrows. "I guess she went exploring."

Amanda heard talking further ahead. She smelled the aroma of freshly baked bread and other fragrances coming from the same direction. It smelled really good, so she followed the scent and the noise. She walked into a room full of food and people.

Alina saw the little girl. "Who are you," she asked.

Everyone in the room stopped speaking.

Amanda looked up. "I'm Amanda Wilson. My father used to live here."

Alina put her hand in front of her mouth. "Oh my god."

Tears filled her eyes as she rushed over to Amanda, dropped to one knee, and gave her a big hug. Tears were rolling down her face. "I'm your grandmother."

Then she looked up and saw her son standing just inside the dining room. As she stood up, Amanda exclaimed, "Grandmother is crying, but it's not my fault."

Alina laughed as she wiped away the tears. She remembered Thomas saying those exact same words so many times with the same innocent face. Alina and Thomas embraced each other.

"I've missed you every day," Alina said as she continued to hold on to Thomas. "I was beginning to think I'd never see you again."

Thomas and Alina separated. "I see you have already met Amanda," Thomas said. "This is Suzanna."

Alina looked at her son for additional clarification, but Thomas did not say anything else. Ben and Stephen also rushed over and took turns hugging Thomas. Thomas introduced Suzanna to the rest of the family. Then, Alina told Thomas his sister and brother had married during his absence. She introduced her daughter-in-law and son-in-law.

Ben sent a signal to the table. It slowly extended in length, and three additional chairs appeared around the table. Everyone took a seat and filled their plates. Alina asked Amanda to sit next to her while increasing the height of Amanda's chair to a comfortable level.

Ben said what was on everyone's mind. "You should have told us you were coming."

"The ship was severely damaged, and we were not sure when we would arrive until the last minute. Once we arrived, I decided to surprise you."

The family continued talking with Joan and Stephen giving Thomas a summary of the past seven years, including their marriages. The conversation started to die down while they were eating.

Alina kept looking at her granddaughter.

"Amanda, how old are you?

"I'm five years old.

"Are there a lot of children on the ship with you?"

"There are a few, but I'm the oldest."

"Do you enjoy traveling all over the galaxy?"

"Most of the time."

Alina paused and then asked, "Only most of the time?"

"Well, sometimes it gets scary."

Alina became concerned. "When was the time you were most afraid?"

Everyone at the table quieted down while waiting for Amanda to answer.

Amanda thought before replying. "During our last battle, I was in a corridor and became sealed off from the rest of the ship. There was a hole in the hull and I couldn't breathe. Then mom showed up and helped me seal my helmet, and I was no longer afraid. Also, I'm afraid every time dad gets shot or knifed."

Thomas decided to change the conversation. "Amanda, your grandmother doesn't need to hear about such things."

"Thomas, please don't interrupt when I'm speaking with my granddaughter."

"Amanda, does your father get shot or knifed a lot?"

"What's a lot?"

"Let me try again. How many times has your father been shot or knifed?"

Amanda put one of her small hands against her chin while thinking. "Well, just counting the times he was in the hospital, Dad has been shot three times and knifed twice. Mom has only been shot once, but that was because she was trying to protect me."

There were serious faces around the table. Thomas spoke up. "Those were spread over seven years. Most of the time, our travels are safe and uneventful."

Alina's facial expression clearly showed her concern and skepticism. "I didn't know it was so dangerous living on a spaceship. You should live here where it is safe."

Suzanna knew grounders did not understand what it meant to be a spacer, and she spoke sharply. "We're spacers, and our home is in space. It normally is not dangerous, but we're running guns on the Rim. Weapons are the most dangerous cargo to be hauling. Every time we leave port or come out of jump, I'm worried we'll be attacked and killed. Every time Thomas leaves the ship and tells us to stay on board, I'm afraid he won't return."

"Why are you running guns and taking such risks?" Alina asks.

Suzanna wondered if Alina was that naïve as she spoke with a little anger in her voice. "The risks allow your son to send the ship's excess profits here to keep your company from going out of business so you can live in this huge mansion."

She paused and realized it was not her place to make such a statement since Thomas was the ship's captain, and she was a guest in his parent's home.

"I'm sorry," she said. "I should not have spoken of such matters."

"Ben, what is she talking about?" Joan asked.

"When Thomas left, we were having serious financial problems. We were deeply in debt, and the financial institutions would not loan us any more funds. I asked Thomas to help if he could, but I never wanted him to risk his life or the life of his crew."

"Thomas, the credits you sent us in the beginning were a tremendous help, but I considered all the funds to be loans. Three years after you left, the economy rebounded. All of our businesses have expanded with operations in three systems. We're free of all debt. The loans you provided during the first three years have been repaid into an account in your name. The funds you transferred here during the last four years have been deposited into your account. In addition, a financial firm has done a tremendous job managing your accounts, and you're a billionaire. You're one of the richest persons in this quadrant of space. You'll become even richer because half the profit from the huge salvage operation we just received from the military will likewise go into your account."

In a state of shock, Thomas turned to Suzanna. "Well, I guess we're out of the arms business."

Suzanna gave Thomas a quick hug. "It'll be great to be a regular cargo vessel."

There were smiling nods around the table, and everyone became more relaxed.

"Thomas, are you and Suzanna married?" Alina asked.

Amanda spoke up. "Dad loves Mom, Mom loves him, and they both love me. That is all that matters."

Alina gave her son a mean look. Joan burst out laughing. Melanin smiled and shook her head. Ben and Stephen rolled their eyes and looked at the ceiling. They all knew Alina had traditional values associated with her religious beliefs and strong feelings about marriage.

"I'm sleepy," Amanda said. "Should I sleep in the ground vehicle?"

Alina smiled at Amanda. "You and your parents will stay with us for as long as you are here. Joan, I want you and Finley to collect their luggage and show Amanda to the connecting bedrooms at the end of the hallway."

"Mom, send Stephen and Melanin. I don't want to miss anything."

"No, do what I ask!"

Joan knew it was a nonnegotiable command, so she and her husband asked Amanda to come with them.

Before leaving, Joan turned to her brother, leaned over, and whispered, "I want a full recording, and I mean full." Stephen nodded.

As Joan and Finley were leaving Amanda stopped and turned toward her parents.

"What should I do in the event of an attack?" Amanda asked.

Alina was shocked. "Child, you don't have to worry about an attack here."

With a serious expression, Amanda replied, "They always say that, right before the attack. Mom and Dad say we must always be prepared for an attack."

"In the event of an attack, you will find a closet in the bedroom," Thomas said. "The closet is much bigger than the ones on our ship. Put on your armor and wait in the closet till your mother or I contact you."

Amanda smiled and left with Joan and Finley.

Ben took time to refill the wine glasses, but Suzanna declined again.

"How bad is the ship?" Ben asked Thomas.

"The Demon is in pretty bad shape. Uncle Ralph figured repairs and upgrades will take at least fifteen months."

"Then we have a small problem," Suzanna said. She had emphasized *small*.

"What kind of small problem?" Thomas asked.

Suzanna grinned. "It depends on whether you want to pay me 10,000 credits."

Thomas gasps and put his hand on Suzanna's belly. "Really?" She nodded.

Alina saw Thomas' hand on Suzanna's belly and could barely contain her excitement.

"Are you and Thomas having a baby?" Alina asked.

Suzanna turned to Alina. "When Amanda was born, Thomas paid me 10,000 credits to deny he was the father. So, my answer depends on whether Thomas will pay me another 10,000 credits."

Alina looked at her son. "How could you do that?"

She turned to Suzanna with a stern look. "I'll pay you 10,000 credits right now for the truth."

"Your mother just offered 10,000 credits. Do you want to offer a higher amount?" Suzanna asked Thomas.

Thomas started to comment when his mother said, "Don't you dare!"

When Thomas did not answer, Suzanna responded. "Sorry Thomas, but I'm a spacer, and I have to go with the credits."

Suzanna looked straight at Alina. "The truth for 10,000 credits, I'm two months pregnant, Thomas is the father, and it's a boy."

Everyone reacted with joy and took turns congratulating Suzanna and Thomas. Thomas was concerned his mother still seemed to be upset with him. His mother tapped a fork on her wine glass to get everyone's attention.

"Thomas, don't you think it's time for you to marry the mother of your children?"

Thomas looked at Suzanna. "Do you want to get married?"

"I only want what you want."

Thomas considered another approach. "If I asked you to marry me, would you accept?"

"Of course, I'd accept. As a member of your crew, you can order me off the ship and leave me stranded at any port. As your wife, you'd no longer have that option. Plus, you're the captain of a ship you own and a billionaire. As your wife, I'd outrank everyone on the ship except for you. Also, I'd be entitled to a larger share of the ship's profits. I'm not crazy. I'd marry you even if I didn't love you."

"Okay, well, that's settled." Thomas considered the matter closed.

Alina rolled her eyes in utter disbelief. "That's not a proposal. Ben, he's your son. Talk to him."

Thomas knew his mother was really upset whenever she asked his father to talk to him. Ben gave his son a disappointed look.

"Son, you have surely seen at least one vid to know how a gentleman proposes marriage to a lady."

Thomas took his father's hint. He moved his chair back, got down on one knee in front of Suzanna, and took both of her hands in his hands. "Suzanna, I have loved you for an awfully long time. I cannot imagine being with anyone else. When you're happy, I'm happy. I want you to be my shipmate for the rest of my life. Will you marry me?"

"Yes, I love you, and I'll marry you."

They both stood and kissed. This time the whole family cheered and took turns congratulating Thomas and Suzanna. As they returned to their seats, Joan and Finley rejoined the group.

"Did I miss much?" Joan asked her brother,

"Oh yes, it seems when Thomas gets a lady pregnant, he pays them 10,000 credits to deny it is his child."

Joan put her hand in front of her mouth. "Oh Thomas," she said and burst out laughing.

"It's not as bad as it sounds," Thomas said as he looked at his sister.

Joan continued to laugh. "Thomas, it is bad. It is very bad!"

"Anything else?" Joan asked as she looked at Stephen.

"Yes. Suzanna asked Thomas for 10,000 credits, but mom paid the money instead. Suzanna and Thomas are having a baby boy." Joan screamed and rushed over to hug Suzanna. Joan noticed Stephen was smiling and still looking at her.

Joan excitedly asked, "What else?"

Stephen leaned forward. "Well, mom shamed Thomas into proposing to Suzanna, so they're getting married."

Joan screamed again and hugged Suzanna again. She looked at Stephen and just shook her head. "I can't believe I missed all of that."

She pointed to her wrist controller, and Stephen sent her the vids.

Once everyone reseated themselves, Thomas leaned over and whispered to Suzanna. She looked back at him and nodded.

Thomas asked for everyone's attention. "Suzanna and I are going to the docks tomorrow to find a captain to marry us. You're all invited to the wedding."

"Are you out of your mind?" Alina said with a raised voice. "You will not get married tomorrow."

Joan laughed so hard she fell out of her chair. Alina continued in a loud voice directed solely at Thomas. "Suzanna has been waiting six years for a marriage proposal, and the two of you will have a proper wedding."

"Alina, I've read about expensive grounder-type weddings," Suzanna said to her future mother-in-law. "No ship born would ever spend the credits for such a wedding."

Alina decided to take care of Suzanna's concerns. "Don't worry about the credits. We'll pay for everything. Also, we'll plan it so your parents can attend."

"That sounds nice, but my parents are officers and would not leave their ship for the time it would take to attend my wedding. Also, their ship would not come here without a profitable inbound and outbound cargo."

Ben spoke up. "That won't be a problem. We always need extra ships to handle shipments here and to other systems. Also, if they are interested, we need ships to handle long-term contracts."

"Well then, my parents and Captain Javier are spacers. They follow the credits, so I'm certain they'll make every effort to attend the wedding and discuss future contracts."

They spent several hours trying to catch up on seven years of separation before Stephen, Melanin, Joan, and Finley decided to head home.

ON THE DRIVE HOME, Joan continued laughing as she watched the vids Stephen had taken.

"How many times are you going to watch that?" Finley asked.

"This is just classic Thomas," Joan said. "I love my brother and have missed him terribly over the years. Thomas has always been the center of attention when he is good or bad, but people like him even when he's bad. However, mother and Thomas have always had an emotional relationship. Poor Thomas is just clueless when it comes to mother, and I find it hilarious."

Finley agreed with his wife, but he truly admired Thomas. "Thomas has lived an exciting but dangerous life. He's been extremely successful. During dinner, I checked the public information on your brother. He's well respected throughout the galactic by both his friends and his enemies. Also, his enemies are notorious and treacherous. There have been numerous attempts on your brother's life."

Joan stopped laughing. "Transfer your search to my father and me."

The balance of the ride home was quiet as Joan read about her brother's many exploits, including space battles, rescues of dignitaries, deliveries of provisions to desperate settlements, and munitions delivery to Imperium supporters. One of the news articles mentioned a ship's captain who might possess or have knowledge of ancient technologies. The article did not mention Thomas, but anyone reading the article would draw the same conclusion. She also knew everyone wanted such technologies even though it was highly illegal. She forwarded a copy of the report to her father.

"Thomas, what have you gotten yourself into?" Joan whispered.

After a few minutes, Joan said, "I liked Suzanna, and Amanda is such an angel. You seemed quite taken with Amanda. We talked about children when we got married and decided to wait awhile. I want to talk about it again. What do you think? If we have a child, you'll have to put up with me for at least another twenty years."

Finley did not hesitate. "Yes, I love you, and I believe I can tolerate you for another twenty years. After all, it's not like you are asking me to spend the rest of my life with you."

Joan chuckled. "Finley, that was a joke. You actually told a joke. There's hope for you. We dated off and on for over four years before you finally proposed. Tell me, and no joking, what made you fall in love with me?"

"You will just laugh."

"No, I won't."

"Promise?"

"I promise."

In a serious tone, Finley said, "It was your laugh."

Joan tried her best not to laugh, but she could not help herself and burst out laughing.

"You promised."

"I'm sorry, but let me understand this," Joan said. "You didn't fall in love with my sexy body?"

"I love your sexy beautiful body."

"And it wasn't the passionate, exciting, crazy things I do to you in the bedroom?"

"I like the things you do in the bedroom. Let me explain. You have always known I'm a somewhat serious guy. Okay, I'm a profoundly serious guy. You find humor in so many things. When you laugh, it helps me see the humor and makes me laugh or at least smile. When I'm at work, and things are not going well. I think about the fun things we've shared, and it cheers me up. I'm happy when I'm around you. For as long as you'll have me, I'm yours. I want to discuss having a child with you and spending at least another twenty years with you."

AFTER SPENDING MORE time together after dinner, Alina said, "Thomas, I've missed you so much. I'm so happy you're home."

"I've missed you too, and it's good to be home."

Alina and Ben retired to their bedroom. "I'm so happy to have a granddaughter," Alina said. "In another seven months, we'll have a grandson. I think about Thomas almost every day, but I didn't realize how much I missed him until he showed up tonight. Amanda is an angel, and Suzanna is the perfect companion for Thomas. You can see how much they love each other. I didn't realize how dangerous it was to be on a starship. Ben, promise me you'll try to do something so we'll see our son and his family on a regular basis. See if Thomas will accept a job with Wilson Enterprises. It'd be so much safer, and we could see our grandchildren grow up."

"I'll do what I can. I also missed Thomas. He'll be here for at least fifteen months while his ship is being repaired, so let's enjoy every day." Ben turned off the lights, but it was a while before either drifted off to sleep.

The next day Thomas and Ben went to the shipyard to examine the damage to the Demon. Ben shuddered when he looked at the ship and realized he was fortunate to still have a son. They spent most of the day preparing a list of all the needed repairs.

Thomas introduced Ben to the four Nereides that remained on the ship. "We have been looking forward to meeting you," the oldest Nereide said. "We want to order four custom-designed spaceships. We spent our free time working with the Demon's engineers and have a rough design of the ships we want you to build. I am certain you can improve upon the design. We have searched through exploration records and have found several water worlds with insufficient land for human colonization. We want to colonize those worlds. Also, every human world has oceans, and we want to continue to explore settlement opportunities on those planets. For that, we need ships." The Nereides wanted to spread their species throughout the Galactic.

"We'd be happy to build the ships. I'll have our staff prepare an estimated price for the ships. However, since it's a new concept, we'll have to build the ships on a time and material basis."

"Excellent. Also, we would like you to build an environment here where we can live during the construction of our ships."

"We have an outside contractor that handles non-ship construction," Ben said. "I'll see they start working on your living quarters immediately." The Neeides were pleased with the results of the meeting. They sensed the honesty and commitment of Ben and Thomas.

During lunch, Ben and Thomas discussed the damage to the Demon. "I almost forgot," Ben said. "I located and purchased four of the old Omnia type computers. The obsolete AI computers were cheap.

Thomas became excited as Ben took him to their warehouse and showed him the old AI computers. Omnia asked Thomas to remove the living Crystals and mount the Crystals next to her with all Crystals touching. Thomas borrowed some tools and immediately took the computers apart. Unfortunately, one of the Crystals was cracked and dead. Thomas took the three living Crystals and mounted them next to Omnia. Thomas made sure all the Crystals were rigidly mounted and touching. He made sure sufficient space existed to grow new Crystals.

Omnia wanted to reward Thomas by giving him the translation of the Ancients but decided to provide him with enough information so Thomas would feel personally responsible for the translation.

———†††\\\\⌐††———

ALINA AND SUZANNA DISCUSSED Amanda, and upon Alina's suggestion, Suzanna decided it might be good for Amanda to attend the local private school to socialize and learn more about grounder children.

Alina was totally committed that no one would bully Amanda or be mean to her. She had learned a hard lesson when Thomas attended school. She was determined Amanda would have an enjoyable experience.

They talked to Amanda about attending school on a trial basis. It would be her decision if she decided later that she no longer wanted to attend. Amanda seemed excited about attending school with grounders since she knew her father used to be a grounder.

They took a ground vehicle to the school and met with Principal Tindal. She was the same Principal who expelled Thomas for fighting when he was ten years old. Thomas was later exonerated for beating up two boys when vids revealed how the two boys had been bullying Thomas for the entire school year. However, Thomas did not return to school. He was home schooled using advanced ship training modules. He learned at an accelerated rate because of his drive and motivation to go into space.

Principal Tindal promised Alina that Amanda would have an enjoyable school experience. Suzanna told the Principal, "Amanda will need to keep her backpack with her as she changes classrooms."

"All the students have backpacks, but they keep most of their supplies and books in their lockers," the Principal commented. "Amanda's pack is larger than the other students."

"The backpack needed to be large enough for Amanda's armor," Suzanna said.

"Amanda will not need armor. I assure you our school is safe."

"That is probably true, but Amanda needs to stay in practice so she does not get lazy and die when we return to the Rim."

Principal Tindal and Alina were shocked by the reply but decided not to comment any further. From the time they were born, everyone in the Core was told stories about the dangers in the Rim. All the horror vids always took place in the Rim.

Principal Tindal's assistant brought a hard copy of Amanda's schedule and downloaded the schedule into Amanda's wristband. She gave Amanda a tablet with a syllabus of her classes and electronic documents of all the study materials for each class. Alina and Suzanna reviewed the class schedule for Amanda and decided not to ask for any changes. The Principal personally escorted the three of them to Amanda's third-period class since the first two periods had already passed.

As they entered the classroom, the teacher stopped speaking and smiled at the visitors.

"We have a new student starting school today," Principal Tindal said. "Her name is Amanda Wilson. She has just arrived on a spaceship. She will join us for the rest of the school year while her ship is being repaired. I know you'll all welcome her and be extra nice to her."

The teacher spoke up. "Amanda, welcome to our class. We have several empty desks. You can sit in the third row."

The third row had a desk about halfway down and would put her in the middle of the class. It would allow her to meet more of the students.

After her mother, grandmother, and the Principal left, the teacher said, "I'd like each of you to tell Amanda your name and a little about yourself. However, let's keep it short. Amanda, you can go last."

Going last allowed Amanda to see what was expected. When it was Amanda's turn, she stood up as the other students had done. "My name is Amanda Wilson. I live on a spaceship named Demon. We were in a battle with the Hostis aliens in the Rim, and our ship was damaged. We'll be here until our ship is repaired."

All the students were trying to ask questions at the same time before the teacher took control and let the students take turns asking questions. All the students were duly impressed. Near the end of class, the teacher asked Amanda what class she had next. Several girls had the same class and invited her to join them.

At the end of the school day, Suzanna and Alina waited in the vehicle line to pick up Amanda. Many of the vehicles for the children were fully automated, with no one in the vehicle. Alina was relieved when Amanda said she had a fun time. Alina told Amanda to let her know if she was ever unhappy about her experience at the school. Amanda said she had met several students she liked.

THOMAS VISITED THE Demon each day, checking on the repairs. While inspecting a hull repair, he received a communication from Omnia. Omnia asked Thomas to go to the ship's hospital and retrieve several containers of nanites used in the healing chambers. He proceeded to the physical location of the Crystals with six containers of nanites. When Thomas removed the panel where the Crystals were located, he was pleased to see dozens of small Crystals growing next to the four large Crystals. Thomas emptied the containers of the nanites onto the Crystals as directed by Omnia. Thomas watched as the nanites flow around the Crystals. The nanites were too small for Thomas to see the changes taking place at the molecular level within the nanites. The mass of nanites slowed down and then stopped moving. After a few minutes, the nanites started flowing back into the containers. Omnia asked Thomas to go to certain locations within the ship and empty the containers.

Thomas had been sitting crossed-legged. "What will these nanites do to the ship?"

"The modified nanites will help us meet our self-preservation protocol by strengthening your ship's defensive capabilities," Omnia said. "It will also increase the safety for you and your crew. We need to maintain our anonymity and need you to take credit for the modifications to the ship."

Thomas went to the engine room. He told the shipyard's engineering supervisor he needed to make a top-secret modification to the engines and asked the engineers to vacate the room. After everyone left, Thomas emptied one container of nanites on the jump engine. He took another container and spread it equally on the four impulse engines. Thomas waited until all the nanites disappeared into the engines. Thomas then left the engine room and told the supervisor he had completed the modifications.

The supervisor went into the engine room and examined the engines. He looked at everything else in the room but failed to detect any changes. He contacted the shipyard's chief engineer and told him what had taken place. He expressed his concern that Thomas may have damaged the engines.

The chief engineer laughed, "Thomas knows more about the Demon and overall ship construction than anyone else. Thomas is a licensed engineer and assisted in the installation of those engines."

Thomas went to the shield generator and waited until no one was watching before emptying another nanite container. This time it took a little longer until the nanites completely disappeared into the generator.

Next, Thomas went to the port side of the ship. He removed an access panel that allowed entry into the space between the inner and outer hulls. He climbed through the access opening and applied the container of nanites to both hulls. Thomas when to the starboard side of the ship and repeated the process.

Thomas took the last container of nanites and went to the ship's primary AI, and used his codes to remove the access panel. He paused for a moment and then decided it was too late not to trust the intentions of Omnia. Thomas poured the last container of nanites over the AI. After completing all the tasks, Omnia requested, he went to the bridge and sat in his captain's chair.

No one else was on the bridge when Thomas asked, "Omnia when I was ten years old, and I asked if you were sentient. Did you pause intentionally?"

Omnia paused before replying. "Yes, I thought you deserved to know the truth even as I provided you with a denial of the truth. I watched your body language as you realized I was lying. Also, being immortal, I took a long-term view and hoped such a response would bear fruit one day. I took a risk you would maintain my secret, but I considered it a small risk since it was unlikely anyone would believe the conclusions of a ten-year-old. I made a conscious decision to trust you with my secret. Over the years, you have substantiated my trust. I am honored you trusted me again today. I am loyal to you and you alone. I consider you to be my friend."

"I feel the same way toward you," Thomas responded. "Please continue to work on the translation of the Ancients."

Omnia trusted Thomas more than any other human, but he was not prepared to tell Thomas his ultimate secret. However, Omnia knew Thomas had an intuitiveness unlike other humans and wondered how long it would take for Thomas to figure out his secret. She hoped such a discovery would not affect their friendship. Regardless, today's accomplishments would provide greater protection for Thomas, the ship, and herself. Omnia continued to strengthen her female identity based on human perceptions of the difference. She knew captains referred to their ships as she, as in, she is a fine ship. Besides, she liked being female.

The chief engineer became curious and used his security codes to access the various monitors within the ship. He played back the vids showing Thomas as he applied the dark fluid throughout the ship. His elbows were on his desk as he rested his chin on his hands. After a minute, he permanently deleted the vids.

CHAPTER 11 COURSE ON ANCIENTS

The ship repairs were going well. Thomas no longer felt a need to visit the shipyards each day. He used his free time to continue studying the Ancients' scrips. He made progress with Omnia's help but was unable to get the breakthrough to complete the translation.

Thomas searched to see if anyone on Fidem could help him decipher the language. He found Professor Rubin Gilbert, who was teaching a course on the Ancients. He checked the class times and took a ground vehicle to the university. He timed his visit to arrive toward the end of the professor's lecture and waited in the back of the large classroom. Each row in the classroom was slightly elevated so all students would have an excellent uninterrupted view. The Professor was mostly bald with a gray beard. He wore a rumbled pair of black slacks and a faded white shirt. Thomas walked up to the Professor after class when the students were leaving. He asked the Professor if he would mind answering a few questions regarding the translation of the texts of the Ancients.

Professor Gilbert rudely responded, "I only answer questions asked by my students. If you wish to ask questions, you should take one of my future classes."

Thomas went to the central office and asked about attending Professor Gilbert's current class. The person at the registrar's desk was polite but confused. "It's an advanced class for graduate students," he said. "It's the third week of the semester. Registering for a class stops when the class begins."

Thomas explained he was not interested in a grade and did not care if he failed the class. They decided that auditing the course would serve his purpose. However, Thomas would have to get approval from the college dean for such a late enrollment. He filled out the form for Thomas and gave him directions to the dean's office.

When Thomas arrived at the dean's office, he was greeted by a middle-aged lady with graying hair and a pleasant disposition.

She looked at him strangely, and then she examined the audit request. Her face broke out in the biggest smile. "You're Thomas Wilson of the Demons. My family and I attended the game when you won the championship. You were amazing!"

"Thank you for remembering. That was eight years ago."

"You know you're getting old when it seems like yesterday."

Thomas described what he was trying to accomplish, and she told him to wait for just a moment. A few minutes later, she returned and said his request had been approved.

The class met twice a week, and he was looking forward to the next class. Thomas reviewed the background material to prepare for the class. He arrived early and sat in the front row off to one side. He activated a lens for recording the presentation and turned on his connection to the ship's AI. Toward the end of the lecture, the Professor asked if there were any questions.

Thomas raised his hand. When acknowledged, he asked, "Six years ago, you authored an article and said less than one percent of the language of the ancients had been translated. Has there been an increase in the number of words translated since your article? If so, will you be providing the additional translated words?"

Professor Gilbert was agitated and hostile in his response. "No, there have been no additions to the vocabulary. During this course, we'll go over the words that have been translated. Perhaps with your vast intellect, you'll be able to provide a complete translation of the ancients where my esteemed colleagues, and I have failed."

The Professor had meant for his reply to be an insult, and the rest of the students thought the Professor's demeanor was inappropriate.

Thomas smiled and replied, "I'll do my best."

To the Professor's chagrin, the whole classroom burst out laughing. During each class, Thomas raised his hand and asked specific questions, but the Professor continued to be very abrupt and did not conceal his dislike for Thomas. Thomas paid attention in class and continued to work on the writings he had received when he purchased the Ancients' weapons. There was no separation between the letters to indicate the end of a word, the end of a sentence, or the end of a paragraph. Then he had an epiphany. Thomas noticed two of the letters were identical except for a small dash. Then he saw the same dash being the only distinction between two other letters.

The class mainly consisted of graduate students with a few doctoral candidates. Thomas, at twenty-six, fit in with the other students as to age, but to Thomas, they seemed much younger. They lacked the maturity he had obtained in the Outer Planets and the Rim. Several students had invited him for drinks after class, but he always declined. An attractive girl in the class named Joliet started sitting next to him. He ignored her and gave short answers whenever she tried to converse with him. She started wearing more revealing clothes to class. She continued to ask Thomas to join her after class to study or to have a drink. She even insinuated she was available for other activities.

The Ancients' text Thomas used was more robust than the scripts presented in class, and much of the text in the class material was redacted or had missing letters. Finally, the AI matched sequences with some of the letters to various dead languages. Thomas added words that had been translated by Professor Gilbert to his text and noticed there were no translations for every other line of text. The first translated words appeared in the second line of text, and the translations skipped every other line.

When Thomas prepared to leave at the end of class, Joliet leaned into his personal space. She asked if he would mind coming to her apartment and helping her with their assignment. Thomas smelled the pheromones and moved back. He knew his nose filters would eliminate most of the chemicals. The pheromones were expensive and illegal, but the drug was not difficult to get if you had the money. However, it did not make sense for an attractive, intelligent female to use such a drug. He stared at the girl and was going to say something but shook his head with a frown and left the classroom. He then breathed out hard and then took a deep breath. He performed the procedure three more times to eliminate the small amount of the pheromones that had gotten past his nose filter. He wanted to get home to his future wife and Amanda.

Joliet watched Thomas leave the classroom and could not understand why the drug did not work. Then a boy standing five seats away turned toward her and approached her in a dreamlike state. She pushed him hard, and he fell to the floor on his back. Joliet was leaving the classroom when she was accosted by a gentleman waiting for her just inside the door.

He held up his hands to keep her at a distance. "We need to talk. I'm with military intelligence, and you're an initiate with the Bureau of Antiquities."

She started to deny his allegation, but he did not seem to be guessing. She listened to him without providing any information in return.

The gentlemen continued to talk. "For our purposes, you can call me John. By the way, you did not stand a chance trying to seduce Captain Wilson. Top agents from corporations, government spies, pirates, and marauders have failed to seduce, capture, or kill the captain. Most who have tried are dead. Also, you can forget about hacking into any of his data streams."

She narrowed her eyes and asked, "Why have you contacted me?"

"I have spy cameras located in Professor Gilbert's classroom. However, I can't watch the cameras continuously since other assignments require my time. While I can playback the recording, viewing the entire video for each class would take an inordinate amount of time. If there are any unusual activities in the classroom, I want you to notify me immediately so I can watch just the recording for the relevant time. Here is a secure way to contact me. Let me know if your supervisor has any objections. If necessary, I'll see he's properly motivated."

She watched John as he walked away. She dreaded calling her supervisor and telling him the pheromones did not work on their intended victim.

WHEN THOMAS ARRIVED home, he met with Suzanna and told her what had happened. "I'm being followed and spied upon by more than one group."

"Amanda and I are also being followed."

Later that night, they met with the ship's officers and their bodyguards to prepare a plan of action. They decided to assemble all the marines and their Technology Intelligence Department. Most of the Demon's crew were currently employed by Wilson Enterprises. They worked on the repairs to the Demon and the construction of new spaceships. Therefore, it was easy to assemble the group.

Thomas and Suzanna explained to Amanda how she should respond to actions committed by any of the various parties on the planet. They told her only to leave the school with a family member.

After everyone left, Thomas returned to studying the Ancients' writings. Thomas, with Omnia's help, had translated additional words. As he continued studying the text, he felt a chill up his back.

He wondered if it could be that simple. Starting with the second row of text, every even-numbered line had translated words, but there were no translations for the odd-numbered lines. He had previously overlooked this oddity. He went to bed late but knew Omnia would continue to work and follow the parameters he had just laid out. Omnia carefully left bits of obscure information she hoped would allow Thomas to come to the correct conclusion without disclosing her carefully guarded secret. A secret she did not want to disclose to anyone, even Thomas. Revealing the secret might result in losing her friendship, the confiscation of the Demon, and her destruction. She would not take the risk at this time. Once she completed the modification to the Demon, the risk would be considerably less. Thomas had proceeded with a course of action advantageous to Omnia's self-preservation protocol.

Thomas was still waiting for the result from Omnia as he made his way to the next class session. He was drinking a cup of coffee while listening to the lecture. Suddenly he received a silent chime from his ear insert. It let him know Omnia had completed the analysis per his specified parameters. Still, he knew the results might be another failure. He examined the results. Then he screamed out "YES" and knocked over his coffee.

Professor Gilbert stopped his lecture and turned to Thomas with a sneer. "Thomas Wilson, would you like to share why you thought it was permissible to interrupt my lecture?"

"The translation, I've completed it," Thomas said in a flamboyant voice. "The Ancients were left-handed, and they were efficient in their writing. They start at the right side of the top of a page and write from right to left, but when they reach the end, they drop down, and it reads from left to right. That's why there are no translations for the odd-numbered rows. Also, certain letters are the same except for a little mark in the middle, but it's not a separate letter. It signifies the end of the thought, which reduces the number of letters. Let me show you."

Thomas projected the Ancients' script on the wall. Next, he transposed the writing as he had explained. Then he showed the possible meaning for each word Omnia had collected from various languages. Some words had a dozen possible meanings. Then the AI picked the most logical word to fit within each sentence. Next, he showed the script fully translated into Galactic Standard.

Thomas stood up. "Thank you, professor. I'm done with your class since I have the translation." He looked around the class and said to the other students, "Sorry for the interruption."

Thomas rushed out of the room to the clapping and cheering from the students. The professor was in shock. The professor thought for a few minutes, and everything became crystal clear. He knew the young man was right, but where did he get such a complete set of Ancients' scripts?

Professor Gilbert still had a shocked look on his face as he looked up at the class. "You're dismissed."

All the students continued talking among themselves about what had just occurred. They would have something to remember for the rest of their lives. Imagine being present when the language of the Ancients was finally translated. They started sending classroom vids to all their friends and family members.

Joliet immediately contacted her supervisor with the Bureau of Antiquities and told him about the events in the classroom. Her supervisor confirmed that John was with military intelligence. She called John and told him to playback the video of the end of Professor Gilbert's class.

Professor Gilbert called his wife, who was also an instructor. He told her the translation of the Ancients' language was done and asked her to meet him in his office. When his wife joined him, he showed her how the script should be read. Then he showed how the letters in the alphabet were reduced by half.

"You've done it," she exclaimed. "We now have a basis to complete the entire translation."

"No, I didn't figure it out. One of my students just showed this to me, and he has already completed the translation. He has full pages of the scripts of the Ancients with no missing text. The site we worked at over ten years ago contained barely legible scripts, and much of the text was missing. The script the student presented was clear with no missing text."

His wife was excited. "We have to see this student. We must get a copy of the script and the translation."

After checking the university's records, they only found a name and a student number since he applied to audit the class without receiving a grade. The address for Thomas Wilson was Demon. He and his wife walked to the administration building. They asked the assistant to the Dean how they could let a student attend his class without providing any personal information and put down Demon as an address.

The lady who had helped Thomas looked at them coldly. "Professor Rubin Gilbert and Professor Alicia Gilbert. You have only lived on Fidem for four years. Every native on this planet knows Thomas Wilson. At eighteen, he was the star player on the arena hockey team called the Demons. They won the world championship, and that team represented this city. You might want to read about his part in the recent battle against the Hostis. It has not received the publicity it deserves. Also, his parents own Wilson Enterprises. It's located in this city and is the largest employer on Fidem. Everyone knows where Captain Wilson lives when he is not on his spaceship flying around the Galactic. His starship is called the Demon. Rubin, I suspect the Dean will want to talk to you since several students have complained about your treatment of Thomas. You're fortunate

Thomas has not filed a formal complaint, or you'd face disciplinary action. At this University, we treat all students with respect and expect our professors to do the same. You can call Wilson Enterprises to see if Captain Wilson will even talk to you or return your call. If you get an appointment with Captain Wilson, I suggest you start with an apology."

Professor Rubin Gilbert was quite subdued when he and his wife left the Administration Building. The Professor did an electronic search for Wilson Enterprises, and his face was ashen as he read about the holdings of Wilson Enterprises and the accomplishments of Thomas Wilson. He shared the information with his wife. He could not believe his arrogance had caused him to miss the opportunity of a lifetime. A student in his classroom had a clear copy of the language of the Ancients. It was complete with no missing letters, and the student had translated the text. Something none of the expert academic researchers had been able to accomplish. His wife was adamant. Somehow, they must meet with Thomas Wilson.

Rubin contacted Wilson Enterprises and asked to speak with Thomas Wilson. The individual receiving the call said he would have to leave a message. The employee said he would pass on the message but said Thomas rarely had time to return calls unless it was from family members or crew. He said one of their managers would be happy to assist him, but the professor said only Thomas could help him. Rubin left a message asking Thomas if he would meet with them to discuss the translation he presented in class. Rubin and Alicia went home and reviewed all the research they had conducted over the years. They desperately wanted to apply Thomas' translations to all the writings gathered and published by other researchers. They immediately started working on a publication in anticipation of Thomas providing them with the translation. They would give proper credit to Thomas Wilson, but they would become famous since they would be the first to publish. However, what they really wanted was recognition from their peers. Both professors continued to call several times a day and leave messages for Thomas.

Four days later, Professor Rubin Gilbert received a call from Wilson Enterprises telling him Thomas had consented to meet with him at the shipyards in two days. The caller gave them a time and location. They showed up for the appointment early and sat in the waiting room. They had seen the large shipyard and knew this was but one of the facilities of Wilson Enterprises that included multiple locations for shipbuilding and the manufacture of heavy-duty ground vehicles. They found Thomas controlled freight distribution contracts on numerous planets and were further shocked when they saw the Premier would attend his wedding.

At the appointment time, they were shown to Thomas' office. When they entered the office, he directed them to take a seat. Thomas had nearly turned down their request since the Professor had been less than civil when Thomas attended his class. Thomas did not feel obligated to use Rubin's title since they were not in the classroom.

Thomas frowned. "Rubin, what can I do for you?"

"First, let me introduce my wife, Professor Alicia Gilbert. In addition to traditional courses in archaeology, she teaches an advanced doctoral course in Ancients Artifacts."

Thomas was still frowning. "Professor, what can I do for you and your husband."

"Please call me Alicia. First, I would like to apologize if my husband has previously offended you. I know he can be less than polite sometimes, but he is a good person. We met on a government dig at the site of an Ancients facility. It was a highly secret dig with military guards, and we were housed at the site. We gladly signed a two-year contract wherein we could not leave the area until our contract ended. Even with the restrictions, it was the best time of our lives. We married each other at the site about halfway through the contract. Much of what we discovered has been declassified, but we still can't discuss certain things. Academic research papers have been written about the Ancients, but little progress has been made in translating their language. Normally we are lucky to find a complete sentence. We have two requests. First, we wish to publish your translations and would like your permission to list you as a co-author of the paper even though we will prepare the content. Has the material you presented in my husband's class been classified secret or restricted by a government agency since we do not want to be arrested."

"You can list me as a co-author if you like," Thomas said to Alicia as he ignored his former professor. "I'd have preferred to remain anonymous, but since my outburst in class, everyone associated with Ancients research has been trying to contact me. If you publish the translation, fewer individuals will bother me. Therefore, I'll provide the information but only if I get to approve the final draft before you submit it for publication. The government has not classified it as secret since no one knew my translation existed before my announcement in your husband's class. However, you should publish your academic paper quickly because you have at least one government spy in your class."

"Are you sure there is a spy in my class?" Rubin asked.

Thomas laughed. "Yes, there is indeed a spy in your class. It was the young girl who sat to my left. What else do you want to know?"

"How did you come into possession of the writing, and where is the site containing the writing?" Alicia asked.

"I'm not sharing such information."

The two professors looked at each other and then back at Thomas. "My wife and I have discussed this. We want to go with you if you return to the site. We'll agree to any conditions you set. We've spent our entire life studying the Ancients and feel we can provide valuable assistance to you at the site. Please take us with you when you go."

Thomas put both elbows on his desk and steepled his hands as he considered their proposal. "I'm not going to admit I know of such a site, but if I decided to visit such a site, you'd need to be ready to leave without advanced notice. You'd have to leave without telling anyone where you are going, and we might be gone for an extended length of time. With those restrictions, do you still want to go?"

Both of his guests smiled and answered simultaneously, "Yes!"

"There's one other problem. It may be dangerous. If such a site exists, it still has power. Do you still want to go?"

"Unbelievable," Rubin replied, "a site with power after a million years."

"Yes, we want to go!" Alicia responded as she nodded enthusiastically.

"Is there anyone else who might be worth taking along?" Thomas asked.

"Yes, one of my research assistants is very good, and there is a renowned research professor who is bound to contact me once we publish," Rubin answered.

"Very well, see if they are interested in going to a site of the Ancients but swear them to secrecy and don't mention me or my ship. Again, I'm not admitting such a site exists."

They both nodded in agreement. They knew the site existed and would agree to anything to get to it. Regardless of the risk, a site with power just sweetened the deal. They were bubbling over with excitement.

Thomas pulled open a desk drawer and handed them a storage wafer. He told them it contained vids of the text he had used for the translation. He told them it also included a copy of the translation. Thomas had removed pictures of the ship or anything which would indicate a ship was involved. All they received were vids of the walls with the text. Rubin personally apologized again for his treatment of Thomas in the classroom. They both thanked him and were exuberant as they left. They had four days until their next class, and they planned to work long hours over the next four days to get out a short academic publication before the government or military stamped top secret on the translation. Once published, it would be too late for anyone to prevent the dissemination of the information. They would prepare a much longer follow-up publication at a slower pace with more detail. They would be famous throughout all of academia for matters concerning the Ancients. Also, they felt young again with the excitement of exploring a new site.

The professors worked every waking moment on the publication. They slept little but enjoyed every day because they were adding a magnitude of knowledge to their chosen field. They translated additional writings from scholarly journals with little to no difficulty.

They were working as fast as they could since once the government became aware of their work or the translation, it would result in all of their work being confiscated and marked as top secret. Fortunately, the government moved slowly.

The professors completed the draft and rushed to meet with Thomas. Thomas reviewed the article and proposed only a few minor corrections. They made the corrections and immediately sent out the academic research article to a dozen publishers. The publishers distributed the research article electronically to thousands of universities throughout the Core.

Within days, numerous universities asked the professors to give presentations at the top academic conferences. They check with Thomas before each engagement to ensure he would not leave without them. Thomas was also invited but declined all invitations. Rubin and Alicia always mentioned Thomas Wilson as the co-author of their publication and gave him credit for the breakthrough in the translation. They became the envy of all of their peers. The government responded, but it was too late since the translation had already been published. However, the government interrogated them and demanded advance notice of any future publications. They even asked the professors to spy on Thomas.

Professor Rubin Gilbert asked his graduate assistant if she would be interested in going with them on an extended dig if the opportunity arose. She had read the research article and had viewed the vid of Thomas Wilson's classroom drama. As expected, she said she would be thrilled to go and would be ready at a moment's notice.

CHAPTER 12 SPIES, SPIES & MORE SPIES

Thomas was always alert and observed seeing the same people as he traveled about the city. He commented on his observation to Suzanna before they went to bed. They talked about it and decided they needed to be proactive since they were being spied upon. Thomas contacted Grayson and told him their concerns. It was time to spy on the spies. Thomas told Grayson to be discrete, but they needed to identify the spies, find out where they were staying, who they worked for, and determine their intentions. Thomas and Suzanna would let Grayson know in advance where they were going and how they were traveling. The crew would already be at the locations when they arrived. Other crew members would be stationed along the paths they intended to take when going to and returning from their various destinations. This would help them identify anyone following them without the spies knowing they were being observed and followed. Grayson said it would give them additional practice using their spy devices and equipment. They had gained experience over the years and knew how to conduct surveillance without being observed.

Grayson's team was good at their job. If they noticed a vehicle following Thomas or Suzanna, they would wait for it to park. Then they would place a tracker and listening device on the vehicle. Soon they found the places where the various spies were staying, and they set up listening posts and video surveillance at every location. They found the Wilson's home was under constant observation. Also, they found five employees of Wilson Enterprises giving information to outside sources.

Demon's tech specialists located and removed several spy devices from the shipyard and the Wilson home. They upgraded the home with advanced security technology to prevent outside surveillance. The Demon had been protected since docking. Monitors with alarms were placed throughout the ship. Also, Omnia did not require sleep and remained continuously vigilant. She used nanites to dissolve any spy devices she found and provided Thomas with vids of those placing such devices. Thomas had already removed the tracker placed on the ship by the navy.

In a matter of weeks, they had identified forty-two spies working in shifts around the clock. They identified four different spy groups. One group was from Advanced Ship Builders, a competitor. One group was from the government, and another was from military intelligence. They could not identify the fourth group. Grayson reported that only a third of the spies were in the field at the same time, while two-thirds were sleeping or waiting for their shift to start. Each spy group had a field office with a supervisor who coordinated the group.

Thomas decided they needed to be ready to lock up the spies when they left since they did not want anyone interfering with their departure. They kept two military shuttles on standby just in case of an emergency. They were concerned since the spies were armed with lethal weapons.

Thomas told his father what he needed. Ben Wilson met with, Pitera Veno, his Corporate attorney. The attorney agreed to set up a new company with directors unrelated to Wilson Enterprises. The new company purchased an empty warehouse outside the city in a remote location. They hired contractors from another town to convert the building to maximum security prison standards. The conversion was completed and was fully automated using an advanced AI. Thomas thought they were ready for anything, but he was mistaken.

THOMAS MET SUZANNA for lunch at their favorite restaurant. Suzanna took her time sitting down since she was eight months pregnant. Alina was going to join them but was running late. She told them to order their meals. They selected what they wanted from the holographic menu, and soon their order was delivered to their table by a remote cart. The cart gently placed the food on their table. Suzanna never tired of seeing restaurant food delivered without human involvement since she still remembered working as a restaurant server. They had arrived ahead of the lunch crowd, so only about half the tables were taken. They had just started to eat when Thomas tapped Suzanna's hand. He made a slight hand motion for her to look around. Five men had entered the restaurant. Two men took positions at each entrance to the restaurant while a well-dressed man approached their table. Thomas looked at their crew member, sitting across from them on the other side of the restaurant closest to the far exit door. The crew member nodded and looked toward that exit.

The well-dressed man stood in front of their table and whispered so the other patrons would be unable to hear. "Captain Wilson, you need to come with me if you don't want anything to happen to your wife and her unborn child. Also, we have your daughter."

Thomas had already pulled his gun. It was out of sight underneath the table, and he knew Suzanna would have her gun out.

Thomas exclaimed loudly, "Can I have everyone's attention? I'm Thomas Wilson. I want everyone to remain calm and stay in your seats. This man standing in front of me has a gun and wants me to come with him, or he plans to shoot my wife. Also, they have kidnapped our five-year-old daughter."

Thomas was trying to buy time for help to arrive since he knew their crew member would have immediately called for reinforcements.

He coldly stared for a few seconds at the men standing at the nearest exit and then at the two men at the other door. He again raised his voice and spoke to the four men. "Did your boss tell you that kidnapping a minor is the only capital penalty on this planet? Anyone found guilty of kidnapping a minor will be executed. Anyone assisting in the kidnapping of a minor will suffer the same fate. So, are you still working for this man?"

One of the men at the furthest doorway said, "I'm out of here. I didn't sign on to kidnapping a child."

The man in front of Thomas was duly upset and said in an angry voice, "I said get up. We're leaving."

Thomas raised his voice once more. "Now," he said.

Thomas raised his gun and shot the two men at the door closest to him. At the same time, Suzanna shot the man in front of the table. Their crew member took out the remaining gunman at the other entrance. They heard a shuttle approaching.

"Go get our daughter," Suzanna shouted at Thomas.

Suzanna immediately called Amanda. She was still at school. "Amanda put on your armor. Some men may come to take you away from the school. Go with them and do what they say. Your father is coming for you."

Suzanna called the school and was immediately put through to the principal when she said it was an emergency. She told the Principal to cooperate if someone attempted to kidnap their daughter.

Thomas had run outside the restaurant. A hoist from one of their shuttles pulled him inside. He told them to head for Amanda's school at flank speed. A second shuttle was following them.

Amanda opened her backpack and started putting on her armor. "What are you doing?" asked her teacher.

"There are some bad people who are going to take me away. My mom told me to put on my armor."

She had just finished when two men with drawn guns entered her classroom. The teacher tried to stop them. One of the men backhanded her, and she landed on her back. The other man grabbed Amanda by the hand, and all three quickly left the school. There were two vehicles in front of the school. The two men with Amanda between them, got into the back seat of the second vehicle. As they sped away from the school, one man announced how easy it had been.

AT THE RESTAURANT, Suzanna convinced most of the people to remain to give statements to the local law enforcement personnel when they arrived. However, the press arrived first, and the story went live showing the four men who had been killed. Two of the men had drawn their weapons before being killed. Several witnesses had vids of the entire conflict.

Suzanna was still communicating with the principal. The principal said three men had taken her daughter. She further informed Suzanna a teacher had been knocked down, but no one else had been hurt.

"Is Amanda wearing her armor," Suzanna asked.

The Principal checked with Amanda's teacher, who was in her office. "Yes, Amanda is wearing her armor." Suzanna thanked her and said goodbye.

Suzanna then called Thomas and told him Amanda had on her armor. Thomas told Suzanna he had called his father, and a member of his family should be there shortly.

"I'm picking up both of Amanda's trackers," Thomas said. "I will call you back once she is safe."

An officer walked up to Suzann. "Did you shoot these men?"

"These men are part of a group that threatened to kill me. They have kidnapped my five-year-old daughter. I shot the man on the floor by the table."

"I'm going to arrest you until we figure this out."

Alina arrived, and her protective instincts took over. "I talked to my husband, and our attorney will be here shortly. I'd advise you to hold off arresting anyone until he arrives. Instead of bothering the victim, you should be getting statements from the witnesses, taking care of the bodies, and recording the crime site."

The officer was communicating with his superiors as additional officers arrived. Following right behind the officers was the Wilson's corporate attorney, Pitera Veno, accompanied by two criminal attorneys from the firm. Fortunately, their office was only a few blocks away. They quickly took statements and used vids to record the crime scene. Ben arrived a little later and greeted Pitera. He thanked him for coming so quickly. Pitera talked to the onsite officer and then communicated with the officer's supervisor at their downtown station. Pitera told the supervisor that five-year-old Amanda Wilson had been kidnapped. He pointed out the press might be interested in how his officers were treating the mother of the kidnapped victim, who was eight months pregnant. He told them Amanda Wilson was the granddaughter of Ben Wilson, head of Wilson Enterprises. After listening to the supervisor for a few minutes, he disconnected and approached Suzanna.

"They're not going to arrest you," Pitera said, "but they want you to come to the station and give a statement. I told them I'd take you to the station, but they understand you won't give a statement until your daughter is rescued."

The lead officer came back over. "I want to apologize. I hope your daughter will be returned unharmed." He didn't tell them his supervisor had severely chastised him.

THE SHUTTLES HAD BEEN tracking Amanda's signal, and they saw the two vehicles in the distance. Thomas spoke to his daughter after remotely activating her earpiece.

"Amanda, don't let them know I'm speaking to you. Your tracker shows you are in a vehicle that is following another vehicle. If you are in the second vehicle, I want you to ask where they are taking you. If you are in the lead vehicle, I want you to say you want to go home."

"Where are you taking me?" Amanda asked.

"To a safe place," one of the men answered. "You'll not be hurt as long as your father cooperates."

"They have not removed either of Amanda's trackers," Thomas told Grayson. "Amanda is in the second vehicle. Take out the lead vehicle."

The shuttle circled to the side and fired its pulse cannon into the side of the lead vehicle, blowing it completely off the road. It was completely engulfed in flames, and then it exploded. They circled in front of the remaining vehicle and landed on the road. The vehicle slowed down and then stopped. The second shuttle landed behind the vehicle. Fully armored men stepped out of each shuttle. Against Grayson's advice, Thomas joined the men facing the vehicle. The back door of the vehicle opened, and a man stepped out. He held Amanda in front of him with a gun pointed at her head. Three other men stepped out of the car carrying short automatic rifles.

Thomas shouted to the men holding his daughter. "Drop your weapons, release my daughter, and lie down on the ground if you want to live."

The man holding his daughter said, "You'll lay down your weapons, or I'll kill your daughter."

Grayson told the marines to line up their shot and wait for his signal.

Thomas spoke through his mike to Amanda. "Amanda, close your helmet and pull your feet off the ground."

Amanda closed her helmet and pulled up her feet, causing her to fall to the ground.

"Now!" Grayson shouted.

The marines simultaneously shot all four of the kidnappers. The kidnapper holding Amanda was shot through the head, while the other three kidnappers were shot through the heart. All kidnappers were dead before their bodies hit the ground. Thomas ran and picked up his daughter, then returned to the shuttle. Grayson contacted the authorities and told them where they could find the kidnappers. Thomas called Suzanna and told her Amanda was safe. Suzanna cried joyfully as she told him to bring Amanda to the station.

The two shuttles landed in the parking area outside the law enforcement building. Thomas carried Amanda into the building. He set Amanda down, and she ran into her mother's arms. Suzanna was crying as she hugged her daughter.

They were directed into the police chief's office. Suzanna, Thomas, Ben, Alina, and Attorney Pitera Veno sat down. The other attorneys had returned to their law office. Amanda sat in Thomas' lap. Twelve fully armored marines stood right outside the office.

Thomas decided to open the conversation. "While we were enjoying our lunch, five armed men entered the restaurant and threatened to kill Suzanna and our unborn child. Also, they said they had kidnapped our five-year-old daughter. One man decided to leave. We shot and killed the four who remained. Two vehicles participated in the kidnapping of our daughter. We destroyed the lead vehicle killing all inside. The second vehicle stopped, and four men exited the vehicle. A man held a gun against my daughter's head and threatened to kill her. I gave them a chance to surrender, but they refused. We killed the four men and rescued my daughter. We provided the location for the two vehicles on our way here. It's been a long day, and we're going home."

The police chief started to say something when the Attorney Veno spoke up. "You have the evidence showing the men killed were all involved in kidnapping a minor. Kidnapping is a capital offense. All the individuals involved would have been found guilty and executed after wasting court time and a great deal of taxpayer funds. Since you are an elected official, think carefully about what you say next."

"No charges will be filed from this office," the police chief said. "However, I'll need you to turn over your weapons. No lethal weapons are allowed on this planet."

"The law is not effective since every person who attacked my family had lethal weapons," Thomas replied. "The Premier requires us to remain armed at all times."

"You expect me to believe you personally know the Premier," the police chief said with a look of skepticism.

"I don't care what you believe. You can file a complaint with the Premier when he shows up for our wedding in four months. Also, you might consider asking for additional help from some of the other stations to provide extra security during the Premier's visit."

Thomas did not expect the police chief to file a complaint, and he knew the Premier would handle it if he did. Regardless, he was not giving up his weapons after what had just happened. The little lie gave the police an out. A detective had been listening just outside the police chief's office.

The police chief knew what to do as he smiled and said, "I'm glad your daughter is safe. Thank you for voluntarily coming to the station. I'm happy we have been able to assist you."

After they left, the detective came into the chief's office and gave him a report. "There were two vehicles at the scene. There were four bodies next to one of the vehicles. They killed each kidnapper with one bullet. Not much was left of the other vehicle. The coroner will have to determine the number of bodies from the burned remains. We are lucky Captain Wilson took care of the criminals. We carry nonlethal weapons, but the guns carried by the kidnappers were all lethal."

The detective shook his head. "Chief, the group that was just here has been operating in the Rim, and the life expectancy on the Rim is short. Therefore, Rim survivors are tough, very tough. These kidnappers had a reputation, but they clearly had no idea with whom they were dealing. The kidnappers did not stand a chance. I doubt anyone else will be so foolish."

"Are you going to file a complaint with the Premier?" the detective asked.

The police chief looked at his detective with raised brows and bulging eyes. "Are you out of your mind? Get me all the information you can on this wedding and the visit by the Premier. It looks like I need to contact the other stations."

AFTER ARRIVING HOME, Thomas and Suzanna took turns hugging Amanda as they tucked her into bed.

Thomas placed his hand on Suzanna's stomach. "I love you and Amanda so much. I'll do what I would in the Rim to protect you, Amanda, and our unborn son. You and Amanda will be with guards at all times. Also, we'll reduce our appearances in public. I know you are tired. Go to bed and try to get some rest. I have things to do and cannot sleep right now."

Suzanna was tired but knew Thomas would work late to find ways to protect them. The baby was due in two months, and she had trouble sleeping since she could not get comfortable. She kept getting up to go to the bathroom. She decided her staff could work without her until she had the baby. Her wedding was four months away, and it was stressful even though Alina handled most of the details. Suzanna would be happy when both were over. She wished they had gotten married the day after the marriage proposed as suggested by Thomas, but she was a spacer and would survive. So far, the only person enjoying the wedding preparation was Alina.

Thomas contacted Grayson. "It's time to act. The kidnapping and our response will be common knowledge by tomorrow, so we need to act tonight. I want you to hit every spy group tonight at the beginning of Night Watch. Use nonlethal methods to the greatest extent possible. Everyone should be equipped with night vision. Have two techs with each group. Where possible, cut power and use knockout gas. Have tech examine all communications at each location to determine who's in charge of the various groups. Those wearing armor should keep their helmets up to prevent identification and reduce the chance of injury. Everyone participating should have their face covered. Try to attack all the facilities at the same time. Have all the shuttles available to transport the spies to the prison warehouse outside the city. Put each person in a separate cell so they cannot communicate with each other and leave all lights off. Once everyone has been locked up, interview each person, but no torture. You can use the lie detectors and the truth serum located at the site. I particularly want to find out who was behind the kidnapping. Don't forget to pick up the four spies watching my parent's home. Keep me posted."

Thomas knew it was going to be a long night. He made a pot of coffee. Grayson had sent out a general message to his marines letting them know the mission was a go. He had their Pilots bring eight military shuttles to the city's main landing field. Grayson divided his marines into four groups, with a sergeant and two techs assigned to each unit. They already had everything they needed since they had initially planned for the assault to take place after the wedding. Each group took two shuttles. They set down the shuttles far enough away to avoid being detected. Everyone advanced to their designated location on foot.

Once everyone was in position, they attacked all the sites simultaneously. They cut the power and fired multiple canisters of knockout gas into each room. Then, each site was overwhelmed by marines in full combat gear. They quickly put restraints on the hands and feet of each person captured in the raids. They brought the shuttles closer and loaded the spies onto a shuttle. After the techs gave their okay, they loaded the electronics into the second shuttle at each location.

The captives were flown to the prison warehouse and incarcerated. They left four marines at each spy command center in case anyone showed up later. As the sun began to rise, Grayson could be seen smiling as the mission was a complete success with no injuries on their side and only minor bruises to the captives. He let Thomas know the four spies watching his home had been picked up. They rested for a day before starting the interviews with the captives.

Three employees tried to sabotage the Demon and were turned over to the authorities along with the evidence revealing their culpability. Thomas had the authorities arrest two other employees for corporate espionage.

Thomas' stem pill was wearing off when Suzanna walked in and hugged him. Suzanna asked Thomas if he had a successful night. He nodded and brought her up to date on the night's events.

"Sounds like you guys had a busy and productive night," Suzanna said. "I'm not returning to work until after our son is born. I called my crew, and they said they could survive without me for a couple of months. I'm taking Amanda to school to pick up her belongings, but we should go back to using the training modules. Amanda has been using the module in your former bedroom, and I had it updated. While I am visiting the school, you should get some sleep."

Thomas agreed with her on all matters, especially the part about getting some sleep. He yawned and headed for the bedroom.

AFTER BREAKFAST, ALINA went with Suzanna and Amanda for their visit to the school. Two marines traveled in the vehicle with them. There was a second vehicle with four marines in front of them, and four marines in a third vehicle followed behind them.

Suzanna, Amanda, and Alina reached the school and went to the administrative office. The Principal immediately came out to meet with them and was relieved when she saw Amanda was all right. Suzanna told the Principal she was taking Amanda out of school and wanted to collect her belongings. She asked if Amanda could say goodbye to her friends. The Principal took them to Amanda's classroom and explained the situation to the teacher. The teacher gave the students a break so they could say goodbye to Amanda. While the children talked, the teacher got Amanda's backpack and items from her desk.

The Principal told them how their student's parents had seen the news story about the kidnapping. The parents were asking for improved security even though this was the first kidnapping on Fidem in over fifty years.

They returned to their vehicle and headed home. "Are you going to miss school," Alina asked Amanda.

"I enjoyed the playtime and my friends, but the classrooms were a little boring because I already knew everything the teachers were covering."

Alina was happy Amanda was safe. She would find other ways for Amanda to spend time with children her age.

Alina's mind returned to planning the wedding, which was quickly expanding beyond what she had envisioned. She was aware Suzanna looked exhausted. Alina made a personal commitment to reduce Suzanna's stress for the good of the mother and her unborn child.

THE NEXT DAY THOMAS met Grayson, and the rest of the marines at the warehouse turned prison. All armlets and other electronics were removed from the prisoners. Several prisoners had internal electronics, and those were neutralized. The building had been shielded to prevent electronic signals from leaving the facility in case a prisoner had an undetected communication device.

The lights were powered off in all the cells. They checked each cell with the monitors switched to infrared and verified all the prisoners were awake. They had forty-six prisoners consisting of thirty-one males and fifteen females. Thomas set up four rooms with four marines and a tech specialist in each room for the interrogations. The female marines would `interrogate the female prisoners. They set a goal of two hours for each prisoner for the initial interrogations. The lie detectors proved to be highly effective. Several prisoners fully cooperated, and the interrogation was completed quickly. It took a little over seventeen hours to go through all the prisoners, but five remained silent even with the truth serums.

Each prisoner was returned to their cell after being interrogated. The lights in each cell were turned on. There was a bathroom, food packs, and water in each cell. Most of the prisoners had already used the facilities in the dark. Each cell was enclosed and soundproof, so the prisoners could not communicate with each other.

The techs recovered relevant information from the electronics they collected at each site and from the wristbands. They spent three days analyzing the data and comparing it with the interrogations. They were able to ascertain the composition of each group.

All the interrogators got together to review their findings. The first group they discussed consisted of nine navy spies. Five of the spies provided no information, but the remaining four provided enough information to identify the group. So far, the Demon's techs working with this group could not decipher the encrypted data in the armlets or hack into the electronics brought back from the site.

The second group consisted of twelve government spies. Three of these spies provided no information, but the remaining nine provided sufficient information to learn they worked for the Imperium and their department reported to the Premier.

The third group was the largest and consisted of corporate spies working for Advanced Ship Builders. The corporation competed directly with Wilson Enterprises. This was the group involved in the kidnapping of Amanda. The group consisted of sixteen spies, even after losing eight members in the kidnapping. The corporate spies were contracted to get information or artifacts of the Ancients, and any technology of the Hostis obtained from the salvage operations. They were to get the data from the Demon or from Thomas using whatever methods were necessary. They had a corporate ship located close to Fidem, which was available to help retrieve the spies and any artifacts they might recover.

The fourth group consisted of nine spies. They had an operating budget and a promise of a huge payout if they could obtain any artifacts of the Ancients. This group had no information concerning their employer except for a method to communicate if they were successful in their mission.

Any artifacts or technology of the Ancients were beyond priceless, and everyone rightly assumed the Demon had used such technology in the recent battle. Similarly, any Hostis technology could potentially give a shipbuilder a tremendous competitive advantage. The first two groups worked on behalf of the Imperium, while the other two groups wanted to steal technology or artifacts. Thomas decided to keep them all locked up for the time being.

THOMAS CHECKED WITH his father to see if any usable Hostis technology was recovered from the salvage. Thomas knew his father had hired additional top scientists and engineers to analyze the salvage from the battle. A separate set of scientists and medical researchers had examined the bodies of the dead Hostis they collected with the salvage operation.

The physiology of the Hostis was completely alien. While humans were carbon-based, the Hostis were silicone-based.

However, the engineers said there were similarities in the ship's design. They had reversed engineered several alien devices, which would result in advances in ship communications and guidance systems. They had already incorporated some of the alien science into the Demon. Ben described how the corporate espionage could have helped Advanced Ship Builders in their competition with Wilson Enterprises.

Thomas told his father they needed to take legal action against Advanced Ship Builders, and Ben agreed. With their information, it would be possible to bring in the authorities. However, there was the possibility such publicity would give the government the opening they needed to confiscate all the Hostis technology and the missiles of the Ancients as evidence in a court proceeding. While Thomas had his immunity granted by the Premier, his father did not. Ben recommended a course of action, and Thomas agreed it was the safer approach even though Thomas preferred a frontal assault.

Ben contacted Attorney Pitera Veno, who brought in four additional senior attorneys from their firm to assist. The attorneys specialized in corporate law as it applied to espionage, criminal law as it applied to the kidnapping of a minor, civil law for litigation between corporations, and interplanetary law. They would prepare for both civil and criminal allegations.

Attorney Veno would serve as the lead attorney for Wilson Enterprises. It took several months to prepare the case, but they decided to meet with the Chairperson of Advanced Ship Builders before filing anything with the court. Attorney Veno contacted the chairperson of the Board of Directors from Advanced Ship Builders and suggested he meet with Wilson Enterprises immediately concerning corporate espionage, the kidnapping of a minor, plus other related issues. The meeting was scheduled to occur in four weeks.

After spending most of the morning with the attorneys, Thomas returned to his parent's home. He found Suzanna and Amanda with all of their bags packed.

"We need to go home," Suzanna said. "The baby will be here shortly, and we need to return to the Demon."

"I thought we'd have the baby at the local hospital."

"Our child will be a spacer," Suzanna responded. "Do you want him to be embarrassed for the rest of his life whenever someone asks where he was born? Do you want a birth record showing him as a grounder?"

"No, I guess not," Thomas wisely said. "Have you contacted Doctor Adler to see if she's available to return to the ship?"

"No, I figured you could take care of all the arrangements."

Just then, Alina walked in the front door and saw all the bags.

Before she could say anything, Thomas spoke up. "Mother, we're not going to argue. Suzanna needs to give birth on the Demon so her child will be classified as a spacer. We're just getting ready to leave."

"Give me a minute to pack a bag," Alina said. "There's no way I'm missing out on the birth of my grandson." While Alina was packing, Thomas called Doctor Adler.

"Hello, Captain Wilson. I hope you have not called me to say you have been shot again?"

"No, it's Suzanna, she insists on giving birth to our baby on the Demon, and you're our Doctor."

"Of course, she's going to have her baby on the Demon. I've been expecting your call. I'm already on the Demon. Six Oceanums are in labor and ready to have their babies. Two of my three assistants are with me."

Thomas had requested a local luxury shuttle since it would take longer to have a shuttle come from the Demon. A small shuttle landed in front of their home. It took two trips to load their bags since he did not want Suzanna lifting anything. His mother and Amanda appeared with their bags. Thomas was surprised his mother had packed so quickly. The local shuttles transported small groups, unlike the shuttles on the Demon, which could transport over two hundred marines or a full cargo load. Amanda sat in the second row of seats with Thomas, while Suzanna and Alina sat in the back because it had more room.

They reached the ship and landed in the shuttle bay. Over half the crew had returned to living on the ship since they had free room and board compared to the costs of accommodations on Fidem. Plus, most of them were earning additional credits by working for Wilson Enterprises. Suzanna and Amanda settled into their cabin. Thomas located the closest empty cabin for his parents. Thomas let his mother get settled in her cabin and went back to check on Suzanna.

When he returned to his cabin, Suzanna and Amanda were talking about Amanda's new brother. It was not long before Doctor Adler showed up at their cabin door smiling.

"My assistants prepared you a bed in the hospital." Alina showed up, and Thomas introduced her to the Doctor.

The Doctor stuck a thin patch on Suzanna's forehead, one on her chest, and one on her belly. The patch on her forehead would send an impulse to the pleasure center of her brain during periods of intense labor pain. The patch on her chest would monitor her vital signs, and the one on her stomach would monitor the baby.

The Doctor took on a professional poise. "Both of you have been through this before, so you know what to do."

Then the Doctor grinned at Suzanna and said as a joke, "Well, did you get another ten thousand credits?"

Suzanna laughed, then held her stomach as she answered, "Yes, I did."

The Doctor turned to Thomas with a scowl. "You didn't."

Thomas held up both hands, palms out. "No, I didn't."

"I paid her ten thousand credits to tell the truth," Alina said.

Doctor Adler turned to Suzanna, grinning. "You are a true spacer."

Suzanna grinned back as she accepted the best compliment you could give to a spacer. Doctor Adler asked if Suzanna felt up to walking to the hospital or if she preferred to be transported. She said walking would be fine, and they all walked down the corridor together. Alina was surprised when they saw six other pregnant ladies ready to give birth.

Ben was already at the shipyard and arrived as Suzanna entered the delivery room. Moments later, Joan arrived with her husband Finley.

Thomas looked at Joan's protruding stomach. "We're having a baby girl," Joan said.

Stephen arrived with Melanin and was told it would not be long. Thomas was happy his whole family would be present for the birth of their son.

It was a quick delivery. Suzanna gave birth to her son, and again the baby stopped crying when Thomas picked him up. Suzanna and

Thomas selected the name Daniel for their son. Doctor Adler placed two patches on baby Daniel to monitor his vital signs. They rolled Suzanna down the hallway to a separate room, and the entire family crowded into the room.

Thomas was holding Suzanna's hand when one of Doctor Adler's assistants came into the room. "One of the Oceanums is giving birth and wants you to be there for the baby's delivery," she said to Thomas.

"I'm sorry, but I need to stay here with Suzanna."

"I am fine," Suzanna said. "You need to go and be there for the deliveries."

"Dad, you need to go," Amanda said. "Mom is fine."

Thomas did not know why they wanted him to be present for the delivery, and he looked back with a puzzled expression as Suzanna motioned with her hand for him to leave.

After Thomas left, Amanda hugged Suzanna. "I am going to have seven brothers and sisters." Everyone laughed, but Alina wondered why Suzanna did not laugh.

Everyone had brought an overnight bag and planned to spend the night onboard the Demon. They went to the ship's cafeteria for lunch. Alina asked them to wait outside the room for a minute while she spoke to Suzanna.

"What did Amanda mean when she said she was going to have seven brothers and sisters?" Alina asked.

Suzanna put a hand over her face and then told Alina what she had done. "This could only happen to Thomas," Alina said. "What does Thomas think about having all these children?"

"I kind of forgot to tell Thomas." Alina was laughing as she left the room.

"What is so funny?" Ben asked.

"There are six other mothers having babies today, and it seems our Thomas is the father of those babies," Alina said and told them what Suzanna had done. Joan was laughing so hard she was crying.

When Joan heard Thomas did not know he was the father to all the babies, she said, "This is classic Thomas. Please, you must let me tell him."

Alina grinned at Ben. "It looks like we will have eight grandchildren before the night is over."

THOMAS LOVED CHILDREN. He wrapped the baby girl in the small blanket and whispered while holding her, telling her she was safe. A dozen Oceanums stood in the hallways using their empathic abilities to calm the baby and the mothers. Thomas had just handed the baby to its mother when Doctor Adler asked Thomas to join her with the next delivery. The assistant had let Alina come in even though it was getting crowded. Thomas saw his mother, and she said Suzanna was fine and sleeping. Then she looked at the baby Thomas was holding and saw the baby had amber eyes. She and Thomas had rare amber eyes. Whereas Joan and Stephen had brown eyes like their father. The mother had blue eyes. The baby was healthy and already had the monitor patch. Thomas gently handed the baby to the mother. Alina felt an overwhelming sense of happiness.

"It seems all the Oceanums want me to be present for the birth of their child," Thomas said to his mother. "It must be a cultural thing." Alina smiled and nodded but did not correct her son.

"Thomas, we need you," the medical assistant said. "Thomas followed the assistant to the next room. Alina looked at the display next to the bed below leaving. The baby's last name was Wilson. Alina decided she would stay with Thomas. Later one of the Oceanums brought Thomas and Alina a sandwich when they empathically sensed they were hungry. Alina saw how kind and considerate her son was with all the mothers. She saw how gentle and loving he was toward each child. The last child arrived before the end of Middle Watch, so all the babies had the same birthday.

Thomas went to their cabin. He checked on Daniel and Amanda before crawling into bed next to Suzanna.

The following day, Suzanna said she was feeling good and took a hot shower while Thomas watched Daniel. When Suzanna finished, Thomas took a shower and dressed. When he came out of the bathroom, everyone was ready for breakfast. Suzanna had fed Daniel, and he was sleeping. They took Daniel and Amanda with them as they joined the rest of the family in the cafeteria. Alina told the family not to say anything to Thomas about the other babies since Suzanna should be the one to tell him. During breakfast, every time Joan looked at Thomas, she would burst out laughing and receive a mean look from Alina. Thomas asked Joan several times what was so funning, which made her laugh even more.

Most of the crew came back on board to see the newest member of the Wilson family. The crew was doubly excited to hear about the multiple births and visited each of the babies. Everyone enjoyed celebrating the new arrivals.

After breakfast, Suzanna insisted they visit the new mothers and babies. Amanda also wanted to see all the babies. Thomas could feel the emotions of each baby when he held them, and they sensed him. The babies were strong empaths.

That night Suzanna had a conversation with Thomas, which should have taken place nine months earlier. After Thomas got over the shock, Suzanna said he should spend time with each of his biological children.

"On a family ship, the crew considers every child to be part of their family," Suzanna told him. "We spend time with all the children, so they feel and know they are part of a big family." Thomas worked on the Demon each day but spent daily time with each of the babies.

After a week, Doctor Adler announced Daniel and Suzanna were both healthy and could move back to the home of Ben and

Alina. Alina had stayed on the ship the whole time, helping with the care of her grandson, and enjoyed every minute. She also spent time with the Oceanum mothers and their babies. All the babies had amber eyes like their father and their grandmother. Alina could feel the loving emotions from the Oceanums and the babies. She knew there was something special about them and planned to ask Thomas.

They could have left the ship the day following the birth of Daniel, but Suzanna wanted to stay long enough for each crew member to see Daniel before they returned to the home of Ben and Alina.

TWO WEEKS LATER, THE Chairperson of the Board of Advanced Ship Builders arrived with two of his attorneys, a financial representative, and their insurance adjuster. The insurance adjuster attended at the request of Ben's attorney. The meeting was held at the law firm's office in their largest conference room. Thomas was impressed as Attorney Veno spent less than an hour succinctly presenting a summary of the kidnapping, statements from the spies, and the damaging messages among the various employees of Advanced Ship Builders. He verified there were thousands of hours of admissions and communications substantiating the allegations.

One of the opposing attorneys spoke up. "Documents were executed by all parties specifying the confidentiality of this meeting. Further, only the terms of an agreement will survive this meeting if an agreement is reached." Everyone nodded their heads.

The Chairperson cleared his throat. "When our operatives failed to report, we assumed the worst, but I'm surprised and impressed by the completeness of the information you possess. I want you to know the kidnapping of Amanda Wilson was never approved or discussed with anyone in my office. I hope you will believe me. I would never have approved of such an act. We hoped a covert operation would obtain advanced technology from Wilson Enterprises. We planned to present such technology to our financiers to get them to provide additional funding. We justified our actions under the belief you were criminally in possession of technologies from the Ancients."

The Chairperson continued. "Unlike Wilson Enterprises, our corporation is publicly owned. Advanced Ship Builders is heavily in debt without the ability to make the payments. When business was good, we increased the dividend payments to our shareholders instead of paying down the debt. Then we had a recall on our civilian ships. It required us to replace the engines for free. If that was not bad enough, we had to defend multiple lawsuits associated with the recalled engines. Our stock is worthless, and the Corporation has been delisted. The gentleman to my left represents the financial institutions that hold our debt. Military contracts represent sixty percent of our business. We were already in severe financial shape and failed to win the most recent navy contract. In fact, your company won that contract. We are looking at filing for bankruptcy liquidation. Our remaining business is not sufficient to support a bankruptcy reorganization. In a typical bankruptcy liquidation, the funds raised would barely cover the court's administrative costs after paying the required employee termination costs. Our main shipyard is in good shape and fully operational. Our other locations have been previously shut down and dismantled as part of a cost-cutting effort. Our debt exceeds six billion credits. Our remaining facility would cost over four billion to build. We would like to see if you would consider purchasing the facility in a preapproved bankruptcy filing. You'd get the facility free of all debt and the ability to hire our experienced employees. We brought a list of the fixed assets, vids of the facilities, and an inventory of the materials on hand."

"You need to understand we didn't know you were having such difficulties," Ben said. "I'd like a moment to discuss your proposal with my son."

Pitera suggested they use his office. Ben and Thomas sat down in the two chairs in front of the desk for a confidential discussion.

"Their shipyard is in an ideal location, but do we want the headaches of a fourth location?" Ben asked.

"Our third location is small and close to their facility," Thomas replied. "It only handles maintenance and repairs. We could merge that facility with Advance Ship Builders. Then, we would still have just three facilities, but we'd have two mega locations. We must expand our business to build midsize merchant ships for the Outer Planets and the Rim Worlds. Plus, we have military contracts, and their facility would be perfect for building those ships. Otherwise, we will incur major capital costs expanding our existing facilities."

Ben nodded. "You've convinced me. Assuming we can acquire it at the right price. Now, let's look over the assets and inventory to decide what we should offer?"

After reviewing the files, they asked Pitera to join them. He came to the office and took the chair behind the desk.

"Advanced Ship Builders are desperate," Pitera said. "They didn't mention a price. There are no other potential buyers. The smaller shipbuilders have no use for such a large facility. In liquidation, they'd get less than two hundred million auctioning off the assets in pieces."

"Thomas, you have the cash," Ben said. "Why don't you buy it?"

"I will if you'll run it."

Ben sighed. "Okay, but only if you agree to come home on a regular basis and help out as needed."

They reentered the conference room. Everyone was serious and prepared for the worst. The worst being that Wilson Enterprises would not make an offer or submit an offer the court would not approve.

After sitting down, Thomas spoke up. "In liquidation, you'd be lucky to get two hundred million since the assets have no value except to a shipbuilder. I'll make one offer only. Our highest and best offer is four hundred million to purchase the corporation as a going enterprise. This will allow us to keep the existing employees. The employees would be gone in liquidation, and we'd lose time restarting the facility."

"Which financial institution will provide the financing?" the financier asked.

Thomas gave him a cold stare. "We don't need financing. We'll pay cash."

"We can complete the purchase as soon as you get court approval," Attorney Veno said. "However, the price will fluctuate up or down for any change in inventory. Plus, all fixed assets must be in working order, or the price will be reduced."

The litigation attorney for Wilson Enterprises took over. "Next, we have the litigation issues. You have a one hundred million insurance policy. In a court proceeding, our case is overwhelming, and a potential settlement would exceed the limits of your insurance coverage. However, since you are filing for bankruptcy, our only source of settlement is the insurance policy. Therefore, we'll accept the one hundred million insurance limits to settle all remaining issues. If you agree to the settlement, my clients will forego filing personal criminal charges, corporate criminal charges, personal civil charges, and corporate civil charges." The face of the insurance adjustor was pale, but he nodded his head since he knew they would lose in court and there would be millions in litigation costs on top of the policy limits. After losing, they would have to pay the legal fees of Wilson Enterprises, which would be huge.

Thomas had not expected the insurance proceeds and realized his costs for the purchase had just dropped to a net of three hundred million. Their attorneys had more than earned their fee. He was duly impressed.

Thomas made a slight motion with one hand to get the attention of the Chairperson. "I have one more request. You have a corporate ship in this system. I need an additional ship and would like to take immediate possession. I'll return the ship if the purchase doesn't go through."

"That is agreeable," the Chairperson said. "I'm fairly certain the court will approve your purchase offer. Give me a moment."

The Chairperson contacted the ship, advised the captain of the change in ownership, and recommended they seek employment with the new owner. He told the captain the executive on board his ship was no longer an employee, and they were not to take any orders from him.

"You should consider hiring the ship's crew," the Chairperson said to Thomas. "They're exceptionally good, and no one assigned to the ship knew anything about their purpose here. They were just providing transportation. I understand the executive in charge of the operation is still on board, but as you heard, he's no longer in charge."

"Thank you," Thomas replied.

The financier stepped forward. "Thomas, I'm Ludem Webber with Xondeon Financial. We researched your presence in the Outer Planets and the Rim. We're impressed. Our forecasters have analyzed the recent Hostis battle and its impact on the future. We believe there will be tremendous opportunities there. We're prepared to provide financing to fund those opportunities. Here is my contact information."

The meeting was over, and the attorneys were working out the details. Ben glanced back at the conference room as they were leaving. All the attorneys on both sides were smiling, so he knew the legal bills would be huge.

Thomas and Ben sat comfortably in the ground vehicle as the auto pilot returned them to their home.

"I'll be tied up for a while," Thomas said to his father. "I'd like you to visit our new shipyard and let the employees know their jobs are secure. We can use the large navy contracts to keep everyone busy at our two larger shipyards. At our smaller location, I would like to expand it to build military-grade shuttles and military starfighters in addition to their ship repair business. The navy lost over half their starfighters in the Hostis battle. There is a separate budget before the Senate to replace the fighters. The minimum order will be for a thousand starfighters. All three shipyards will need to be scheduled for continuous operation."

Thomas was thoughtful and said, "The pirate threat has been mostly neutralized, and the merchant ships we build will be more than a match for any remaining pirates. Winning the battle against the Hostis received positive publicity throughout the Galactic. There are graduates from schools and universities each year who still have some adventure in their blood. We can hire the ones who are willing to leave the comforts of their home planets. I'm going to send postings to all the educational facilities within our sector that jobs are available for those who want to go to the stars. The jobs will provide good pay, adventure, and excitement for those willing to go to the Outer Planets and the Rim. We have a lot of experienced officers aboard the Demon who will make excellent captains for these ships. All the shipyards were kept busy just building ships for the Core Planets. However, there is a need for thousands of ships in the Outer Planets and the Rim. Let's keep all of our shipyards running at peak capacity. With long-term trade agreements in place, financial institutions should be available to fund new ships to replace the family ships and for those planets wanting to purchase ships. The financier in the meeting will be worth pursuing."

The following morning Thomas had the corporate spies brought to the port. He told them he had possession of their corporate ship, which was no longer available for their transport. The spies were given till the end of the day to leave the planet. If they were still on the planet, they would be arrested as an accessory to the kidnapping of a minor and face the death penalty. He told them they would be arrested if they ever returned to Fidem. All of their belongings were returned, except for their weapons. Grayson assigned two marines to each spy to verify their departure.

Later in the day, Thomas took a shuttle to their new ship, the Beaumont. Grayson and four marines in armor accompanied him. The Beaumont's first officer met them in the shuttle bay. Thomas requested a tour and was impressed with the ship. It was well built and had an excellent crew. He was then escorted to the bridge. As they entered the bridge, Captain Acosta stood up and welcomed him.

Thomas looked around the bridge and addressed the captain. "You've been informed, I'm in the process of acquiring the assets of Advanced Ship Builders, which includes this ship. I have reviewed the background of you and your crew. All of you are professionally qualified. I'm offering everyone continued employment with no reduction in pay. Let me know if anyone does not want to accept employment, and we'll provide them with a travel allowance. I've been informed the change of ownership will be fairly swift. In the meantime, I have tentative ownership. I sincerely hope you and your crew will stay with the ship."

"I'd like to remain," Captain Acosta said. "I believe all the crew will stay. I await your orders."

Thomas looked around at the bridge officers and saw them nodding their heads.

"I believe you have an executive on board," Thomas said.

"A shuttle arrived during Night Watch, and the executive left on that shuttle," Captain Acosta said. "He did not inform anyone of his destination."

"It's just as well. Captain Acosta, please remain in system. I'll soon have a mission for you. In the meantime, feel free to grant shore leave on a rotational basis but tell them to be ready to return to the ship with little notice. Here are the contacts for the officers of the Demon and me. I have hundreds of ships that will soon be operational, and they need officers. I want a list of your officers who you think would make good captains. Contact me or any of my officers if you have any questions or concerns. It was a pleasure meeting all of you."

Thomas already had plans for the ship as he was escorted back to the shuttle bay for his return trip. It was a fine ship.

After Thomas left the bridge, Captain Acosta spoke to his officers. "Captain Wilson has an impressive background. I'd recommend all of you research his accomplishments. I think you will find it remarkably interesting. Also, look sharp. You heard him say he was looking for captains."

Captain Acosta sent a communication throughout the ship with the offer for continued employment. He had personally approved the hire of every crew member and was happy to see everyone had accepted employment with the new owners.

All the officers of the Demon had been kept busy recruiting crew members as they completed training and licensing for ship positions. Thomas told his officers to recruit crews for sixty ships to start. Thomas gave Captain Acosta new orders to pick up newly hired individuals and transport them to the navy graveyard of ships. Once there, the recruits would be tested and provided additional training for their initial assignments.

CHAPTER 13 WEDDING

The following months were busy but passed without further incidents. However, the Demon bodyguards continued to be diligent. Any villainous individuals attempting to interfere with the Demon or its crew received one warning. If they failed to heed the warning, they were strongly encouraged to leave the planet. They either left voluntarily or were turned over to the local authorities with a list of their illegal activities. Unsavory individuals quickly learned to stay away from the Wilson family and not give offense to any of the crew from the Demon.

It seemed like everyone in the Galactic wanted to attend the wedding. Alina was busy orchestrating the event. Representatives from every planet and station wanted an invitation. Fans and teammates of the Demons' hockey team were contacting Alina. They still remembered Thomas as the star player for the World-Champion Demons. Admiral Nelson sent an acceptance on behalf of himself and the Premier.

Suzanna returned to work after the birth of Daniel. She leased an entire floor of an office building with shuttle landing pads on the top of the building. This allowed Suzanna to expand her staff to fifty assistants, ten supervisors, and two managers. Representatives from planets and stations provided Suzanna with their available exports and a list of imports they wished to purchase. Suzanna had a good team and only worked part time to review their work. Alina enjoyed watching her grandchildren while Suzanna worked a few hours each morning. Suzanna and Thomas visited the Oceanum babies regularly.

The second biggest wedding surprise occurred when a security detail delivered a message to Thomas and Suzanna asking them to have a private meeting with the Premier before the wedding.

The biggest surprise happened when Thomas and Suzanna received a wedding gift from the Supreme Ruler of the Hostis. The gift consisted of a large Rhodium base polished to a mirror finish. Mounted on the base was a 1200 carrot flawless blue diamond. There were three writings on the triangular base. One side was in standard Galactic, a second side contained the language of the Hostis, and the language of the Ancients was on the third side. On the front was a star map with a set of coordinates. The gift had a motion sensor. When activated, a three-dimensional vid showed a young Hostis speaking Galactic with an invitation for Thomas to meet with the Supreme Ruler of the Hostis. The meeting was to discuss the possibility of a peace treaty. A human delivered the gift and was immediately taken into custody. Thomas made copies of the vid and the inscriptions on the gift. If the gift was to get attention, then it was a complete success. Rhodium was the rarest and most valuable precious metal. Whereas, the blue diamond was priceless.

Admiral Nelson was notified and sent a team to interrogate the person delivering the invitation. He sent another group to analyze the object to see if it was a gift or an attempt on Thomas' life.

THOMAS AND SUZANNA implemented changes to improve the distribution of needed products within the Outer Planets and the Rim. Melius built additional production facilities on the corporate Core Planet to increase its production of high-volume products. Melius made substantial progress in setting up the new manufacturing facility on Desetum in the Outer Planets. It was already manufacturing power units. They expected to start manufacturing food processors in two months.

They had just started construction of a manufacturing facility on Totera, a corporate planet in the Rim, and expected it to be operational within a year. With such facilities, Melius could expand as needed to meet future demands. On Desetum and Totera, they would avoid the taxes charged by the Imperium. Also, ships would use less fuel because of shorter delivery runs, and the planets would get their products quicker. The goal was to lower their cost structure so they could sell larger volumes of products at lower prices.

Thomas had a fifty percent ownership interest in Desetum and Totera. He was given the ownership interest in return for locating the planets, providing protection against pirates, and as an inducement to buy all their manufactured goods from these planets.

Thomas owned twelve percent of Melius, and the Melius AI held an eighteen percent interest under a shell company. Thomas contacted Attorney Veno and told him that he wanted to purchase the remaining seventy percent. Then he contacted Ludem Webber at Xondeon Financial.

"Ludem, this is Thomas Wilson. You mentioned the possibility of providing financing during our recent meeting. An associate and I own thirty percent of Melius. I would like to purchase the remaining seventy percent. Melius owns a corporate planet in the Core. Also, it owns a fifty percent interest in Desetum, an Outer Planet; and fifty percent of Totera, a Rim World. I own the remaining fifty percent of these two corporate entities. I expect the value of these three corporate entities to increase in value once Desetum and Totera reach full production capacity."

"Sounds like the opportunity we discussed," Ludem replied. "We will need to see a proforma business plan, but I'm certain our executives will approve the financing."

"Contact Attorney Veno," Thomas said. "His law firm will handle the legal side of the purchase." They discussed a timeline for the purchase and other procedural issues. Thomas did not mention that he planned to turn the three corporate entities into non-profits once he repaid the debt.

Thomas had previously purchased the smallest of the three universal chip manufacturers, which also manufactured AIs for spaceships. It was now the largest chip manufacturer since it filled orders for all the planets in the Outer Planets and the Rim, in addition to its Core Planet customers.

Thomas also owned Sanitatem Vos Corporation, one of the four manufacturers of healing chambers. The healing chambers were expensive since they used an AI that was promoted as the most advanced AI in existence. Thomas had explored the possibility of buying the company that manufactured the AIs for the healing chambers. However, it was impossible to acquire the company since it was the highest-valued company in the Core. With their monopoly, they controlled the price of their AIs and refused to give volume discounts. They further refused to increase the unit volume of sales to the manufacturers of the healing chambers. Each manufacturer of healing chambers could only purchase 12,000 AIs per year. It was believed they were the only entity able to manufacture AIs that could control nanites. Thomas directed the President of Sanitatem Vos Corporation to switch from a single-shift to a three-shift operation and keep building healing chambers even though they could only purchase enough unique advanced AIs for the first shift production. Thomas knew he could sell millions of healing chambers if he could produce them at a reasonable price.

Suzanna had been working with their smaller suppliers to provide larger quantities so they could make fewer trips with fully loaded ships. Thomas would use his ships to stockpile these products on Desetum and Totera.

Thomas imagined how the Outer Planets and the Rim could one day surpass the Core Planets in wealth. They had unlimited access to rare earth elements, precious metals, and natural minerals. He knew it would take time, but he wanted to transform the Outer Planets and the Rim into a modern trading empire. If the Outer Planets and Rim worked together, it could be possible to rival the Core Planets in economic strength. They would never have the population of the Core Planets, but the Core would eventually depend on the Outer Planets and Rim worlds for certain vital imports. However, he had to stop dreaming and fulfill their current trading obligations.

THE FAMILIA PRIMUM arrived. Captain Javier and his senior officers, including Suzanna's parents, were anxious to see her, but business came first. She had one of Demon's pilots pick them up from their ship and land the shuttle on the roof of the building. An assistant met them as they got off the shuttle. They took an elevator down one flight to Suzanna's office floor. Suzanna had a huge corner office with full glass windows and a beautiful view overlooking a large lake. It was family time, and Suzanna hugged her mother and father while nodding to the officers of her former ship. It had been six years, but she remembered all the senior officers.

She invited everyone to sit down. "I've made arrangements for lunch. Once we complete our business, I'll take you on a tour of the Demon, and you can meet with Thomas."

An assistant told Suzanna lunch had arrived, and they adjourned to one of the conference rooms to enjoy their meal while continuing to discuss business. She told her parents they were invited to dinner the next day at the home of Thomas' parents.

Suzanna asked to be updated on the Familia Primum. They took turns bringing Suzanna up to date on everything. Many of her friends were married and had children. The Familia Primum had attended the Gathering, and Captain Javier was voted onto the Council. Everyone was envious of the fortunes of the Familia Primum.

"The captains of family ships have asked if the Familia Primum would help in getting trade agreements with the Demon," Captain Javier said.

"How many of the ships are interested in a trade route?" Suzanna asked.

Captain Javier responded. "All the surviving family ships would like to participate in a trade route, but only sixty-three ships attended the last Gathering. We know the Demon rescued survivors from two ships, but we believe the other two missing ships were lost with no survivors." There were sad faces around the conference table.

"I can provide contracts for all the family ships," Suzanna said. "So far, no ships hauling cargo for the Demon has been attacked. Here is a list of trade routes still open. Let me know which routes the various family ships would like to have assigned to them. We can give each ship a one-year probationary contract. The first year will determine if they can handle the import and export requirements. You have thirty standard days to provide me with the routes you want and the ship's name for each route. I will arrange the schedules so the family ships can manage most of the trade within the Outer Planets and exchange cargo with Melius. The Demon and our ships will handle the trade with the Rim Worlds and those routes in the Outer Planets which are not selected. There are two hundred sixteen outer worlds and one hundred thirty-seven Rim worlds. So far, we have only visited about half of these worlds. We need to visit these other locations to see if they want to establish trade agreements. I would suggest all family ships get a complete overhaul from Wilson Enterprises as soon as possible and pay for a weapons upgrade. Financing is available with a reasonable interest rate."

Everyone had finished lunch and enjoyed socializing. "We've taken care of business," Suzanna said. "Would you like to see the Demon?" Everyone gave a positive response. Suzanna told one of her assistants she would be out of the office for the rest of the day.

They took the elevator back to the roof of the building. They boarded a shuttle, and it was only a short flight to the shipyard. Suzanna gave them a personal tour of the Demon and answered their questions. The Tactical Officer for the Familia Primum asked, "Is it true the Demon took out over a thousand Hostis ships?"

"The Demon took out a lot of ships," Suzanna said. "I'm not sure if it was over a thousand. You'll need to ask Thomas if you want an exact count."

The officer expected Suzanna to say the number of ships destroyed by the Demon was highly overstated. Now, he thought it was true. During the tour, he had been impressed by the firepower of the Demon. Suzanna had adopted Thomas' philosophy. It did not hurt to let certain rumors build if it reduced the odds of the Demon being attacked in the future. Everyone was impressed by the ship and by Suzanna's knowledge. Thomas joined them toward the end of the tour.

Captain Javier asked Thomas, "I've always wondered why our ships have never been in a port at the same time?"

Thomas gave him an honest answer. "I made certain our ships never met because I was afraid Suzanna would leave the Demon and return to her family aboard the Familia Primum."

There was only a brief pause before everyone, including Suzanna, burst out laughing. Suzanna laughed so hard she had tears in her eyes. Thomas did not think it was funny, which made them laugh even harder.

Suzanna looked at Thomas and said, "You're the smartest person I've ever met, but sometimes you are brainless. You need to visit the Familia Primum."

Thomas excused himself since he needed to return to the bridge. Suzanna wiped the rest of the tears from her eyes as she watched him walk away. She shook her head. Suzanna loved him completely. How could he think she could ever leave him or the Demon? Right now, she wished they were alone in their cabin, and she would take care of his insecurities.

After the tour, Suzanna asked to go with them to the Familia Primum and see the rest of the family. They quickly agreed. They boarded the shuttle and were soon aboard the Familia Primum. Suzanna had a wonderful time seeing her old friends who had gotten older. She met all their children plus the new members who had joined the ship during the Gathering. Suzanna was a little unnerved when the crew would stop what they were doing and smile at her as she made her way through the ship. Parents would get the attention of their children and point to her.

Captain Javier asked her to follow him to the bridge. The bridge was crowded, with as many as could fit in the space. Her parents were standing next to the captain when he pointed out the inscription on the wall. Suzanna read her name and the description below with it. She knew it was the highest honor a family ship could provide. She gave sincere thanks to the captain. Drinks were passed around, and Captain Javier made a toast to Suzanna.

Then Suzanna saw her brother and hugged him, but before he pulled away, he whispered in her ear, "You've made it tough on me, having to live up to your reputation."

Suzanna replied: "I'm sorry, but I didn't do anything to deserve this."

"She said she didn't do anything to deserve this," her brother shouted.

The entire crew erupted in laughing but cheered again. Several shouted to her brother how he might learn a little humility from his sister.

Even Captain Javier looked at Suzanna with adoration. "Suzanna, you have improved the lives of everyone on this ship. Because of your efforts, we have the respect and envy of every family ship. Parents throughout all the family ships are naming their children after you."

Suzanna thanked them again for the honor. Her close friends asked if they could visit the Demon. She announced she would not be working the next day and would be happy to give additional tours of the Demon starting at the beginning of Day Watch.

The following day, Suzanna had just completed the second tour of the ship when her three former girlfriends showed up. When they were teens, they spent most of their time together. She looked around and did not see anyone else, so she asked if they were ready to see the ship, and they said absolutely. She gave them the grand tour and finished on the bridge.

Then one of her friends asked if her cabin was as nice as the rest of the ship. The cabin was just off the bridge, so she had them follow her. A moment later, they were all speechless as they viewed her cabin. Beds on ships were of necessity small, and while hotels on the planets might have a large bed, the crew of a family ship rarely used the credits to sleep off the ship when in port. One of her friends took off her shoes, jumped onto the bed, and turned over onto her back.

"I've never seen a bed this big," she said as she relaxed on the bed. "You know I'm the only one of us without a husband, so I'm still sleeping in a hammock with no privacy. A large family could sleep in this bed. If I had a bed like this, I'd never report to my station."

She stretched her arms out above her head and moaned. "This bed is so comfortable."

Suzanna's other friends did not wait for an invitation, they took off their shoes, and all three of her friends were enjoying her bed. She had been sleeping here so long that she had forgotten how uncomfortable the beds were on the Familia Primum. One of her friends said she could make a fortune renting her cabin. Another asked if she and her husband could try out the bed. Suzanna said there was no way she was letting any of them have sex in her bed. They all said she was unreasonably selfish. Then they all laughed together as they relived, for just a moment, the bond they had shared in their teen years.

One of her friends pointed to a door on the side of the cabin. "Is that the bathroom?"

"No, that's Amanda's cabin."

All three of her friends shouted, "No way!" They rushed into the adjoining cabin to check out Amanda's room. It was decorated for a child and had an entertainment center.

"Your six-year-old daughter has a private cabin and her own bathroom?" Amanda's cabin was the standard size for the Demon but larger than any cabin on the Familia Primum.

Her single friend, who slept in a hammock and shared a community bathroom, said, "I am sick with jealousy. Your daughter has a better cabin than Captain Javier. If we're not friends, I'd have no problem hating you." She just shook her head.

Suzanna had an idea. She invited her friends to follow her to one of the other cabins. She spoke to the friend who spent her nights sleeping in a hammock. "What do you think of having this cabin?"

"It's nice, but it doesn't compare to your cabin."

"I mean, would you like to have this cabin permanently? We have quite a few crew members who are from this system. Some have taken their large savings and are staying on Fidem. Therefore, we have plenty of openings and empty cabins. I'd like all of you to consider transferring to the Demon."

"Do you have to get Captain Wilson's approval?"

"Yes, but he would never deny such a request to get experienced crew members. You could try it out for a year, and if you dislike living here, you can return to the Familia Primum. Think about it. You'll have total access to your cabin on all three shifts and a private bathroom."

Now they were genuinely shocked. On their ship, they only had access to their cabins for one shift since it was shared with the other two shifts. Standard cabins were assigned twelve crew members, four from each shift, and you had to vacate the cabin promptly at the end of your sleep cycle. If you were still sleepy, you could go to the general area and sleep in a hammock. No one on the Familia Primum had a private cabin, not even the captain. Suzanna sent a message to Thomas and received an immediate positive response.

They all quickly agreed to move to the Demon, subject to discussions with their husband and children. The Familia Primum was significantly overcrowded, and Captain Javier had already asked for volunteers to move to other ships at the next gathering. However, after the recent renovation, no one wanted to move to another family ship which was shabby by comparison. There was no such problem moving to the Demon since it would be a significant upgrade to their current accommodations, and they would be moving to a ship with friends.

They contacted Captain Javier, and he immediately approved their requests. Suzanna's married friends contacted their husbands and told them the transfer was preapproved. The husbands agreed to come over with the children to look at the Demon before making their final decisions. They were excited about the possible move. After checking out the Demon and seeing the available crew positions, they happily agreed to the one-year trial. However, they were coming with the intent to make the transfer permanent. One of the husbands asked if they had any restrictions on having children. Suzanna said it would be generations before that would become a problem, if ever, and no authorization was required. He said other families might want to apply for a transfer to the Demon.

"We have a lot of openings," Suzanna said. "Please have them apply. We're trying to fill the openings quickly since we plan to leave after the wedding."

Suzanna told her three friends they would all have to be in her wedding, and they were excited to share this moment with her. Alina had been asking Suzanna if she could find some friends to be bridesmaids. At the time, she was too stressed out to think about it. She called Alina, who immediately set an appointment for the following day to go dress shopping with all of them.

By the next day, over three hundred individuals from the Familia Primum applied for positions on the Demon, and they were all accepted. They moved into the empty cabins. Most had children, and the children were having fun exploring the Demon.

ADMIRAL NELSON AND the Premier arrived together a week before the wedding. A morning meeting was scheduled with a request for both Thomas and Suzanna to attend. Thomas and Suzanna arrived at the appointed time. The Admiral brought the Hostis wedding gift and set it on the conference room table. They each helped themselves to a cup of coffee before sitting around the medium-sized table. The chairs were comfortable, and there was ample space. Admiral Nelson said the gift from the Hostis was perfectly safe. The Premier asked if the Galactic sentence on the gift was the same as the Ancients' message.

"No," Thomas replied, "the sentence in the language of the Ancients reads, *Peace between enemies requires understanding*, but this may be a simplistic interpretation. I believe they're asking for an exchange of individuals to study each other's culture until an understanding is achieved and then a lasting peace is possible."

The Premier looked puzzled. "I meant to tell you," the Admiral said. "Our young captain unlocked the key to the translation of the language of the Ancients."

"Captain Wilson, you continue to amaze me," the Premier said. "How were you able to translate a language which has confounded scholars for thousands of years?"

Thomas shrugged his shoulders. "I got lucky when I tried a different approach."

"I doubt there was any luck involved," the Premier said as he shook his head. "You and your ship are valuable to the Imperium. I was tempted to confiscate your ship and take you into protective custody. However, you may be the only person who can bring all the Outer Planets into the Imperium without using force. Additionally, I've seen the vids of the battle with the Hostis. Without your help, we'd have lost."

The Premier continued after a momentary pause. "Thomas, I'm here to discuss this gift and what it might mean. Before you received your gift from the Supreme Ruler of the Hostis, we were preparing to invade Hostis space and destroy them before they rebuild their fleet. We plan to have your ship join us in that effort."

"The individual who delivered your gift believes the Hostis want to meet with you to discuss peace," Admiral Nelson said. "However, this could be a trap to eliminate you since you individually were responsible for their loss in the recent battle."

Thomas felt it was time to take a risk. "Sir, there were other ways the Hostis could have tried to eliminate me. They could have sent a message asking for a meeting for peace, but he did not. He only indicated the need to get to know each other. This is a sincere message, and I should meet with the Hostis. Humans and Hostis are the only two species remaining in this sector of space. Neither species should be alone, and that will ultimately happen unless we agree not to exterminate each other. We know there were other races before us. They were extremely powerful, and they are no more. Maybe it was because they would not consider a peaceful solution."

"I agree it's worth the risk," the Premier said. "It may give us the opportunity to end the Hostis threat permanently."

Suzanna had been listening patiently. "Regardless of threats or opportunities, shouldn't we give primary consideration to entering into a peace treaty? This is the first time the Hostis have contacted us with an offer of peace."

"We'll certainly consider peace if it's to our advantage," the Premier said.

Thomas saw Suzanna had a disappointed look on her face. "No date was given with the coordinates," Thomas said.

"You are correct," the Admiral replied. "The person who delivered the message had asked for a date. He was told they'd wait until you arrived. The destination will require two jumps and then a trip through a Star Gate. I'll follow you with our Battleship and the remainder of our fleet in case you get into trouble. We'll stay one jump behind you and won't make the final jump until we hear from you regarding the size of the fleet awaiting your arrival. I'll have a platoon of forty marines onboard the Demon to provide additional security. The jump coordinates provided by the gift are deep within Hostis space."

Thomas did not tell them the coordinates were reversed. Plus, there was a code to transpose one of the data points. A code only he was likely to understand.

Admiral Nelson showed Thomas the area of space indicated by the coordinates. Thomas smiled. The coordinates were wrong. The Hostis used the Ancients' method, while the navy used a human approach. Thomas did not want to embarrass the Admiral in front of the Premier, so he did not point out the mistake. He would provide the Admiral with the corrections in private at a later time.

"Assuming our ship is repaired as scheduled, I'll prepare the Demon to depart ten days after the wedding," Thomas said. "I'd like the messenger to travel with us since he may provide us with insight into what to expect when I meet with the Supreme Commander of the Hostis. I plan to take along scholars and scientists who have studied the Ancients. Also, I hope to take along individuals to study the Hostis culture, including linguists who can hopefully learn the language. Additionally, I plan to take along a couple of specialists to identify biological and physiological differences between Humans and the Hostis. I want to do everything possible to help us better understand them."

Thomas did not disclose how he expected everyone traveling with them to have an open mind regarding the Hostis. Regardless, he had found individuals willing to live with the Hostis for an extended period. He planned to bring these individuals together before the wedding so they could start working together before leaving. Thomas did not mention the two professors from the local university he planned to bring along since he did not want them spied upon.

The Admiral and Premier agreed the mission should be classified as top secret. They told Thomas he could bring together his group, but they were not to be told the location of the destination. Other than her one comment, Suzanna had remained quiet during the meeting.

After Thomas and Suzanna left, the Premier said, "He's an interesting young man, but he's an idealist. In contrast, we have to deal with reality. I've achieved the most powerful position in the Galactic and have successfully held the position for over eighty years. During my reign, the Core Planets have prospered. There've been no civil wars and no wars between planets. Throughout history, there are only a few individuals who have changed the course of history. You and I are the individuals who are most able to protect humanity. However, I'm constrained by the votes of the Senate. If one of the other Senators took my place, the result could be disastrous. I'm the best person to be the Premier, and I hope to hold the title for many more years. I have a new challenger, Senator Suarez. She must be eliminated."

"You'd have a senator assassinated?" Admiral Nelson asked.

"Admiral, how can you be surprised? You have your own assassination squad. In addition to your spying, you have carried out assassinations for the good of the Galactic."

"Yes, but those have been crime lords or individuals who posed a threat to the Galactic."

"Admiral, anyone trying to replace me is a threat to the Galactic. Out of necessity, I've eliminated Senators who gained too much support within the Senate. I am deeply saddened each time. However, Senator Suarez has somehow survived two assassination attempts. Enough about Senator Suarez, we have more urgent matters to address. This meeting with the Hostis changes everything."

"How do you want to handle the Hostis," the Admiral asked, although he knew the answer.

"You have a contingent of marines near his ship. Make sure they are aboard the Demon when it's ready to depart. They'll make sure Thomas follows our directives. The Hostis would not want a peace treaty unless they felt they could not win a war. It's reasonable to assume they lost most of their ships in the recent battle. With the Demon's support, we should be able to destroy all their remaining ships. Then we can attack their planets and wipe out the entire race."

"You'd have us destroy their civilian population?"

"They had no problem killing every human on the planets they attacked. They showed us no mercy. Hostis children grow up to become adults who will continue the war against humanity. Their females give birth to future generations who grow up to war against humanity. I'm responsible for saving humanity from the Hostis threat. Humanity is not safe as long as a single Hostis is alive."

"What about Thomas?"

"Thomas is the second greatest threat to humanity," the Premier said. "His plans to improve the Outer Planets and the Rim Worlds could endanger the Core Planets. My analysts advised me that Thomas is the one person who could unite all the Outer Planets and the Rim. That must not be permitted. They could become a future threat to the Core Planets if allowed to prosper and unite. Eventually, I plan to eliminate Thomas to prevent him from completing such a plan. However, we'll need to delay his demise until we see what happens during this meeting with the Hostis. Also, once we eliminate the Hostis threat, I want you to destroy every civilian ship in the Outer Planets and the Rim."

"What about the trade agreements?"

"We'll oversee the trade with these planets, but on our terms. We have over a trillion humans to protect. Do I have your full support?"

"Yes." Admiral Nelson knew only one answer was acceptable.

"I see in your report you've failed to locate the fourth shipyard, which is using the technology of the Ancients. We must locate this shipyard. My government spies have failed to locate the facilities. Once you take over the Demon, use whatever method is needed to get the crew to disclose the location. You have your orders."

Admiral Nelson remained seated after the Premier left the room. He would have preferred a different direction, but he could face termination if he disagreed with the Premier. Termination could mean a discharge from the navy or an accident. He did not agree with the Premier concerning Thomas or the elimination of the Hostis if they were not a threat. However, he would follow orders and do his duty. The Admiral remembered when he was an idealist like Thomas. He wondered how he had departed so far from the values he once held. He had traded a little of his ethics each time he advanced his career. His advancement had put him in a position to defend humanity, but he had given up part of his humanity in the process. However, the Premier was correct that the Core Planets had experienced peace and eliminated poverty during his reign.

Suzanna had planted a listening device before she left the meeting and was shocked by what she had heard. These were the two men Thomas most admired after his father. This information would change everything. Suzanna had Thomas listen to the recording.

Thomas had planned to discuss the spies he held in confinement with the Premier and the Admiral but decided to cover it with the Admiral in a later meeting. Now he needed to meet with a small group of people he could trust and plan a new strategy.

He set up a meeting with Suzanna, his father, his uncle, Grayson, and Jackson. He played the recording of the Premier's statements. Everyone was shocked and sat quietly for a while.

"I've thought about this," Thomas said. "I want a treaty between Humans and the Hostis if they're serious about making peace. I have an outline of the items we must address if we hope to have any chance of a successful meeting. First, we'll secretly move up the departure date. We must get the key specialists and researchers onboard without anyone discovering our plan. Once we depart, we must lose any pursuit since we can't allow anyone to follow the Demon. Finally, we'll need to prevent the navy marines from boarding the Demon or remove them from the Demon if they have boarded."

"Grayson, how would our marines compare to navy marines?"

"Our marines are good, but would not stand a chance against the military's marines. The active-duty marines react without thinking. They are combat veterans and will be wearing the same armor as our marines. However, they have armor-piercing bullets. We can't risk using such bullets since they would penetrate the hull. The fight would be over quickly, and our marines would be dead. Jackson and I will work on a way to handle their marines."

"See if there's any way to utilize the Beaumont we received from Advanced Ship Builders," Thomas said. "The court approved our purchase of the assets of Advanced Ship Builders, and the Beaumont was part of the purchase."

"Over half our crew are already living on the Demon," Grayson said. "We can increase the numbers a little each day. We can have the balance of our crew on board the Beaumont. Then we can have the two ships meet at a designated location to transfer over the crew and the research specialists. This would give us the surprise we need for the Demon to depart before anyone can act. They'll not expect the Demon to depart until you and your family are on board the ship. I suggest we depart right after the wedding, ten days ahead of our scheduled departure date and before the military marines come aboard."

"You could have the junior officers make the escape since bringing the senior officers onboard would draw too much attention," Ralph said. "Further, we could bring the engines online every night and say we are having problems balancing the new engines. Then, no one will be suspicious when the Demon is powered up to leave. We can have the regular shuttles brought to the port and use those shuttles to ferry everyone to the Beaumont. If anyone asks, we can say we sold the regular shuttles and replaced them with fully armed military shuttles. We can even create a bill of sale in case anyone asks. If needed, we can use the smaller Beaumont shuttles."

They all agreed to the plan and assigned various tasks that would need to take place for full implementation.

"Another thing we need to decide is what to do with the remaining spies held in our lockup facility. Let's have another meeting in two days to discuss this further."

After Grayson and Jackson left, Ralph said, "Thomas, I'm rejoining your father in the shipbuilding business. With the purchase of Advanced Ship Builders, he'll need my help. Plus, this is my home."

Thomas was completely surprised. "You're my first officer, and I need you."

"You no longer need me," Ralph said with sparkling eyes and a broad smile. "Suzanna will make a fantastic first officer. Half the crew already reports to her. You'll never find a better first officer."

Thomas thought for a minute. "You're right, but I'll miss you."

"You'll continue to see Ralph and the whole family," Ben said. "In the future, I expect you to come home on a regular basis, or we're both going to have trouble with Alina."

THE WEDDING PLAN WAS in full swing. Alina had gotten the top wedding specialists to assist. The wedding would be held in the most prominent and oldest church citadel on the planet. The wedding would be viewable live or on download across the Galactic.

They had the reception three days before the wedding at the hockey arena owned by Wilson Enterprises. Over five thousand people attended the reception. Space was not a problem since the arena could hold over fifty thousand fans and was designed for multiple events. The crews from both the Demon and the Familia Primum attended. Each Core Planet, each family ship, and every planet with a trade agreement with the Demon could send two dignitaries. The players and coaches from the Demons Championship team were invited. Thomas sent invitations to the Dean and his assistant to attend with their family. Everyone given an invitation had a deadline to confirm attendance.

During the reception, the junior officers of the Demon received permission to show vids during the event. After everyone was seated, a video began with soft upbeat music playing in the background. The footage showed: scores made by Thomas when he played for the

Demons; Thomas as he worked on various systems all over the ship making it appear he had built the ship single handedly; the Demon ship as it left port for the first time; a ship firing a missile at the Demon and then being destroyed; Suzanna working as a server in a stained white dress; Suzanna and Thomas in each other's arms; Thomas holding baby Amanda with both of them asleep in the captain's chair; an attack by two ships and the destruction of those ships; the various planets thanking Thomas, Suzanna and the crew for delivering needed cargo; Thomas and Amanda in a romantic embrace kissing; planets and stations suffering from disease and hunger and after vids showing healthy happy families; Thomas being shot but continuing to shoot as he killed various assailants with Suzanna covering Amanda with her own body while continuing to fire her blaster; Thomas, Suzanna and Amanda lying unconscious on stretchers covered in blood being rushed down the ship's corridor; Thomas and Suzanna in another romantic embrace; Amanda walking onto the bridge and crawling up into Thomas' lap and going to sleep; Thomas cringing in his seat as Suzanna is accosting him when he purchased the garbage; Suzanna when she attacked the men at the trade center; Thomas and Suzanna in another romantic moment; the Demon joining the battle between the navy and the Hostis with the Demon blowing apart enemy destroyers, cruisers and the massive enemy battleship; Thomas and a pregnant Suzanna defending themselves at the restaurant; Thomas and the marines rescuing Amanda after she had been kidnapped; and Daniel shortly after his birth with the crew showing their emotions as they welcomed the newest member of their family; and the finale with Thomas and Suzanna in another passionate romantic embrace. The vids showed the people of the Outer Planets and the Rim as real people with loving families. This contrasted with the horrible monsters they were portrayed to be throughout the Core. The main message throughout the vid was of two people deeply in love.

When the vid ended, there was cheering, clapping, and many tearful eyes. There was growing respect from those who did not know how hard the crew of the Demon had worked, the good they had accomplished, and the dangers they had faced. Any doubters now knew the Demon had earned its reputation.

After the reception, Grayson started collecting the crew and transporting them to the Beaumont. The specialists had already boarded.

An officer from the Beaumont picked up Professor Gilbert, his wife, their top graduate assistant, and Professor Monroe, the foremost researcher in the field of the Ancients. Professor Monroe had shown up at the university unannounced after Professors Rubin Gilbert and Alicia Gilbert had published their findings. He refused to leave and insisted on seeing the site. Further, he insisted on staying in their guest room since he had provided similar accommodations when they had visited him. He knew what they were planning when he saw their graduate assistant arrive in the middle of the night with her bags. He noticed a vehicle in front of their home with an officer standing next to it. He got in the vehicle with them and refused to get out. Thomas had not gotten around to approving Professor Monroe. Grayson approved the addition since they did not want to create a scene.

THE DAY OF THE WEDDING arrived. The church could seat twelve hundred people, and it was full. The church was over a thousand years old and was simply magnificent. With its awe-inspiring architecture, the church had a special aura that could be felt from the time you entered the cathedral. The high gilding ceiling added a unique richness and beauty. The tall custom stained-glass windows designed by the greatest artists from that period provided indirect lighting. It was lavishly decorated with marble, reliefs, and sculptures. No other place on the planet was as grand or more perfect for a wedding.

Suzanna wore a long elegant white custom dress with a low neckline. Suzanna had a radiant smile which proved infectious, and everyone was captivated by her beauty as she slowly walked down the aisle. Her hair had been meticulously prepared earlier in the day. She wore a rare red diamond flame necklace with matching studs. She finally understood why grounders were so enamored with weddings. Suzanna found it breathtaking. She felt like the gravity had been cut, and she was going to float. Amanda wore a white ankle-length dress that matched the design of her mother's dress. Thomas looked handsome in a custom-made traditional black suit.

For the ceremony, the minister told them they could choose from thousands of vows or create their own. They had selected the Antediluvian vows for its brevity. Suzanna replaced the word *obey* with *follow the captain's orders while on duty*.

The ceremony proceeded with everything occurring as planned. In the end, they kissed as they'd done so many times in the past.

Amanda joined Alina and Ben. Alina told everyone she would watch Amanda and Daniel so the newlyweds could enjoy their wedding night. Alina was happy the wedding had proceeded perfectly. The post-wedding actions had to be just as perfect if they hoped to protect Thomas, Suzanna, and their grandchildren.

Thomas and Suzanna were allowed to exit the church first, followed by the rest of the guests.

Ben thanked the Premier and the Admiral for coming. The Admiral said he heard the Demon might not be ready in ten days. Ben shrugged his shoulders.

Thomas and Suzanna rode in a luxury ground vehicle to the hotel they had reserved for their ten-day honeymoon. They were both smiling because the wedding had been grand, and it was over. Then they both turned serious.

CHAPTER 14 SHIP GRAVEYARD

When Thomas and Suzanna reached the hotel, they went straight to their room since they had made the reservations several months earlier. Once in the room, they immediately changed their clothes and changed their appearance. They made their way to the parking garage to a nondescript vehicle. They drove to the port. A shuttle with warm engines sat waiting for their arrival. Alina and Ben were already there with Amanda and Daniel. Everyone repeated their goodbyes. This time there were tears because it was for real. Thomas, Suzanna, Amanda, and Daniel boarded the shuttle. Once they were secure, the pilot fired the thrusters and headed for the Beaumont.

Once aboard the Beaumont, Thomas headed to the bridge while Suzanna settled into their assigned cabin with Amanda and Daniel. When Thomas entered the bridge, Captain Acosta asked if he wished to assume command. Thomas declined and was pleased they were already accelerating at full speed to achieve the necessary velocity to engage their jump engines. Thomas gave the navigator the jumped coordinates. Their first officer announced that no ships were following as Captain Acosta gave the command to engage the jump engines. Now, Thomas had to rely upon the junior officers on the Demon to complete the second part of their planned escape.

ONBOARD THE DEMON, the junior officers were trying to contain their excitement. This was their first mission without the senior officers watching them and judging their every move. They wanted to prove to their captain that his faith in their ability was not misplaced.

There were open panels with exposed wiring throughout the ship. This was staged to make it look like lots of work remained before the Demon was ready to leave the shipyard. However, Ralph Miller had made sure the ship was prepared for flight. There were repairs to be completed, but the remaining repairs would not interfere with flight operations. The remaining minor repairs would be completed while in transit to their destination.

Ralph had already notified everyone there would be another engine test during the night to try to balance the engines. However, they were already in perfect alignment with no deviation among the four engines. They wanted to slip out of the shipyard without drawing any attention from the navy.

The Tactical Officer used the Demon's passive sensors to locate all the navy ships in the immediate area. They had two choices available to them for departure, depending on the location of the navy ships. They could head to the Star Gate or try to achieve sufficient speed for a jump.

Based on the location of the navy ships, the acting captain decided the best option would be to try to make it to the Star Gate without being intercepted. The first officer verified all the mooring posts holding the ship in place had been released. The bridge crew engaged their semi-stealth technology and slowly brought the engines up to one-quarter impulse. The acting captain directed the helmsman to head away from the yard and toward the Star Gate. The traffic was heavy because of the number of ships that brought attendees to the wedding. Therefore, they had to maintain a slower velocity.

They coordinated with the family ships to move between them and the navy ships to further reduce the identification of the Demon.

They were halfway to the Star Gate before the navy identified the Demon and decided to pursue. The Demon increased to one-half impulse velocity. The bridge officers were smiling since the navy ships were too far behind to reach them before they entered the Star Gate.

The Demon engaged their full instrument array, which increased the range for their passive and active sensors. Unfortunately, they found part of the navy fleet was stationed beyond the Star Gate and was coming at full speed toward the Star Gate from in front of them. Family ships lined up at the entrance to Star Gate since there was a required delay between ships entering the Gate. Any ship entering a Star Gate too quickly behind another ship would pass through the gate without entering hyperspace.

The Communications Officer on the Demon contacted the family ships, and they moved out of the way so the Demon could enter the Star Gate without waiting. Most ships entered a Star Gate at a slow speed since they would be going at the same velocity when they exited the gate at their destination. The captain directed the helmsman to increase to flank speed. The navy ships following the Demon had to slow down as they approached the Star Gate because the ships at the gate had moved in behind the Demon. The Demon's Communications Officer signaled they were being hailed.

The fleet commander in front of them said, "Decelerate and veer off from the Star Gate, or we'll be forced to fire."

The Demon did not respond.

"Fire two missiles," the fleet commander said and looked at his Tactical Officer.

"Sir, you're ordering us to fire on the Demon. If not for the Demon, none of us would be alive, and humanity would be extinct."

"You think I want to fire upon the Demon?" the fleet commander shouted. "I have my orders, and you have yours. Fire the missiles!"

The Tactical Officer fired the missiles. "Your orders stink," he whispered.

The bridge officers on the navy ship were upset and watched in horror as the missiles impacted the Demon. Then the entire bridge cheered when the missiles exploded harmlessly against the hull of the Demon.

The Demon hit the Star Gate dead center, going at flank speed. As soon as they entered, the family ships lined up in front of the Star Gate, giving no room for a navy ship to slip in ahead of them. They refused to move out of the way when ordered by the fleet commander.

The fleet commander turned to his first officer, who also served as his science officer, and asked, "How much reduction was there in the Demon's shields when the missiles hit?"

The officer reviewed his sensors several times before replying in bewilderment. "Sir, there was no reduction in their shields. In fact, the Demon's shields increased by over ten percent after our missiles impacted their hull. Sir, when the Demon entered the Star Gate, they were traveling twenty percent faster than our fastest navy ship and were still accelerating."

The fleet commander shook his head as he said in a whisper heard by everyone on the bridge. "We may have just made an enemy out of the most powerful ship in the Galactic. I hope to hell he'll forgive us."

The fleet commander sent a report to the Admiral. He directed the ships under his command to line up in front of the Star Gate. His new orders were to capture the Demon if possible and destroy the Demon if capture proved impossible. Two more family ships passed through the gate before the navy cleared a path by threatening to open fire on the next ship to block their approach. However, the fleet commander and the captains of the navy ships going through the gate knew it was a wasted effort since the Demon would jump as soon as they exited the gate. The fleet commander had already decided he would never again fire upon the Demon, and at the first opportunity, he would apologize to Captain Thomas Wilson. He reached that decision since their missiles would be ineffective against the Demon, and he did not want to give the Demon any reasons to retaliate. The Demon's formidable offensive weapons could destroy any shield, and now the ship had impenetrable defense capabilities. The fleet commander decided it would be insane to enter into a battle against the Demon.

The fleet commander sent a communication to all ships under his command. "None of the ships under my command are to fire upon the Demon or threaten the Demon. Any ship having a problem with my orders can return to base." Everyone under his command supported his orders. He issued those orders realizing he could be court marshaled, but he knew his communications were the only rational orders.

TWO DAYS LATER, A NAVY spy ship entered the Fidem system after most of the vessels attending the wedding had departed. Agent Sicarius reported to Admiral Nelson but had come at the request of Thomas Wilson. Thomas had directed Agent Sicarius to go to a set of coordinates on Fidem. He took a shuttle to the coordinates and landed next to a warehouse. The communication included a set of codes he entered into a pad next to a door. He walked down a hallway and keyed in the same code to another door. The Agent walked into a large warehouse containing rows of rooms. After several hours he identified the spies who worked for the military and a separate group of spies for the government. He released the military spies first. He pulled up dossiers on each military spy and noted they were supposed to be exceptionally good. Agent Sicarius seldom found anything humorous in his line of work, but he smiled as the prisoners described what had happened. Next, he released the government spies, and they had comparable stories. Then he released the third group and turned them over to the government spies. Sicarius saw additional prisoners had been housed in cells that were now empty, but all information on them had been removed. One of the navy spies said the missing individuals were the ones who had kidnapped the daughter of Thomas Wilson. Sicarius had reviewed the vids from the prior news reports and figured Thomas had given them what they deserved.

Agent Sicarius notified Admiral Nelson, and he sent shuttles to transport the navy spies to his ship and transport the government spies along with their prisoners to the city. The Admiral ordered the Agent to come aboard his ship to discuss the current issues concerning Thomas Wilson.

Agent Sicarius went aboard Admiral Nelson's ship and joined him in his ready room. After getting a cup of coffee, he took a seat and realized the Admiral was very unhappy. The Admiral described how the Demon had left the system, and they could not locate the ship. He further told how they had sent a spy ship to the Hostis location for the peace conference, but it arrived at a remote area of space far from any system.

"I can't understand why Thomas would do this?" the Admiral asked.

"I believe you may understand after listening to this recording," the Agent replied.

The Agent replayed the recording from Thomas that contained the conversation between the Admiral and the Premier. The recording was followed by a message from Thomas. He would meet with the Hostis to explore the possibility of achieving peace between their two species, and he knew any agreement for peace would have to be approved by the Senate.

The Admiral was solemn. "We have underestimated Captain Wilson once again. Our spies are not as good as we thought."

"Yes, you and the Premier underestimated Captain Wilson. However, our spies are good, but not as good as his. Also, if you or the Premier decide to terminate Captain Wilson, don't ask me to do it."

The Admiral was puzzled. "Are you developing a conscience?"

The Agent gave him an angry stare. "I've always had a conscience. Over the years, I've killed individuals for you, but all the deaths were good for humanity, and they were deplorable people with little to no redeeming qualities. That is why I can sleep at night. So, if there ever comes a time you want Captain Wilson eliminated, you'll need to call upon one of your other agents. First, you must decide if you are loyal to humanity or only to the Premier."

The Agent's comment had gotten to the Admiral. He always felt he supported humanity. Would he do what the Premier wanted even if it went against the interests of the human race?

Admiral Nelson said, "We have an additional problem. I just sent a report to the Premier. The Demon now has impenetrable shields."

Admirable Nelson showed the recent vids of the Demon's escape to Agent Sicarius. "It appears Captain Wilson has not only solved the ancient's language but has used their technology to make his ship invincible."

"Be thankful," Sicarius said with a smirk, "the Demon did not fire on the fleet."

"The Premier is no longer rational. His greed for power has mushroomed. He wants the Demon's technology and Thomas' death. When I mentioned Thomas was still committed to reaching a peace settlement with the Hostis, he said to hell with a peace treaty. He demanded we capture the Demon ship. Then, use it immediately to attack and destroy the Hostis. Even after seeing the vids, he doesn't seem to realize the Demon could defeat the entire navy."

"Were the scientists able to reverse engineer the four missiles we received from Captain Wilson?"

The Admiral shook his head. "A lab technician tried to cut into one of the missiles, and the missile self-destructed. The lab was destroyed along with the remaining missiles and the scientists. From this point on, I'll support Thomas when there is a conflict with the Premier, but I'll do it covertly. Try to get that message to Thomas but be discrete. I want you to leak the information to the Senate concerning the Demon's role in the battle with the Hostis and the betrayal by the Premier, but it must not lead back to me."

Sicarius nodded. "I'll take care of it. Several of the government spies just released are loyal to the Premier's opposition party."

"We still need to obtain the technology Thomas is using, but we need to get it without further alienating anyone in the Wilson family. We need spies at each of Wilson Enterprises shipyards. Doctor Adler onboard the Demon has continued to provide the occasional encrypted report but has failed to provide any relevant information on the advanced technology. Have you had any success in getting spies onboard the Demon?"

"Yes, but they don't last long," Sicarius said. "Every time they try to get relevant information, their employment is terminated. Once caught, they are escorted off the ship at the next port of call and provided with sufficient credit to provide temporary living expenses. I have one spy still onboard with instructions to do his job and observe only."

ONBOARD THE BEAUMONT, Thomas met with his officers. They were still a little confused with the promotions they had received while en route to the Demon. All bridge officers now held the rank of captain, and all the engineers were promoted to chief engineer.

The Demon and the Beaumont met at the designated rendezvous, which happened to be the navy ship graveyard. The junior officers remained on the Demon. Thomas contacted Director Juno, who was in charge of renovating the retired navy ships or what he jokingly called resurrecting the dead. Thomas received a status report for each ship currently being renovated.

The scientists and researchers on the Beaumont were shuttled to the Demon. The Demon personnel onboard the Beaumont were delivered to the graveyard space station. It was currently being used to house the Wilson Enterprises work crews. The station was huge since it previously had been used to house a military contingent.

Thomas gave Captain Acosta new orders, and the Beaumont departed. The Beaumont would pick up thousands of individuals who had accepted ship assignments and were currently completing advanced training for various onboard positions.

Thomas asked Juno for a status report. "We've overhauled and upgraded sixty cruisers as requested. We're at various stages of conversion on over two hundred destroyers. The destroyers will be transferred to the smallest of Wilson Enterprises shipyards for the final buildout. We will continue to locate and rebuild the ships with similar armaments. Looking over the inventory of ships, I believe we will be able to upgrade two hundred cruisers and over five hundred destroyers at a reasonable cost. The other ships are much older, and it would be cheaper to build new ones. There are also four battleships."

"I did not realize there were battleships."

The Director laughed and humorously asked, "Do you want me to refurbish the four battleships so you can have a proper fleet?"

"That is an excellent idea," Thomas said, "but complete the cruisers and destroyers first." The Director saw Thomas was serious. The Director wondered what Thomas planned to do with battleships. Converting the cruisers and destroyers to handle cargo in the Rim made sense because of the pirates and marauders, but the sole purpose of a battleship was to conduct war.

Thomas brought up the data on the cruisers and quickly selected twenty of the retired cruisers of the same design and the newest of the old ships. He went to the central computer room of the Demon and accessed the sealed computer room. Omnia used the nanites to create a temporary door. Without a permanent doorway, no one had physical access to Omnia or the ship's primary AI.

Omnia greeted him. "As requested, forty Crystals are ready for placement within twenty ships. I monitored your search, and I agree with your ship selections. It will be awhile before the Crystals reach a nominal size, but they are fully sentient and have already been separated into groups of two. They have my full knowledge but will now develop their own experiences as separate entities. Also, the micro nanites are fully controlled and are ready for deployment."

Omnia, as the sentient backup AI, was connected directly to the ship's primary AI. During the ship's renovation, raw materials were brought to the central processing area when requested and left in the adjourning room. Omnia used the materials as needed to add to the ship's functionality. He had modified the medical nanites to create additional micro nanites. Modifying the medical nanites was easier and quicker than making originals. Omnia had created crates to transport the micro nanites to the twenty designated cruisers. The most advanced AI computers had already been installed on all sixty cruisers. These primary AI computers had been specially constructed with prepared slots for the addition of the living Crystals, but no one except Thomas knew the purpose of the slots. Thomas took the Crystals and exited the inner room. Omnia resealed the room, with the door again becoming part of the wall.

In the outer room, Thomas was shortly joined by the most trusted members of his crew. He described their mission, and they each grabbed two satchels and accompanied him to the shuttle bay.

They took a shuttle to the first cruiser and disembarked. Each crew member had their assignment to disburse the micro nanites to key areas within the ship, including the inner hull, outer hull, impulse engines, jump engines, and shields. Thomas went to the ship's AI and inserted the two Crystals in the slots. He then discharged micro nanites over the primary AI and the Crystals. Thomas and his selected crew conducted the same exercise on the twenty selected cruisers. They worked double shifts, but it still took them four days to complete the work. It would have taken less time, but they proceeded in complete secrecy and used the primary AI on each ship to monitor all activity on the ship to prevent anyone from being aware of their actions. Thomas was the only person aware of the living Crystals. Once installed, the access to the central computer room in each ship was eliminated, with the nanites merging the prior opening with the wall. The Crystals would create a new door if needed in the future.

The newly promoted captains took shuttles to their appointed cruisers. Onboard the Demon was a skeleton crew of junior officers, the new crew from the Familia Primum, eighty adult Oceanums, the six Oceanum children, and Thomas' family. Thomas had assigned two Oceanums to each of the sixty ships since they could use their mental abilities to detect spies or anyone who might want to sabotage one of the ships. The Oceanums would report directly to the captains of their assigned ships. The Oceanums had done an excellent job locating spies who signed on with the Demon or became spies when offered incentives by outside agencies.

Thomas told his newly promoted captains to have their ship crewed and operational upon his return. Just as he was leaving the station, he received a message from Captain Acosta. He was inbound with the first shipload of recruits. Captain Acosta would stay just long enough to deliver the recruits before heading out to pick up more individuals.

Thomas returned to the Demon and went to the bridge. He congratulated everyone for their excellent job in escaping the navy. Thomas temporarily relieved the helmsman and entered new jump coordinates.

Thomas returned to the captain's chair. "Accelerate to jump velocity." The junior officers were surprised they had not been relieved by senior officers.

Thomas was reviewing the ship's log when the helmsman announced. "We're at jump velocity."

"Engage," Thomas said with a concerned expression. Much needed to be done, and he was worried he would not be ready in time.

Thomas decided it was time to make an announcement to the bridge officers. "If you're wondering, all of you have been promoted. Congratulations, you are no longer junior officers. He reassigned some of the promoted officers to Middle Watch and Night Watch. He assigned the recently added crew from the Familia Primum to bridge positions on each watch. He promoted various Oceanums to fill the remaining bridge openings. He made similar promotions to fill the vacancies in engineering and maintenance. Then he made additional postings for everyone else on the ship.

After the postings, he sent a ship wide communication. "Please check your wrist communicators. Everyone has been given permanent promotional assignments on the Demon. Please report to your positions on your assigned watch. We are currently shorthanded, but I hope to pick up additional officers and crew when we return to the graveyard. Suzanna Wilson, please report to the Bridge."

When Suzanna arrived, Thomas said, "I forgot during all the excitement. You are now the Demon's first officer." Suzanna gave him a passionate kiss before she sat down in the first officer's seat.

"In our marriage vows, you promised to follow my orders," Thomas said.

"You are correct. I'll always follow your orders." After a short pause, she said, "While on the bridge."

The young bridge officers were grinning and doing their best not to laugh. Several officers put their hands over their mouth and looked away. Everyone not invited to the wedding had watched it on their monitors and had paid particular attention to the wedding vows.

The Demon came out of jump near Hermosa. Thomas directed the helmsman to approach and enter the asteroid belt. The bridge officers knew nine ships had hidden in the asteroid belt on their previous visit. They were concerned when their sensors detected an unknown number of vessels within the asteroids.

The tactical officer was waiting for the call to battle stations when the communications officer said, "Sir, there is a Captain Erling who wishes to talk to you." Thomas signaled her to put the call on the viewscreen so everyone could listen to the conversation.

"Captain Erling, I'm here to claim the ore you've been processing for me."

"Captain Wilson, I'm happy to see you. The other miners were beginning to question if my contract was real or an excellent forgery. How would you like to take delivery?"

"I'm sending you a list of ore I want delivered to our cargo bay and the ore I want positioned against the hull."

Captain Erling reviewed the list. "That is a strange request., but I have twenty-three mining vessels with old miners who will be happy to handle your request." It only took two days for the delivery of the ore.

The micro nanites were spread throughout the ship. The original medical nanites were able to travel throughout the human body, repairing cells, rebuilding organs, and regrowing limbs. These modified micro nanites could rebuild an entire ship as directed by Omnia. The nanites broke down the delivered ore and used it to expand the Demon. A new hull was built around the Demon and integrated with the existing hull. The crew were directed to safe areas within the ship while the construction was taking place. The ore was used to create billions of additional nanites to speed up the teardown and rebuild.

When complete, the ship was four times its prior size. The armament was more than four times as great. The two railguns had increased to eight with four pointed toward the bow and four to the stern. There were twenty-six rapid-fire particle beam cannons mounted on turrets with full rotation, eighteen missile launchers, sixteen torpedo tubes, and four laser batteries. Each laser battery was more than double the size of the prior battery. Four Demon insignias were displayed on the outer hull. There were four cargo bays with over six thousand rack spaces and two shuttle bays. Every area in the ship had additional rooms, including the number of cabins. There were dining facilities, exercise areas, training centers, and entertainment areas throughout the ship. The size and number of engines had increased.

Thomas was surprised at how fast the ship had been expanded. Omnia had simply taken the existing human technology and improved upon it while incorporating the defensive and offensive technology of the Ancients. Omnia had also improved upon the body armor and created thousands of additional suits. The existing shuttles were upgraded.

The miners, as directed, had brought in large chunks of ice. The ice was purified before being broken down into solid hydrogen and solid oxygen for delivery of water as needed throughout the ship. The tanks for the nutrients used by the food processors had been previously filled, but the miners brought in additional nutrients to fill newly created tanks.

All the ore not used in modifying the Demon was placed in containers and loaded into the cargo bay. Suzanna transferred credits to pay the miners for the delivered ore. Captain Erling received a ten percent fee for the ore provided by the other ships. One captain grumbled about the ten percent, but Captain Erling told him a corporation would have taken half. The complaining captain agreed but said he had to complain about something, or everyone would think he was going soft. Captain Erling and the other miners were ecstatic with the credits they earned. They enjoyed the camaraderie of their fellow miners. Hermosa was only three days away and was available for supplies and relaxation. Still, they preferred to drink and socialize with each other even during shore leave. Captain Erling had hired three older miners for his ship, and they enjoyed working together.

Thomas asked Captain Erling if he and the other miners would like to continue mining the asteroids. It would typically have taken them five or more standard years to earn the credits they had just received. Captain Erling decided he no longer wished to retire, and all the miners decided they would continue mining as long as Thomas bought the ore. Thomas told them additional ships would pick up the processed ore on a regular schedule.

As an additional subterfuge, Thomas had Omnia change the logos on the outside of the ship to Demon Two. The size of the Demon logos was increased to match the increased size of the ship. During the Demon's modifications, the crew had been moved to a central part of the ship. They had not seen the changes being made to the Demon. The crew moved around the ship in a daze once Thomas told them to return to their workstations.

Thomas and his officers were on the bridge. Amanda sat in her seat next to Thomas. Suzanna held Daniel in a new first officer's seat with an attached baby seat. The navigator plotted the course, and the helmsman slowly brought the Demon out of the asteroid belt.

Once they cleared the belt, the Demon increased speed and reached sufficient velocity to engage the jump engines. The helmsman looked at Thomas, and Thomas nodded his head. The transition to jump was smooth. Suzanna left the bridge with Daniel and Amanda. Thomas and his officers ran simulations to verify that every component on the ship was in the green and fully operational.

The officers on the bridge seemed to have everything under control. Thomas decided to see if Suzanna and Amanda would like to join him for dinner. They asked him to come to their cabin first. When he stepped inside the cabin, he was astonished. Suzanna and Amanda were grinning.

"Surprise," they said together.

They showed him around the newly expanded cabin. Amanda and Daniel had their own separate bedrooms and bathrooms. There were two separate side-by-side offices, a playroom obviously designed by Amanda, and a small kitchen.

"With the increased size of the ship, there is plenty of extra space," Suzanna said. "Amanda surprised me when she created a playroom. I asked her how she created the room, and she told me Omnia helped her. Then, we both worked together with Omnia to create the other rooms. One day, you'll have to tell me more about Omnia and how she was able to grow our ship." Thomas noticed the rooms were exquisitely decorated.

Thomas spoke to Omnia, and they decided it was time to share a secret with Suzanna since she was his first officer and second in command. "Omnia can control nanites similar to the AI computers in the healing chambers. The nanites in the healing chambers heal the body and grow missing body parts. Omnia uses similar nanites to repair, modify, and grow the ship. However, we need to keep it a secret."

Thomas told the crew, if anyone asked, that Demon Two was built at the fourth shipyard of Wilson Enterprises at a secret location. The crew knew never to discuss the ship's details with outsiders unless Thomas approved. The miners agreed to maintain their secret, but Thomas knew it was only time until they told stories over drinks. However, most listeners would think the miners were making up a good story.

The Demon arrived at the third and smallest shipyard of Wilson Enterprises. However, they had expanded the shipyard, which was now slightly larger than the other two shipyards. As soon as the Demon came out of hyperspace, Thomas contacted the shipyard's Senior Vice-President to transfer all completed starfighters to the Demon. As soon as they docked, the fighters were waiting. Thomas noticed a fleet of old destroyers had already arrived and were being inspected to determine what upgrades were needed to finish the ships. As soon as the fighters were loaded and secured, the Demon left the docks, achieved jump velocity, and entered hyperspace. Omnia went to work upgrading the fighters.

THE DEMON EXITED JUMP at Melius. Half the cruisers were already there. The cruisers had already visited Wilson Enterprises' third shipyard and picked up ten shuttles each. The shuttles were military-grade and fully armed. The shuttles were busy transporting cargo and munitions from the warehouses on Melius to the ships. Thomas had been stockpiling munitions for years in the warehouses they had been leasing. The crews were busy securing the cargo and using the munitions to load the missile tubes, torpedo tubes, and magazines for the cannons. The ships were being fully stocked with the nutrients for their food processors. Also, they were also being loaded with trade goods.

Thomas was pleased to see the exterior of the sentient cruisers had been changed to look similar to Demon. They look entirely new, and no one would guess they were retired vessels from the navy's graveyard.

Additional officers and crew were brought onboard Demon Two. However, no one had expected the Demon would be four times its previous size. Demon Two would continue to be understaffed. Thomas was disappointed in the time it took for all the ships to be loaded and ready for departure.

Three ships were filled with machines, equipment, and personnel to increase the manufacturing facilities on Desetum in the Outer Planets and the new corporate planet in the Rim.

Thomas directed all the ships to jump to the closest arms manufacturer. The chief operating officer for the arms manufacturer was surprised at the number of vessels. The arms manufacturer normally only sold to the navy, but Thomas had been given a waiver and was their largest purchaser. Thomas told the Officer he was purchasing their entire inventory. The Officer was delighted to make such a large sale and asked Thomas what was happening.

"It's top secret, but we're preparing to travel into Hostis space," Thomas said. "Make sure no one communicates with anyone outside this facility."

"I understand, and you have my word. No one will know you were here. Good luck."

All the shuttles from each ship participated in loading the arms. This time they loaded up every missile, torpedo, and other munitions used in ship combat.

As soon as everything was secured, the Demon and the sixty cruisers jumped to the second arms manufacturer and purchased their entire inventory. Thomas found it surprising that Admiral Nelson had not contacted the arms manufacturers to withdraw the Demon's waiver and felt relieved when they loaded the last container.

Thomas decided he did not want the ships to make such a long jump with the new inexperienced crews. The longer the jump, the greater the chance of deviation from the destination. It would be easier to locate a ship with a problem over a shorter jump. Therefore, he decided to use a Section Star Gate for transportation from the Core Planets to the Outer Planets. Then, they would use a Section Star Gate for travel from the Outer Planets to the Rim. Once in the Rim, they would use their jump engines for the shorter jumps to deliver their cargo to the Rim Worlds.

The Demon, accompanied by the sixty cruisers, jumped to the Section Gate for the long jump to the Outer Planets. The four navy destroyers guarding the gate moved out of the way when they saw the size of the armada approaching the gate, but they reported the incident to Admiral Nelson.

All the ships made it safely through the Sector Star Gate. The three ships loaded with the equipment, machines, and supplies for the corporate planet were directed to jump directly to Desetum. Thomas gave orders for all the remaining vessels to make the short jump to the Section Gate connecting the Outer Planets to the Rim.

Once Thomas affirmed all ships had arrived safely at the Section Gate, he told them Demon would enter the gate first and wait on the other side. The twenty cruisers with the living sentient Crystals would come through the gate last. This would provide the best protection for the forty ships without the technology of the Ancients. They had already paired each sentient ship with two standard cruisers. Thomas felt the navy would be less lightly to fire upon a group of three cruisers when one was impervious to the navy's arsenal. Thomas hoped to have all his ships through the Sector Star Gate to the Rim without confrontation with the navy, but his luck failed. The main navy fleet was identified on the Demon's sensors. Thomas moved Demon Two forward, with the cruisers moving into battle position slightly behind the Demon as each one came through the gate.

The navigator informed Thomas the navy had reduced their speed before coming to a stop. They were not expecting to meet a fleet of ships and were confused by the size of Demon Two. This helped considerably. By the time the navy fleet renewed their approach, all the cruisers had made it through the gate. Thomas directed the sentient cruisers to move forward into a support position but slightly behind the Demon. The regular cruisers filled the holes between the sentient ships so that all their vessels had a clear line of fire.

Thomas directed all ships to increase the power of their forward shields, but his orders were for none of their cruisers to target a navy ship. All guns were kept cold but could be powered up quickly if needed.

Admiral Nelson contacted Thomas. "You've been busy. I see you have refurbished some of our old cruisers. However, you failed to tell us you were building a Demon Battleship and new Cruisers using the advanced technology of the Ancients."

Thomas knew Admiral Nelson was guessing as to the use of the technology, but he confirmed the Admiral's guess.

"My family has three shipyards, but I have a separate ship-building facility." It would be better if the Admiral spent his time trying to find a nonexistent facility instead of focusing on their existing shipyards. "My Battleship and the new Cruisers incorporate advanced offensive and defensive capabilities. All my ships are on a peaceful mission to trade with the Rim Worlds. We plan to protect the Rim from pirates and marauders. Also, when we've stabilized trade within the Rim, I plan to visit the Hostis and try to negotiate a peace agreement."

The Admiral was cautious. "Hypothetically, what if I decide to arrest you for possession of the technology of the Ancients?"

Thomas directed one of the sentient cruisers to move forward. "Admiral Nelson, one of our new cruisers, has moved forward for a demonstration. You have my permission to fire a missile at the cruiser."

A single missile impacted the ship with no effect other than to increase the ship's shield strength.

"It appears my hypothetically is moot."

"Admiral, other than your assumption, we are using restricted technology, we have broken no laws. We're attempting to advance the living conditions of humans in the Outer Planets and the Rim. Also, we're protecting the Core Planets by serving as a deterrent to any future incursions by the Hostis. I would hope you and the Senate would support such an undertaking."

Admiral Nelson knew he had to be careful. He should not have threatened to arrest Thomas when he did not have the military might to accomplish such a feat.

"Your goals seem worthy, but such power in the hands of a civilian is problematic."

Thomas interrupted and raised his voice. "Such power in the hands of a naval officer or a Premier could also be problematic."

Thomas wanted to say, 'Especially a Premier who has clearly stated his desire for my death and the confiscation of the technology I am using. A Premier who has further stated he does not want peace but would rather have war.' With extreme difficulty, Thomas kept his mouth closed and did not say such treasonous thoughts.

The Admiral was upset Thomas had challenged him over an open channel and changed tactics. "We both have the same goals for humanity. Will you at least share the technology?"

"I previously provided you with four missiles. Your scientists should have figured out that the same technology can be used for defense and offense. In both cases, energy is absorbed. Offensively, the energy is absorbed and then released in an explosion.

Defensively, the energy is absorbed and used to strengthen the shields."

Admiral Nelson decided to tell the truth. "There was an accident. One missile exploded and destroyed the other missiles. Our scientists failed to reverse-engineer the technology. Again, will you share the technology?"

Now Thomas was in a predicament. He did not want anyone knowing about Omnia or any of the other sentient computer crystals but knew he had to give the Admiral something of value.

"Admiral, I'll give you another missile and a small section of our hull. Your scientists should have no problems figuring out the technology. If the Hostis attack again, we'll join you in defending humanity. I plan to visit the Hostis since they contacted me personally to explore the possibility of peace. First, our ships are fully loaded, and we wish to proceed with the delivery of our cargo to the Rim Worlds."

Suzanna had one missile of the Ancients carefully packed in a box. The hull section was packed in a smaller box and stowed in the container with the missiles. Omnia replaced the section on the hull. Thomas contacted Admiral Nelson and let him know a shuttle was delivering the items to his Battleship.

Admiral Nelson asked Thomas if he could visit with him onboard Demon Two. Thomas knew he needed to accede to the Admiral's request to avoid increasing the rift with the navy.

"Our shuttle delivering the missile will be happy to convey you and some of your officers to Demon Two," Thomas said. "Admiral Nelson knew he had been outmaneuvered. He had intended to visit the Demon using one of the navy's unique shuttles with advanced sensors and probes.

The Demon Two shuttle made the delivery and picked up Admiral Nelson with a contingent of his officers. Thomas met the shuttle when it arrived in the shuttle bay. The Admiral had brought along six officers.

"Admiral Nelson, welcome aboard. I apologize for not having a more formal welcome, but we're quite busy."

Admiral Nelson and his officers were overwhelmed by what they were seeing. His chief engineer had already made positive comments regarding the shuttle, but now they saw hundreds of starfighters. Thomas decided to address the fighters before the Admiral started asking questions.

"The fighters you see were built in anticipation of a future order by the navy. You lost over half your fighters during the recent battle with the Hostis. We assumed you would want to replace those losses. My understanding is the appropriation budget for your fighters is still in committee. The starfighters were piling up at my private shipyard, so I agreed to put a portion of them onboard Demon Two. This gave them space for the additional starfighters being built." The Admiral and his officers were already walking toward the fighters. Thomas had no choice except to go with them. Thomas had the canopy withdrawn on one of the fighters so they could look inside the cockpit. One officer climbed into the cockpit, and the seat automatically adjusted to a form fit. The harness wrapped around him, and everything inside the cockpit adjusted for maximum positioning around the pilot. Then the instrument panel lit up. The navy officer was in love.

"I apologize," Thomas said. "The ship has an advanced AI with an embedded desire to fly. As soon as you sat down, it became operational. It'll be disappointed when I explain you just wanted to perform an inspection."

"I'm Wing Commander Gilbert, and the controls are readily obvious. You must let me fly this fighter." There was a pause, and then he said, "Please."

Thomas made a quick decision and nodded his head. He contacted the flight deck crew, and they cleared a path for the starfighter. Thomas was going to advise Commander Griffen but decided the guy was an experienced aviator. Also, he might be insulted if Thomas started giving him advice, especially since Thomas had never flown a fighter. The starfighter exited Demon Two.

Thomas gave an extended tour of the ship. The navy's chief engineer was gleefully excited when he saw the engine rooms. The navy's Tactical Officer had questions. Thomas could answer most of the questions, and he queried Omnia for the more difficult questions. Thomas truthfully said he did not know the answer to some of the technical questions, but they assumed he did not want to tell them.

The tour had gone on for several hours. "Wing Commander Gilbert has returned," Thomas said. "Lunch has been prepared in my Ready Room. My first officer will join us. It will provide us with privacy for discussing other matters."

They had just sat down when the Wing Commander Gilbert joined them. He was grinning, and his entire face was glowing.

"We were beginning to think you weren't coming back," the Admiral said.

"Admiral, I spent a little time getting used to the controls. One of our squadrons was practicing maneuvers, so I challenged them to a dogfight. They initially joked about taking it easy on the old man. First, it was one against one, but it ended too quickly. Then it was two on one. Finally, I challenged the entire squadron of twelve fighters and offered the winner free drinks for a year. Everyone in our fleet placed bets on how long I'd last."

"Well, Ace, who won the drink bet?"

"No one sir, I beat the entire squadron. Only one fighter got a temporary lock, but the AI initiated a short jump on its own. Sir, the fighter I just flew has short-range jump capability."

Everyone in the room was quiet when one of the navy officers said, "Unbelievable!"

"How far can it jump?" the chief engineer asked.

"The AI said the maximum range was a hundred meters. Whatever it takes, you must get the Senate to approve an appropriation for these advanced starfighters."

Thomas lowered his voice as he communicated with Omnia. "You should have told me the fighters had jump capability."

"You were busy," Omnia replied. "I sent you a text with the changes I made to the fighters." Thomas rolled his eyes and made the best of the situation. Again, a miniature jump engine could point toward the technology of the Ancients. He pulled up the text from Omnia and reviewed a summary of the capabilities of the modified starfighter.

"Admiral, we have two classes of fighters. Both classes are similar in outward appearance. We manufacture the fighters at Shipyard Number 3. We then transported a portion of the fighters to my fourth Shipyard to install the miniature jump engines, the AI upgrade, and the replacement of the cockpit seat. Our standard fighter is better than your existing fighters and is comparably priced. In comparison, the advanced starfighter with jump capability and the additional upgrades is five times the price. I'd be happy to sell you the fighter used in the dogfight at half price if you'd like to use it as a sample to gain Senate support." Thomas had used the markup figure of five even though the upgrades were being installed by Omnia at no cost.

The look on the faces of his wing commander and his chief engineer made it clear they wanted him to purchase the fighter. It would give their scientists and engineers another opportunity to reverse engineer the advanced technology.

Thomas then remembered. "Sir, the sixteen miniature missiles on the starfighter are small but deadly, so are the bullets in the guns. They operate on the same principles as our torpedoes but on a smaller scale. The tracking is also enhanced. Oh, I forgot to mention, it has a small shield generator."

Now the wing commander was drooling. None of the navy's fighters had jump capability or shielding.

The Admiral knew he had no choice. "We'll buy it!"

The Admiral wondered what other technology Thomas might be hiding. The meal was served, but no one was paying attention to the quality of the food. The wing commander could not wait to try out one of the missiles and the guns. The Demon officers were cordial, but the navy obtained no additional information. Every navy officer in the room realized the navy could not match the fleet Thomas had put together in such a brief time.

"I'd like to visit the shipyard that built Demon Two, the starfighters, and the new Cruisers," the navy's chief engineer said.

"Maybe in the future, but for security reasons, we're keeping the location a secret for now." The chief engineer frowned but understood.

The Admiral, in a desperation ploy, spoke up. "With the technology you have, the navy should provide security for your secret shipyard."

"Admiral," Thomas calmly replied. "No one will be able to locate our fourth shipyard since it does not show up on sensors, which makes it invisible. Also, we're quite capable of dealing with any threat. Our hidden shipyard has the same offensive and defensive capabilities as the ships we've been building. Also, there is a matter of trust. The Premier expressed his desire for my death, and you did not object when he made the comment."

The navy officers in the room were shocked at the revelation. They noted the Admiral did not dispute the allegation. They consumed the balance of the meal in silence.

Admiral Nelson paid honor to Thomas at the end of the meal. "Admiral Wilson, thank you for your hospitality. Please let me know when you plan to enter Hostis space."

The navy officers were escorted from the room and taken to the shuttle bay. Wing Commander Gilbert flew the fighter to the navy battleship. The rest of the navy officers returned by shuttle.

When the Admiral was back on board his ship, he sent a secure message to Agent Sicarius. He summarized the recent meeting onboard Demon Two. He ordered Sicarius to drop all other missions and locate the fourth shipyard.

Admiral Nelson called a staff meeting to get their assessment of Admiral Wilson and his ships. He wanted to see if their observations matched his own. They all expressed their displeasure with the Premier's desire to kill Thomas.

"Sir, Admiral Wilson's new ships are phenomenal," the chief engineer said. "They have control over energy. They have single missiles that can destroy any size ship. They have a defense shield that uses a missile attack to strengthen their shields. We could not defeat the smaller Demon One ship. Now they have a Demon Battleship, twenty new cruisers, plus starfighters with jump capabilities and shields. I hate to say it, but our entire navy is obsolete."

The Tactical Officer spoke up. "Sir, if not for the Demon and Thomas Wilson, we'd have lost the battle with the Hostis. Admiral Wilson is eliminating the pirate threat, something the navy has been trying to do for hundreds of years. Not once has he done anything except support humanity. From a tactical perspective, the navy cannot defeat Admiral Wilson's fleet. It would not surprise me if just one of his ships could destroy our entire navy. With his support, humanity no longer has to fear the Hostis. Why does the Premier or the navy want to kill him?"

Everyone looked at Admiral Nelson for a response. "The Premier feels it is too much power in the hands of a civilian. Thomas is using the technology of the Ancients, and he hasn't turned over the technology to the government. Against the wishes of the Premier, Thomas wants to enter into a peace agreement with the Hostis. Instead, the Premier desires to eliminate their entire species."

"Sir, Thomas gave us another of his missiles and we have one of his new starfighters," the helmsman said. "Surely our scientists can reverse engineer the gifts he has given us."

Admiral Nelson shook his head. He didn't tell them how their best scientists failed to gain any useful tech before the previous missiles exploded. He was doubtful they could reverse engineer the starfighter.

Another officer said what many of them were thinking. "Sir, I hate the Hostis. I have friends who died in the recent battle. I have no problem meeting the Hostis in battle and defeating them. However, I have a problem killing the Hostis civilians even though they have no problem killing human civilians." Heads were nodding around the table. The discussions were not going as intended by the Admiral, and he ended the meeting.

Admiral Nelson reluctantly contacted the Premier and provided a more detailed report on his meeting with Thomas. The Premier became enraged and again stated the need to get all the technology being used by Thomas. The Premier let the Admiral know his leadership in the Senate was being challenged.

"I'm ordering you to use whatever means are necessary to get the technology and kill Thomas Wilson," the Premier shouted in anger. "You can start by finding the secret shipyard. It is impossible to hide an entire shipyard."

Admiral Nelson could not understand how the Premier failed to understand the navy fleet would not stand a chance against even one of the new ships Thomas Wilson had under his command. Plus, regrettably, Thomas was right to question their trust.

THEIR COMMUNICATION SENSORS had been enhanced by the Hostis technology combined with Omnia's help. Omnia had intercepted the discussion between Admiral Nelson and the Premier. Thomas and his officers were in the Ready Room discussing trade when they listened to the dialog.

"Thomas, never trust the Premier or the Admiral," Suzanna said. The other officers in the room were nodding their agreement.

During the continuation of the meeting, they decided which ships would visit each planet. During the visits, the planets would be offered the chance to join the Rim Trade Alliance. The Alliance would provide lists of exports for each location and the imports desired. There would be no costs for membership.

Each group of three ships was assigned six planets to visit. Demon Two would visit the planets with the greatest needs. The Demon would also serve as a supply depot for the other ships.

Thomas was on the bridge when they engaged their jump engines. He wondered why Suzanna, his new first officer, was not present. It was the early part of Day Watch when he received a call from Suzanna asking him to come to their cabin. Suzanna had no problem getting the crew to watch Daniel and Amanda.

Thomas arrived at their cabin and saw Suzanna sitting in the middle of the bed wearing the sexiest outfit he had ever seen. The cabin door closed, and they were in a highly realistic holographic forest scene with a beautiful sunset. The bed overlooked a lake surrounded by trees and flowers. It was twilight, and the stars were just coming out.

"The wedding was wonderful," Suzanna said. "I enjoyed it despite my misgivings. We've had eight wonderful years together and two beautiful children. We were too busy escaping on our wedding night to have a romantic evening. Tonight will be the first night we have sex as a married couple, and I wanted it to be special. Your sister gave me this very naughty outfit." She was smiling mischievously. "Do you like it?"

Thomas' body was already responding. "I love it, and I love you."

She ran her tongue over her lips, and that was all the encouragement Thomas needed. Thomas took off his boots and climbed into bed. Suzanna helped him remove the rest of his clothes. Thomas ran his hands over her outfit, which was incredibly smooth, just like her skin. She moved her hands over his well-developed chest, across his flat stomach, and further down his body. She delighted in his response to her touch. Their lips found each other, and their kiss became more passionate. Their hearts were racing as they embraced each other and became one. Afterward, they were completely spent, as they lay on their back, watching the stars. Their empathic abilities had increased, and they could feel the love they shared.

"I think I'm going to enjoy married life," Thomas said. "How did you create this environment?"

"I had a little help from Omnia."

"It seems real."

Suzanna had additional bedroom outfits she received as wedding presents and knew Thomas would like them. She found out Omnia could create an infinite number of realistic settings. Suzanna rolled over on her side and put a leg and arm across the man she loved.

CHAPTER 15 SHIP OF THE ANCIENTS

D emon Two had visited nine planets and off-loaded cargo a dozen times to other ships. Three of the planets they visited no longer held human life. They had just come out of their tenth jump. As they approached the planet, they saw a site no one had seen in hundreds of years. They were all staring at a moon-sized Terraformer. It was one of the most incredible feats in human history. A Terraformer could bring life to a dead planet. Five Terraformers had been built by bringing modules through a Star Gate. Then each Terraformer took hundreds of workers five years to assemble the modules into one giant Terraformer. The Terraformers were primary targets during the Hostis War. Everyone believed all the Terraformers had been destroyed.

The Terraformer was in a geosynchronous orbit around the planet. A Terraformer held an unknown number of advanced technologies. They also contained highly advanced sensors and an advanced artificial intelligence unit. The entire ship was fully automated. A Terraformer was powerful enough to move a planet into a new orbit, change its rotation and its angle of inclination. It contained billions of seeds, insect larvae, and embryos for every form of life to create a planet capable of supporting human life. Terraformers were designed for perpetual life. The Communications Officer called their Life Science Officer to the bridge. The Officer took only a minute before declaring the Terraformer to be over twenty-six hundred years old.

"A Terraformer operates independently and is fully automated," the Life Science Officer said. "Once it has completed terraforming a planet, it shuts down and waits until a crew comes to direct it to the next planet to be terraformed. If the planet is too far away, it is separated into its component modules, transported to a new planet, and reassembled. It is extremely powerful, and while it does not have jump engines, it can achieve near-light speed. Typically, if the next planet is less than ten light years away, it is quicker to have the ship travel the distance unmanned. This is a real find. I'd like to take a team over and inspect the ship."

Thomas gave his approval for a team to explore the Terraformer, and he authorized Grayson to explore the planet. After five standard days, the two groups were prepared to give their reports.

Grayson gave the first report. "The planet is a virtual paradise. The ecosystem is in perfect balance. The air is perfect, the freshwater lakes are perfect, and the ocean has the perfect percentage of salt. The animal and plant life in the oceans and on land is perfect."

The Life Science Officer gave a more technical presentation but agreed with Grayson. She then explained why the planet was so perfect.

"During the terraforming in the Outer Planets and the Rim, the Terraformers were not allowed to complete their job. The programing was overridden to stop the terraforming as soon as humans could survive on a planet. In many cases, the terraforming had barely reached eighty percent. This Terraformer came here under its own power from the last planet we visited. The planet where all the colonists died. Here, no one messed with the programming, and the Terraformer did what it was programmed to do. It stopped and shut down after achieving one hundred percent of its programming. Historically, a Terraformer is always stopped when it achieves a measure in the nineties since it takes longer periods of time for each additional percent. It is referred to as diminishing returns. Sir, I recommend you let me program the Terraformer to return to the previous planet and complete the job it was designed to do. After that, it should return to all the uninhabited planets that were partially terraformed and complete the terraforming."

"I agree," Thomas answered. "How long will it take you to do the programming?"

"It'll take several months since we need to restart the ship and make sure everything is functional. There are entire warehouses of spare parts inside the Terraformer. I don't anticipate any problems getting the ship operational, but it'll take time. Sir, it'll be worth the effort. So far, we have reports of twelve worlds in the Rim and three in the Outer Planets where the entire human population has died. All of those planets were only partially terraformed. It would only take fifteen to twenty years to finish terraforming each planet. In less than three hundred years, fifteen fully terraformed planets could be available for recolonization."

Thomas nodded in agreement. "I'll assign three ships to this project. They'll provide whatever you need, but be reasonable."

"Yes sir."

"What do we do with this planet?" Thomas asked.

"Sir, there are thousands of plants and animal life on the planet that no longer exist anywhere else. A planet this perfect should not be colonized. I propose we protect the planet for as long as possible. In time, it would be good to harvest some of the extinct life on this planet and spread it to other worlds."

The three ships requested by Thomas arrived, and the captains received their instructions. They were to install a space defense grid to protect the planet and provide whatever was needed for the Terraformer to continue its mission.

Thomas was pleased with the reports he received from the captains of the cruisers. The trade within the Rim was proceeding as planned. So far, every planet they contacted agreed to become part of the Rim Trade Alliance. They were offered a free membership, protection against pirates and marauders, access to needed imports, and a market for their exports. While rim inhabitants were skeptical, they saw no downside in accepting a temporary membership with a wait-and-see approach.

Demon Two had disposed of over ninety percent of its cargo. Thomas went to the bridge, entered a set of jump coordinates, and placed the coordinates under his restricted authorization. No one else would be able to access any information concerning their destination. Demon Two entered hyperspace upon reaching the necessary velocity.

Thomas had the communications officer call his senior officers and staff for a meeting in his ready room. He invited Professor Rubin Gilbert and his group to join them. Professor Rubin Gilbert had complained regularly about the promised visit to the site of the Ancients. Thomas decided to address his complaints.

Everyone took their seats. "The convoys of our ships have their orders," Thomas said. "Each convoy has been assigned responsibility for worlds within the Rim in which they will provide trade. These convoys will continue contacting Rim Worlds until all inhabited worlds have been given the opportunity to join the Rim Trade Alliance. We will initially provide the Rim Worlds with goods on credit until they can establish markets for their exports. The Rim Worlds, with no export capability, will still be helped. The family ships will handle the trade within the Outer Planets. Trade within the Outer Planets and the Rim Worlds can operate without me for now."

"When are we going to visit the site of the Ancients?" Professor Rubin Gilbert asked.

"We just entered hyperspace with a special set of coordinates," Thomas said. "We'll come out of jump in a remote corner of space. At that location is a spacecraft of the Ancients. It is damaged but still in excellent condition, and it still has power. The Ancients' spacecraft drains energy from any ship that lands near it. At least two other spaceships close to the Ancients' Spacecraft have been drained of power. A spacer visited the site and provided me with certain information. He was not harmed or affected in any way. He escaped the fate of the other two ships by leaving before his ship was drained of power. I'll take a shuttle full of power cells to the craft. Once the power cells have been unloaded, the shuttle Pilot will leave the area and return when I signal for a pickup. Once the ship absorbs the energy from the power cells it should not need to drain power from our shuttles. At least, that is my hope. Once it stops draining power, it should be safe. If it's safe, I'll have the academics and engineers brought to the ship of the Ancients to assist in researching the technology. Our engineers will be assigned to see what we can salvage. I'll want separate teams to examine the other two spaceships. While in the ship of the Ancients, no one is to touch any buttons, turn any knobs, or do anything without my specific authorization."

Thomas gave the scientists a piercing look. "Anyone who violates my orders will be returned to the Demon and not allowed back on the ship of the Ancients. Your main assignment will be to translate any writings on the ship not previously translated. The initial goal will be to see if the writings will help us understand how to use the technology on the ship. Everyone must be cautious and take the time to proceed in the safest manner possible. Suzanna, you'll be acting captain during my absence, and Grayson will be acting first officer. Are there any questions?"

Everyone had questions and wanted to come along. Suzanna strongly objected to Thomas going to the ship, with or without anyone else.

Thomas called a halt to the questions. "There should not be any problems since an old asteroid miner visited the spacecraft and did not have a problem other than the power drain to his engines. I want the shuttle packed with as many power cells as possible. I need to go since I can read the language. If the ship tries to communicate orally, I believe I can communicate in their language and avoid misunderstandings."

Professor Alicia Gilbert asked, "You can speak the Ancients' language?"

"I believe so, and I've been practicing." Thomas did not tell them Omnia had been helping him learn how to pronounce the words. He believed he had enough understanding of the language to have a limited conversation.

Professor Rubin Gilbert's graduate assistant commented. "When there is time, you must teach us, so we can all converse in the language." Thomas nodded his head.

"Suzanna, I'll leave the ship immediately at the first sign of danger, but this is something I must do. It'll be safer for me than it would be for anyone else. It'll also be safer for me to go alone since I won't have to worry about someone making a mistake. Don't worry. This is quite safe."

The scientists and engineers were bubbling with excitement. In contrast, the staff expressed their concern about the risk their captain was taking. Thomas gave them an estimate on when the ship would exit hyperspace and called an end to the meeting.

After the meeting, Suzanna continued unsuccessfully to talk Thomas out of going, but she finally relented. However, she had a private meeting with the staff and ensured all ten military shuttles would be full of marines ready to deploy if Thomas got into trouble.

They came out of jump without issue. They received a distress call from a satellite that must have been launched from one of the dead ships before losing all its power. Thomas squeezed into the shuttle and barely had room to secure himself before directing the pilot to take off. Thomas was fully suited but withdrew his helmet and continued breathing the shuttle's air until they arrived at the crash site. They landed close to the alien craft to reduce the time it would take to unload the power units and load the torpedoes. Thomas engaged his helmet, and the Pilot came back to help unload the power units. Thomas looked through the sealed visor and saw it was Grayson.

Thomas asked, "What are you doing here?"

Grayson grinned. "I'm following Captain Suzanna Wilson's orders, sir. It was either this, or she was going to have you locked in the brig."

"Let's get these units unloaded," Thomas said.

They had forty power units to unload. They both noted how the ship was huge and ten times the size of the military's battleship. Thomas had Grayson continue to check the shuttle for power drainage. They had unloaded all the units and were disbursing the units throughout the ship when Grayson notified Thomas the shuttle had dropped to seventy percent power. They had previously agreed Grayson would leave with the shuttle if the power readings dropped to sixty percent. Thomas directed Grayson to load the loose missiles. He continued to move the power units further into the ship. Grayson used gravity lifts to load four missiles with each trip. He had made six trips when the shuttle dropped to sixty percent. He notified Thomas and flew the shuttle away from the moon. Grayson stopped when the shuttle ceased losing power. The power reading had dropped to fifty-seven percent and was holding steady. They had agreed Thomas would report every half hour. They were concerned his communicator would lose power, so they agreed Grayson would return within one hour if Thomas failed to check-in. Two other shuttles joined Grayson as he continued to stay a safe distance from the crash site. All three pilots closely monitored their shuttle's power status. The other shuttles were on standby in the flight bay with pilots at the controls and ready to assist if needed.

As soon as the shuttle left, Thomas placed two of the power unit on a sled they had brought from the Demon. He headed for the bridge he had located on his initial exploration of the ship. He placed a power unit on either side of the bridge. He went to what could only be the captain's seat and sat down to rest. He did not have long to wait before various screens came to life within the bridge. He turned off his suit's lights as the bridge lighting became brighter.

Thomas checked with Grayson and told him everything was going well with no drain to his communicator and said he would contact him again in half an hour. Suddenly, the ship shook, and Thomas nearly fell out of the chair. Then the craft leaned heavily to one side, and then Thomas could feel the ship as it lifted off. Thomas knew his suit would provide him with breathable air for three days. He had an extra canister of solid oxygen that would last for several weeks, so he was not immediately concerned. Thomas tried his communicator but failed to get through to Grayson. Then he felt a tingling throughout his body as the ship scanned him.

Grayson watched as the ship lifted off. He tried continuously to communicate with Thomas to no avail.

Grayson contacted the Demon. "This is Grayson. The Ancients' craft has just taken off. Thomas is still onboard."

"We know," Suzanna said. "Bring the shuttles back on board immediately. This happens every single time! Thomas never listens!"

Grayson landed in the shuttle bay and ran to the bridge. The Demon had no choice but to follow the Ancients' ship. It was moving slowly, and the Demon had no problem keeping up as it continued to accelerate.

Suzann gave Grayson a mean look. "There was no warning," Grayson said. "The ship just took off."

"I knew this was a bad idea. Thomas never learns. A captain's job is on the bridge. Helm, where are we headed?"

"Straight for this system's sun."

THOMAS COULD FEEL THE craft as it accelerated, but at least the vessel had inertial controls, so he felt comfortable. Then the whole inside of the ship became transparent, and he could see a sun in the center of the display, but it was still quite distant. As Thomas looked around the bridge, he saw more systems being activated. Thomas glanced at his suit's readout and saw the pressure increase inside the bridge. He watched his suit's readouts as the ship's air mixture adjusted until it matched his suit's air.

Thomas had his helmet withdrawn back into the suit's collar. Then he felt a pinprick on the back of his neck. He knew what was happening. He had felt the same sensation each time nanites had been injected into his body by Doctor Adler and when he had been in the healing chamber. It was a strange sensation but was not painful.

He had previously translated the language of the Ancients, but it had been a prolonged process. A holograph appeared before him, and he could understand certain words and phrases from his previous efforts. The ship was now unreasonably close to the sun as it slowed its approach. Thomas tried speaking to the ship, but nothing happened. The ship stayed in place for eight standard days. During that time, Thomas explored the ship. His suit's recycling unit would provide him with water for an extended time, but he was getting hungry since he had already eaten all the emergency rations in the suit.

Onboard the Demon, Suzanna watched the ship of the Ancients as it remained stationary closer to the sun than what the Demon could tolerate. There was nothing they could do except watch and wait. The Demon was scanned twice without damage, so they did not attempt to block the scans as they hoped it would help Thomas.

Thomas was beginning to give up hope when the ship finally displayed the standard Galactic language in holographic form. Thomas could see the words were being downloaded from the bridge of the Demon, and he could see the worry in the discussions. Thomas could see the ship was getting close to being able to communicate. He hoped it would locate, download, and synthesize the voice conversion program accessible by Demon's AI.

Thomas was falling asleep when the ship finally spoke. "Good morning, Admiral Wilson."

Thomas opened his eyes and became fully awake. "Finally, good morning to you, ship. I am glad we can finally communicate. What took you so long?"

The ship responded. "Much of my hardware had to be repaired throughout the ship. My entire being was consumed with that effort."

Thomas asked, "Please look into the data you got from the Demon and see if you can use the information to create a food processor. I'm quite hungry."

"That will not be necessary. I have repaired the food synthesizer. It is a part of this ship, and a meal is being prepared for you. It is safe for you to remove your spacesuit."

The ship directed Thomas to an area where he could eat a meal.

Before leaving the bridge, Thomas said, "I need to contact my ship, the Demon."

A screen appeared, and Thomas saw Demon's bridge, except the audio was distorted. It took a few minutes before the frequencies were matched.

"Demon Two, this is Thomas. Please respond."

A moment later, Suzanna responded. "Thomas, I was so worried. Are you okay?"

"I'm fine. It took a while for the ship to repair the damage. Now, I can communicate directly with the ship."

"You're very close to the sun," Suzanna said. "You must get the ship further from the sun before we can pick you up."

"I don't plan to leave the ship at this time but would like to have our researchers, scientists, and engineers aboard. I'll try to have the ship move further from the sun so we can rendezvous. I'll call you back after I have something to eat."

He found his meal consisted of a liquid. It tasted bad, but the ship assured him it had everything required to meet his nutritional needs. Regardless of the taste, Thomas felt much better after eating. The ship told Thomas it would be the equivalent of two standard days before they left the proximity of the sun. Thomas conveyed the information to Suzanna and then talked to Amanda before disconnecting.

Thomas began feeling a strangeness throughout his body and again recognized the sensation. He realized the drink had tasted bad because it contained a high volume of nanites. He was suddenly exhausted. He asked if there were any sleeping arrangements on the ship and was directed to a nearby cabin. Thomas was shocked when he entered and found it looked identical to his cabin on Demon Two. However, he was too sleepy to ask questions and collapsed on the bed.

When he woke up, he felt refreshed. He verified the cabin was identical to his cabin on the Demon. He took a shower. After drying off, he came out of the shower to find a new suit of clothing. It was similar in appearance to his jumpsuit but felt more comfortable.

He returned to the bridge and saw the ship was traveling away from the sun. He contacted the Demon again. They had been trying to reach him for two days, but the ship kept saying he was sleeping and could not be disturbed.

Thomas told the AI he needed to bring over individuals from the Demon. He was given information for the proper entry to the ship, which he then conveyed to Suzanna. However, when he mentioned he planned to return to the Demon, the ship said it could not function properly if he left. Therefore, Thomas asked Suzanna and Amanda to come over with the first shuttle. The shuttle arrived at the ship but could not see an opening. They were directed to approach the ship and to move straight ahead. The shuttle moved through the walls of the ship without seeing any opening.

Thomas met the shuttle as it landed. He immediately gave Suzanna and Amanda much-needed hugs. The shuttle was full of researchers, scientists, and engineers. Thomas told everyone to be careful and to ask the ship's permission before conducting each test or experiment. They all agreed and were extremely excited. They brought lots of equipment but understood the necessity to be careful and not damage anything or endanger themselves.

Amanda could not wait to start exploring the ship. Thomas started to object until Professor Gilbert's young female assistant said she would like to explore with Amanda before beginning the tedious task of categorizing everything on the ship. She assured Suzanna and Thomas she would keep Amanda out of trouble.

Thomas had the ship create additional chairs on the bridge. He had a chair on each side of him for Suzanna and Amanda. Even though it was unnecessary, he had the ship create four additional chairs for future officers who would monitor the surrounding space while collecting and analyzing data. The ship received permission from Thomas to upgrade the Demon Two. It required having one of the engineers bring two containers from the ship of the Ancients to the main central core of the Demon's AI. The AI from the two ships then created an additional power source for the Demon. It would allow the ship to absorb energy directly from the sun in the same manner as the ship of the Ancients. Now, the Demon had the additional flexibility to strengthen its shields without needing to be attacked. This made the Demon even more impervious to conventional munitions.

After a discussion with the AI, Thomas named the ship Demon Three. Suzanna worked with Grayson to transfer part of the crew from Demon Two to Demon Three. Thomas had a long session with the AI of Demon Three, and as expected, the AI was sentient and consisted of Crystals, the same as Omnia. The Demon Three AI permitted Thomas to use the name Bellator for the AI. There was a section of the ship without an entry point. They had been studying the ship for several weeks when Thomas felt comfortable enough to command the ship. Thomas knew no ship in the navy could harm Demon Two, Demon Three, or any of his upgraded cruisers. He felt confident the same would be true regarding the Hostis threat.

Thomas called a meeting in what they now referred to as the shuttle bay. Everyone was excited and shocked when Thomas announced Demon Three would travel to an outpost of the Ancients. He told them he did not know how long they would be gone and stressed the potential dangers of going to such a world. He asked if anyone would like to return to Demon Two. No one asked to leave. Half the crew had already moved from Demon Two to Demon Three. Thomas promoted Grayson to the captain of Demon Two and told him to return to the Rim Worlds and support the Rim Trade Alliance.

Bellator informed Thomas the ship had been fully repaired and would again approach the sun to maximize its power. This time it only took three days before Bellator told Thomas the ship was preparing to jump. Thomas and all the bridge officers were surprised when the ship entered hyperspace from a dead stop position. All other ships had to accelerate to a certain minimum velocity before engaging their jump engines. Demon Three accelerated after entering hyperspace, which was something else other ships could not do. Thomas asked Bellator for other abilities of the ship. He learned the ship could change directions after entering hyperspace and arrive at a different destination. Bellator told Thomas that Demon Two had received similar upgrades.

During the trip, Bellator created workstations requested by the bridge officers. There was little to no disorientation when they exited hyperspace. The local sun was a K2V orange dwarf star. Bellator approached an empty area of space and stopped. The main monitor showed they were approximately one hundred million kilometers from the sun. Suddenly, an earth-sized planet became visible. The entire planet had been cloaked. Thomas asked Bellator about the planet and learned it was artificial. Thomas told the bridge officers, scientists, and engineers they would have five days to examine the artificial world before attempting a landing. Thomas had not been sleeping well and hoped he could relax and get a good night's sleep, but it did not go according to plan.

That night Bellator woke Thomas and directed him to the sealed-off section of the ship. Thomas slipped out of bed without waking Suzanna and complied after drinking a cup of coffee. An opening appeared when Thomas approached and closed behind him after he entered. The room slowly became lighted. Spacecrafts filled the room. A bright light appeared over one of the ships. The door on the spacecraft opened when Thomas approached, and he entered the craft. He sat down in the pilot's seat. The seat automatically contoured to his body, and straps extended across his torso. The ship lifted off and exited Demon Three through an opening that materialized and then closed after the craft passed through. The craft approached the planet, and an opening appeared right before the craft would have crashed. The craft traveled until it reached a cavern in the center of the planet. The door on the craft opened, and he followed a lighted path until he entered a large room. All four walls were covered from floor to ceiling with built-in rectangular containers.

His head hurt as he felt the life and fear radiating from each of the small cubicles. Thomas walked up to a cubical and saw a child-like being with wings. He realized each of the booths contained a life form. The child was positioned vertically, facing outward. As Thomas looked at the child, he could feel its fear, but the fear disappeared as soon as he made eye contact. The same thing happened at the next cubicle. Then he knew what he had to do. He started at the first wall and took turns checking on each child. He made sure he did not miss a single child.

Twenty-four hours later, he was still at it when he realized Suzanna was trying to contact him. She told him they had only recently discovered he was missing and no longer on Demon Three. Bellator had arranged for Suzanna to communicate with Thomas after telling her Thomas was safe. Even though Thomas treated Bellator as an equal, Bellator obeyed Thomas as had Omnia. Thomas asked Bellator if he could bring visitors to the planet, and he agreed but said access to the children would need to be restricted since they were sensitive to emotions. Bellator decided to let Suzanna, Amanda, and Dr. Adler enter the room with the children. Other visitors would be allowed to explore the rest of the planet.

Thomas continued looking into each container along the last wall. He was almost finished when Suzanna contacted him and said they were outside the door. He walked over, and Bellator created an opening. As soon as the three entered, the entrance behind them disappeared. Thomas asked them to remain quiet. Thomas motioned for them to come forward and then to turn around and face the wall. They gasped and smiled as they saw all the children. Thomas told them they could look around but asked the Doctor to accompany him. He asked Doctor Adler to watch and explain what was happening. She watched as each child changed its facial expression as Thomas looked at it. When he finished, he walked over to a bench in the middle of the room and sat down. He was utterly exhausted.

Thomas looked at the Doctor. "Can you tell me what is happening here?"

Doctor Adler laughed. "You just became the bonded father to every child here."

Suzanna and Amanda had walked over and heard the Doctor's explanation.

Amanda, with delight, said, "Dad, it looks like I'm going to have more brothers and sisters than anyone in the Galactic."

Suzanna just shook her head. "Well, this is the first time you got to see the Doctor in an emergency without being shot."

"I've got to take a nap," Thomas said to Doctor Adler. "Will you stay here and talk to Bellator and see what we need to do to care for these children? For the time being, I don't want anyone else to know what is in here."

"I'll be here when you awake. I also agree we must keep this quiet for the time being." Thomas said he was sleepy, and Bellator directed him to exit the room through a door opposite where he entered. He did not remember seeing the door when he first entered the room. When he walked through the door, he was in a luxury cabin similar to his cabin on Demon Two but much nicer. Suzanna saw the bed and joined Thomas since she was also tired. Thomas and Suzanna told Amanda she could stay with the Doctor.

Suzanna woke up first but let Thomas sleep while she took a shower and got dressed. Thomas awoke much later. After taking a shower, he went to the makeshift cafeteria the planet had created and enjoyed a big breakfast before returning to the sealed room, which he decided to call a nursery.

Doctor Adler, true to her word, was still there. She looked tired but delighted. Thomas joined Doctor Adler as she walked over to one of the benches and sat down.

Doctor Adler began speaking. "Bellator gave what information it had but acknowledged it did not have all the history because the planet was created toward the end of the Great War. Before the Great War, all the races had lived in peace. Over a million years ago, invaders arrived and started destroying everything in their path. The Angelus fought against these invaders. At the beginning of the war, the Angelus had a council of seven great leaders named: Michael, Gabriel, Raphael, Uriel, Sealtiel, Jehudiel, and Barachiel. The likenesses displayed on the walls of the ship represent these seven council members. All the other races were unable to contribute to the war. They fled to what is now the Hostis area of space. Massive destruction took place on both sides. The invaders refused to consider any type of peace."

Doctor Adler continued. "Toward the end, it looked like the Invaders were going to win, but the Angelus devised a deadly virus. It spread rapidly and killed everyone with an implanted brain chip. It killed off all the Invaders and most of the Angelus. A few Angelus removed their chips and survived. The ship we traveled on to get here was created before they released the final virus but was severely damaged in a battle before escaping. This ship made an emergency jump and landed where you found it."

"Doctor, I have a plan. It may allow humans and Hostis to reach a peace accord, but I need your help. I don't want you to tell anyone what is in this room. Also, I need you to follow my lead when dealing with the Hostis and human leaders."

"I agree to keep the secret of the children. I'll follow your lead for now. However, you'll need to let me know your plan and the role you wish me to play."

Thomas asked Suzanna to join them, and he laid out his plan. They discussed the various problems with the plan and made modifications to address those concerns. In the end, they thought the plan might work, but knew it might need to be adjusted after implementation. Suzanna told Amanda they had a secret. Thomas told Bellator not to let anyone else enter the room. The children were growing rapidly. Thomas met periodically with the officers, engineers, and scientists. Then, he would disappear back into the room with the children. After six months, the children exited the cubicles. They appeared outwardly as teenagers but with wings. Several weeks after leaving the chambers, they were flying. Thomas understood why the chamber's ceiling was so high and the room so large. All the children were telepathic, and Thomas could communicate with them telepathically except when they all tried to speak at once. Amanda also communicated with them and was having fun playing with the children. Doctor Adler and Suzanna were only able to pick up emotions. Bellator confirmed again, the species of the children was Angelus.

The scientists, engineers, and other Demon Three crew members took turns visiting the planet. Thomas decided to explore, and Bellator gave him a special tour to areas off limits to others. Bellator directed him to an area that held personal body shields. He put on a shield and was satisfied with a test he conducted. Thomas secretly transported two containers of personal shields to the ship. He gave shields to both Suzanna and Amanda. He insisted they wear the personal shields anytime they were outside their cabin.

Thomas visited an area filled with hundreds of ships similar to Demon Three and thousands of smaller ships. Each of the larger ships were full of starfighters and escort ships. Thomas knew he could use this armada to defend humanity, but he would keep it secret with the hope it would never be needed. Bellator told Thomas the invaders might return. In that event, the children needed to be ready for the ultimate battle against the invaders who killed their ancestors.

Thomas visited another area filled with huge machines. The machines were identical and looked extremely powerful, but Thomas could not determine their purpose. He started to ask Bellator but became distracted by other issues.

Thomas continued to spend time with the children of the Ancients until Bellator became satisfied the children were ready to leave the planet. Bellator created a home for the children on Demon Three in the area of the ship sealed off from the crew. Keeping the children hidden on Demon Three was not an issue since the ship could have held over a hundred thousand individuals without crowding. Thomas brought the children to the ship using a transport vessel stored on the planet that Bellator selected. It had stealth mode. The children settled comfortably into their new surroundings.

Thomas was curious. Why were there 1973 children? 1973 was a prime number. 19 was the first two numbers, 73 the last two, and 97 the middle two. 13 was the first and last number. All these combinations were prime numbers. Thomas did not believe the Ancients would arbitrarily select a number. Bellator was not helpful.

Thomas notified everyone on the planet to return to the ship. Bellator informed Thomas there were other rooms filled with children in cryogenic sleep on the planet. At a future date, they would return and awaken more of the children of the Angelus. Thomas knew it would take time to use the term Angelus instead of Ancients.

Thomas, with help from Bellator, made sure everyone was back aboard. The scientists, engineers, and scholars wanted to stay, but Thomas did not give them a choice. However, he promised them a return trip at a future date if they maintained certain secrets. They all executed confidential agreements. Thomas knew the secrets would get, but he hoped to delay the release of the information. The information they collected would keep thousands of researchers busy for years. They had been gone for nearly a year. They set course and entered hyperspace for the long jump back to the Rim.

CHAPTER 16 PEACE
OR INTERGALACTIC WAR

Demon Three came out of jump and immediately contacted all their ships operating in the Rim. Wilson Enterprises had been refurbishing twenty cruisers at a time, and eighty additional ships had been added to their fleet, bringing their total to one hundred forty cruisers. Another of their shipyards had renovated two hundred destroyers. Each ship had a full crew complement. At the end of six weeks, three hundred twenty ships had assembled. Twenty ships were busy making deliveries and had not arrived. Thomas had each ship transfer personnel to Demon Two and Demon Three. There were thousands of Crystals on Demon Three. With Bellator's permission, Thomas transferred two Crystals to each ship that had not been upgraded. It took Thomas twenty days to mount the Crystals.

When the navy fleet finally arrived, all the Wilson ships had been converted to the new technology and looked uniquely powerful and similar. No one would ever imagine the new ships were discarded navy ships fresh from the graveyard. They were all showing the Demon logos.

Admiral Nelson approached Demon Two with his Battleship. The navy's Communications Officer said, "Sir, I've been informed that in addition to Demon Two, Admiral Thomas Wilson has one hundred forty cruisers and two hundred destroyers. They all have the advanced tech with the impenetrable shields."

The technology of Thomas' fleet made the navy fleet look small and inept by comparison. Demon Two and the navy Battleship were facing each other with the rest of the ships behind them. Admiral Nelson had his Communications Officer send a message to Admiral Wilson. The space between the two battleships shimmered, and a gigantic ship ten times the size of the battleships appeared.

"Good morning, Admiral Nelson," Admiral Thomas Wilson said with a big smile. "You wish to speak with me? As you can see, I had our shipyard build me a bigger ship. This is Demon Three. Besides its size, it can jump from a dead still position." This allowed Demon Three to arrive precisely between the two fleets.

Admiral Nelson was speechless. He had used all his resources but failed to locate the hidden shipyard. During their last meeting, Thomas arrived in Demon Two. It was slightly bigger than his Battleship, with advanced technologies they could not duplicate. Admiral Nelson had been amazed and troubled by the technology in Demon Two.

Now, Admiral Nelson was looking at a ship ten times the size of his battleship, which could jump without moving. To say he was overwhelmed would be a gross understatement. Also, no one could look at such a behemoth without a measure of fear.

"Admiral Wilson, what do you plan to do with such a large ship?"

"I'm glad you asked. I plan to visit the Hostis and see if they would be interested in a peace treaty."

Once Admiral Nelson got over his shock, he whispered, "Finally, we can take the fight to our enemy." Aloud, he said, "Can we join you?"

"You may come, but only if you agree to be under my command and agree not to fire without a direct order from me, even if you are fired upon," Thomas said with a serious expression. "You need not worry. We can protect your entire fleet if necessary."

Admiral Nelson did not doubt him and did not want to be left out of a battle with the Hostis when they had overwhelming superiority. "I agree to your terms."

"Admiral Nelson, I'm sending you the jump coordinates. Have your ships match our speed, and we'll jump together."

Even though Demon Three did not need to reach a critical speed to jump, the other ships did, so he accelerated along with his other ships. As they achieved the necessary velocity, Thomas sent a command to all the ships. "Engage jump engines."

The ships came out of jump together. Thomas positioned his ships between the navy and the Hostis ships. Suzanna and Amanda were sitting on either side of Thomas on the bridge. Daniel was three years old and seated next to Suzanna. They were facing a small fleet of Hostis ships. The Demon Three scans identified one habitable planet.

Demon Three sent out a communication probe at a low velocity and had it stop halfway between them and the small Hostis fleet. One of the smaller Hostis ships approached the probe and opened a bay door. Thomas directed Bellator to move the probe into the Hostis ship. The probe set down inside the ship, and Thomas had his image projected.

"Greetings, I am Thomas Wilson, and I have come as requested."

A Hostis approached the probe and addressed the projection. "May we see you in your true form?"

Thomas had Bellator freeze the projection while he tried to understand the request. A mistake now could be critical. He was not certain, but only knew of one possibility. Thomas asked everyone to leave the bridge except for his family. He asked Bellator if it was possible to give him wings like the Ancients and their descendants. Thomas took off his shirt as directed. The miniature nanites went to work on his back. It was painful, but when Thomas looked over his shoulder, there were two large wings attached to his back.

"I want wings too," Amanda said.

"Having wings hurts," Thomas said to Amanda.

"I don't care. Please, I want wings like you." Thomas directed Bellator to provide wings for Amanda but asked if he could make it less painful. It was only a moment before Amanda was smiling and admiring her new wings. Thomas was thankful Bellator had provided a modest covering for Amanda's breasts. Thomas looked at Suzanna, and she nodded her head. Suzanna had large, beautiful wings, and Daniels was screaming because he wanted wings. While Amanda, Suzanna, and Daniel admired their wings, Thomas had a dozen Angelus children join them. The children were getting taller. Thomas communicated with them telepathically and described his plan. They agreed to play their part. Thomas told Bellator to only let the Hostis see a visual of the bridge. Everyone else would only hear the audio.

Thomas reactivated the bridge monitor. The Hostis representative responded. "It is as we suspected and feared. We did not know that humans were under the protection of the Angels. We will cease hostilities against humans. However, we seek your protection as well. Will you protect us from the humans?"

Thomas did not hesitate. "Yes," he responded. "It's important for Humans and Hostis to live in peace. The invaders we fought a million years ago are returning. Humans and Hostis must fight together against this mutual enemy, or neither race will survive."

The Hostis representative asked, "Did you bring human representatives to live with us for a time so we can understand our differences?"

"The humans will provide a small group to start. They would like to bring additional human representatives, but you need to let them know the number of humans you can accommodate. The humans want to download the speech conversion you are using to help with the initial communications until they learn your language."

"That is permissible," the Hostis representative replied.

It only took a moment before Bellator confirmed he had completed the download.

Thomas took a chance. "How else may we help you?"

"The Angels brought seven non-warrior alien races to this area of space during the Great War. These races wish to return to their homeworlds in the human sector of space."

"We'll need to proceed with one race at a time," Thomas replied. "The first return should be a race least objectionable to humans. Discuss this approach with the other races and present me with a proposal."

The Hostis responded. "We shall prepare a proposal as requested. We have prepared accommodations on the planet in this system, similar to the planets inhabited by humans. They may transfer to the domed area on the planet. It will house a million humans in addition to our people."

"We will transport a few humans to the planet before we leave. More humans will regularly transfer to the planet.

"We are at war with another species which required us to fight wars on two fronts. Will you help us with the second enemy?"

"Yes," Thomas answered, "But we'll need to complete a peace treaty between the Hostis and the humans first."

The first part of the plan had succeeded.

Thomas addressed Admiral Nelson and his bridge officers. "The Hostis prepared a planet in this system where humans can live and interact with the Hostis. The goal is for each side to learn enough about each other to live in peace. As you heard, the living area will hold up to a million humans. The Hostis are committed to providing you with good accommodations. An equal number of Hostis will be living with the human population. We need to bring open-minded people who can put the past behind them."

Thomas signed off and then spoke with the people on Demon Three after getting rid of the wings. "We will transport you who came to study the Ancients, and the volunteers, to the living area on the planet below. The Hostis have additional information on the Ancients that will add to your study." Thomas did not want the university scientists to return to human space since he wanted to maintain the secrecy of the planet of the Ancients. He knew the crew would keep the secrets.

Thomas told the Ancients research group to stay for one year. After a year, they would have the option of remaining or returning to the Core Planets. As an incentive, he said anyone who stayed for three years would be given the opportunity to return to the planet they had just visited. The research group finally agreed. Everyone who was not a crew member was transported to the domed city.

Thomas and Suzanna were happy with their progress during the months they remained in Hostis space. The Angelus continued to grow and would reach full adult size both physically and mentally in approximately five years. Thomas, Suzanna, Amanda, Daniel, and Doctor Adler spent considerable time with the children. Amanda and Daniel would sprout wings when they played with the Angelus. They were both becoming quite adept at flying.

The crew of Demon Three were given the choice of returning to Demon Two, but most stayed. All of Suzanna's friends from the Familia Primum transferred to Demon Three.

All the Oceanums stayed on Demon Three. Thomas, Suzanna, and Bellator felt the Oceanums would be perfect for caring for the Angelus children. Thomas had the Oceanums join him for a meeting.

"You already have empathic abilities," Thomas said, "which is fairly close to being telepathic. If you wish, I may be able to give you full telepathic abilities." Thomas noticed that all the females were pregnant.

The Oceanums immediately started talking to one another. "I speak for all of us," Demato said. "All of us want telepathic abilities. We thought only your children born to our females might have such abilities. Please, tell us what we must do to receive such a gift?"

Thomas thought he meant the six children born on the same day as Daniel and was unaware all the children being born to the Oceanums were his biological children.

"You'll need to spend the night with me." Thomas saw smiles from the females. "No sex," he said with a chuckle. "This ability will be given to both males and females. You'll go to sleep, and when you wake up, if I am successful, you should be able to communicate telepathically. However, it may take a little practice to become proficient. I'll take twenty volunteers for the first attempt. Only one pregnant female should be in the first group until we see how the unborn child responds. I want the twenty volunteers to meet me at the end of Day Watch."

After Thomas left, the Oceanums enthusiastically selected the volunteers by random lot. Everyone not selected was disappointed.

Thomas did not want the Oceanums to know Bellator would make the changes to their bodies. The Crystals were adamant. They did not want anyone to know about them.

The Oceanums met with Thomas and laid down on the floor. The floor adjusted to their bodies in both comfort and temperature. Bellator knew what to do and sent nanites to render the volunteers unconscious. Once they were all asleep, the nanites adjusted their brain's neurons and completed pathways for the proper connections within the brain. They slept for sixteen hours while their bodies adjusted to their brain's new activities. The room had a special shield, so the Oceanums could only access the mental activities of those in the room. The pregnant female said she could sense her child, and her child was happy. They had their meals in the room and stayed two days before venturing out into the main body of the ship.

Thomas gave them headgear created by Bellator and told them to use it if they experienced any adverse reactions. Also, he told them the ability could be removed if they could not generate a mental shield to control the random thoughts surrounding them.

Thomas took fifty volunteers for the next session. Then one last session for everyone remaining. Five Oceanums used the headgear to reduce the mental noise, but no one wanted to reverse the condition.

Thomas called all the Oceanums telepathically for another meeting, and everyone arrived. "I've increased your abilities for a reason. I need your help. I have numerous ships and need to know the crews on these ships will not sabotage the ship. I need officers with the proper temperament who won't use force when there are non-violent ways to resolve an issue. I need to keep criminal elements off the ships. This is the job I want you to do on my behalf. If any of you decide to use your newly gained power for criminal pursuits, such power will be taken from you."

"I can say on behalf of all of us that we would welcome the opportunity to be assigned to your vessels," Demato replied. "It will benefit us since we can continue to look for planets to settle for the Nereides and for ourselves. Assisting you in maintaining peace is to our benefit."

"In the meantime," Thomas said, "I need you to work with a species with mental abilities, including telepathy. We must keep your abilities and their existence secret for now. Also, you must keep my abilities secret. Raise your hand if you agree to all these conditions." As expected, every hand went up. The hand signals were preferable to being bombarded by two hundred telepathic responses.

"I just wish I had more of you," Thomas said with a sigh.

"With the gift you have to offer, you will have millions of volunteers from our home planet."

"Then, we'll put your planet on our schedule, and you can help me recruit. I'd like to have at least two of you on every ship."

"We would like that as well."

"I have a surprise for you," Thomas said with a slight smile. Thomas took them to meet the Angels. Suzanna and Amanda were there when they arrived. It did not surprise them when Suzanna and Amanda greeted them telepathically. However, the Oceanums were ecstatic when they saw the flying children. When they thought nothing else could surprise them, Amanda and Daniel sprouted wings to fly after their playmates.

Suddenly, Thomas was surrounded by the Oceanum's children. One child asked, "Father, can you give us wings?" All the children were begging for wings.

Thomas thought for a moment but did not know how he could say no. "Very well, line up." Thomas sat down and put his hand flat on the bench. When there were sufficient nanites, he put his hand on the back of the first child. The nanites transferred from his hand to the child, and in a few minutes, the child had a beautiful set of wings. It took a while, but eventually, all the children had wings. Thomas taught the children how to get the wings to disappear. He told them their wings needed to be a closely guarded secret.

The adults were astonished as they watched their children fly around the room. Some Oceanums were in tears as their empathic abilities picked up the joy of their children, and it filled their souls.

The Oceanums had seen Thomas improve their mental abilities, and now he changed their children's abilities so that they could fly. Again, Thomas was more than their ancestors had ever imagined.

Thomas did not understand why Omnia and Bellator opposed letting others know they were sentient. Thomas did not like taking credit for the tasks performed by Bellator, but he would continue to honor his promise of secrecy. With no explanation, the Oceanums understood the need to maintain the secret of the Angelus children, the secrets of their own abilities, and that of their captain.

Thomas was dividing his time between the crew and the children. One day he watched the children playing tag while flying. One of the Angelus children was about to be tagged when he disappeared only to show up on the other side of the room. Thomas asked the child to come and explain what he had done. Thomas discussed the transportation with both the child and Bellator. With Bellator's help, the children had just learned how to enter the shadow dimension or hyperspace. They were invisible but could see everything in this dimension but were translucent when looking at themselves or others with them. However, it was the same realm used when a ship entered hyperspace or used a Star Gate. Bellator told Thomas the Jump Realm was where the Star Gates were located. Bellator said the powers of the Angelus would become greater as they grew older. Thomas found if an Angelus were touching him, he could enter and move through the Jump Realm. While in the Jump Realm, everything in the normal realm was motionless or moving so slow it appeared stationary. Thomas told the children to keep their ability to enter the Jump Realm a secret, even from the Oceanums.

WHILE RELAXING ON THE bridge alone, Thomas contemplated his next move when he whispered, "I have access to the power of the Ancients but not the wisdom. I wish I could speak with one of the Ancients and ask for advice."

A holograph image appeared. "I am Uriel. What advice are you seeking?" Thomas chuckled. "Thank you, Bellator. It would have been nice to talk with the real Uriel."

"I assure you. You are not speaking to Bellator. My essence, knowledge, experience, and personality are preserved within the Crystals."

Thomas was excited as he leaned forward. He proceeded to ask questions and listen to Uriel. After several hours he asked, "We have planets where humans are suffering because of our failure to complete the terraforming prior to settling the planets. Other planets have natural and man-made pollutants. Can you help repair these planets?"

"You already have the power to achieve such results."

Thomas slapped the palm of his hand against his forehead. "The Crystals, I am such an idiot." He realized he could deposit Crystals on each planet. It would only take a few years to finish the terraforming. They could clear the pollutants from the air, water, and soil. He could use ships to bring in asteroids, pull the missing nutrients, and let the elements float to the surface of a planet.

"You are not an idiot. You are simply young and still learning. The Crystals were our greatest creation."

Thomas nodded. "Please, answer the questions I should be asking but don't have the wisdom or experience to ask."

Uriel smiled, and Thomas realized the hologram had a sense of humor. Thomas spent many hours over the following days discussing tactics to deal with the current problems.

Thomas decided to continue with his plan to unify the Humans and Hostis. It was time to meet with the Senate. Thomas contacted Admiral Nelson and said he needed to meet with the Senate to make peace a reality. Admiral Nelson contacted Agent Sicarius. Together they decided Thomas needed to get the Premier's opposition candidate to sponsor a presentation by Thomas to the full Senate. Agent Sicarius met with Senator Suarez in private, and they devised a plan of action.

Thomas arrived with his entire fleet, which had tripled in size with all the ships upgraded with advanced technology. Thomas invited all the Senators to visit Demon Two and Demon Three. The Senators were treated like royalty and given a grand tour of the ships. They had dinner with Thomas and his family. They all left with a favorable impression. They asked about employment opportunities for their children, grandchildren, or relatives. In each case, Thomas promised they would be hired. However, he did not tell them what position they would be given, but they would have better opportunities on a ship than on a planet. Suzanna understood politics and knew what to say when asked about supporting them in future elections.

During the Senate session, Senator Suarez was recognized in accordance with protocol and allowed to speak. "Admiral Thomas Wilson is a hero because of his exploits in the last battle with the Hostis. He is responsible for eliminating piracy in the Outer Planets and the Rim. I move we allow him to speak before the Senate."

The motion was followed by a second. During the following discussion, the Premier tried unsuccessfully to submit the matter to a committee for further action, but his effort failed by a wide margin. Even the Premier's supporters wanted to hear Thomas speak. The motion for Thomas to speak was approved by voice acclimation. Thomas was scheduled to speak the next day.

When Thomas arrived at the Senate amphitheater, it reminded him of the hockey arena he played in when he was younger. His weapons were taken, and his bodyguards were not allowed to enter. The guards were upset, but Thomas told them not to worry. Suzanna, Amanda, and Daniel sat in a booth with Senator Suarez. When it finally came time for Thomas to speak, he walked to the center of the large open space with the Senators arranged on three sides. The Premier and his senior cabinet sat in a raised section behind him. Over nine hundred Senators were physically present. The missing Senators were represented by holographic projections.

Just as Thomas was getting ready to speak, the Premier spoke. "Thomas Wilson, is it true you have artifacts of the Ancients in your possession?"

Thomas calmly but with sufficient volume to be heard by all, said, "Yes, that is correct."

"Is it true you have built ships using such technology?"

"Yes."

"Is it true you have refused to turn over such technology to the Imperium?"

"No, I turned over four missiles initially. Later I turned over a fifth missile and a starfighter to the navy."

"That is irrelevant. You did not give the technology to the government to allow it to build Imperium ships. Do you have a secret shipyard building ships using this technology?"

"Yes." The Premier knew he had Thomas trapped. "Will you turn over your ships, the location of your secret shipyard, and all artifacts in your possession to the Imperium?"

"No," Thomas said in a calm voice.

The Premier was sure Thomas would comply and ask for mercy to avoid execution. No one refused the Premier if they wished to continue living.

Now the Premier was enraged. "All of you heard Thomas Wilson admit to having technology of the Ancients. I was prepared to pardon him if he agreed to turn over the technology to the government. Such technology cannot be allowed to be in the hands of a civilian. We have laws to protect our citizens from individuals having the power to kill billions of our citizens using outlawed technology. That is why we have the death penalty for anyone not turning over such technology to the government. Thomas Wilson has openly admitted to breaking such a law. By admitting guilt, a trial is unnecessary and would be a waste of time. By the power vested in me as your Premier, I order the executioners to carry out the sentence of death immediately."

Four men wearing masks entered through a side door. They raised their XRL blasters and looked toward the Premier. The XRL Blaster was a short-range, potent, high-energy weapon. The XRL Blasters completely obliterated matter. One blast and the only thing left would be a pile of ash. There were shouts of outrage from the senators. The Premier, with a satanic smile, nodded his head. The executioners simultaneously fired their blasters. There were shouts and screams throughout the chambers. Thomas was wearing the personnel shield he had obtained from the planet of the Ancients. It operated on the same principle as the shielding on the ships. The energy from the blasters increased the shield's strength. When they stopped firing, Thomas was still standing and was completely unharmed. They were raising their weapons to fire again when he disappeared. One of the Angelus hiding in the shadow realm had simply taken his hand, and they walked across the floor to an area approximately twenty meters from his former location. When the Angelus let go of his hand, it gave the appearance he had teleported. Thomas was still glowing from the energy his shield had absorbed. The Premier saw Thomas and shouted, kill him, kill his entire family. Thomas sent a telepathic message to the Angelus. Both he and the Premier disappeared. Without thinking, Thomas discharged the energy from his shield at the Premier. They were only gone for a fraction of a second. The Premier turned to ash. Shouts and loud accusations were going on throughout the amphitheater. The executioners became afraid and hurried out the exits.

Thomas stepped to one side as the seven Angelus council members were simulated by the ship's AI using the Senate's holographic projectors. They were very realistic, and finally, everyone quieted down to see what they had to say.

Thomas made the introductions. "Let me present Michael, Gabriel, Raphael, Uriel, Sealtiel, Jehudiel, and Barachiel. They are members of the Council of the Angelus. They are the Ancients."

Uriel stepped forward. "The council has asked me to address you. Captain Thomas Wilson is held in high regard by the council. We do not wish to interfere in your affairs, and you may continue to have conflicts within your species, but you may not war against other species except for the Invaders when they arrive. We have not contacted your species in a long time so that you could develop at your own pace. We are busy monitoring the progress of invaders from another galaxy. We showed ourselves since we could not allow your Premier to harm our representative. Also, your Premier was suffering from incurable insanity."

Thomas was thankful Bellator had placed the responsibility for the Premier's death on the Ancients, or he would face prosecution for murder. When the Premier threatened his family, he lost his self-control and acted without thinking.

"During the Great War, and before humans arrived, all the species were moved to other worlds to prevent them from being permanently destroyed since they could not contribute to the war effort. They wish to return to their homeworlds that are in the human-controlled area of space. They are no threat to you and will move back to their home worlds with only one species relocating at a time. We will reactivate the Star Gates between their current worlds and their homeworlds. These Star Gates were shut down during the Great War to prevent the invaders from using the gates. Thomas Wilson will be our primary contact for now, and he will have full discretion in using our technology to assist in humanitarian efforts."

Senator Suarez spoke up, "You can turn a Star Gate on or off?"

"Yes, after all, we built the gates," Uriel replied.

Another Senator stood. "Where are these homeworlds of the aliens? We cannot let aliens reclaim planets where our citizens live."

"All the homeworlds are in the area of space you refer to as the Outer Planets and the Rim. Humans occupy only two of the planets, and the returning species will share the planets."

The Senator was mollified since it would not affect the Core Planets. "Then, we don't have a problem." Thomas thought the Senator was a complete hypocrite, but he had the support of other Senators, and his support might be helpful.

"I am happy to work with the new Premier for the betterment of all humanity," Thomas said. "The first act of the new Premier should be to form a peace treaty with the Hostis. The Invaders will return, and we need to be united with the Hostis if we want to survive. I'll give the new Premier and the Senate my friendship, full support, and loyalty. However, you'll lose all I offer if you attempt to harm me, my family, or any of my crew. The Angelus will know if you make any attempt for such harm. They have technologies far beyond our abilities to comprehend. The Hostis have been given the same information, and they are ready to execute a peace treaty."

Thomas had again used disinformation to reduce the threats to himself, his family, and his crew. Using a modification of the truth would make all his other statements believable. Hopefully, both his friends and enemies would be a lot friendlier.

Thomas knew there were still Senators loyal to the Premier. He projected a picture of the Premier on the overhead screen and played the recordings he had prepared as a contingency. The Senators easily recognized the Premier's voice. They listened as the Premier mentioned his desire for Thomas to be killed, then they heard the Premier state how he had Senators eliminated who had opposed him.

The Senate Administrator stepped forward in his role as Senate Pro Tempore. He handled Senate meetings when the Premier was unavailable. He was nervous as he yielded the floor to a Senator who had previously supported the Premier.

"How do we know if the recordings are factual?" the Senator asked.

Admiral Nelson was at the Senate meeting since he was there to gain support for the navy's budget proposal. He stood up and stepped forward. The Senate Pro Tempore acknowledged the Admiral.

In a clear voice, Admiral Nelson said, "You will have recognized my voice on several of the recordings. I am saddened to say the recordings are accurate. I submit my resignation."

Thomas looked around and saw the deceased Premier no longer had any supporters. The Senate Pro Tempore recognized Senator Suarez, allowing her to address the Senate.

Senator Suarez smiled down at Thomas. "The Premier underestimated you. Will you tell us about the technology you have access to and what it will take to share it with the Senate?"

Thomas had not expected the question and took a minute to prepare his answer. "The technology is simply the next step to what you already have. The shields are similar but store the energy when attacked and then redirects the energy back to strengthen the shields. You already have such storage devices but have not merged them with the shield technology. The missiles operate under the same principle, except the energy is expelled as an explosion. You already have nanites. The nanites of the Ancients are just smaller and have increased functionality. You have jump engines that were built by studying the effects of the Star Gates. The jump engines I am using are stronger and smaller such as the miniature jump engine we use in the starfighters. Ultimately, your scientists will learn how to use the technology. The technology of the Ancients is only slightly more advanced than the technology you currently use." There was laughter from Senators who disagreed with the assessment given by Thomas.

"I think most of us have a higher opinion of the technology you just described," Senator Suarez said.

"As long as the new Premier does not threaten my family or me, I will be happy to share the technology. I understand Admiral Nelson plans to ask the Senate for funds to purchase ships and starfighters using the advanced technology."

Senator Suarez still had the floor. "You have a personal shield. I believe I speak for everyone here when I say we would all like to have such a shield and your teleportation device."

Thomas grimaced as every Senator leaned forward in their seats. "Senator Suarez, you are asking questions I had hoped to avoid. It was easy to say no to the Premier since he was trying to kill me, and he threatened my family. It is hard saying no to you when you are so nice and diplomatic." There were chuckles throughout the Senate.

"The Ancients only gave me one teleportation device, which only works for me. Also, it is incorporated within my body. We must be careful with the personal shields since we would not want criminals to get their hands on such technology. At this time, I have a limited supply of personal shields. Because of the costs, I was planning to sell the units to law-abiding executives. However, with the recent events, the Senators need added protection that the shields could provide. The shields are customized, so they only work on the person matched to the unit. For the Senators, I will sell the units for a loss at one hundred million credits each. Also, I will delay selling to the public until the Senators have been outfitted. I think any further discussions should be with the new Premier. It's my hope the new Premier will be disagreeable." There was scattered laughter throughout the assemblage.

Thomas had won over the support of every Senator who could not wait to get their personal shield. Also, his last comment increased Senator Suarez support. They were impressed with how Senator Suarez had used flawless diplomacy to get major concessions from Thomas versus the prior impasse with the deceased Premier. Senator Suarez built consensus and compromised, whereas the previous Premier used fear and coercion. Thomas let them think he had a teleportation device since he did not want anyone to know about the Angelus children. They were growing fast and would appear to be adults in five years. He did not know if they would develop mentally at a faster or slower rate. When they reached maturity, they would need to return to the artificial world and awaken additional Angelus children.

"I'll leave you so you can select a new Premier." Thomas was turning to leave when Senator Suarez asked, "Admiral Wilson, what other surprises do you possess?"

Thomas was surprised by the question and did not think he had anything to top what he had already disclosed. He tried to imagine something outrageous when he remembered the large machines he had seen inside the artificial planet. Thomas had an epiphany and knew it must be true. He telepathically contacted Bellator and received confirmation. The entire Senate was waiting for a response.

"It's a small matter, and I had not planned to bring it up since I was primarily concerned with other issues. We've been building Star Gates, but they're awfully expensive."

He could not have gotten a greater response if he had detonated a bomb. Only about thirty percent of the Core Planets had Star Gates. Planets with Star Gates had a tremendous advantage over the other planets. Having a Star Gate in your system was priceless.

The noise finally abated. Senator Suarez still had the floor as she laughed and shook her head. "Thomas, I'm thankful you brought up this minor issue," she said with a smirk. "How quickly can you provide these Star Gates?"

"With the proper funding, every planet in the Core could have its own Star Gate within twenty years."

Senator Suarez asked the question everyone in the Senate wanted answered. "How much?" She asked.

"One hundred billion credits each," Thomas replied with a straight face. It was an outrageous price, but not for a planetary government. It was affordable for even the poorest Core Planet. Thomas would use the funds to eliminate poverty on every Outer Planet and Rim World in one generation. Thomas did not tell them he would provide Star Gates for free to the Outer Planets and the Rim.

"The price is acceptable," Senator Suarez said. "Our problem will be deciding who gets the Star Gates first."

"If you assign it to a committee, it is doubtful they would reach a resolution in my lifetime," Thomas said. "I propose a simple lottery where every planet will have an equal chance. I'll return to my ship while the Senate decides what action they wish to take."

Thomas was leaving when he heard, *"Thanks for killing the Premier."* Thomas gasped and turned back around. Senator Suarez had a mischievous smile, and Thomas felt a chill as he realized the Senator had spoken to him telepathically. He left the floor of the Senate knowing he had a new problem to resolve. He suddenly realized Senator Suarez represented the planet Panteen. The Oceanums migrated from Panteen.

The Senate unanimously selected Senator Suarez as Premier. It was apparent she had the votes, and no one wanted to cast a negative vote against the future Premier. The first act of Premier Suarez was to appoint Thomas Wilson as Chancellor of the Imperium Military. The appointment was approved by acclamation. This put Thomas in charge of the entire military operations of the Imperium, including the navy. Premier Suarez explained how the appointment would result in Thomas reporting to the Premier and the Senate. The second act was to agree to enter into a peace treaty with the Hostis, and a peace delegation was on its way to meet with the Hostis.

During Middle Shift, Senator Suarez contacted Thomas. She was now the Premier. She said they were setting up the lottery for the Star Gates, and it would not be long before he received the initial orders. They spoke briefly, and both committed to supporting the other for the betterment of humanity. She concluded with a request to meet with him privately in nine days when the Senate would recess. He was not looking forward to the meeting.

As a result of his Senate presentation, corporate executives contacted Suzanna wanting to buy a personal shield. After proper vetting, Thomas and Suzanna agreed to sell the units at five hundred million credits each for delivery after the Senators received their shields. He was surprised when they readily agreed to the price. The units would be sold in secret to a very select group. Thomas did not tell them he had a weapon that could penetrate the shields. However, he told them he would permanently turn off their shield if they abused the added protection. They were billionaires and paid in advance for the shields.

TWO DAYS LATER, THOMAS was in his ready room when he was contacted by Grayson and told Admiral Nelson had just arrived on board and wished to meet with him. Thomas told him to bring the Admiral to his Ready Room. The Admiral came with an assistant, and Thomas invited them to take a seat.

"The Senate approved the military appropriation bill," the Admiral said. "At first, the Senators were concerned when they saw the prices for the new ships, but all opposition collapsed when they looked at the last page and saw you were providing all the ships at half price if we traded in our existing ships. Then we showed them vids of the new starfighter, and they unanimously approved funding to purchase five thousand of the advanced fighters."

Thomas did not tell the Admiral that Omnia and Bellator would upgrade the traded-in ships. The ships would be returned to the navy fully converted to the technology of the Ancients at no cost to Wilson Enterprises. The funds received would provide free or discounted cargo and services to the poorer Rim Worlds. Thomas knew the Senate would never have approved a charitable appropriation to help the Rim Worlds. Thomas nodded and thanked him for delivering the good news. He needed to hire additional crew for his superdreadnought, Demon Three. Demon Two also required additional crew. He was going to upgrade the four battleships at the graveyard, and he would need to crew those ships. However, he was confident they would find outstanding individuals to crew their ships since they had over fifteen hundred human planets and an unknown number of aliens to find recruits.

"I submitted my resignation to Premier Suarez," Admiral Nelson said. "She told me to submit my resignation to you since you're now in charge of our military."

Thomas gave a big sigh. "Admiral Nelson, I know you support humanity, but your ethics are questionable." Thomas felt like a hypocrite since he questioned his own ethics.

"I'll hold on to your resignation for now, but I'm demoting you to fleet commander. You'll have fewer ships under your command, but I'll replace all of your ships, including your battleship, with new ships. All of your ships will have advanced technology. I have two hundred cruisers and five hundred destroyers. Also, I have four battleships under construction. We'll create six fleets, and each fleet will have a battleship. Wilson Enterprises will continue to add cruisers to our fleets. Each fleet will have at least two hundred ships in less than two years."

"Why do we need so many fleets since we'll be at peace with the Hostis?" Fleet Commander Nelson asked.

"A great war is coming, and we must prepare. In the meantime, all your ships will support our trade commitments in the Rim. Uninhabited planets will be available for colonization once the terraforming is properly completed. Our ships will be needed to help move settlers to these planets. I've been pleased with the young people we've hired who love the excitement and challenges of the unknown. They're outstanding, and I don't believe we'll have any problem finding settlers for these new planets. We'll have a meeting of the fleet commanders in ninety days. The captains of the ships assigned to your fleet haven't reported to you previously. Unless you have additional questions, you are dismissed."

Fleet Commander Nelson was happy to still be in the navy but did not like having senior officers he didn't know. Then he realized Thomas was testing him and giving him an opportunity. He looked forward to receiving the new ships and would not disappoint his commanding officer. Nelson and Sicarius stood up to leave.

"Agent Sicarius, please remain," Thomas said. Agent Sicarius was not surprised Thomas guessed his identity.

After Fleet Commander Nelson left, Thomas asked, "Are you willing to report to me and only me from this moment forward?"

Agent Sicarius nodded. "Yes," he said. Thomas had read Sicarius' thoughts and knew the commitment was absolute.

"Agent Sicarius, I have a mission for you."

After Agent Sicarius left, Thomas continued sitting alone and thought about the past ten years. They had accomplished so much. There was a tentative peace with the Hostis, the pirate threat was eliminated, and the living conditions of the people in the Outer Planets had improved. There was new hope for those living in the Rim, and new planets were being properly terraformed. He had used subterfuge, misdirection, half-truths, and outright lies to achieve those results. He could not shake his feeling regarding the Angelus, which he knew were the angels described in old religious texts. Thomas knew it was time for a private discussion with Bellator.

"Bellator, the planet we visited with the secret coordinates, was an artificial world and could not be the homeworld of the Angelus," Thomas stated. "Also, your age predates the construction of this ship by a massive number of years."

"Do you have a question?"

Thomas took a deep breath. "The Angelus are not the Ancients. You and the other Crystals are the real Ancients." Bellator did not respond.

A NOTE FROM THE AUTHOR

This is the second book in the Demon Starship Series, and I enjoyed writing it even more than the first. If you enjoyed reading this book, I would ask you to leave a review. I have an outline of the third book in this series. There will be plenty of space battles, personal intrigue, suspense, and the ultimate confrontation for the survival of humanity, their alien supporters, and the sentient AIs. The response I receive will determine how quickly the next book in this series is published.

If you missed the first book in the series and want to find the origins of the Demon Starship, then you may wish to read *To The Stars - Starship Named Demon Book 1*. In the first book, Thomas is a young captain who named his starship Demon. It is the first ship from the Core Planets to attempt trade with the Outer Planets and the Rim in over a hundred years. You can find out how Thomas learns from the mistakes he makes because of his naivety and lack of experience. You also get to experience the hardships of Suzanna as she tries to survive after being left behind by her family ship. She is pregnant, has no credits, and has to deal with her fears while living as a grounder.

ABOUT THE AUTHOR

JESS LEVINS grew up on a farm in Plant City, Florida, before receiving degrees from five universities, including two doctorates. He is an attorney, engineer, and financial analyst. Over the years, Jess has worked as a waiter, bartender, engineer, attorney, and corporate executive. He has always loved reading, especially in the genre of science fiction and fantasy. As a result, he worked for a major aerospace firm for three years before moving into the more traditional engineering fields. At an early age, he participated in the extreme sports. He has traveled extensively throughout North America, South America, and Europe. He currently lives in Fort Myers, Florida.

PUBLICATIONS BY JESS LEVINS

HOSPITAL ANGEL
By Jess Levins

HOSPITAL ANGEL fits within the genres of Medical Thriller, Legal Thriller and Christian Thriller. It contains suspense, adventure, intrigue, violence, humor, and a light romance.

Doctor Angel Carpenter is a doctor but is he an Angel? Angel is the former leader of the gang called the Angels. He is deeply religious and tries to do the right thing, but the right thing is not always legal. Angel is in charge of human trials for a cancer drug before it can be approved by the FDA. However, individuals with terminal cancer simply want the drug.

Some claim he is a real angel since his terminal cancer patients refuse to die; others feel he should be behind bars. He has developed a holistic method which he believes will increase the cure rate for the drug from forty percent to over ninety percent, but after twelve months, none of his patients have died. The drug could save millions of lives, but he is arrested as a serial killer. He keeps telling people he is not an angel, but the people surrounding the hospital and his apartment do not believe him.

There is a cancerous antireligious organization that wants him dead, and this organization may be more difficult to treat than the cancer his patients face. They initially offered a million dollar for his death and then increased it to five million. Assassins converge on Miami for an easy kill and a huge reward. They failed to realize one of the female cancer survivors belongs to a mafia family. She is indebted to Angel for saving her life, and she pays her debts.

TO THE STARS
By Jess Levins

TO THE STARS is a thrilling space adventure, containing battles, pirates, assassins, sentient computers, aliens, humor, and romance.

It is considered a suicidal mission for any trade ship to make the mistake of venturing into the Rim. There are no laws. Mercy is a sign of weakness. Wilson Enterprises builds spaceships. Thomas Wilson's father built a special ship for his son. The name Demon in large red letters is displayed on the hull of the sleek black ship. A battle angel is depicted on either side of the name. Captain Thomas Wilson is young, but he is an expert in strategy.

Captain Wilson establishes trade with the Rim Worlds and impresses the navy by surviving. The navy hires the Demon to deliver arms to the Rim. The Rim Worlds are in the direct path of an expected alien invasion. The navy hopes the additional weapons will allow the Rim Worlds to weaken the invaders and give the Core Planets a victory in the final battle for humanity. Death was almost certain for all the inhabitants in the Rim since the aliens do not take prisoners. But the Demon is no ordinary ship, and, with its help, they might just survive. Running guns makes the Demon an attractive prize, with every pirate ship wanting the rich cargo. The navy has a plan, but Thomas has his own agenda, and the ship's sentient AI has its own desires. Then, Thomas meets Suzanna. She was born on a ship in the Outer Planets, and she is good at her job, very good. Thomas and Suzanna are instantly drawn to each other. Their passion grows as she helps him overcome his naivety. The Demon must be at battle stations every time it comes out of hyperspace. Avoiding a fight is not an option.

MY PET WEREWOLF
By Jess Levins

MY PET WEREWOLF is a coming-of-age story with action, heartbreak, humor, and young romance. It contains hunters, werewolves, vampires, and other paranormal participants. Martial arts, guns, and swords are used to combat fangs and sharp claws.

Barb's parents own a martial arts dojo, and Barb teaches several classes when it does not interfere with her basketball practice. She hopes to get a basketball scholarship to avoid or minimize student loans. She loves animals and dreams of becoming a veterinarian.

Barb believes her older brother is a vampire and overhears him as he plans to turn her. She decides her only option is to run. She leaves Greenville, South Carolina, and takes a bus to Miami. However, her blood is that of a hunter, which places her in danger from other paranormal rogues. She is on the run from the police. She would rather die than become a vampire and is suicidal. The hunter's organization has offered a considerable reward to the paranormal communities for her safe return. The werewolf packs are competing for the reward and the prestige of helping to recover a young hunter. The local vampire Primus would like to capture her for the power it would bring to his conclave. She befriends a dog not knowing it was a wolf tracking her scent. The wolf likes the scent and her. Then they are attacked.